BAD WORDS

Ríoghnach (pronounced ree-uh-nock) Robinson grew up in North Carolina, studied economics at Kenyon College, and now lives in New York City. She is also the author of several YA novels, most recently the Lambda Award winner *Come Home to My Heart. Bad Words* is her debut novel for adults, which she drafted predominantly whilst visiting her parents in Ireland.

Ríoghnach Robinson

BAD WORDS

HarperCollins*Publishers*

HarperCollins*Publishers* Ltd
1 London Bridge Street
London SE1 9GF

www.harpercollins.co.uk

HarperCollins*Publishers*
Macken House, 39/40 Mayor Street Upper
Dublin 1, D01 C9W8, Ireland

First published by HarperCollins*Publishers* Ltd 2026
2

A catalogue record for this book is available from the British Library.

ISBN: 978-0-00-880175-5 (HB)
ISBN: 978-0-00-880176-2 (TPB)

Printed and bound in the UK using 100% Renewable
Electricity by CPI Group (UK) Ltd

FSC
www.fsc.org
MIX
Paper | Supporting
responsible forestry
FSC® C013604

To everyone I've ever loved

Thank you for teaching me how

John Keats, who was killed off by one critique,
Just as he really promised something great [. . .]
Poor fellow! His was an untoward fate;
'Tis strange the mind, that very fiery particle,
Should let itself be snuff'd out by an Article.

—LORD BYRON,
DON JUAN

One real reader is enough to persuade me
of the meaningfulness of my work.

—DUBRAVKA UGREŠIĆ,
A MUZZLE FOR WITCHES

Chapter One

Parker Navarro

I arrived home on a crisp October morning to find my roommate, Arthur, heralding disaster.

He was sitting in our apartment's front room, typing so furiously at the dining table that the laptop's keystrokes ran together like a snare roll. This was the first warning sign—not so much the frenetic typing as the fact that he was out of bed. The clock had just hit 10 AM, and Arthur Leung was the kind of borderline nocturnal computer person who never crawled into the sunlight before eleven except for emergencies.

The second red flag: his full-body twitch when I opened the door. Cat meets spray bottle. His head jerked up, and for a moment, he didn't move.

Then he shook back his hair and declared, in the voice of someone whose kidnapper has told them to act natural, "Oh, hey, Parker! What's up! How was"—his eyes lit on the bags in my hands—"the grocery store!"

"Um," I said, toeing off my shoes on the doormat. "The store was normal."

"You were going to get yogurt, right? Did you get yogurt?"

"I did." I paused. "Was the yogurt an urgent thing for you?"

"No! It's fine, it's all good."

I set the bags on the kitchen counter, still watching Arthur. In an interrogation room the guy would have folded like wet cardboard. He avoided my eyes, his foot bouncing so that reverberations went through all six foot three of him. Within seconds, a pale sheen had developed on his forehead.

"So," I said slowly. "What's going on, man? Is everything okay?"

A muscle ticked in his jaw. Before I could ask if his friends and family still had all their limbs, he slammed his laptop shut and said, "Don't go online."

My concern shriveled into a hard pit of dread. "Arthur. What happened?"

But I already knew the answer.

I knew that somehow, despite the emails I'd sent to my publisher begging them to prevent this exact scenario, Selina Chan at *City Magazine* had gotten hold of an advance copy of my second novel.

Four summers ago, you couldn't get within spitting distance of the publishing industry without hearing about my debut novel. The book was called *These Extraordinary Times*, and three days after I'd started pitching it to literary agents, Bill Owens of the legendary Owens Agency had flown out to me in the Bay Area, plied me with hundred-dollar sushi, and told me—almost flippantly—"Oh, this book will be huge. I'll see to that."

A week later, he'd sold the manuscript for $1.2 million in a nine-publisher auction.

That month blurred with celebrations. Texts poured in from friends I hadn't spoken to in years: holy shit dude just saw your instagram thats so sick lol!!! Emails arrived from my college professors: Dear Parker: I was pleased to read the good news about your novel. Many happy regards from the department. Best, Elias.

I could barely believe it—that after years of scraping rare minutes to write, of agonizing over every page, this dream I'd had since childhood was about to be realized.

These Extraordinary Times had sold to Lauren Nilsen, a seventy-year-old industry veteran at Coronation Books who spoke in long, elegant sentences over the phone, like she'd lifted her lines out of Daphne du Maurier. By January, a velvety-covered advance copy was commanding lines out the door at bookseller conventions, and by May, I was sitting for overwhelming interviews in which I tried to talk about the book and interviewers insisted on talking about me. Three months from publication, *These Extraordinary Times* was set to be the book of the year.

Then, on the morning of June 11, a critic named Selina Chan published her review in the online edition of *City Magazine*. It was my first major review.

This was its kindest paragraph:

> *These Extraordinary Times* is a stupefying misfire, ten thousand fine sentences that heroically join forces to say nothing. Hardly does a scene begin to take shape when it's blasted to pieces by some postmodern pyrotechnic—six pages of footnotes! an interlude told in the form of an Excel spreadsheet!—as though Mr. Navarro were embarrassed to catch himself engaging in that pedestrian work of the author: writing a paragraph that might interest a reader.

Within hours, the review was gaining traction, cross-posted everywhere online with gleeful commentary:

> **@wolvescandlesfelt**: So glad publishers are spending $1.2 million on Baby's First MFA Workshop Project, starring lines like "Through the delicate skin of her eyelid the organ itself felt grapelike." Vomit :)

@servingkant: only two directives remain in contemporary literature, if indeed our modern letters can still be termed literature, which are to eagerly plumb new depths of the facile and to blithely elevate muck dredged from the collective artistic nadir

@sierrasnax: Lol this is why I hate when Asian authors write books aimed at white people . . . the self-hatred is strong with this one

@Patriot27Max: Don't you love to see the left eat itself? This is what publishers get for selling out to woke novelists!

@LanaLanaLand: Okay but like, are we shocked? Yale is right there in his bio. What IS publishing if not watching rich, talentless straight men make millions living off their family's money and using Ivy League connections to get their execrable books on shelves?

"But I didn't *make* any publishing connections at Yale," I sputtered to Bill over the phone. "My family doesn't have—look, can I just reply to say—"

"*Absolutely not.*"

"But if I just—"

"Parker! No. You don't say anything to these people."

"But they have no idea who I am! They're making up this idea of who I am!"

"It doesn't matter. This is beneath you. There's always been an element of complete idiocy in the culture. Repeat after me: It doesn't matter."

I splayed my hand against the wall of my apartment, the fresh paint squeaking under my fingertips. The response of the reading public seemed to matter a lot, actually. It mattered because I'd bought an apartment in North Brooklyn three weeks ago, when I was confident I'd have a steady income from writing, instead of, potentially, no writing paychecks for the rest of my life. It mattered because people were making assumptions about my parents, who had felt embarrassed enough when I'd paid off the mortgage on my mother's house, and then on the soup-stained one-bedroom where my father had lived in the two decades since their divorce. That was the truth about my "family money," and the truth, as far as I was aware, mattered.

"It doesn't matter," I said, keeping my voice low and controlled.

"Correct," said Bill. "Look, Parker, in some ways you're lucky. These things are essentially unserious, but they can get nasty."

"Nasty? And this is, what, fun and enjoyable?"

"No, of course not. But one critic who doesn't like your style? You have to expect that if you write anything remotely interesting. What counts is that she didn't go ad hominem."

"I'll write her a thank-you card."

Bill barked out a laugh. "It's tough, I know, but you've got to ride this out."

So I sat back and watched the *City* review smash its way into the far corners of the internet. That was the Selina Chan effect. Two years ago, one of her raves in *City* had skyrocketed a future Booker Prize winner out of obscurity. On the flip side, her vicious pans induced this sort of instant backlash, like the recoil on a shotgun. You'd have thought she was some longtime titan of criticism, but in reality, she was only a couple of years older than me.

I began to feel a furious clench in my stomach at the sight of her headshot, an unrealistically flattering picture that some photographer had probably tweaked for hours in Photoshop: Chan with her arms folded on an enormous desk, wisps of black hair escaping from an artfully messy topknot, dark eyes set deep above high cheekbones, her mouth exactly symmetrical and unsmiling.

And, one by one, the rest of the critics followed her lead. "Bloated and exhausting," they said. "Fails to justify its own existence." In the end, the book I'd labored over for six years became a once-in-a-century flop, slinking in at number eighty-seven on the *USA Today* bestseller list for a single week before disappearing. I'd cost my publisher millions.

Still, I had two things that most writers didn't: time and money. When I'd finished spending full days in bed and half joking about jumping in front of a train, I opened a new journal, and two years later, Lauren bought my next manuscript, *High and Dry*, for fifteen thousand dollars.

Obviously I'd asked Coronation not to send a copy to *City*. Still, sometimes, in weak late-night moments, I'd imagined Selina Chan reading *High and Dry*. I pictured her sitting in a Chesterfield armchair in some underlit mansion, turning pages with that uncrackable expression. I imagined her realizing that, to her shock, she loved what she was reading.

I fantasized about the rave she'd write, whose cool, precise sentences would admit how wrong she'd been about me. She'd write that I was in fact a once-in-a-generation talent, possibly a genius.

Then I reminded myself that I had better things to do than fixate on one smug, overpowered member of the literati, and I went back to loathing every atom of her being.

"Parker?" Arthur said. "You okay?"

I barely heard him. I'd sat down on our sofa and was staring through the window, watching the park across the street with its laughing families. The autumn light suddenly felt thin, as though each sunbeam were gliding down the length of a spiderweb.

"Hey."

The concern in Arthur's voice brought me back to myself. One look at the way he was approaching me, edging along the border of our rug with slow, cautious steps, and I knew he was mapping out strategies for the next weeks, shortlisting friends to invite me out, planning tactful questions about whether I'd taken my medication. He might even try to cook for us, a sign of real catastrophe.

"Yeah, no, I'm okay," I said quickly. "Thanks."

"You sure? Don't get depressed over this, Park. She's not worth it."

"I'm not depressed. I'm just . . ." Outside, the yellowing oak leaves trembled. I pushed myself to my feet. "I'm kind of pissed off."

"Really?" Arthur sounded pleasantly surprised.

"Yeah." I strode to the kitchen and began wedging groceries into our overfull fridge. "I mean, she didn't have to do this. She—she could have ignored the book. Right?"

"Right."

"So *why* is she still punching down at me?" The freezer wailed as I forced in a sleeve of plant-based burgers. "Did I murder her in a past life?"

"Bro, this is exactly what I've been saying for three years! My theory is that she hates all books now. Like, she's read too many of them and can't feel things like 'enjoyment' anymore, so she has to take out her bitterness on the nearest target."

"Maybe. I don't know . . . Her other pans don't feel the same." I shut the freezer door and pressed my forehead against its cool surface, my frustration flickering out as quickly as it had kindled. "God, what am I going to do? Bill's never going to sell anything else I write. I have a mortgage to pay."

Arthur settled against the counter next to me. "Good thing the first one made you an overnight millionaire, right?"

I didn't answer.

"Hold on," Arthur said. "*Hold* on. Parker. Please tell me you didn't secretly gamble your whole advance on fantasy football or something."

"No, no. It's . . ." I sighed. "So, my agent's cut was fifteen percent, and forty percent of the rest went to taxes, right?"

"Right."

"Then I paid off my parents' places, and zeroed out my sister's student loans, and—"

"Wait, for real? Elena or Christi?"

"Elena. Christi and my brothers paid theirs off already." I gestured to the apartment. "And then there's this place. I did a thirty-five percent down payment to save on interest."

Arthur had never asked how much our apartment had cost, but he knew as well as anyone else that in this part of New York, a million dollars was pocket change. I could see him doing the math, realizing that my bottomless windfall would be gone within a couple of years.

"I'm so stupid," I muttered. "What was I thinking?"

Arthur recovered. "Hey. Come on. You didn't want your family drowning in debt, and you've wanted to live in New York your whole life. That's what you were thinking." When I didn't speak, he shook me by the shoulder. "The *City* thing is going to blow over, okay? The book comes out in . . . January?"

"February."

"February! Nobody's going to remember this in February. Selina Chan is a professional name-caller. You can't let her get to you."

Despite everything, the righteous set to Arthur's chin made me smile. He was a righteous person in general, a perennial activist who could never quite turn off the air of canvassing you for something. I'd always envied his certainty.

Arthur and I had met in a writing seminar at Yale. We'd both been working on irredeemable short stories revolving around "shocking" coincidences, which would have shocked no person with a working prefrontal cortex. He was a book publicist at Macmillan now, and he always managed to discover weird little novels I wound up half in love with. As long as Arthur liked what I was writing, I could cling to my self-respect.

He was still looking at me expectantly.

"Thanks," I said. "Yeah. Maybe nobody will care."

"There we *go*." Arthur clapped me on the back and looped his shaggy hair into a ponytail. "We're going to go to that cocktail thing tonight and not even think about it, all right?"

I let out a tired laugh. Arthur had been invited to a party celebrating the hundred-year anniversary of a publisher called Maynard-Roth Editions, and he'd been angling all week for me to join him. Right now, I felt about as sociable as a Carthusian monk, but if I'd learned anything from the last go-around, it was that sitting at home and marinating in self-pity wasn't actually a useful coping mechanism.

"Okay," I said. "I'm in."

Then I retreated to my bedroom, pulled up the *City Magazine* website, and braced for the worst.

In Parker Navarro's Sophomore Effort, a Search for Meaning in a Bus Driver's Daily Route

BY SELINA CHAN

Life is full of punishing routine. Parker Navarro's new novel, *High and Dry*, reminds us of this inescapable fact, though likely not in the way he intended. Over these six hundred pages, Navarro invites readers into the life of Dave Hernandez-Gretzky, a Houston bus driver who circles a single route, morning to night. When forty days of rain hit Texas, Dave holds fast to his preestablished patterns, retracing his assigned streets even while the water level climbs across the city.

A fertile enough premise . . . [U]nfortunately, the Parker Navarro writing *High and Dry* is very much the same writer who, three and a half years ago, perpetrated *These Extraordinary Times*, that paean to hysterical realism that felt plucked from the trenches of the early 00s. Navarro would like to use Dave's routine to skewer the absurd circularity of the way we live. Instead, he winds up doing what he does best: subjecting the reader to hundreds of pages of shapeless musings . . . [a] maddeningly oblique, non-confrontational approach to what should be vibrant, dramatic material. . . . [I]f a writer can't look uncomfortable realities in the eye, how can he satirize them? How can he expose the absurdity of life if he's palpably frightened that people might call him absurd? How, most mysteriously, can Navarro write so much and communicate so little?

In one memorable scene, a lost seven-year-old boards Dave's bus . . . [a] humane moment cut short by—and I wish this were a joke—the boarding of a mutant alligator who's acquired the power of speech. Readers of *These Extraordinary Times* will remember this tic: the way Navarro subverts every promising moment, displaying a kind of miserable hypervigilance that makes even a skilled stylist painful to read. Possibly, if *High and Dry* were less desperate to make neurotic apologies for its own contents, it could adequately explore any of the thousands of thoughts that fly pell-mell through its shallow and obnoxious protagonist's head.

With its unforgivable length and wild tonal inconsistencies, this is another novel in search of an idea from an author who mistakes bombast for wit. The most punishing routine of all might be opening a new book by Navarro, still wondering if he's found something to say.

Chapter Two

Selina Chan

"It's up."

I reluctantly lifted my eyes from my book. "What?"

Kellie Cade, *City Magazine*'s other senior editor, had angled herself into my office in the usual way, her chin hooked around the doorjamb. "Your *High and Dry* review," she said. "It just went up."

"Ah."

Kellie snapped her fingers. "Hey. Don't do the face. It's a good piece."

"A piece that should never have been assigned to me."

"Probably. People online are having fun with it, though. Maybe it'll keep the click overlords off our backs for a week." She tossed a glance down the hall. "Speaking of which: Hayden's here for the meeting."

"What? Why?"

"I don't know. Firing the rest of us, maybe?"

"Thank you for that inspiring theory."

Kellie cracked a smile that compressed her eyes into sly green dashes. "I try. See you in there." Her hair whipped out of sight.

Alone, I exhaled and let Lauren Groff flip shut in my lap. Kellie had always been much more attuned to the thoughts and feelings of people online than I was; the closest thing I had to social media was a Venmo account. And contrary to what the internet surely thought about me, I didn't relish the idea of people cheering on a negative review, especially for a book I'd never wanted to read.

I swept the advance copy of *High and Dry* from my desk. One look at its dusky, rain-shot cover, and my frustration began to simmer again.

I would never pat a writer on the back for what they might someday accomplish. That was a job for the supportive English teacher, for generous friends and relatives. But if I'd been forced at gunpoint to talk about that dubious concept, *potential*, I would have had to admit that Parker Navarro had it. The man could write a single-punch knockout of a sentence. The kind of description that makes a reader look up with new eyes at the room around them, freshly aware of texture, color, and sensation.

He also seemed perversely uninterested in making any meaning out of his balletic turns of phrase. He was Pavarotti singing on a nonsense word. Van Gogh run through a paper shredder.

The dizzying height of his potential—and the corresponding depth of the loss that these god-awful books represented.

I stood and tossed *High and Dry* onto the desk face down, exposing Navarro's brooding headshot. Charcoal-gray sweater pushed to his elbows. Soft-looking hair that rose above his forehead. For an instant I imagined his shadowed eyes following me, a glint of accusation in that glossy black and white.

Ridiculous. I swept my laptop beneath my arm and strode out of my office, down the hall. To my left, the misty silhouettes of fact-checkers paced behind frosted glass doors. On the right, framed *City Magazine* covers lined the wood-paneled walls. Warhol-inflected sixties duplication. A screaming neon mouth from 1987. By the time I rounded the corner, I'd pushed Parker Navarro out of my mind.

I believed in criticism too much to waste time on guilt. When critics wrote honestly, the public could use us to cut through the chatter and find the books that would illuminate their worlds. But if we shrank back from our feelings, apologized and demurred, we were of no use to anybody.

I had one life. I wanted to spend it surrounded by excellence, by fine wine and dark chocolate and great reads. I wanted everybody else to have that, too. How many books could a person read in a lifetime? A thousand, five thousand, ten? A world without criticism looked like the thirty-million-title Amazon catalog.

Without criticism, I'd have died unaware of *Asylum Piece*, Anna Kavan's strange, clinical story collection shot through with isolation and incomprehension, which Marcy D'Artagnan had raved about in *City Magazine*—a book that had saved my life at sixteen.

In a world without discernment, in the attempt to give everything a chance, you could die without tasting chocolate. I was not sorry.

I entered the library at 10:59 to Hayden singing out, "*There* she is. Our killer queen!"

I moved my mouth into something that could technically be called a smile and looked to the armchair in the corner. Seated there was a tall, sharp-chinned woman in her midforties wearing beige cashmere and scrolling through an iPhone the size of her face. Her name was Hayden Fairbanks. Back in April, when *City* had been bought by a venture fund named Nextward Capital Associates, she had become our handler.

We'd never seen her in the library, though. Her presence felt intrusive. Bookshelves ran corner to corner in this inner sanctum of the *City* offices, displaying the hundreds of authors—Ellison, Faulkner, Sontag—who had published work in our pages.

"The reactions are *so* good," Hayden went on, to her phone screen.

"I can't believe you didn't want to write this. Didn't I say you were the perfect fit?"

Of course she had. I was used to the euphemisms. The perfect fit. The viewpoint we need. The truth was, as *City*'s only Asian American staff writer, I was all but required to write our opinion on everything from the continental diaspora.

No matter that Parker Navarro was third-generation Filipino American, the Californian son of Californian parents, while my parents had moved from northern China to Minnesota in the 1980s. Our backgrounds had never come within one and a half thousand miles of each other. But no one really seemed to care about this.

"Thank you, Hayden." I sat stiffly at the round table, a pitted oak slab fifteen feet in diameter whose feet, four heavy claws, had notched deep footholds in a century-old Persian rug. When I'd started here, twenty-six of us had sat around this table during editorial meetings. Now we were down to fourteen.

"Deep breaths," Kellie murmured, spinning her pen over the back of her hand.

"Working on it," I said under my breath.

The clock hit eleven, and the door swung open. In swept our editor in chief with the embattled air of a general on day one hundred of the siege. Scott Goodwin had been *City*'s editor for twenty years. Every year he looked more and more the part, with his trim, graying beard and his rotation of well-cut suits.

He lowered himself into his chair, shook his expensive sleeves up his forearms, and interlocked his arthritic knuckles. "Good morning, all," he said. His eyes strayed to Hayden but didn't linger. "Let's kick right off with features. Joyce, what have you got?"

We looked to our features editor, Joyce Crafton, a pixieish woman in her sixties whose tufts of silver hair stuck out from her scalp in every direction. This combined with her wide, unblinking eyes gave her a look of recent electrocution. "What do we think about Teresa Cagle?" she said. "I have an idea for her latest, *Pathogenius*—you know, with the alien frame narrative? I want to put it in conversation with *War of the Worlds*."

"What's the gist?" Scott asked.

"So"—Joyce adjusted her reading glasses with a jittering fingertip—"with the pandemic in mind, I've been thinking about barren environments. Safe from disease, but hostile to life: Is that more comforting or menacing? The way that both books—"

Hayden cleared her throat. The fourteen of us looked to her corner. She was still holding her phone near her face, as if she were about to return to an unmissable video call.

"Hi." She broke into a wide smile, as apple-cheeked as a cursed Victorian doll. "I'm *so* sorry to interrupt the pitch sesh. So great to see you guys again!"

Nobody answered.

"I was wondering . . ." Hayden looked to Joyce. "Who's this Teresa Cagle person? *Path*—what's this book?"

"Oh, it's wonderful, it's called *Pathogenius*," said Joyce quickly, shifting forward in her seat so that her glasses skittered back down to the tip of her nose. "It came out in July."

"Okay! So, like, a summer blockbuster? Book of the season?"

"Well . . . not exactly. It didn't get the attention it deserved."

"Ooh. Bummer." Hayden's smile flagged. "And the author is . . ."

"Teresa Cagle. A real talent. Her first collection was in 2003. Then a novel in 2012 that, I think, was a finalist for the National Book Critics Cir—"

Hayden, who'd gone back to her phone, said, "Right, I'm seeing the book. Wow. A dozen reviews on Amazon." She scrunched her face into an apologetic wince. "I'm not sure, Joyce."

I aimed a wearied look at Kellie, who bobbed her freckled shoulders.

Apparently Nextward was no longer satisfied with emailing Scott twice a week to complain about our traffic. They'd stationed Hayden at the source to make sure our coverage had all the intrigue of unbuttered toast.

"Point taken, Hayden," Scott said with audible restraint. "That said, *Pathogenius* is an excellent book. I'd be happy to send you a copy."

Hayden laughed. "Okay, but seriously, what about the Top Ten lists Alicia did last month? Those performed." She aimed an encouraging look at Alicia, one of our editorial assistants, who flinched. "What if you jumped in on those for a week or two, Joyce? We could use a few more in the pipeline." Her nails clattered against her phone screen. "And I just forwarded everyone a list of books I've been seeing around. It'd be great to pop out some reviews for them while they're hot."

A dozen laptop track pads clicked as we opened the email, and Kellie disguised a laugh as a cough. Hayden's list was immediately familiar, culled half from Barack Obama's reading list and half from October's highest-profile book club selections.

I kept my voice even. "Hayden, unfortunately we don't have the bandwidth for this. Our review calendar is blocked out for the next few weeks."

"Ah. You know, I'm *so* glad you mentioned output. I've been wanting to break open this conversation: How do we feel about using AI to increase the team's content production?"

Deafening quiet dropped over the round table. Beside me, Kellie's pen stilled in the middle of a doodle of Hayden. A blot of ink widened until it engulfed her left eye.

"We do not feel good," said Scott, in a voice that suggested he wanted nothing more than to tar and feather her.

Hayden looked from shocked face to shocked face and let out a small laugh. "Everybody, come on! Let's be realistic, right? You're up against sites that are packed with AI. Of course we want to preserve the spirit of the whole *project*, but at the end of the day, this is a business. Dollars in, dollars out. We need more eyes on the site if we're going to keep paying for"—she gestured at us—"*this*."

She rose, hoisting her purse onto her shoulder. "Think about it! No one's saying you can't add your own little personal touch."

As she headed for the door, she spared a brief downward glance for Scott, as though he were her unpaid intern rather than a man who'd shaped American culture for decades. "Thanks *so* much for letting me sit in, Scott." She paused, keen-eyed, on the threshold. "It's been so illuminating."

The door shut, leaving crushing silence in her wake.

After work, I met my friend Jacob for a drink in the Meatpacking District, at an Italian restaurant as long and thin as an alleyway. We drank matching happy-hour glasses of house white, ten dollars per anemic pour.

"Scott won't let that happen," said Jacob. "Will he?"

"Scott would set fire to our office before touching AI."

"Good. I need to know that your pans are made from all-natural, homegrown loathing."

I managed to smile. "So, you saw the *High and Dry* review."

"Yep." Jacob laughed. "It, uh, didn't sound like a very good book."

"We don't have to talk about it."

"My lips are sealed," he said. We clinked and drank.

Jacob and I had met on our first day at Columbia orientation through alphabetical fate: Selina Chan, Jacob Chau. Even then, he'd been handsome in a professorial way. Thick wavy hair, relaxed blazer, stubble. He'd been the sort of person you'd expect to adjust his glasses while reciting facts about Sartre. Which he'd frequently done.

Everybody thought something sordid was going on between us, despite Jacob's five years of blissful marriage. True, we'd dated for about a month in our senior year, but it was hard to express the lack of romantic feeling I'd had for him since then. His passive, go-with-the-flow style of partnership had felt like some torturous psychological test—how could someone have so few opinions on how we spent our days?—and the sex had appalled me, a kind of limp-touched, romantic-whisper lovemaking that had made me want to go to a boxing class.

I'd known the fling was doomed forever when he'd asked me, with genuine curiosity, why I cared so much about the other students' comments in a seminar I'd been taking.

"Because they haven't done the readings, Jacob," I'd said. "I can look at their faces and see they didn't read the book."

"So?" he'd said with a good-natured laugh. "Does that hurt *your* understanding of the book in some way?"

I hadn't even known where to start with that. Jacob, Upper East Side–born and bred, might not have related, but I'd moved halfway across the country and taken on eighty thousand dollars of debt for that degree. It was fucking Columbia. I was supposed to be sitting in a room full of exceptional people who would try, who would *care*, in exceptional ways, not legacy admits who started every sentence with "Um, going off what Addison said." But I could have tried for hours to explain my frustration, and it still wouldn't have registered with Jacob in any personal way.

I loved him, of course. He was my best friend, and every day I admired his kindness and humility. I adored his wife, Cassie, a molecular biologist and rock climber who, with her mile-long list of travel plans and her desire to micromanage every detail, had always been a self-evidently perfect match for Jacob. And I loved walking into their apartment to see their one-year-old daughter, Lyra, finding new and creative ways to destroy their imported furniture.

"How's Cassie?" I asked. "Wait—did she like the Isa Serrano book?"

"Not really her thing. She said it was 'too crime-y.'"

"*Too crime-y?*"

Jacob made a calming motion. "Easy, easy. It's the thought that counts."

He was baiting me. I gave him an unimpressed look and sipped my wine.

"What, you're not going to say it?" He sat up out of his usual slump to imitate my posture. "'It's not the thought that counts, it's the execution!'"

"It *is* the execution that counts," I muttered.

Jacob laughed. "Got her."

I broke into a smile. "What about the gremlin? Has she developed ethics yet?"

"No. I think she might actually be getting more evil." Jacob covered a massive yawn with the back of his hand.

"You two still aren't sleeping?"

"Nope," he said dully. "She's been having nightmares again."

"I'm so sorry. Can I do anything? Edit anything?" I asked. Jacob was a grant writer for a global health nonprofit. Whenever he sent me a proposal for a final polish, I was acutely reminded that there could, in fact, be more urgent aspects to writing than beauty of language. "Or—let me know if I can babysit. Buy you and Cassie some time to nap."

"Thanks, Lina." Jacob rubbed at one eye with his knuckle. "I miss sleeping, but I miss *doing* things more. We spend half our lives, like, mumbling about when we used to go on dates. Let alone ride horses in Croatia."

"That's what you get for bringing the miracle of new life into the world."

"Yeah, our bad."

Once we'd finished our wine, we gathered our coats and edged down the restaurant's slender artery. "Which way are you headed?" Jacob asked.

"FiDi. There's some publishing party. Scott made us all swear to come."

"*You're* going to a party? On a *Wednesday*?"

"I know. But one drink and then I'm home." As we emerged onto the sidewalk, the wind combed the cool evening air through our hair. I leaned up and hugged Jacob.

"Good luck," he said. "Text me if you start hyperventilating in a bathroom."

"Jacob."

"Oh, how I miss College Selina." He waved and walked north.

With the breeze humming in my ears, I watched him move lightly, purposefully back toward his beautiful life. We were thirty-four now and the novelty of Jacob having a kid wasn't so shocking anymore, but sometimes, in moments like these, the difference between our lives hit me afresh. I'd be standing somewhere like this, alongside a road full of cars, in the black space beneath the old train line, watching the world move and change, feeling pinned in place. I'd wonder if I belonged in any real way to that world, where people tumbled pleasantly along in love, or if something about me was just askew enough to put me on the outside.

I caught myself before I got too wistful. Perspective, after all, came from being on the outside of something. Better to be out here and objective than inside and lost.

I buttoned my coat and headed for the subway.

The Maynard-Roth party was held at Cipriani, a venue whose two levels of gray granite columns loomed over Wall Street. In publishing, the place was best known for hosting the National Book Awards every November, but tonight the atmosphere was more casual. The cavernous ballroom had been cleared of the usual lavish dining setup. Instead, a hundred small high-top tables formed long aisles down the hall, and teak easels, at intervals, displayed four-foot blowups of Maynard-Roth book covers. Hundreds of people in neutral coats stood grouped around them, chatting over drinks, their profiles lit by the racks of stage lights that hung suspended from the seventy-foot ceiling.

I wound between groups and ignored the eyes that strayed to me. One person in my wake said, in a lowered voice, "Was that—?" I increased my pace.

At the curtained front windows stood tables of hors d'oeuvres, plus the bar. I bolted a few slices of cheese and swept up a glass of bubbles, but before I could retreat, an eager voice said, "Excuse me, are you Selina Chan?"

I turned, bracing myself. A pair of women holding champagne flutes were gazing at me with expressions of morbid fascination.

I managed a taut smile. "Yes. Hi."

The woman who'd spoken was close to six feet tall and cupped her champagne glass as though it were a mug of hot cocoa. Bending toward me like a reed, she said, "I'm Eileen. I do data at Harper. I read all your pieces."

As her friend's head bobbed, my shoulders relaxed. So they didn't hate me. In criticism you never knew who was carrying one of your less flattering sentences around in their pocket, nursing it like a bottle.

"Thank you," I said. "I appreciate that."

Eileen exchanged an uninterpretable look with the small blonde friend. Had I somehow, in five words, said something abnormal? That would be a record, even for me.

But then Eileen said, "This is my friend Courtney Mitchell." Panic spread over Courtney's face, but Eileen forged on: "Courtney's an author. Her debut comes out next August and it's brilliant."

"Ah." I nodded to Courtney. "I'll keep an eye out. What's the title?"

Her face turned bright red. "Oh, wow—thank you so much. It's called *Mean Streak*. I hope you like—if you read it, I mean, not that I expect you to—"

"I'll read it," I said. "Congratulations on the sale."

A profusion of giddy thanks, and they disappeared into the crowd. I wrote Courtney's name into my phone and breathed. That could have been much worse.

After a full circuit of the ballroom and mezzanine, I'd found nobody from *City*. Inconvenient, since Scott needed to see I'd been here before I could escape. Moments later I'd been roped into conversation with an editorial director asking if I'd slide his author's latest into my queue. "Selina Chan, out in public!" he exclaimed with the rare, brash confidence of literary extroverts. "A review from you, I know Jack would be thrilled . . ." Meanwhile, from over his shoulder, two men's venomous glares were burning into my forehead.

None of it surprised me. I was less than beloved among novelists. Occupational hazard. Six months ago, Christian Gatehead had referred to me—on the record with *The New York Times*!—as "an insufferable little whiner delivering undergraduate-level analysis with the self-righteousness of a youth pastor." Better characterization than anything in his past three books.

I did another round of the mezzanine with my glass emptying. I hadn't eaten enough. What was I doing here, in a hall of people who looked at me and saw either a tantalizing shortcut to commercial success or the literary Antichrist? I never felt so far away from the point of literature, an art form built on honesty and intimacy, as I did at these events. To my left, a group of authors burst into laughter over a comment made by the bestselling writer among them. They gazed at her like they wanted to eat her.

I wished I were at home. As usual, I wished I were alone.

And when I stopped at the mezzanine rail and glanced back down at the ballroom, I wished I were anywhere on earth but here, because stepping over the threshold in a dark felt coat, spots of color high in his cheeks from the cold, was none other than Parker Navarro.

My breath stuck in my throat like a bone. I was seized by the absurd urge to run. Instead I stood utterly stiff, hammered down into place like a nail.

Navarro slipped out of his coat. He was lean and angular, the first author I'd ever seen whose headshots didn't overstate his appearance to the point of unreality. He actually looked like that: debonair, something sorrowful about his mouth, like he was made for black and white.

Before I could move, he looked up, across the ballroom, and his eyes locked onto mine.

Chapter Three

Parker

It was her.

Selina Chan, in the flesh.

I stared up at the mezzanine as her eyes lasered down into me. She had one crimson-nailed hand curled over the rail and the other cradling a nearly empty champagne flute. Shadows the color of honey fell down the long lines of her throat, while a teaspoon of light pooled in the divot between her collarbones. Her hair was swept over one shoulder, a dark accent to her serious, delicate features.

Time distended. We might have looked at each other for a second or an hour.

Then the ghost of surprise vanished from her expression, and she looked away from me with a disdainful little turn of her head—and at that slight motion, such a powerful hatred pulsed through me that I felt as though my diaphragm had contracted.

Arthur nudged me. "Parker? What's up?"

"Nothing," I managed to say, but actually I felt like I was having a Joycean epiphany. For three years, I'd thought of Selina Chan as some force of nature, halfway between a celebrity and an omniscient literary god, but in reality, she was this: just some *person*, alone at a party in a well-cut jacket, who happened to have strong opinions.

What gave her the right to ruin people's careers? Had she ever even tried to write a book?

What the fuck did she know?

Arthur was eyeing my expression warily. "Let's get a drink, all right? The bar's over there."

"Right. Cool." I followed at his elbow as usual, trying to appear normal. If Arthur found out Selina Chan was here, that'd be his night down the drain, too.

When Arthur left to check his coat, I knocked back the last of one old-fashioned and got another. *No*, I told myself, like I was my own disobedient dog. No, I wouldn't approach her. I wouldn't demand to know how she could have been more offended by *High and Dry* than by Christian Gatehead's unreadable latest book. I was going to be a good little author who held his tongue and suffered in silence.

It was occurring to me that this second drink might have been a less than brilliant idea when Arthur returned. "Okay," he said, rolling up his shirt sleeves. Arthur did pretty well with women already, being tall, but he'd read somewhere that women liked it when men rolled their sleeves to their elbows, and now he did so with an almost pathological consistency. "Sarah and Brady are here somewhere. Want to find them?"

"Sure, I just . . ." I scanned the crowd. Selina Chan could be leaving as we spoke, slithering back into her lair. I might never get this opportunity again.

I made up my mind. "Sorry, man, I need some air. The subway got me motion sick."

"Oh, shit. Want me to—?"

"No, don't worry! I'll catch up with you guys."

Outside, the cool air smelled of smoke, and a dozen people stirred on the sidewalk, cigarettes dangling from listless hands, drawing red shapes in the dusk. She wasn't here. I retreated inside, moving faster.

No sign in the ballroom or on the staircase to the mezzanine. If I'd blown this chance, I would seethe in bed for hours tonight. I'd wind up rereading her *City* profile for the hundredth time, hate-scrolling Google results for her name, looking for anything incriminating.

There was nothing to find, of course. She was too composed, too cryptic. She didn't even deign to have social media like the rest of us sheep.

On the mezzanine level, a group of familiar-looking authors were draped over the balcony railing. Spotting me, one of them murmured to her friend, amusement playing around her mouth. I plowed deeper into the mezzanine. This was Chan's fault, too. Thanks to her, I couldn't meet anyone new in publishing without wondering if they thought I was some talentless avatar of privilege who'd never worked a day in his life.

I stalked down a deserted side hall and shouldered locked door after locked door. Then, suddenly, a door came open, revealing a long catwalk that spanned the back wall of the ballroom. At the far end, an exit stood ajar.

I crossed the catwalk, head low in the shadows of the columns. When I peered through the crack of the exit door I found, of all things, a small library. Rows of books leaned against each other in tall walnut bookcases, and above, paired chandeliers hung from the ornamental molding.

There, by one of the floor-to-ceiling windows, an empty champagne flute glinting on a table to her side, stood Selina Chan, her head angled down at her phone.

I pushed through the door. She looked up and saw me.

She grew still and alert, like a lioness hunched low in grasses. For several long, silent seconds we stared at each other.

Then she said, "I don't think you want to do this."

"Do what?"

She let the question hang, idiotic, in the air. We both knew why I was here.

"I'm serious," she said. "Don't start this conversation. Walk away."

Her voice was exactly what I'd imagined: a cool, crisp alto. She seemed to use her tongue and teeth more actively than most people, reminding me of a snake's hiss, a cat baring its gums before it spits.

On any other day, I might have taken her advice. But I could feel the liquor in my blood now, in my capillaries, rolling close to the surface of my cheeks.

"No," I said, stepping deeper into the library. "I think you owe me an explanation."

"The only thing I owe you is an honest evaluation of your books. That's my job. And your job is to react professionally to reviews of your work, which means turning around"—she nodded to the door—"and leaving."

Something began to beat rhythmically in my gut. "You want to talk to me about professionalism after what *City* published this morning?"

Chan dropped her phone into her purse with a casual flick of her wrist, then turned from the window to face me. Under the black satin blazer was a green dress that shimmered when she moved, and as the light played over her features I was disgusted to realize how attractive she really was, even more attractive than the evidently unphotoshopped picture on her *City Magazine* profile. How was this fair? Why was the worst person in the world allowed to look like this?

"So," she said, "you think my review was unprofessional."

"Completely."

"Okay. Tell me: What should I have done differently? Should I have lied? Should I pretend to enjoy every book I read? Is that what you want *City Magazine* to turn into?"

"No. Come on. Obviously not."

"Then what do you want from me?"

"I want to know what your real issue was with my books!" I said, my voice rising. "I've read your other reviews, and—"

"What, all of them?"

"Yes. All of them."

For the first time, Chan looked surprised. Her eyebrows flinched toward each other.

"And," I barreled on, "you didn't write about other people's books like you wrote about mine. I want to know *why*."

In the small contractions of the muscles around her eyes, I could see her deciding whether or not to give me a real answer. I felt a pulse of impatience, hating her composure. The slight tilt of her chin. For a single bizarre moment, I imagined reaching out, disrupting the perfect sweep of her hair.

Finally, she said, "I don't know what you're talking about."

"Bullshit."

She shrugged. "My reviews speak for themselves. Obviously you can hang pretty little sentences on every paragraph just because you feel like it, but don't expect to earn my respect like that."

"I'm not trying to earn your respect!"

"Fascinating. Then why are you still talking to me?"

I set my empty glass on a desk with a clatter. "Maybe I want to know how you sleep at night. Maybe I want to know if you ever take a single second to think about the actual *people* writing the books you read."

"Oh, here we go." Chan snapped her purse shut, slung it over her shoulder, and stalked toward me. "Yes. Since you ask: I think about authors constantly. I think about what you say and how you say it. I think about what you wanted to accomplish, and how you failed to accomplish it." She stopped feet away. Her eyes, as cold and dark as deep seawater, utterly devoid of remorse, bored into mine. "I don't do retractions. If you tracked me down looking for an apology, it's not happening."

I'd never been a confrontational person. Growing up, I'd been the kid hiding in the back of the neighborhood bookstore, having slipped away from my parents' dinner-table arguments, and well into my twenties I'd hovered around the fringes of every social circle, dancing out of my friends' personal lives. The idea of me picking a fight was ludicrous.

But as I stood there, staring into Selina Chan's eyes, loathing her with an almost nuclear force, I suddenly understood the appeal. In that moment I detested her in such a pure, uncomplicated, almost exhilarating way. It was an anger that gave me a clear vision of myself. No, I wasn't a saint, but at least I wasn't *this*: a condescending narcissist who apparently thought that being intelligent and beautiful gave you license to look down your nose at the rest of the world. At least I built things rather than knocking them down.

"You must be such a miserable person," I said, my voice shaking, "to get this kind of joy out of ripping people's work to shreds."

"Joy? You think I got *joy* out of your books? I was assigned to them."

"But you could have said no to *High and Dry*!"

"Oh, really?" Her voice grew brittle. "I'm guessing you don't subscribe to *City*."

"Of course not."

"So, you read the articles with a paywall remover."

"Yes. I do."

"In which case, maybe you shouldn't be shocked that the magazine's up against a wall, and the writers can't do whatever we want." Chan made a noise of cold disgust. "*Authors*. I don't even know why I'm surprised. You pretend to care about the rest of the literary world, critics, bookstores, journals, everything—but at the end of the day, all that matters to you is flying to ten-thousand-dollar residencies and getting puff pieces in the media and padding your sales figures."

"And you think that's, what, frivolous? You think it's shallow to care about being successful?"

"Yes. Shockingly, I'd hope that authors would care more about literature than moneymaking."

I couldn't help it. I laughed. "Oh, my God, are you serious? Could your ivory tower *get* any higher? Authors have to care about moneymaking! Before I got that book deal, I worked two jobs and trying to get a hundred words on paper was like pulling fucking teeth. So, yeah, excuse us all for caring about our futures. Excuse me for wanting to keep writing novels instead of going back to bagging groceries and living paycheck to paycheck."

"*You're* talking to *me* about paychecks?" Chan snapped. I'd finally struck a nerve. The mask slipped, her cheeks flooding with red. I felt an odd thrill, looking at the contorted shape of her mouth. "Is that a joke? The author with the seven-figure advance wants to make this conversation about finances?"

"Yeah, Selina, I do," I said with a kind of savage pleasure. "You're the one who brought up money like it's so far beneath you, when—sorry, what do you think the point of a review is? The whole exercise is to tell people where to put their time and money."

"Oh, please, tell me more about the point of criticism!"

"I'll stop telling *you* about the point of criticism when you stop telling *me* how to write a book."

"I'll stop telling you how to write a book," she said through her teeth, "*when you write a good book!*" She slammed her purse down on the table beside us. A lock of hair toppled across the side of her forehead. "How dare you stand there and act holier-than-thou about paychecks and profits when you, *a millionaire,* read the entire archive of my work by illegal download? Thanks to assholes like you, *City* has to answer to a bunch of venture vultures who haven't read anything longer than an Instagram caption since high school. We've lost half our staff in the last two years. We can hardly buy the paper to print our magazine."

"Good!" I spat. "The type of trash you've been publishing, I can't wait until you go under!"

Chan's sudden silence was unnerving. The redness receded from her cheeks as she considered me. The quiet hummed in my ears.

She smoothed the stray lock back from her forehead, then twisted her hair up into that shining bundle at the back of her head. The motions of her long pale fingers, the crimson shine of her nails, the gleam of the light on her hair seemed calculated and hypnotic. "You want to know my problem with your books, Parker?" she asked, soft and scathing. "Look at what just came out of your mouth. No, you don't want *City* to go under. You'd have been thrilled if we gave you a rave. But you'll say anything, do anything, to get a reaction."

She took another step toward me in her dangerous-looking high heels. We were barely two feet apart now, eye to eye. I could see the thin, jet-black curve of her eyeliner. "That's spineless," she hissed. "Noncommittal. Just like your books. They have no guts, no loyalty to anything, there's a void at the center. God, I can't stand people who refuse to put anything on the line."

Face burning, I scrambled for a rebuttal, but to my humiliation, she was right about *City*. I'd read the magazine since I was a teenager with pretensions, acting like I understood their poetry, imagining my work in their pages someday. I'd wanted so badly for them like me.

I'd wanted everyone to like me.

In that moment, with a sickening plunge of my stomach, I wondered if that was the only thing I'd ever wanted while writing.

Selina Chan lifted one red-nailed finger and jabbed it into the center of my chest. A wave of heat issued out from the point of contact. "People like you," she said, "pretend to want real critics. Serious readers. But it's all for show. If anyone dares to dislike *your* precious novel, *your* darling little self-indulgent doorstopper, then surprise, surprise!

We suddenly turn into unqualified gatekeepers. And you'll blame us for your problems. And you'll stand back and wave in a future where the only 'reviewers' in the world are people getting backdoor payments from publishers to recite pitches for books they haven't read." She leaned so close that I could feel her breath on my cheek. "If you want the critical equivalent of an upvote, Parker, go the fuck back to the internet and filter for five-star reactions. It's not my job to like you."

And with that, she stalked out of the library and slammed the door behind her.

Parker

8:20 PM

Hey man, so sorry to flake, but I'm heading home. The motion sickness didn't get any better

Arthur

8:21 PM

That suuuucks. Get some sleep. I can pay for your Uber since you only came to this bc of me?

Parker

8:22 PM

Oh, no, really no need for that lol. Tell Sarah and Brady hi for me :) hope you all have fun :D

Arthur

8:25 PM

We will, see you tomorrow!

When I woke up, nothing about the night seemed real. Who had that man been, that author who'd stormed through a party to yell at his generation's most prominent critic? Surely I couldn't have done something that reckless, that impulsive.

I couldn't even blame the alcohol. When I rose from my bed, I discovered that I had no hangover. The world felt sun-touched, like some knob had turned to increase the brightness of everything around me, but my head was clear, my body relaxed.

As I washed my face and showered, I marveled at how good, exactly, I felt. Every motion in the mirror looked calm, confident, as I folded my glasses, pressed in my contact lenses, and tapped out my antidepressant. Chan had gotten the last word, but hadn't I said what I'd meant to say?

I'd even dug under her skin. That was the most satisfying memory: her face reddened, her mouth twisted. Maybe I'd never wanted restitution, or an explanation. Maybe I'd only ever wanted to make Selina Chan as angry as I felt.

I returned to my bedroom and picked up my phone from my bedside table.

That quickly, every drop of calm evaporated.

I had eighty-six notifications. A text from Bill at 7 AM that said, Call me. Arthur had linked me a video at three in the morning with the single word, Dude.

My heart began to drum. I loaded the video, which had been posted last night around ten o'clock by an account whose username was a twelve-digit string of random numbers.

Walnut bookshelves. Glittering chandeliers. Selina Chan and I were standing feet from each other, my fists balled and shoulders straining, her face tilted disdainfully toward me. I was snarling at her, "You must be such a miserable person."

"Oh my God," I choked out, checking the timestamp. The video was six minutes long. This person had seen nearly the whole thing.

I called Bill in a nauseated trance, pacing, careening, from my bathroom door to the window and back. The hangover had hit, pulsing behind my temple. As the phone rang and rang, nightmarish brightness throbbed around me.

"Parker," came Bill's gravelly baritone. The climax of Mahler's fifth symphony cascaded behind his voice. "I was just going to give you another call."

"I'm so sorry. It was so stupid. I shouldn't've—"

"Sorry? Why are you sorry?"

I stopped midpace, wondering if I'd misheard.

"Because I wrecked my career by confronting Selina Chan on video?"

To my amazement, Bill laughed. "Parker, you're behind the times. Read the reactions and call me back. And *The New York Times* wants to talk to you."

Chapter Four

Selina

Search results for: Selina Chan

1m ago wow, **Selina Chan** really is that mean irl, lol . . .

1m ago Did any of you WATCH the video? **Selina Chan** didn't do anything that deserved a confrontation. She reviewed a book. Leave it to some entitled man to take issue with a woman doing her job.

1m ago **Selina Chan** thinks she's that bitch but she's just a bitch. Like girlie you are not that important sit tf down.

2m ago My opinion on The Video is that both **Selina Chan** and Parker Navarro could get it

"Have a seat," said Scott.

I balked. He was sitting in his usual place at the round table. Beside him, wearing a fixed smile that promised death, sat Hayden.

"We're not firing you," Scott added.

"Yet," Hayden said.

This clarified nothing about whether I'd ruined my life.

I lowered myself into a chair. "Before you say anything, I'm sorry."

"Obviously." Scott leveled an uncomprehending look through his glasses. "I mean, for goodness' sake, Selina. Why didn't you just leave?"

I folded my hands on the table. It wouldn't sound professional to plead temporary insanity, or to admit that even now, the memory of Parker Navarro's martyred expression made me want to shatter something. Poor baby, rolling in his piles of hundred-dollar bills!

"You're right," I said stiffly. "Yes. I should have left."

"But you didn't," said Hayden. "And now we all have to try to salvage the situation. Even us . . . what was it? 'Venture vultures'?"

I winced.

Hayden crossed her arms and leaned toward me. She'd tinted her lips in that gradient style, the inner edge darker than the outer. She looked like she'd recently drunk somebody's blood. "Luckily for you, Scott's been reminding me how much of a value add you are to this team, in terms of engagement."

"Right. Thank—"

She held up a hand. "Here's what's going to happen. You're going to write a statement. You'll apologize to Parker Navarro. You'll apologize to our subscribers. You'll remind everybody that thanks to Nextward, *City* is in a better spot financially than it's been for a decade—which is true, in case you forgot."

I bit down on my cheek. Yes, technically, our financials had stabilized, after six months of watching our ferociously talented coworkers pack their desks and say they'd go into marketing.

"And," Hayden went on, "you'll publish a retraction about Parker Navarro's new book."

The words hit like a slap. "*What?*"

"You heard me."

"I can't do that," I said.

"Yes, you can. Or you can hand in your resignation."

"Hayden, I can't retract a review. It'll cast doubt on our entire editorial process."

Scott broke his silence. "Selina's right. Moving to change the piece suggests that we might have published it to target Parker Navarro. Our credibility would suffer enormously."

The frustration ballooned in my chest. "I'm sorry, but I have to say this: *Any* apology is going to suggest there's something questionable about our process. Or that there's something remotely acceptable about an author tracking me down at a party to pick a fight about a review." I moved to the edge of my seat. "Hayden, I shouldn't have had the argument. I know that. But backing down isn't the answer. It's a disservice to our readers."

"Oh, please—our readers? Don't pretend you were thinking about our readers last night. Do you think they wanted you to say any of that?"

Scott held up an index finger. "Actually, Hayden . . ." He rotated his laptop to show her a graph, a line tracking along at the bottom of the screen. "The data team sent me our subscription numbers this morning." Scott prodded the final point, which leaped halfway up the screen. "*City*'s had more new subscriptions in the past twelve hours than in the last two weeks combined."

Hayden seemed unimpressed. "Well, yeah. That video is everywhere. More awareness means more subscribers. That doesn't mean people like anything Selina said."

"But they do," Scott said. "The reactions aren't universally positive, but . . ." With another few clicks, he pulled up a couple of posts on Bluesky:

@narizsuperlativa: Was **Selina Chan** wrong? Every corner of publishing has become obsessed with hype, buzz, and relentless bite-sized positivity to the point that criticism is existentially endangered. Sorry your feelings got hurt, Parker, but if you don't have sharks in the literary ecosystem, you get fifty thousand minnows, where every minnow is some terrible book that publishers are trying to sell to you as the Second Coming of Sally Rooney.

7,187 likes **1,320 reposts**

@arslonga_vitabrevis: Hilarious that people are offended by **Selina Chan** talking about paywalls, like a journalist's livelihood has no relation to her publication's financial solvency.

5,226 likes **522 reposts**

"Yes," I said, pointing to the posts. "*This* is who we're writing for. If I go back on everything I said last night, it's going to alienate these people, who probably make up our whole subscriber base."

Scott nodded. "When op-eds come out about this, I'm expecting journalists to sympathize with Selina, too. Critics need to write honestly about what they feel."

Hayden's pale blue eyes bordered on bloodshot. They studied the graph of subscribers, unblinking. "So, you think we can build on this? How?"

"By refusing to let Parker Navarro dismiss our work," I said immediately. "People have clearly forgotten why magazines like *City* matter. That's a conversation we should be having."

"I'm not interested in what you think is culturally important, Selina," Hayden said. "I'm talking about *City*'s bottom line. I'm asking if sticking to your guns is going to grow our market or shoot us in the foot."

"Well, I don't think defending our worth to people is going to *lose* us any subscribers." I let out a short breath. "Look, haven't you been telling us for months to . . . to use socials more aggressively for cross-platform content engagement?" The effort it took me to speak these words with a straight face was incredible.

"Yeah," she said slowly.

"Well, if I'm going to bat for *City*, I'll finally have something to say on social media. I'll—I'll sign up for"—I waved at Scott's screen—"this stuff."

Hayden shook her head. "The optics are only going to get worse if you waltz onto socials to double down while Parker Navarro writes out some heartfelt apology."

"Apology?" said Scott. "He's not apologizing, Hayden. Haven't you seen the *Times*?"

"What?" said Hayden.

"What did he say in the *Times*?" I said.

Scott navigated to a new tab and opened the article. Hayden and I hunched closer to read.

By the bottom of the page, my hands had curled into fists on the table. "This is what I'm talking about!" I said. "We can't just sit back and let him say *this* about us to millions of readers. People have to see that he's not some brave truth teller who's right about the future of media. He's just another entitled, mediocre writer with an ego the size of Siberia."

Hayden raked her fingers through her glimmering highlights. Her eyes narrowed on the *Times* interview. In that moment, I knew that however much she hated me, Navarro's comments had just made him the bigger threat.

"Fine," she said. "Get him."

Excerpt: "Viral Video Captures Face-Off Between Bestselling Author, Critic"

This article has been updated to reflect additional commentary.

. . . "[O]bviously, I'm not thrilled that our conversation was filmed," said Navarro, "and I think Selina would agree. But this could be the threshold of a productive dialogue. Authors aren't allowed to respond to even the most virulent, ad hominem criticism. The aftermath of a negative review can be destructive and isolating."

And the future of *City*? To that, Navarro said, "I have nothing but respect for *City* as a historical institution, but personally, I don't see a place in any reasonable literary future for teeth-bared takedowns like Selina Chan's, which encourage gleeful dogpiles instead of artistic open-mindedness. In an industry designed to separate the wheat from the chaff at every level prepublication, you have to ask yourself what the function of a negative review is. A simple buyer beware? Hobbyist academic analysis? An exposé on the critic's precious feelings? More and more, it seems like the latter, like this brand of prescriptive criticism is designed to reduce the scope of literary culture and chastise those who dare to enjoy the difficult or offbeat."

In a request for comment, Chan replied, "I see that Parker Navarro, as usual, has used two hundred words where he could have used twenty."

"I can't believe he's saying all this," I muttered as Jacob slid a mug of chai over to me. "Thank you."

"Want one of these?" asked Cassie, withdrawing from a cabinet with a shortbread cookie sticking out of her mouth.

"Yes, please. You're the best."

"I know." She shook a cookie into my palm before dropping back down on the rug, where Lyra was thrusting wooden animal heads into a board painted to look like a zoo enclosure. "No, baby," said Cassie encouragingly. "Look, you're making a cursed chimera again."

I'd come straight from work to Jacob and Cassie's apartment. This was one of my favorite places in the world, a brick-walled loft with a subzero sense of visual unity. The rug that Lyra and Cassie sprawled upon was an enormous, psychedelically colored diamond with one point under a midcentury sofa and the other under an antique vinyl stand. The lights were black metal cones suspended from eight feet of cord. A steel counter ran along one wall toward a set of modular plastic bookshelves, giving the far corner a retrofuturistic look. It was a place with no self-control, crammed full of every beautiful thing Jacob and Cassie could imagine. The same way they lived their lives.

Jacob and I were sitting at the kitchen island, halfway in and halfway out of our phones. "Why wouldn't he keep this going?" Jacob said, scrolling. "Look at the benefits."

"What benefits?"

"Uh, Exhibit A." Jacob showed me his screen—the Amazon page for *High and Dry*—and pointed to the sales ranking: #12 in Books.

At this moment, Parker Navarro was selling more copies than the Bible. More copies, even, than Colleen Hoover.

"What the *fuck*," I said to Amazon dot com.

"What?" said Cassie. "Share with the class."

Jacob handed over his phone, and Cassie let out a bemused murmur. "Wait, is this just because of the video? No offense, Selina, but who outside publishing thinks this is interesting?"

"Lots of people," said Jacob. "It's on the front page of Reddit. It's all over Bluesky and Threads and Twitter. The internet loves taking sides."

"Great!" I said. "So people have decided to take the millionaire's side. Very reasonable."

Cassie laughed. "Dude, take the win. Just think about those sweet, sweet subscribers."

She was always calling me "dude" or "bro." Cassie Katayama was a native New Yorker, like Jacob, with a bottomless well of gym-rat affectations. At the moment she was wearing a T-shirt emblazoned with the words HIIT. LAB. REPEAT. Gaping holes where its sleeves had once been showed a slice of neon sports bra and rib tattoos.

I sighed. "I know, you're right." With a listless swipe I unlocked my phone. The apps now littering my background were pockmarked with red notification circles. They looked diseased. Since I'd joined Threads several hours ago, five thousand people had followed me. My mentions were full of strangers calling me names that I hadn't been called since I was a teenager, although Scott was right. There was a fair amount of support here, too.

In fact, near the top of my notifications was a post that almost twenty thousand people had liked.

"What?" said Jacob.

"Someone called Lola Xu tagged me in something."

"Who's Lola Xu?"

"I don't know. A book person, apparently." I tapped through to her colorful profile. "God, she has a hundred and twenty thousand followers."

"Does she hate you?"

"I don't think so." I scanned the post.

@LolaXu: Wow, so, the book world has reached a wild new low if this many people are defending Parker Navarro. He didn't have to read @SelinaChan's review! This is just like last year with the Hazel Samuels debacle in my comments lol. Friendly reminder for the millionth time: Reviews aren't for authors, they're for readers!! Authors, LEAVE US ALONE!

I hesitated, then hit Reply.

@SelinaChan: @LolaXu Thank you. I appreciate the support. I'm sorry to hear you had a similar experience online.

Within a moment, she'd replied:

@LolaXu: @SelinaChan Omg I can't believe you replied. You're a huge inspiration to me! I'm sorry this is happening. I can't understand how people are defending a man cornering a woman in a back room, yelling at her to change her opinion.

I set my phone down, a headache pulsing at the crown of my head. The day had been so loud, so fast, so unrelenting.

"Hey. Drink your tea," Jacob said. "Maybe help the gremlin make an animal that isn't an unholy monster."

I glanced down at a delighted Lyra, who had managed to force a snake's head onto the body of a fox. "Amazing," I said. "Right out of Revelations."

"Selina, I don't know why you're so miserable," said Cassie, unplugging the snake head from the board while Lyra stared at her with deep betrayal. "I thought you'd be thrilled to tear the guy's head off in the *Times*."

"Well, no, I don't mind that. Since it's him." I paused. "But I've never wanted to get involved in all this public-facing, personality-politics stuff."

"Why not?"

I gave Cassie a questioning look. "Would *you* like it?"

"Not at all." She leaned back against the sofa, hands behind her head. "And that's why I go into the lab every day and scrape my bacteria out of a centrifuge, instead of getting into a ninety percent public-facing field like, say, literary criticism."

I couldn't help a smile. "Okay. Yes. I want to share my criticism with people. That doesn't mean I want to share anything else, though." I gestured with my phone. "I mean, *this* is why. Overnight, hundreds of thousands of people have opinions on who I am. What am I supposed to do with that?"

Cassie shrugged. "Nothing. Those aren't informed opinions."

I didn't reply. It wasn't like I was so beloved among people with informed opinions, either.

Jacob must have followed my train of thought, because he asked, "Did you text your parents?"

"No."

"You don't think they'd want to hear ab—"

"Not really, no." I went back to my phone as Jacob and Cassie exchanged a glance in my peripheral vision.

Then my timeline reloaded. At the top, the algorithm suggested a post by Parker Navarro.

> **@ParkerNavarroWrites**: Wow. Thank you so much, everybody, for your kind messages. I'm trying to reply to everyone, but it's been an intense day, to say the least—in the best possible way. I couldn't have anticipated that The Video, haha, would resonate with so many of my fellow authors and

"Jesus *Christ*," I said, slapping my phone down on the island. "He's *loving* this." I stood up and strode to the world map mounted on Jacob and Cassie's travel wall. I seized the cherry-red head of an unevenly positioned pin and pushed it harder into Île de Ngor. "This whole circus act! He's lapping it up."

I stormed back to the island, grabbed my phone again, and tapped through to Navarro's profile, seething. The man was truly everything that was wrong with publishing. Bad books. Big ego. That obnoxious, brooding profile picture, like he was auditioning to be on the cover of *Vogue.*

Even more infuriating was the stream of fawning replies to every one of his paragraph-long posts. *Everyone who's ever created something knows how you feel, Parker! Who needs a bunch of elitist tastemakers telling us what to read?*

Even as I stared into the abyss that was Navarro's profile, a button reading 1 New Post appeared at the top of his feed. I hit the button, and the post materialized:

> **@ParkerNavarroWrites**: Curious how the Selina Chans of the world would feel if their hypothetical future novels were subjected to unrelenting, worldwide mockery?

I'd always assumed that "seeing red" was a rank cliché, but now it actually happened: a livid crimson flash over my vision.

My heart pounding in my throat, I began to type.

@ParkerNavarroWrites: Curious how the Selina Chans of the world would feel if their hypothetical future novels were subjected to unrelenting, worldwide mockery?

2,187 likes **85 reposts**

@SelinaChan: @ParkerNavarroWrites I have no desire to write a book, and it's childish to expect critics to "graduate" to fiction writing, as though the only way to love something is to imitate it. Hope that helps.

1,899 likes **59 reposts**

@ParkerNavarroWrites: @SelinaChan Amazing! You'd think someone whose career is built on reading comprehension would understand that I wasn't trying to imagine some hideous alternate universe where you try—doubtless, with all the empathy and delicacy of an electric chair—to write a novel. My point is that a career critic, someone who's never put artistic work into the world, can't imagine the vulnerability involved.

2,487 likes **44 reposts**

@SelinaChan: @ParkerNavarroWrites And it will be so brave of you to make yourself vulnerable once you've hounded the world's critics into silence.

2,287 likes **33 reposts**

@ParkerNavarroWrites: @SelinaChan I've never asked for anyone to be hounded into silence! You're acting like it's unreasonable to ask that human beings—and, maybe overgenerously, I'm including you in this category—show a little consideration toward their fellow human beings, even when they're expressing disappointment that they didn't like a book. I'm sure that must be hard for you.

1,922 likes **39 reposts**

@SelinaChan: @ParkerNavarroWrites Out of curiosity, are you physically capable of writing three sentences in a row without using an em dash?

3,133 likes **194 reposts**

Chapter Five

Parker

Teeth clenched, I paced from my kitchen to my front window and back, into and out of the cloud of steam rising from the stockpot on the stove, trying to think of some way to express how much I hated her, but in a way that would sound vengeful and righteous and not just vaguely pathetic.

I stopped in front of the TV, my vision clear with rage, as though I'd just put in eyedrops. I typed, Out of curiosity, are YOU capable of feeling any emotion besides sneering self-satisf

A red number 1 popped up over my messages tab at the bottom of the screen. I forcibly unclenched my jaw, deleted my response, and tapped into my inbox. An author named Jenny House had sent me a message:

Hi Parker! My name's Jenny. You probably don't know me, but I have a few books out from Penguin. Selina Chan wrote a soulless pan of my last book, too. I'm glad somebody's standing up to that vulture and her pretentious cult of readers who seem to hate all books!

I settled at our dining table, the fist in my gut loosening for the first time in hours.

Hi Jenny. I do know you, haha—I loved your first book! Thanks for the message. Really means a lot.

No way? she said. That's sweet. Nobody read that book!

Her debut had been a crime novel called *Hurricane Cassandra*, and I'd liked nearly everything about it, from its hard, muscular sentences to its unexpectedly pulpy climax. It deserved more attention, I wrote. When I recommend it to people, I tell them it's their new favorite hidden gem. :)

Stop! Jenny said, followed by a few bashful emojis. I've already preordered High and Dry. Can't wait to read it. Review by the Devil Herself notwithstanding.

I sent a laughing emoji back, then looked up as Arthur's keys rattled in the lock. A moment later he'd barged inside, face alert. "Hey. Are you—"

"I'm fine. Everything's fine."

He relaxed as he bumped the door shut. "Okay. Just, I was watching you two get into it."

"Yeah, five minutes ago I was ready to punch something."

"You don't still want to punch something?"

"A little. But this author just messaged me. We're bonding over being Selina Chan victims."

I tapped back to my profile and reread my replies to Chan with a twinge of unease. I'd never talked to anybody this way in my life. I sounded like such an asshole. "Should I delete this stuff I said to her?"

Arthur tossed his jacket onto the hook with an indignant flourish. "What, to Selina Chan? Fuck no. She deserves the heat."

"Right . . . Yeah, you're right. I just"—I let my phone clatter onto the table and rubbed my hands over my face—"it feels so weird to, you know, *say* shit like this."

"Enjoy it. I bet every person she panned would kill to be in your shoes."

I doubted that. Three years ago, I might have been a punchline, but I'd never been hated the way that some people in my mentions seemed to hate me now. You sexist pig, I hope your mother sees the video . . . You are what's poisoning our culture . . . If only someone had paid you $1.2 million to never write again.

Arthur jogged down the hall, I returned to the kitchen to check the stockpot, and my phone chirped again. Jenny House had sent another message:

If you want some commiseration, I know a bunch of authors who are a hundred percent behind you. We could hop in a group chat.

Really? I replied. I'd love that. Honestly, I don't know a lot of other authors.

Omg! Here, two minutes

A new group chat appeared in my DMs. I opened it to see the first notification: Jenny House renamed this group to Chan Pan Support Group.

Jenny House

Hey beauties! Meet Parker Navarro, the man of the hour

Aiden Linville

you mean my hero? defender of the innocent? avenging knight to selina chan's accursed wyrm?

Carla Lew

Parker!! I'm Carla. It is SUCH a pleasure.

Parker Navarro

Wow, it's great to meet you all!

JJ Purnell

I'm imagining you're overwhelmed? Please know that however much hate you're getting, there's an even larger contingent of people silently cheering you along.

Aiden Linville

true. about time this happened. according to selina chan, my second book was "unchallenging" but "blessedly slender"

Jenny House

Put that in your dating profile, Aiden

Giving the stock a stir, I wondered whether to riff or commiserate, but before I could choose, Bill called.

I set down the ladle and picked up. "Bill, hey. What's going on?"

"Parker! I'm getting bombarded with interview requests, that's what. *GQ* wants to meet, and *The Atlantic* asked if you could get on the phone beginning of next week. Good with you?"

"Whoa." I hesitated. "Yes. Sure."

"What is it?"

"Sorry. Just—do they want to talk about *High and Dry*, too? Not just Selina Chan?"

"They didn't say. Krys Badowski's doing the *GQ* piece, and they assigned Ellery Robbins at *The Atlantic*. Good writers. I trust them to get a big-picture view."

"Okay." I turned down the burner. "I just don't want this fight to be my entire personality, you know?"

I could hear Mahler in the background again, the string section twining through Bill's office. Then he said, "I'll level with you, Parker. I have faith in your work to stand the test of time, but the interest this is driving in the new book, that's not something to ignore. I talked to Lauren. Your team at Coronation is happy right now, very happy."

"Right," I said. "Right, of course. I'll do whatever you send me."

"Good. Incoming."

As he hung up, I inhaled the steam from the stockpot and felt my mouth water. For the first time in three years, my publisher had reason not to rue the day they'd learned my name. It was probably too much to hope that if I argued my case strongly enough, *These Extraordinary Times* would undergo a reappraisal, but *High and Dry*'s fate wasn't set in stone. Maybe I wouldn't need to sell my apartment, flee New York, or get another job, or two, or three. Maybe I just had to hold the line.

I spent the days after the video glued to my phone. Time flowed in a lumpy, unsteady way, like mud-clumped water being pumped through a thin hose. I'd look up from my screen and find that the quality of the light had changed and suddenly I needed to feed myself. I'd look down again and feel myself sliding headlong into the evening, obsessively refreshing my notifications, or cracking jokes with the Chan Pan Support Group, or tending to my siblings' group text.

The video had shocked my family. My parents responded in identical ways: They each called me up to worry for half an hour about the professional repercussions, then accused each other of embroiling me in this mess.

"It would be just like Moy," my mom scoffed, "to suggest you bull into this with no forethought."

"So, let me guess," my dad grumbled. "Analyn said you should make that woman's review into a *conversation*."

"No," I said, exhausted, to both. "I did this on my own." To which they reacted with insulting confusion, as though I had never done anything of my own volition in my thirty-two years upon the earth.

My brothers and sisters shared their own opinions in our group text:

Elena

Parker wtf. I thought you weren't allowed to talk to critics??

Christi

He isn't allowed. He was just drunk. How many drinks did you have, anyway, P?

Parker

two

Justin

Hahahhahahahaa

Justin

Lightweighttttttttt

Kevin

Barely recognized you in the video bro. Yelling like that. Who knew you had it in you lol.

Elena

Kevin don't lol at this! It's not funny, Parker's getting harassed online by like thousands of people!

Kevin

Im not laughing at that Jesus

Kevin

Where is the laughing at harassment in what I wrote

Kevin

Show me the bad lols Lena

Elena

You are so annoying and like, a bad brother

Kevin

Wtf why am I the bad brother when JUSTIN is the one who was harassing Parker IN this chat!!!!!!!!!

Kevin

He's literally complicit while Im innocnet

Kevin

innocent

Christi

Parker, this is why I stick to soda water or seltzer when the office goes out to drinks. You never know what might happen.

Parker

Yeah, that's fair.

Elena

Kevin you're NOT funny and you're NOT taking this seriously enough. This is like a national news story???

Parker

Don't worry about me, Elena. I appreciate your concern, but the situation looks worse than it is.

Kevin

See Lena? Looks worse than it is. Im allowed to lol as much as I want

Parker

Yep, feel free to lol

Justin

lol @ you getting drunk off 2 weak ass cocktails

I loved my siblings, but they were an exercise in being overwhelmed. In fact, even the things I felt most grateful for that week—the landslide of exposure for *High and Dry*, the hundreds of supportive messages—overwhelmed me. Sometimes, after two straight hours of refreshing, scrolling, replying, liking, and emailing—Thank you so much! That's really kind. Appreciate you! Thanks. Totally agree!—I'd lie face down on my bed, close my eyes, and envision the thin dirt trails in San Bruno Mountain Park, where I'd started taking walks near the end of middle school, after my parents had split up for good. I'd imagine the antique armchair in the back corner of Poppy Street Books, six blocks from my mother's house in Daly City. These places were silent in my mind, oases. I could barely remember what that quiet felt like.

As the days passed, op-eds cropped up in publications and newsletters, each with a rude title like "Parker Navarro's Big Miscalculation" or "The Obsolescence of the Wounded Critic," and I discovered that the only thing more annoying than Selina Chan was other journalists trying to outcriticize Selina Chan. A week turned into two, and the interviews began to blur together. I was running out of ways to rephrase my loathing.

Chan—unsurprisingly, for someone who'd built a career on rephrasing her loathing—had no such problem. She seemed to think I was some harbinger of the publishing apocalypse, that if she said even one syllable of a mea culpa, the very offices of *City Magazine*, and also possibly the rest of civilization, would crash down around her silver-studded ears. I'd developed this compulsion to check her social media the moment I woke up, groping my phone into my bed in the half-light, thumbing in her handle semi-conscious, until finally I was barraged by whatever self-important bullshit she had to say that day. Two weeks after the video, I woke up to this gem in LitHub:

> **SC:** Some of these op-eds have come dangerously close to suggesting that criticism has been replaced by social media, and that the only articles to punch through therefore have to be disproportionately negative. The implication is that my review of *High and Dry* was negative for negativity's sake, even for publicity's sake. Frankly, this is unfair. *City* remains devoted to writing what we've always written: thoughtful long-form journalism executed to a rigorous standard. Even Parker Navarro has never tried to rebut any point I made in my review, though that might just be because he lacks the conviction.

The line wormed its way under my skin. After reading the interview, I lay in bed with the curtains drawn for three hours, like a frail Victorian dying of consumption, and reread her review dozens of times, trying to come up with rebuttals.

But the worst thing about Chan's review was that while she'd detested the book, she'd understood exactly what I'd wanted to achieve with it. I *had* wanted to skewer the absurd circularity of modern life. I *had* wanted to nod to Kafka and Lucy Ellmann and Virginia Woolf.

This had happened with *These Extraordinary Times*, too: She'd written about my strategies and influences with a crystalline accuracy that had made me feel like she'd X-rayed me, then used that X-ray to puncture my lungs.

That evening, I felt proud of keeping to the plans I'd made. Instead of inventing an excuse to cancel, I dragged myself out of bed and showered and took my medication. I dressed in real clothes instead of depression sweatpants. I took the subway into Manhattan and joined my friends at a tiki bar on the Lower East Side, where you could pay twelve dollars for the privilege of drinking a Corona.

Five of us had made it out tonight, but the overall friend group was twice this size, consisting of everybody from our corner of the Bay Area who'd wound up in New York. Slouched in a booth surrounded by tropical foliage, we kicked off the night chatting about Tyler's residency—he'd gone into neurosurgery and now discussed catastrophic brain injuries with a weird, blithe indifference. We joked around about Julian's millionth new startup idea, which aimed, somehow, to disrupt the airport luggage cart industry ("Would you describe it as Uber for airport luggage carts?" asked Maricel). As for Maricel and Xiangyu, they were both consultants and therefore never talked about their jobs, except to say that they were trying to get new jobs.

I was happy to be three drinks deep by the time the subject turned to me. "Hell of a couple of weeks for our famous author," hollered Julian, ruffling my hair.

"Are we allowed to ask about it?" asked Tyler, sounding more concerned than he had about last Tuesday's subarachnoid hemorrhage.

"Sure," I said.

Xiangyu and Maricel exchanged a look. "Okay," said Xiangyu as they both leaned over the table. "Be honest. Was it staged?"

I choked on my drink. "Was it—what? No!"

"Told you," said Julian, looking satisfied.

"Why did you think it was staged?" I said, staring between Xiangyu and Maricel.

"Uh," said Maricel, "because we've known you for eighteen years and never seen you lose your shit like that?"

"Must have felt good," said Xiangyu, grinning.

"It . . . Yeah." I hesitated. Part of me wanted to admit how I'd spent this afternoon, to paint the range of the experience, but I didn't want to complain. Xiangyu and Maricel regularly described their jobs as exercises in soul death. Julian, alone of the people at this table, was still struggling to pay rent. Tyler worked twenty-eight-hour shifts and saved people's lives. My problems were all fictional.

I told myself, *Relax*. The last thing I needed was to be seen differently by a group of friends I'd had since childhood, and we were having a nice time here, their smiling faces smudged violet by the tinted lightbulbs. Easy.

"It'll blow over soon," I said. "Anyway, I made some author friends from this, which is cool. I'm going to meet them later. One of them is throwing a, like, a house party in Boerum Hill."

A storm of teasing about my attendance at this prestigious literary salon followed, and Julian gave me a fond elbow to the bicep. "I'll tell you what, I would *not* be this silver lining about all this shit happening."

"Well, it's Parker," Maricel said with a laugh, and they agreed that it was Parker, glass-half-full Parker, and I smiled and kept drinking my gin and tonic, and soon they'd moved on to the topics of the subway and that new show they were all watching.

As we parted ways outside the bar, Maricel and Julian and I broke out a little Tagalog to make our goodbyes. I would've liked us to practice together more often, but Julian was self-conscious about his pronunciation, especially around Maricel, who'd lived in Quezon City until age ten and was still near-fluent.

"No, you sound great, Julian," Maricel was saying, and I was agreeing, "Tama siya," when from a heaving group of passing bodies, a voice slopped out, singsong:

"Speak English."

"Fuck off," Maricel said reflexively, and like every one of these encounters I'd ever had, it was over with a surprising abruptness, the faceless guy and his friends already turning the corner, Julian and Xiangyu making annoyed sounds, Tyler cracking a joke about how clearly Julian's Tagalog sounded good enough for dickface over there. Loud sighs and "anyway"s. We laughed, hugged, broke apart.

I wandered toward the train and heard the man's voice echo twice, three times. I thought of the woman who'd once snapped her fingers at me outside a concert hall and said, with a mysterious urgency, "You Korean? You Chinese? No, you Korean?" Remembered the guy leaving a college party who, on his way out, had grabbed the back of my T-shirt and crowed, "*Maaade in Vietnam!*" Why was I always so curious about these people, where they came from, where they were going? Curiosity seemed like the wrong emotion to have. Occasionally these encounters walked out of my fingers when I was writing, but usually upside-down, backward, like I was those people, looking in at myself, finally able to control how other people saw me, or at least able to explore the implications in a way that would mean something. From this side the interactions felt so meaningless.

Weaving through a college-aged throng outside a dollar-slice joint, I felt remote and lightheaded. I'd drunk too much again, which didn't help whatever this disconnected feeling was. When I checked my phone, I was grateful to find new messages to latch on to.

I opened my mother's text thread first.

Mom

8:58 PM

Hi sweetheart How r u?

😌

Parker

9:16 PM

Hi Mom—everything's great over here

Mom

9:17 PM

Everything settling down with the critic?

Parker

9:19 PM

Yep, nothing to stress about. How about you, how are you?

Mom

9:19 PM

Doing OK

Parker

9:20 PM

Just okay?

I descended into the warm stink of the subway, hip-checked my way through the turnstile, head beginning to ache, and then:

Mom

9:25 PM

Took the car to the mechanic, it's having suspension problems 😟

The train roared down the track toward me. Car opened. I stepped in, crumpled down, rubbed my forehead with the flat of my palm.

Parker

9:25 PM

Oh, man. That must be so frustrating—I know you just had it in the shop. Does this help? I don't want you to worry.

Parker Navarro sent $500 with Apple Pay

Mom

9:26 PM

Oh Pijay. You're too generous to your mom 💗💗 I don't know what I did to deserve you

Parker

9:27 PM

Haha, I can think of an entire childhood's worth of things you did. Love you, Mom.

Mom

9:27 PM

I'm sorry to be such an inconvenience

Parker

9:28 PM

You're not an inconvenience at all. This is what kids want to be able to do for their parents. Living the dream, haha 😌

Mom

9:29 PM

Can we call tomorrow??
Love you so much 😌

Parker

9:30 PM

Of course, any time. Talk soon.

As the subway rattled eastward toward Brooklyn, I swiped through photos of my family. My mother in florals with Christi and Elena at a seaside restaurant on her birthday. My father laughing at his retirement party, two thumbs up over a steaming pot of sinigang.

My dad, a former X-ray technician, hadn't retired until last year at age seventy-two, and my mom was still working the front desk at the same hotel that had hired her after my dad had moved out. For how hard and how long my parents had worked, they should have had more to show for it, but they'd had five of us to raise in the Bay Area, where the cost of living had gone from high to sadistic, and their bitter divorce hadn't exactly contributed to our financial stability.

My mom, at least, I could trust to be somewhat open about her problems. The car was a recurring issue. With my dad, I had to ferret around for information through Christi and Justin—the oldest of us—to figure out if he could foot the copays for his blood pressure medication, his ankle therapy, the appointments for his deteriorating vision.

I switched texts to my thread with my father.

Dad

8:22 PM

So f.y.i. your mom is trying to guilt-trip about the holidays

Dad

8:23 PM

I told everyone in Manila you would all be here on the 28th like last year. Somehow this is an enormous problem for her

Parker

9:32 PM

Thanks for letting me know, Dad. I'll talk to her, we'll figure it out.

The train shot underwater. Sympathy and affection pressed in on me as though someone were palpating thick pillows against the front and back of my skull. In some ways my feelings toward my parents verged on pity; I couldn't help it. The divorce had shocked my grandparents and set off waves of discontentment among our extended family in the Philippines, who were all varying degrees of Catholic. Both of my parents had cousins who thought divorce should never be legalized in the Philippines, cousins who hadn't spoken to them in two decades now.

The conductor blared something indistinguishable as we pulled into the station. I navigated around some jacketed teenagers on the platform, checking the address in the Chan Pan Support Group thread.

Ten minutes later, I was jogging up to the third floor of a limestone building on a quiet one-way street. Laughter and conversation swelled as I pushed through the cracked door. There they were, tucked in by a standing chessboard: Jenny, willowy and auburn-haired, dressed in a long velvet wrap, beside Aiden and Carla, clinking a pair of blue-tinted goblets. Jenny seemed to be the youngest—maybe a few years older than me—while Carla and Aiden appeared to be in their forties.

Carla's eyes strayed onto mine, and her face split in an open-mouthed smile. "Parker," Jenny and Aiden exclaimed together as I navigated toward them. "I'm so glad you made it," Jenny said before giving me a voiced kiss on my cheek: *Mwah!* "I wish J.J. were here, we'd have everybody!"

"Yeah, I wish! Thank you so much for inviting me," I said, trying not to ogle the apartment, its extravagant width, the working fireplace and wall of professionally framed prints, whose treated glass didn't reflect the chandelier. As Jenny poured me a glass of red wine, I imagined spilling its contents onto the coffee table, an avant-garde and porous-looking concrete blob. "Jenny, your place is incredible."

"Thank you, you're too sweet!" She craned her neck, sliding a jeweled charm up and down a silver chain at her collarbones. "Christopher's around here somewhere. My husband. You'll have to meet him."

"Is he also a writer?"

"God, no." Jenny laughed. "He's in tech. Thus . . ." She waved around at the apartment.

"Oh, cool! Right. Um—are these people all writers?"

"Mostly, yeah. That group in the kitchen is all Penguin people. Shane, at the table, they're a poet. A lot of people from my class at Iowa wound up in the city." Jenny frowned. "Wait, what year did you go to Iowa? *Did* you go to Iowa? Am I making that up?"

"You are," I said. "I never got an MFA."

"Me neither," said Carla, lifting her wineglass. Her red lips had an impish slant. "I only got into programs without funding, lucky me . . . Aiden, you went to NYU, didn't you?"

"Yep. Eighty grand when I went. It's over a hundred now." Aiden let out a throaty laugh, flattening his skinny tie against his button-down. "Thank God this city is so affordable, to make up for it."

We laughed. "Parker," Carla said, "how have things been with Pannibal Lecter?"

I hesitated, then pulled out my phone to show them the LitHub interview.

"Impressively insufferable," said Aiden, "even for her."

Carla let out a sort of snarl. "Tell me why she always sounds like she's channeling your most out-of-touch modern lit professor who won't take anything after Nabokov seriously?"

"Well, that's her whole thing, Carla," said Jenny. "If she weren't pretending to be New York's reigning intellectual monarch, her little empire would collapse."

I laughed, suddenly glad I hadn't gone into the industry details with my friends from home. "Yeah. To be honest, I got sort of worried that everything she's saying about my new book is true."

"Nope." Carla leveled a manicured finger at my nose. "Stop right there. After she reviewed me, I started gaslighting myself into thinking I was a bad writer because—why? Because she didn't like a book that clearly wasn't even *for* her? She doesn't know anything about you, Parker."

We spent the better part of an hour getting progressively drunker and more outraged. I couldn't believe how satisfying it felt, the verbal equivalent of shattering a glass against a brick wall. By the time I spilled myself into an Uber, my temples were palpitating.

The driver dropped me outside my building. My street was silent and deserted, but the night felt agitated, loud somehow, the noise of the house party and the tiki bar still ringing in my ears. *Speak English.* I could feel the subway plunging onward far below, making the ground vibrate.

My phone buzzed as I let myself into the foyer.

Jenny House

11:37 PM

P, you're a gem. Remember, don't think about it too hard! She's just a bad person. It doesn't have to be interesting or complicated.

I twisted the key in my apartment door. My friends were right: Selina Chan didn't know me. I was ascribing too much insight to somebody who had written a few thousand cursory words in response to 1,500 pages of my work.

Parker Navarro

11:42 PM

Thanks, guys. You're the best.

Parker Navarro

11:43 PM

I don't know why I let Selina Chan, of all people, get in my head

Parker Navarro

11:43 PM

I guess I've just got to remind myself: I might have bad reviews, but at least I don't have to wake up in the morning knowing my broken personality will alienate everyone in my life

Aiden Linville laughed at Parker Navarro's message

Jenny House laughed at Parker Navarro's message

J.J. Purnell laughed at Parker Navarro's message

The messages kept arriving as I sat down at the table, but I lost track. I opened my laptop, and there was the interview again, still glaring out at me from my most recent tab.

That might just be because he lacks the conviction.

I'll show you conviction, I thought, tossing my phone into the sofa. Looseness spread through my body, the kind I hadn't felt all night, and a thrilling clarity pierced the rubbery surface of my drunkenness. At last I was alone. Alone, I could say something. I could speak to *her*.

With a gray haze eating into the edges of my vision, I opened a blank document and began to write.

* * *

I awoke the next morning to find that I'd dragged my laptop into bed with me.

When I moved, the screen lit up, showing me what I'd done last night. I reread, my eyebrows slowly drawing together.

Then I called Bill.

Chapter Six

Selina

> **@ParkerNavarroWrites**: The news is out . . . excited to share my first piece of short fiction soon in @TheParisReview Daily! Keep an eye on this space. :)

Unbelievable. Genuinely unbelievable that the same journal that gave us the Art of Fiction interview series had decided to debase themselves by publishing Parker Navarro. Had he bribed somebody? Had Bill Owens leveraged every ounce of cultural capital he'd earned in four decades as an agent to get a story through the door? Had—

"Selina."

I looked up from my laptop. "What?"

Hayden was giving me her flattest smile. "Are we interrupting?"

"No." I cleared my throat. Shut my laptop. "Of course not."

"Well, I was wondering," she said from her armchair, "what we can do to keep this momentum building."

Down the table, Joyce exchanged a glance with Mike, our global news lead. Mike was a burly seventy-something man, serene and good-humored, who had worn the same pair of orthopedic slippers every day since I'd joined the team. He and Joyce were *City*'s two seniormost staff members, predating even Scott. Easy to guess why they were upset. For the past three weeks, Hayden had interrupted every meeting to review Navarro's press, which podcast had featured him, which influencer had mentioned me, how we could push the feud into new corners of the internet as other corners moved on. I doubted this had been thrilling for two writers who'd been here since the magazine's communications were conducted by fax machine.

"Did you want to add something, Mike? Joyce?" Hayden asked.

"No, no!" said Joyce, fluttering her hands near her face.

"Nothing to add," said Mike with an easy roll of his cardiganed shoulders. "But, well . . ."

Joyce swapped another look with him. "The conflict has been a little disruptive. That's all."

This seemed to delight Hayden. "Disruption is what Nextward is all about! Being change agents. Injecting life into whatever industry needs shaking up. And readers are reacting to this! Page views are up, subscriptions are up—"

"But this can't go on forever, can it?" said Joyce. "Selina's said what she needed to say. When are we going to go back to . . . well, to business as usual? Writing great pieces that connect with people?"

"Joyce, keep up. *Business as usual* hasn't worked for y'all for fifteen years."

The lines in Joyce's forehead deepened. She glanced down at her notepad, her reading glasses performing their familiar downward slip.

I felt the urge to stand, yank the door open, and demand that Hayden get out. From the hard expressions around the table, I knew the rest of staff was having similar thoughts. Saying something cutting to Joyce was like aiming a kick at a rescue dog.

Scott was considering Hayden, stone-faced. "What do you mean by 'building momentum,' Hayden?"

"Well, Selina's always been a bit of a controversial figure," said Hayden, "but now that's a real part of her brand, which is great."

"Is it?" I muttered.

"We should keep her as exposed as we can, keep people coming back. Ooh—maybe we should do this with all the writers! Rebrand *City* as the place where the biggest, boldest personalities go."

"Wait, wait," I said. "I haven't been talking about 'rebranding' in any of these interviews. I've been defending *City*'s mission. The importance of what we *already* do."

"And . . . you think that's what's driving people to the site?" said Hayden. "A friendly reminder that *City* is still here, doing the same old thing it's done for a century, publishing articles it takes half an hour and a dictionary to read?"

"Yes! I think people want a place online that'll—that'll respect them. Their intelligence. Their attention span, which everything else on the internet is trying to degrade." The skeptical tilt to her mouth made my fists curl on my thighs. "Okay, what's *your* theory, then?"

"My theory is that they're engaging because they think you're an interesting person."

"But none of this is about me."

"Of course it is. Are you kidding? It's a feud, Selina. It's all about you."

For once, I found myself speechless. She was wrong. She had to be.

Scott lifted his hands. "We're getting away from the point here. Hayden, what you're saying about a writer's name brand isn't so far removed from our existing coverage. We've always had our staff participate in readings and festivals and so on."

"Like what?"

"Well, let's take a look," said Kellie, making a little lasso-twirling gesture with her pen. She swiped left on her laptop's screen, scanning her calendar. "*n+1* has a sold-out event tomorrow night—I'm interviewing one of the readers there. And the Wiseman Fest is in a couple of weeks . . ."

"What is that?" said Hayden.

"The Wiseman Foundation Literary Festival. They book out a convention center for panel programming, bookseller booths, signings—"

"Okay, yes," said Hayden, rising and snapping her fingers. "I want to hear more about that. Kellie, send me the details, and Selina, keep your game face on."

I left the office in a state of dejection. Ever since I was a teenager, I'd loved the invisibility of the writing process, the feeling that, in this small way, I was allowed to step out of my skin and leave myself behind. I wanted to communicate with readers about art, about ideas, about something with real worth—not about myself.

It was a relief to walk into the weight room at my gym and lose myself in my routine. For fifteen minutes I was a machine among machines. A two-second inhalation through the nose and a two-second release through the mouth. Flicker of muscle in my thigh, prickle of sweat down my cheek. Thoughtless.

Then, during a recovery minute, came the intrusion, a fact I'd forgotten. Parker on some NPR show. Hayden had sent me the link that morning.

Reclined on the bench, I crooked the weights over my head and pushed, trying to focus on the quiver in my triceps.

Useless. The peaceful emptiness had gone. What was the show called? *Jacket Copy*, something like that. What had Parker been spouting about me on nationally syndicated radio?

Before I could stop myself, I sat up, swept my phone from the floor, and found the podcast release of the show. I climbed onto a treadmill, hit Play, and began to run.

I forwarded through fifteen minutes of chitchat about Parker's background before Steve Elgin's mellow voice said, "*So, considering some other literary feuds, I'm hoping this won't end in a Proust-Lorrain scenario, with shots literally fired—*"

Parker's easy laugh echoed in my ear. "*Yeah, let's hope it doesn't go that far.*"

Steve laughed too. "*No! No. But I am curious how you view this battle between yourself and Selina Chan. Would you say the stakes are personal? Financial? More broadly cultural?*"

"*Oh, interesting. I think it has to be all of the above, right? Critical anxiety is always financial anxiety. But with a really punishing review, like . . .*"

"*Like Selina's,*" said Steve.

"*Yes. Like Selina's.*"

"*You can say her name. We don't have her hidden in the supply closet.*"

They laughed. Hilarious.

"*Sorry,*" said Parker. "*It's just . . .*"

"*She's an intimidating woman.*"

"*Yeah. The way she looks at you, it's like facing down a bull shark.*" More laughter. I increased the speed of the treadmill. "*Anyway, reviews like hers are different. Writing and reading and reviewing are—are supposed to be personal relationships, right? And they're supposed to be, like, undergirded by this foundation of communication and connection.*"

"*Right,*" said Steve.

"*Right. So, getting told that you've failed to communicate* and *humiliated yourself trying, and then when thousands of people pile on . . . to get that response feels like, not only have you failed in, you know, crafting the artistic object, it feels like you're also separate from other people. Like other people can't understand you, or maybe you'll never understand them.*"

Navarro hesitated. I was thinking that this was a surprisingly cogent point when he went on, "*And I feel like, with this feud, I'm now in the position to say I don't think authors should be expected to—like—suffer the slings and arrows of outrageous criticism totally voiceless, I guess."*

"Oh—my God—shut up," I panted. The woman on the adjacent treadmill gave me a scandalized look.

"*So,*" Steve said, "*on the topic of your second book . . . I have a copy of* High and Dry *here. The rumors are true, it's six hundred pages, but I tore through it.*"

"*Wow, Steve, that's so gratifying after these past few weeks. Really appreciate it, man.*"

"*I'm not just saying that. It has a whimsical air that I found exceptionally charming.*"

Parker paused for a split second. "*Oh. Whims—really? Interesting.*"

"*Absolutely! These forays into the fantastical, the sentient alligator, the partially submerged bus . . . the book takes on the feeling of a dark fairy tale. Like Dave is an elemental archetype.*"

"*Oh! Um, yeah, I can see that! Yeah. I love hearing people's different interpretations. Thanks again for reading it, thank you.*"

"*You bet, and I want to dive deeper after the break . . . Everybody, this is Parker Navarro, the author of the upcoming* High and Dry, *and—if you're here after seeing his starring turn on video, rest assured—one of the nicest people I've met in a while. We'll be back soon for more.*"

I hit Pause. As the treads slowed, as I broke out of my run and scrubbed the towel across my forehead, Navarro's voice echoed in my ear. *I love hearing people's different interpretations.*

I scoffed. He loved getting fellated, was what he loved. Steve Elgin couldn't have been further from the mark in terms of what Parker Navarro was trying to do with *High and Dry*. Whimsical? Fantastical? That book had been about as whimsical as a documentary about workplace injuries.

But instead of setting the record straight, Navarro ate up the praise.

Why bother clarifying the point of his book when he could pat himself on the back for somebody *liking* him?

I stalked into the gym showers and ran the water scalding. *One of the nicest people I've met in a while*, said Steve's enthusiastic voice in my mind while I scrubbed myself pink. Niceness. The world was drowning in it.

I closed my eyes and listened to the water's drumbeat on my skull, massaging an aching muscle in my forearm. Maybe Parker Navarro was right. Maybe I did look at people the way a shark looked at its prey. Fine. I'd rather do that than gaze at every person I met with a desperation for them to like me.

At my locker, I considered the earbuds sitting atop my wallet. I didn't have to do this to myself. I didn't *have* to listen to seventeen more minutes of Parker Navarro palling around with Podcast Steve. He was so good at this. Eager. Generous, even. He responded immediately, attentively to Steve's every side note; he made socializing seem effortless, the way a figure skater cuts cleanly across the ice. He'd even been born with an appealing speaking voice, a low, warm tenor, like the hum of a guitar string.

Here, I thought, was somebody who had never been disliked, somebody who could walk into a crowded room and expect everyone to turn toward him with a smile. And all it had cost him was his backbone.

Yet here I was, hitting Play and plugging that smiling tenor back into my ears. Apparently the joke was on me.

I returned to my apartment at a gray-black seven o'clock. Daylight saving time had ended, and with it the last of the year's sun-washed evenings, but a flick of a switch and warm light painted over the darkness.

My home was five hundred square feet of pale neutrals. A jute rug ran beneath a pastel pink table, over which a wax paper globe light hovered like a moon. A taupe love seat faced a mounted television and a soundbar on a low, minimal stand. Amid the gentle bump of the radiator and the gurgle of the pipes, I wiped down the narrow counters and set acoustic guitar humming from my speaker. I watered the line of cacti on the windowsill and straightened the photos in the hallway. Jacob beside me in sky-blue robes at our graduation. Cassie planting a kiss on my cheek at her bachelorette party. My parents and my child self, clutching the ends of my sleeves in self-conscious middle school agony.

Then I dressed in sweatpants, sat cross-legged before the apartment's front windows, and began to run a hand sander over the baseboard. Nubs and blobs and drooling lines of old paint flattened out and disappeared. Delicate hillocks of white powder accumulated on the uneven floorboards.

Eight years ago, I'd been lucky enough to land this rent-stabilized one-bedroom in a quickly gentrifying Bed-Stuy. My landlord had learned not to worry when I texted him bulleted lists of proposed improvements. Over the years, I'd wallpapered my bedroom, installed a backsplash in the kitchen, replaced every doorknob and drawer handle and light switch plate. This year's project was to sand off decades of sloppy paint jobs from the windowsills, crown molding, and baseboards, then reprime and repaint with crisp new lines. I'd probably rent until I died, but I refused to live somewhere that would inflict itself upon me.

A meditative half hour passed, the sander's vibrations harmonizing with the guitar, before my phone buzzed on the floor beside me. I unlocked it to find that my cousins in Seattle had finally caught wind of the Parker Navarro situation.

Amanda Lu

Selina! We just saw the video of you fighting with that author?!? Can't believe it! Hope you've been holding up okay!

Peter Lu

Yeah, let us know if we can do anything, wow.

Peter Lu

For what it's worth, I thought you won, haha.

I wasn't particularly close with Peter and Amanda, who were seven and nine years younger, respectively, but we'd always been friendly. Like my Auntie Sylvia, they were ambitious, energetic people. Amanda was a software developer at Google, while Peter was working toward his economics PhD.

I replied, Ha. Thank you, guys. It's been an interesting few weeks, but nothing I can't handle.

They each reacted with a heart. I half smiled. Normally, we only texted at Christmas, birthdays, and Chinese New Year. I'd have liked to see them more often, but nothing ever brought us to each other's respective coasts.

I typed, haltingly, Peter, how's your PhD going? But before I could tap Send, another message arrived:

Peter Lu

By the way, should we mention any of this to our mom?

His unspoken question was, of course, whether I wanted the news to circulate back to my parents. Auntie Sylvia was delightful but not discreet.

Selina Chan

Probably best not to worry her.

Peter Lu

Got it

Amanda Lu

Your secret's safe with us! Only we three and the internet will ever know.

I hit the laugh react, but my smile had gone. I didn't like the idea of the rest of my family caught in the sand trap that existed between my parents and me. I wished that what was between us could stay between us, sealed within the walls of my childhood home, but everyone could hear our silence as distinctly as sound.

I glided my portable vacuum over the baseboard seam and watched white dust swirl up its translucent throat. I pictured my parents at this moment, ghostlike entities drifting through the clapboard house in our Minneapolis suburb. The kitchen table having worked gray circles into the linoleum floor.

When I slid a damp cloth along the baseboard, dust peeled away from the paint above the molding. The lines between materials grew clean and crisp, each wooden ridge perfectly redefined.

Satisfied, I picked up a fresh square of sandpaper. As I was attaching it to the sander, I got a text from Jacob:

Oh boy.

Oh boy what, I said.

A pause.

Jacob, I said. Oh boy, what?

I switched windows into Bluesky and found thirty notifications. When I refreshed, thirty-five.

1m ago **@SelinaChan** What a disgusting and invasive thing to be written about you

1m ago **@SelinaChan** lawsuit when? wtf were they thinking letting him publish that

1m ago **@SelinaChan** hopw u r taking time for sel f care sweetie

I stared at this last post. Self-care? Historically, people on the internet had been more likely to recommend me self-immolation than self-care.

A text dropped down from the top of my screen. Jacob had replied:

Enjoy.

[LINK: "Who Will Know Me When I'm Gone?"—New Short Fiction by Parker Navarro—TheParisReview.com]

Still cross-legged on the floor, I began to read. My mouth drifted open.

Halfway through, I let out a disbelieving laugh, stood up so quickly that I nearly lost my balance, and grabbed my laptop from the table.

Excerpt: "Who Will Know Me When I'm Gone?"

by Parker Navarro

In the concrete heart of the critic's apartment building, three elevators rise to different heights. The first elevator rises as high as the twelfth floor and the business center. The second can take a person all the way up to the pool, assuming that person is worth the pool. The third elevator shaft spans the full height of the building, basement to fifty-third floor, where the critic lives. On the evening of February 3 she slides down the gullet of elevator three and counts time to herself. She lives thirteen seconds above the people who are worth the pool and twenty-nine above those who are worth the business center and forty above the man in the lobby who tells her, Stay warm, ma'am, as he opens the front door for her to pass, unpausing, through.

The critic is on time for her seven o'clock reservation. She carries a black leather bag that holds at all times her uncased cellphone, two red lip stains, three fifty-dollar pens, the current novel, a notebook produced in Japan, a wallet produced in Germany, within the wallet two credit cards with a collective $53,000 limit, and gum. On the street she is never recognized but often admired. She knows that the exact symmetry of her features affords her certain opportunities at host stands and bars. Even the disaffected greeter at the front of the restaurant fumbles his words when she arrives.

At 7:02, the host at the stand, a fragile eighteen-year-old pursuing a degree in literature, says, I'm so sorry, we're clearing your table now, it'll be five minutes still.

My reservation was for seven o'clock, the critic says.

Yes, ma'am. I apologize. But the table over there, you can see, that's the one.

I see a table that isn't ready for a seven o'clock reservation.

Yes. Of course. I understand.

Do you? Are you able to understand?

Yes, ma'am, I understand.

The critic considers the review she will write on each of the major platforms. A beautiful paragraph. An elegant cruelty. Maybe to maximize its reach she should translate it into each of the five languages she speaks. Later, as she teases pieces of the lobster away from its exoskeleton, she thinks with weary disgust that to keep a promise is not so very difficult. The lobster passes into her esophagus, and the current novel lies prostrate on the table beside her. When she was twenty-seven, she flew back to Denver and took up a post at her shrunken mother's bedside. Not an easy promise to keep, but she was there. Her father excused himself regularly to weep and otherwise spent his hours bowed over the bed or entangling himself into her mother's hair or fingers. The critic asked, upright, Do you need the blinds drawn, Mom.

She turns the page of the novel, then swirls her wine and examines its pale red legs running down the delicate glass. Her mother said no and reached for the critic, who enfolded her hand around her mother's knuckles and moved her thumb neatly along the maze of the prominent veins. Her mother said, Would you tell me a story?

When the waiter arrives, the critic says, I've been waiting for this check half my life.

I'm so sorry.

This is a restaurant full of apologies, she says, handing him her credit card. Her mother's eyes closed while the critic tried to think how to begin. Several minutes later the card comes back, and the critic replaces it in the German wallet, then closes the current novel, parsing her dislike. At the next table, some man, his face a blurred brushstroke of rosacea, has split his mouth open to display laughing teeth. The woman opposite plumps her hair with a self-conscious hand. The critic's disgust and impatience intensify, and she carves a path in her black coat through the bobbing lights, the heads of the candles in their crystal jars bowing fearfully in her direction. Fifty-three years later she will die in a hospital bed in San Jose, the only person in the room.

At home, the critic adds resistance to the weight machines and watches the flexion of her deltoids in the mirror. They twitch and gleam and relax, and she counts them into and out of their suffering. Afterward, she spends a quarter hour before the full-body mirror in her bedroom. She inches her fingers down the yielding contours of her waist and wonders why she is still so hungry . . .

The Paris Review: Letters to the Editor

To the Editor:

In response to your story, "Who Will Know Me When I'm Gone?" published yesterday in the Daily:

Thank you for an evening's unexpected entertainment. Imagine my surprise to find Parker Navarro writing a story with a real purpose, the kind of intent I've wished he would bring to the page since his first novel. That purpose may be hopelessly juvenile, and the piece does suggest total creative bankruptcy, but I'm not one to spit in a baby's face as he takes his first tottering steps.

Warmly,
Selina Chan

Chapter Seven

Parker

November cartwheeled into the city, a month of record wind speeds. I buttoned my coat higher and kept walking.

After my mental health had hit its nadir in college, this had been the deal I'd made with myself: that I would walk out into the world every single day for the rest of my life. Three weeks sequestered in my dorm room, surviving on spooned-out peanut butter, Cup Noodles, and delivered mozzarella sticks, pondering nonexistence, interacting with nobody except my increasingly disgusted roommates: If this experience had taught me nothing else, it was that crossing the threshold of my front door could always make me feel more human.

When I'd moved back in with my mother in Daly City for those first years after graduation, I spent my walks listening to indie rock playlists, until my jobs at H Mart and the neighborhood karaoke bar made the quiet feel so valuable that I began to walk in silence. I'd kept that routine to this day, and it felt especially helpful on mornings like this, when I imagined my brain like an animal in a too-small enclosure, hurling itself against the walls.

The Paris Review had published my story yesterday afternoon. Selina Chan's response had been published this morning, and I'd read it over and over, working myself into a froth of indignation. I'd expected her to react with cold fury. Instead, I got this obnoxious equanimity, as though she had distance from even the most aggressive form of ridicule I could come up with. I'd wanted her to be devastated, not *mildly amused.*

And the kicker: *Thank you*, she'd said, for *a story with a real purpose.*

What interdimensional chess game was she trying to play? Why had she complimented a story I'd written to insult her?

I bypassed the park and the green bulbs of the subway entrance, the distant laughs of toddlers harmonizing with sirens. As I walked beneath the elevated train line, I saw the text stamped across my vision. *The kind of intent I've wished he would bring to the page since his first novel.* I imagined her crimson-nailed fingers striking the words into a laptop keyboard in a graceful blur, like a concert pianist knocking out a chromatic run, and here, on the other end, the phrase replayed over and over in my mind, like the strain of some unshakable melody.

I drained the last of my coffee, crumpled the cup in a fist, and threw it in the nearest recycling bin. What did I care what she wished for? Surely I hadn't *wanted* her to like the story—to be, in any way, impressed? You didn't throw a punch in a boxing ring hoping your opponent would admire your form.

Did you?

When I got home, Arthur had a sloppy, overfilled grilled cheese smoking on the skillet. "Hey," he called over the thrum of the ventilation hood. "Good walk?"

I made myself smile. "Yeah. Solid."

"You want a grilled cheese? Mine's burned, but I can make you one that isn't terrible."

"Sure. Thanks, man."

"I'm going to take cooking classes one of these days, and then you'll never know what hit you."

At the counter I sifted through Arthur's stack of mailings. "Is this before or after the driving lessons?"

"After the driving lessons, but before the Chinese lessons." He scraped the spatula over the skillet with a sound like a sled getting dragged over asphalt. "And the personal training will go . . . somewhere in there, I don't know."

I looked through the last of his mail. He'd circled three time slots on a brochure advertising bachata dance lessons—times that I knew he was not even a little bit free—and he'd scribbled a list of canvassing dates on some literature from Ziad Bishara for Congress. Arthur still hadn't accepted that spending ten hours a week volunteering with a Chinatown youth arts organization meant that he had ten fewer hours a week to do things for himself. Math was a cruel and inflexible thing.

"How are the ChiArts kids?" I asked. "Still writing poems about death and knives?"

"Yep. And broken glass. I'm thinking about banning the word 'cruel.'"

"That seems pointed."

"Not as pointed as the knives. Anyway, I wish I worked on books they had literally any interest in reading. They're always saying, can you get us free books? And I'm like, yeah, I can hook you up with a five-hundred-page biography on Schopenhauer."

I knocked his mail against the counter to align the corners. "When you guys publish a Schopenhauer-inspired YA fantasy, you'll finally be cool."

"Please, Parker, you know I'll never be cool." He whirled to face me so suddenly that I startled. "By the way. I read it."

"What? You read what?"

"Your story. The Selina Chan fanfic."

"Oh." I frowned. "It's not *fanfic*."

"True. Hatefic? Anyway, I read it." He snapped his head back like a baby bird about to feed and yowled out a laugh. "It's so *aggro*. It might be my favorite thing you've written."

"It—wait, really?"

"Yeah. There's this snap to it, you know? Reminds me of the stuff you wrote in undergrad."

"Hang on. You didn't also read—I mean—" I set down the mail. "This morning, did you read—?"

"Read what?" He mopped his dripping brow with a palmful of apron, clueless.

He hadn't read Selina Chan's response. He'd arrived independently at her conclusion, that my joke story had a sense of energy and lucidity that neither of my actual books had exhibited.

"What's wrong?" he said. "It was supposed to be fun to read, right?"

"Yes. Yeah." I tried to resurrect my smile. "Sorry, just—it's hot in here."

He studied me.

"That's burning," I said, pointing.

"Oh, shit." Arthur spun back around. I took the opportunity to jog down the hall, calling out something about hanging up my coat.

I shut my bedroom door and pressed my forehead against the exposed brick wall.

So much for gaining the upper hand. All I'd done by writing this story was learn three crucial facts. First, that apparently everyone from Arthur to *The Paris Review* preferred my writing when it was driven by hard-eyed loathing, slammed onto the page with a total disregard for things like beauty and civility. Second, that Selina Chan, cold and lethal though she might have been, was perfectly willing to write something positive—if she thought I deserved it. And third: that counter to everything I'd believed, I *could* impress her, or at the least surprise her.

Pressing my forehead harder into the brick, my neck hot, my hands pushing deep into my pockets, I told myself that this meant absolutely nothing to me.

As all-consuming as the feud had become, Bill was right: It had given *High and Dry* an undeniable sense of momentum. Reviews had begun to trickle in. Grant Kim at the *L.A. Times* had written a rave that should have had me buzzing, but it left me frustrated instead. "Bombastic and celebratory," he'd said. "Ebullient, bighearted, adventurous." And Steve Elgin at NPR, calling the book a "dark fairy tale," "whimsical," "fantastical" . . . Somehow, they didn't satisfy me.

Grant Kim and Steve Elgin had loved my book, but they'd read a different book than the one I'd meant to write.

The book I'd wanted to write had been the one Selina Chan described in *City Magazine*.

The morning of Grant Kim's review, I called Bill. "What if she's right?"

"Parker. What?"

"What if Selina Chan is right, and *High and Dry* is an abject failure of a book."

"It's not an abject fai— Parker, it's a hell of a book, because you're a hell of a writer."

"Good writers can write bad books," I rasped out. "Happens all the time."

"Look. Where is this coming from?"

"The *City* review. No one else . . . I mean, Bill, she described *exactly* what I wanted to do with it. She—"

I turned face down on my bed. The silence that followed was mortifying for us both. I muttered an apology to Bill and hung up, crawling back across the bed to my laptop.

Rereading her LitHub interview, I could hear her smooth, contemptuous voice sliding through the air. *I know what he wants: sympathy, not serious readership.* So confident, so arrogant, as though she knew me better than I knew myself.

I tried to focus on the good: that *High and Dry* wasn't getting a critical drubbing; that, according to an email from Lauren's assistant, the book had already gone into a second printing. The best sign of all came early in the month, when I received an invitation from Kristen Keough—Coronation's director of publicity—to speak on a panel at the Wiseman Foundation Literary Festival. Kristen had handled the launch for *These Extraordinary Times*, but *High and Dry* had been assigned to a publicity assistant named Amanda, who had never contacted me and who I suspected didn't exist.

Now I was back on Kristen's radar. I know this is short notice, her email said, but the festival is at the Arnie Roe Convention Center in the Meatpacking District next weekend. Let me know if you can make it!

Apparently, I had a functioning team again. Maybe even a real marketing plan. An hour later, Kristen had sent me a schedule with the panel's information—The Future of the Novel, South Stage—and the stall where I'd be signing advance copies of *High and Dry*.

I invited Arthur, but he had a letter-writing campaign uptown that afternoon, so I arrived alone around 3 PM, my exhibitor badge clipped to my jacket. The spine of the convention center arced gently above me, banks of LED lights zigzagging southward for half a block as a dull roar of sound echoed through the labyrinth of stalls. On the map in my hand, the space looked like a suburban neighborhood, but in the flesh it was a crush of bodies and bulging backpacks and, everywhere, phones—phones extended for selfies, phones aimed at displays, phones glinting under the harsh light.

I ambled by the first row of stalls, where the Center for Fiction was handing out pamphlets about a new writing course, *The New Yorker* had a roulette wheel involving its ubiquitous tote bags, and the booksellers—McNally Jackson and Greenlight—were being swarmed by attendees who'd trouped over from a nearby stage. I gave the crowds a wide berth. The unfamiliar names interested me more at lit fests and conventions. Every so often, lost in the sea of exhibitors, you'd stumble across something like a hyperlocal press that only published erotic fiction about Santa Claus, staffed by one wide-eyed, beaming person who wanted nothing more in life than to discuss their microscopic niche. I passed a stall for an indie press proudly displaying its inaugural hardback, then a graphic novelist who'd booked out a sliver of space and bedecked it with vinyl stickers of iguanas.

As I approached Coronation's booths, a nearby group of women glanced at me. I kept walking, the back of my neck warm. Only around a fifth of people in publishing were men, and even fewer were straight or under forty. I was never as conscious of being single as when I went to events like this. Sometimes it felt like a trap, like if I spent too much time talking with any of these good-looking, well-read women, people would think I'd come here on the prowl. Even the idea was embarrassing.

I checked my map and made a final turn. At a brightly colored kids' booth, youth librarians with pin-studded lanyards were exclaiming over a fantasy blockbuster, and just ahead stood a romance imprint, Flutter, where a line had formed for T-shirts that read I ♥ 📖♥. Halfway down the row, I reached Coronation's booth.

"Parker!" said Kristen, breathlessly surfacing from a cardboard box full of *High and Dry* advance copies. She was a fidgety, round-shouldered woman whose hunched posture always made her look like she was falling bodily into whatever activity she was doing. "Good, you're early."

"Try to be."

"Yes! I remember from the last go-around." For an awkward moment we faced each other across the displays for next year's spring titles. I didn't blame Kristen for anything that had happened with *These Extraordinary Times*, but it was uncomfortable to see her again, like running into your ex-girlfriend in a grocery store.

She edged around the stall's front counter. "So, your panel is on the South Stage—just past those curtains over there. Walk with me."

We fell into step, the blue velvet drapes growing ahead. "Feeling ready?" she asked.

"Yeah. A little nervous, I guess. I haven't done an event since the whole feud thing started."

"About that. I wanted to warn you that they might ask about it."

"Really? But it doesn't have anything to do with the Future of the Novel."

Kristen puffed out a breath that made her cheeks balloon outward. "Right, but . . ." We reached the blue curtains, and I caught a glimpse of a sectioned-off area where a hundred-odd chairs faced a modular stage.

"Look, Parker," she said. "We got some last-minute news. There have been a . . . a couple of changes with the panel, and—"

I pulled the curtain back, and she broke off midsentence.

"Kristen," I said.

For once in my life, I wasn't the earliest person to an event. Selina Chan, wearing a slim green dress and high-top sneakers, was helping a volunteer set the chairs into place onstage.

I let the curtain fall and revolved on the spot, horrified, to face Kristen.

She held up her hands. "Hey. Stay calm."

A strangled noise made its way from my throat. Stay calm? Selina Chan had probably been preparing all week to decimate me, to make some ironclad case that my books represented a danger to the Future of the Novel, while I wandered in blissful ignorance through my life, assuming I was going to have a normal conversation with another author, not someone who wanted to drain my blood from my veins like one of those dystopian torturers from *Mad Max: Fury Road.*

The audience was starting to take their seats. In fact, I realized, as I stuck my head through the curtain again, a long line had formed. They *knew*. They'd all known.

I withdrew before anyone could see me and stripped off my coat. The exhibition hall was freezing, but sweat had begun to roll down my spine, and I assumed it wouldn't stop until four thirty, when this panel was at its end and I could go back to my apartment to drown myself in the bathtub.

"Parker, it's going to be fine," said Kristen.

"Is it?"

"I talked to the organizer. They're not planning to do anything inflammatory."

"Right. Sure. Good."

"Listen"—she checked her phone—"I need to get back to the booth. I'll see you there for the signing, okay? You'll be great."

I couldn't do anything but nod.

As Kristen retreated into the crowd, I steeled myself, then slipped through the curtains and approached the stage. Selina Chan had vanished. The volunteer spotted me, rushing over with a hand outstretched, her lanyard bouncing against her neon T-shirt. "Parker! You found us. How are you feeling?"

It would have been rude to say anything about throwing up or dying, so I said, "Great! Thank you! Sorry, what's your name?"

"Natalie." We shook hands, and she lowered her voice. "Let me know if you need anything, okay? I know it'll be a little awkward up there, but we don't want any of you to feel uncomfortable."

She glanced toward another corner of the curtained area, where the final two panelists stood. I recognized both on sight. One, a white-haired woman in a canvas jumpsuit, was a National Book Award winner named Tessa Hargreaves. The other was a man in his fifties, slender and unsmiling, his hair slicked back from his prominent widow's peak.

His presence erased any lingering doubts about whether the festival organizers had put this panel together as a publicity stunt. The man was Christian Gatehead, who'd raked Selina over the coals in *The New York Times* last year.

I was beginning to wonder exactly how much blood would be spilled over the next hour when Natalie clapped her hands together in a kind of prayer gesture. "Look, I know this is . . . but the moderator's going to stick to the topic, all right?"

Her anxious expression calmed my ragged nerves where nothing else had. Natalie hadn't had any say in this deranged decision, and neither had our moderator, or National Book Award winner Tessa Hargreaves. They were depending on me, Selina, and Christian to behave like civilized people.

I would ignore Selina Chan for the entire panel. Couldn't go wrong with pointed silence.

"Absolutely," I said. "It's going to be great. Which seat am I?"

Natalie indicated a chair on the far left, beside the chair where Selina Chan's purse hung. Of course. I jogged up the steps, cracked open the water bottle by the seat, and drained half of it in one go.

When I surfaced, Christian Gatehead was standing before me, hand outstretched, wearing a grim smile. "Parker Navarro," he said as I shook. "Nice to meet the only other person in publishing with the balls for some honesty."

"Hey, thank you," I said, not completely sold on discussing my balls. That said, I wasn't sure what else to say to Christian Gatehead, whose books I'd disliked in my teenage years and now hated. He always seemed to be trying to write something spare and incisive, but landed on cold and banal, like Yasunari Kawabata without the grace, or Raymond Carver but pretentious.

Guilt ran through me as I let go of Christian's hand. He was a more important figure in fiction than I would probably ever be. Before I could conjure up something polite to say, Christian's eyes strayed to the back of the seating area. He made a disgusted sound, then stalked to his chair.

Selina Chan was sidling in between the blue curtains. She looked just as unconcerned as she had at Cipriani a month ago, eyes downcast at her phone. Fragments of her writing echoed in my mind as she stepped up the aisle.

Thank you for an evening's unexpected entertainment . . .

I know what he wants.

At the bottom of the steps, she glanced up and caught my eye. I set my jaw and held her gaze.

She didn't slow, didn't falter. She glided up the stairs and into the seat beside me, where she looked out at the crowd with cool disinterest etched into her features. When I inhaled, I caught a faint grapefruit tang on the air. Her shampoo? Perfume? Something she'd massaged into her skin? I looked down at the double knots of her sneakers. She had a scar halfway up one of her shins. The hem of her dress had slipped an inch up her thigh, and her hands were draped over one knee. The gleaming ovals of her nails had been repainted maroon.

I settled back in my seat and forced my eyes away. It was bizarre to be this close to her after the past few weeks. Weeks of holding my phone inches from my face at two in the morning, scrolling through her press, checking her social media as though she were an ongoing breaking news story.

While I stared ahead, her profile picture floated in my mind, the exact angle of her face in the studio light. Now, two feet to my left, she was taking her hair down from that intricate knot and letting it topple over one shoulder, black and smooth like water at night.

The audience filled to capacity, and a tech handed each of us a microphone. Finally, Natalie approached the podium, signaled to the videographer in the back, and said, "I think we're about ready to start!"

As she welcomed the audience, as she thanked the Wiseman Foundation, as she introduced our moderator, a mustached professor emeritus of English at NYU named Tony Gutierrez, my leg jogged and jogged and jogged. I was unrelentingly aware of Selina Chan's total stillness to my side, as though she were a photograph of herself rather than the real thing. Everything she said was going to be a work of perfect accuracy, like a punch to the kidney, and I would have to sit here, defenseless, and take it.

Tony Gutierrez took the podium to a round of applause. I brought my hands together a few times as he beamed at the audience. "Good afternoon, everybody! What a pleasure it is to gather on this blustery Saturday to celebrate literature together. It's an honor to have this distinguished set of writers together on one stage, just a real honor." He snapped out a page of notes. "Now! I'd love this conversation to flow freely between the four of you as we ask ourselves the question that's gathered everyone here today: What might the future of the novel look like?"

Eyes tracked from me to Selina to Christian. People in the crowd whispered. I wondered if they were voicing what I was thinking: *That's not what gathered anyone here today.* They didn't want to witness the civilized exchange of ideas. They wanted to see someone's throat torn out.

But Tony, who with his ponytail and his velour suit jacket looked like the coolest uncle at a wedding, betrayed no unease. He gestured to Tessa and Christian. "Let's start with this side of the stage. Tessa, you first made waves with your novel *White Haven* in the early eighties, and

Christian, your first book, *Arabella*, was published in the late nineties. We can't talk about the future of the novel without talking about the way books have changed in living memory. When you compare your older books to your newest, how would you say your work has reacted to our changing world?"

"Oh, where do I start . . ." Tessa's jumpsuit rustled, her free hand leaping emphatically as she spoke. Beside her, Christian was relaxed in an easy slouch, his elbow crooked over the back of his chair. They each spent a few minutes making comparisons between their novels, and Christian even allowed himself a smile when Tessa complimented his second book.

My heart rate slowed. Maybe this panel *would* just be shoptalk, batting ideas back and forth with Tessa and Christian and Tony and our weird vestigial limb.

This hopeful thought had just clawed its way through the thicket of my nerves when Tony said, "And what would you say is the biggest recent change in the way books are written, read, or discussed?"

"Oh," Tessa said, "I don't think books are written so differently now than when I published *White Haven*. Longhand, typewritten, word-processed, it doesn't matter. You put one word after the other and you try to choose the right ones. It's as simple and impossible now as it has been for centuries."

Christian straightened up from his slump. "Well, I don't know. When readers change, so do the writers. For instance, if you can't assume a readership that can identify a work of any real intelligence, what does that do to a writer?"

Clearly Tony smelled blood in the water, because he stilled behind the podium. "So, Christian," he said, "you think the general readership has changed in the past few decades?"

"Of course it has." Christian massaged the spot where his jaw met his ear, drawing the loose skin against his mandible. "Different appetites.

And different levels of comprehension, obviously. A good writer wants to write for the good readers. The smart ones. But sometime in the past twenty years, the smart readers got clever, and that's a different beast. You can't write for a clever reader. They're always above what they're reading. For instance . . ."

"When you say comprehension," Tony broke in, but Christian rolled on.

"—for instance, one of the readers here on this stage."

Something in the air sharpened. The rustles and sniffles of the audience went silent. Hundreds of eyes turned to Selina Chan.

After a moment, Chan lifted her microphone. "Let's be nice, Christian," she said, smooth and quiet. "There's no reason to insult Parker's reading comprehension."

The tension snapped. The audience dissolved into laughter, and warmth rose into my cheeks, but I glanced out at the crowd and grinned. I'd take a mild dig if it meant all five of us edging past the elephant in the room.

"To your question, Tony," Selina went on, "the biggest change over the course of my lifetime is the rise of the autofiction movement, although I think the trend may be behind us, for which I'm grateful." Her voice sounded different than it had in the Cipriani library. She was barely murmuring into the microphone, her eyes fixed on the back curtains.

"Not a fan?" Tony asked.

"Well, some of my favorite books could be described as autofiction. But if a novel can pull off a Houdini-style escape act, where you watch the author disappear through some trapdoor and leave behind nothing about themselves . . . I'd love more of those books." Selina stroked a loose strand of her hair back behind her ear. "It's also important to me that when the average person walks into a bookstore, they are not confronted with endless shelves of books about novelists."

Laughter rippled through the crowd. "A fair ask," said Tony Gutierrez with a chortle. "Parker? I'm curious about your thoughts."

I lifted the mic. "Yeah. Yes! I—I'm liking all these ideas."

A quiet, scathing sound came from the chair next to me.

I looked over at Chan. A foot away, her eyes bored into mine, disdainful, expectant. *A novel in search of an idea*, I heard her say.

My eyes dropped to the corner of her mouth, which had drawn outward by a matter of millimeters. Anger made my gut contract.

I looked back out at the crowd, feeling suddenly clearheaded. "I don't know if I'll ever write any autofiction. In my experience, a lot of authors come at writing from this feeling like—like you're out of step with the world, like disjunction. Or maybe just loneliness. Anyway—I think, maybe, when autofiction is the prevailing form, it feels like a place you used to visit to explore and connect and wander and hypothesize, not just about yourself, but about all the types of mysteries around you, right, this place becomes a hall of mirrors. Which isn't to say that there's no interest or creativity in the skew," I added. "Just that personally, I'd maybe want to walk out the door, into somewhere I'm not, like, always obliquely looking at myself."

I couldn't help it. I glanced at Selina. She was looking into my eyes, point-blank, a furrow between her brows.

Then she faced back to the podium, chin high.

"Well, look," said Christian, "I agree with all that. It was Faulkner, wasn't it, who said a writer needs observation, experience, and imagination, and if one's missing, the other two can rise up to cover the shortfall. But are we *surprised* that writers these days are banking more on experience than imagination?"

His voice had begun to harden. I could feel my pulse in my hands again. "I mean," he went on, "you say you want writers to take a leap, Selina. But if they're scared to risk writing something out of the box, why do you think that is?"

Impatience flashed across Selina's expression. "I don't know, Christian, but it sounds like you're itching to enlighten me."

"Okay, let's—" said Tony, but Christian was already full steam ahead.

"Yeah, I'll enlighten you. I've been saying it for years. When some glorified blogger with a cult of personality can make or break a book, something's rotten. And it creates a fear culture. And that's creative poison." He nodded in my direction. "Good thing Parker opened the floodgates. When every last warm body in publishing is overjoyed to see a hack finally get treated like a hack, you'd think that person might do some soul-searching."

The crowd's scandalized silence rang out. I sat rigid, gripping my microphone, with no idea what to say.

I started to lift the mic. Selina beat me there.

"Tell me, Christian," she said. "What about my reviews of your books, exactly, made you think I'd be interested in your thoughts or opinions?"

Shocked titters stuttered across the crowd.

"You—" Christian started, but Tony had found his voice.

"All right," Tony said firmly. "Let's move forward here. We've talked a little about the past, a little about the present. Let's look into the future, now . . ."

Time passed uneasily. I didn't think I was imagining that every time Christian spoke, Selina stiffened in her seat.

I didn't know what I would do if he went for her throat again. Technically, Christian was on my side, yet somehow, he'd put me in the ludicrous position of feeling like I needed to defend Selina Chan. A glorified blogger? You could find about two hundred unflattering adjectives for the woman beside me, but nobody could accuse her of being unserious.

Was that how I seemed to the audience, ready to make any claim about Selina to restore my own reputation? That wasn't what I'd been doing—was it?

As the minutes ticked by, though, Christian seemed willing to stick to the subject. It was with obvious relief that Tony said, "It looks like we're nearing our forty-five-minute mark here. Before we move into our Q and A, I want to close by asking you each to name a book you love. Parker, would you like to start?"

"Sure," I said, then immediately forgot every book I'd read in my life. "Um—I—well, this past week I read Aiden Linville's *Desperations*, which was both prescient and terrifying."

For the second time, I heard a reaction from Chan. This time a brief, irritated exhalation. I didn't look at her, paranoid that she would somehow read the truth on my face: that in reality, when I'd read her dismissive pan of *Desperations*, I'd found myself agreeing with her.

But I said, "Yeah. Loved that book." I lowered my microphone and looked at Chan, defying her to respond.

She looked at me with disgust.

Then she glanced to Tony. "I always like to recommend *Asylum Piece*, by Anna Kavan. It's a criminally underread book about a narrator's institutionalization in a Swiss clinic, shown through a series of fragmentary vignettes." A red tint touched her cheeks. "The language is so sensuous and startling and, maybe even more rare for something that occasionally toes the line of surrealism, it's so precise. Every sentence seems to walk down a passageway full of shadows. I really love this book."

Tessa began to speak, but I kept looking at Chan's profile, my defiance withering into disbelief. I'd never met anybody else who'd read *Asylum Piece*, an obscure book I'd been trying to press on my friends since I was fifteen, a book that surprised me every time I opened it.

I didn't even hear Tessa's answer. *I could have said that*, I was thinking.

I could have taken a moment to collect my thoughts, to give my actual opinion.

I'd said something nice. She'd said something honest.

As I looked at Selina Chan, my dislike mingled with a strange, sudden envy. There was something pure and distilled about her, as though she had come from no place, influenced by no person, formed like a pearl in the heart of an oyster. I tried to imagine emerging that way from my childhood, from the fights over borrowed clothes and shattered glasses, from the yearslong feuds I'd moderated between my family, from being tugged in six directions every day of my life, trying to see every side, to satisfy every defendant or accuser, until I got out to college. And even now. Even now, when I picked up the phone.

Of course this marble statue of a woman thought I was spineless and noncommittal. When you saw what a life full of objections turned into, you saw what it was worth to make yourself unobjectionable.

But she made it look easy. She was straight-backed and calm, like she could say exactly what she wanted without an ounce of regret.

She seemed so free.

Chapter Eight

Selina

For the post-festival mixer, the Wiseman Foundation had booked a subterranean cocktail lounge called the Bar Car, located under a warehouse-turned-hotel. Its many spotted mirrors reflected smoky lights, stylish twenty-something waiters, and a long, greenish bar. I liked the place, except for the bookshelves. The books were all turned backward, as though the most interesting thing about books was that they were made out of paper.

After that panel, I'd considered slinking home to Brooklyn, to the Slippery Cork, the neighborhood dive half a block from my apartment. But crucially, the drinks here were free.

I hoped Hayden was happy. "What I want," she'd told me yesterday, "is a good sound bite."

Well, she'd gotten her sound bite. And I'd gotten Christian Gatehead telling New York how much the entire publishing industry despised me.

I slipped into a seat at the end of the rapidly filling bar and arranged my bag of advance copies between my feet. Radiohead murmured over the speakers, and groups of lanyard-wearers jogged down the steps, spilling sunset in behind them. I stretched a hand over the gutter, trying to catch the attention of the closest bartender, a man with a red-brown cloud of a beard and two full sleeves of tattoos. He didn't see me.

Someone leaned over the seat to my right. I caught the scent of cologne, something sharp and smoky—like orange bitters, toasted almond. The man braced his forearms on the back of the seat, two fingers resting on the curve of the bar.

I turned my head halfway before realizing it was Parker Navarro. I had to force myself not to jerk backward.

His chin angled toward me. I could see the dislike on his face. He was readable that way, open.

"Selina," he said stiffly.

"Parker."

A muscle moved low in his cheek. He looked down at my watch, at the crook of my elbow. In the half-light of the bar, these slight motions made shadows glide over his eyes.

Saying nothing else, Navarro looked back to the bartender and pushed a hand through his dark hair. It stayed there for a moment, disheveled, before beginning to settle downward.

I wished he'd stood somewhere else. I didn't need to know he smelled like this, heady, faintly edible. My irritation increased. So easy for a handsome novelist to waltz onto magazine covers and keynote stages, covering up his mediocrity with his articulate hands, his sensitive eyes, the way his soft charcoal sweater stretched at the corners of his shoulders.

Behind us, a hit of laughter. Down the bar, shouts vaulted over the roll and heave of conversation. But the silence between us was as dense as snarled wool.

And as the shock of his appearance faded, my ire mixed with reluctant curiosity. He'd been less shallow on our panel than I'd thought he'd be. I'd expected an hour of bluster and equivocation, laced with insults. But he hadn't joined in with Christian Gatehead's jabs. Maybe even more surprising: He'd had opinions, apparently his own.

The bearded bartender finally pushed his way toward us and crooked his finger at me.

"Gin gimlet," I said. "Thank you."

"And you, man?" the bartender asked Parker.

"Hey, uh, could I get a Jack Rose?"

I glanced sideways. The Jack Rose had been my go-to cocktail in undergrad. It was a sweet, bright drink, apple and lemon, prominently featured in *The Sun Also Rises*. Some strange part of me felt like I should admit this. Confess to having the same literary affectation.

Then a voice from his opposite side said, "Parker?" I watched his shoulders turn toward the woman in floral pants who'd appeared next to him. "I'm Emily Shapiro," she said. "I work at Word Bookstore in Greenpoint. We were emailing a bit about your event?"

"Oh, wow, yeah! Thanks so much for helping me with that. It's so great to meet you in person!"

"You too!" said Emily from the bookstore. One of her curls was tangled in a peacock-feather earring. "I caught your panel. It was great!"

"Hey, thank you. More eventful than I thought it'd be."

"I know, right?"

Navarro laughed. "But I had a good time."

"Good. That's good!"

"Thanks," Navarro said to the bartender as his cocktail came across the bar. He looked back to Emily. "Do, um—I don't know if you're here with friends, or—"

"I'm not!"

"Cool, well, I'm over there with some other people, if you want to join."

She enthused. She seemed sweet and genuine. Navarro retreated with his red-gold glass. I watched him circumnavigate a low table with an old-fashioned globe set into its top.

In a nook between bookcases, he set his camel coat over the back of a low leather chair and sat among a group of cheerfully chatting women. I recognized one of them—Carla Lew, who'd written one of the most unmysterious mysteries I'd ever had the misfortune to read.

Navarro's mouth had tilted into a smile. He listened for a while, jumping in for a few words at a time, flashing his grin around. When Bookstore Emily hurried over to their seating area, he moved sideways to make room, then leaned in over the low glass table as though he were telling a secret. As he spoke, the women broke into peals of laughter that cut through the noise of the bar. Emily touched his arm.

My feelings swung back into dislike. There was the Parker Navarro I'd expected to see all day, luxuriating in the spotlight and the attention from women, surrounding himself with people who'd treat him like the center of the universe.

As he looked down at the spot where Emily had touched him, his short story intruded into my mind. *She inches her fingers down the yielding contours of her waist.*

I imagined Parker Navarro lounging in the dim corner of a coffee shop, that flushed color high in his cheeks, thinking—for some reason—about my waist.

Feeling an unwelcome tug in my stomach, I looked away. I wondered if he believed some of the things he'd written about me. The section of his story where he imagined my expensive organic diet, for instance, which if anything gave me too much credit. And I would have liked to speak five languages, but in reality, in the years since I'd stopped speaking to my parents, my halting, childish Mandarin had atrophied to a degree that I felt embarrassed even swapping conversational basics with cashiers in Chinatown grocery stores.

For somebody who hated me to the point of fantasizing about my death in *The Paris Review*, he seemed to have a strangely high opinion of me.

My lips twitched, and I took a sip of gin. *Fifty-three years later she will die in a hospital bed in San Jose, the only person in the room.* I supposed I understood why that particular line had lit up the internet, but to me it was almost funny. Its frankness, its offhandedness.

Without even knowing it, Parker Navarro had written something that understood me. I'd known for a long time that the most connected people would ever feel to me was through my writing. I wasn't really afraid of dying alone, only of dying without having done the best I could. I thought of this more often than was probably normal, lying awake in my apartment, considering what I would leave behind if I died in my sleep.

I took a long pull of my gin gimlet and picked through my bag of books, but before I could choose, my phone buzzed. Jacob or Cassie, I assumed, asking about the panel.

But when I glanced down, I went still. The bar seemed to rotate around me. A smiling photo had appeared onscreen.

Call from: Charles Chan

My parents hadn't called me in two years. I hadn't seen them in three. But every few days I opened WhatsApp and checked the line of text under each of their names: last seen online 11:22 a.m. Sometimes I imagined this exact situation: a call out of nowhere, an accident, a medical emergency. My father was a nervous driver, and my mother had a weak heart.

I threw a glance across the bar. Packed. By the time I fought my way across the crowd to privacy, the call would go to voicemail.

I hunched toward the wall beside me and picked up. "Dad?"

"Xueyan."

Those two syllables confirmed my fears. My mother and father hardly ever used my middle name. At home I was Xiao Yan in the day-to-day, Selina with company—Xueyan only under serious duress.

I slid forward on my barstool so its edge bit into my thigh. If I got a car back to Brooklyn and it took me fifteen minutes to pack a bag, I could be at LaGuardia in an hour, although God knew if there were any flights to Minneapolis tonight. "What happened?" I said sharply.

"What happened? You tell me. Fred Richards at work said today he see you in the news."

This took me so completely by surprise that for a moment I could only sit there, staring at the bottles of bourbon clustered upon an iron shelf. Thoughts of a rush flight to Minnesota vanished.

I straightened up on my barstool. "Wait," I said. "This is about the *feud*?"

"The feud? The feud!" My father's voice was a reedy, mournful baritone, like a bassoon turned into a sixty-eight-year-old man. "You say 'the feud' like we should know about this. We don't know anything. You have a fight with this writer? You were in every newspaper for weeks? Why didn't you tell us?"

"What do you mean, why didn't I tell you? What was I supposed to—" I hunched over the bar, my bewilderment interrupted by a stab of frustration. "Never mind. Okay. Now you know. Do you have questions, or something? Is that why you're calling?"

Now I heard my mother faintly in the background. "She picked up? Let me talk to her." A moment later, she was saying, "Xueyan. What are you going to do about this? We heard about this fight from your father's coworker! From—"

"I know. Dad already said that."

"—so? So?"

My free hand had curled into a fist in my lap. "I'm handling it."

"How?"

The tattooed bartender had caught my eye. He made a motion toward his ear, a kill gesture across his throat.

"I don't have time for this," I said. "I have to go."

"Where are you? What's all that noise?"

"I'm at a bar. I'm fine. I just have to go."

My father again. "Xueyan, this is—"

"I can't be on my phone in here. Bye."

I ended the call and shoved my phone into my purse. My dress was sticking to the middle of my back. My face, reflected in the mirror behind the bar, looked blank and hard-eyed, but I felt like something inside my torso had bruised. My heart thudded against that soft place again and again as I drained half my gimlet in two long, bitter swallows. The panel, and now this, too? With the low roar of the bar churning around me, I returned to thumbing through the books in my tote bag, needing something beautiful to catch my eye.

Chapter Nine

Parker

"To the feud," said Carla, clinking her martini against my second Jack Rose.

I tipped my drink back. "Glad it's entertaining you."

"Not as much as *this* is. Are you seeing her?" Carla's eyes, clever and quick, a little mortified and a little smug, strayed to the bar.

"Still drinking alone?" I glanced back. "If it were anyone else, I'd feel bad for her."

Emily nibbled her lower lip. "Are we sure she's that awful? It seems like nobody's really talked to her. Not to be a hopeless cliché, but she could just be kind of misunderstood."

"No," I said. "Selina Chan is understood exactly the way she wants people to understand her."

"How do you know?" said Emily.

"I just know." I glanced again at Selina, at the curve of her neck licked by the violet lamp on the bar beside her. Her head had bowed swanlike over her book, a lock of dark hair brushing her cheekbone, her dress's zipper a dot of steel at her nape.

"She doesn't want people to like her," I said. "Or, you know, defend her. She wouldn't care about that." I took a long swallow of my Jack

Rose. "Actually, I'm sure she thinks being liked too much would be a red flag, because it would mean people weren't taking her seriously."

"How long have you two known each other?" Emily asked.

"Known each other?"

"I mean when did you meet? Was it after her first review?"

"Oh, no. That night the video went up—that was the first time we met."

Emily looked confused. "Oh." She measured another sip from her copper mug.

"Sorry," I said, realizing it had been a minute since I'd asked anyone a question. "Um—how are things at Word? Thank you so much for doing my launch, by the way. I can't wait."

Emily lit up. "Of course! We're so excited to have you!"

We spent an hour discussing the ups and downs of running an independent bookstore, but throughout, my eye kept straying to Selina, those long fingers delving between pages, her lipsticked mouth leaving pink arcs on the rim of her glass. She looked as unconcerned now as she had onstage, Christian's insults bouncing off her armor. Nothing like the night we'd fought at the party, when she'd reddened, snapped—engaged.

Something in me kept picking at the idea of that, as though I were picking a scab. She'd looked at Christian like he was nothing, utterly beneath her notice. That wasn't the way she looked at me.

When the bar dimmed its lights, Emily checked her phone and stood. I rose to let her by, and as she slipped past, she said, "It was so great to see you, Parker!"

"Yeah, you too. I'll see you at the store sometime."

"For sure! Or, um . . ." A flush rose in her cheeks. "I don't want to make it weird, but maybe we could trade numbers? We could grab a drink in the neighborhood at some point?"

I felt a pinch of surprise. My eyes, which had been sliding toward the end of the bar, snapped back onto Emily.

"No pressure," she added quickly. "I understand if it's, like, a conflict of interest."

"No, it's okay." I was suddenly very aware of the way Emily was winding one of her curls around her fingertip. "Um, yeah. I can—I'll add myself?"

"Okay, cool!" I created my contact in her phone, and she left with a fluttery wave. I settled back into the sofa feeling both flattered and worried that the group would make some innuendo, but they didn't seem to have noticed.

As the open bar wound down, we ordered a last round, and in the corner of my eye, Selina passed the halfway point of her advance copy. The tipsier I became, the more I caught myself ruminating on the panel, and the more outrageous it seemed that Selina Chan loved *Asylum Piece*. First of all, nobody had read that book. It was *my* obscure book to recommend to people, and she was encroaching on my territory. Second of all—

I stood and headed up to tip the bartender. This time, there was plenty of space, but I stopped at Chan's side again. "You like *Asylum Piece*," I said. "You."

She lifted her dark head from her book. Two deep furrows had appeared between her brows, pointing toward each other.

"What," she said slowly, "are you saying *you've* read *Asylum Piece*?"

"Yeah. Six, seven times."

She stared at me like she couldn't believe I was literate.

"*City* reviewed it when I was a freshman in high school." I set my empty on the bar. "So, was that—I'm guessing you also—"

"Yes," she said.

For another long moment, we just looked at each other. I had an uninvited vision of the woman across from me as some gangly teenager, lying in bed under a band poster she'd find humiliating now, poring over the same issues of *City* that I had, month after month.

It was bizarre to think of her ever having been a teenager. I'd sort of assumed she'd sprung out of her father's head fully formed, like Athena.

"Anyway," I said. "It just doesn't make sense that you'd like that book. Because, you know, I read somewhere that a narrator not having agency is such a dealbreaker for you."

Chan recovered, her surprise disappearing with a single slow blink, like an unimpressed housecat's. "I love a passive narrator. I also love a book that knows its cutoff point should be two hundred pages."

"If I wrote a two-hundred-page book, you'd still find some way to call it bloated and interminable."

"Yes, because if you wrote a two-hundred-page book, it would still somehow feel bloated and interminable." She drained the last of her gimlet. "Your short story felt interminable, and that was, what, three thousand words?"

"I bet you loved reading it."

"Oh?" She looked amused. "Why's that?"

"Because it fulfills the delusion of your life, where you're the main character."

Chan sighed. "Parker, we both know the main character of that story was you. Everyone who read it was forced to spend time in your company, not mine." She marked her page—dog-eared, I hated that shit—and let her book flip shut. "Although I meant what I wrote. It was a nice change to see flashes of . . . what?" She snapped her fingers a few times, lazily. "Cognition, maybe? Drive?"

"You think I don't have *drive*? You think anybody writes a nine-hundred-page book without *drive*?"

"Yes." Her eyes flicked down to my dress shoes, then tracked up to the neck of my sweater. Heat filled my body as though she were pouring boiling liquid into me. "Don't worry, though. I think if you really put your mind to it, you could write a twelve-hundred-page book without drive."

The hot itch intensified up my ribs. I leaned over the bar and tucked a tip into the glass jar. My hand came within inches of her bicep as I withdrew, but she didn't move away. She stilled in her seat, though, some tension in the clean lines of her forearms.

Her gaze lingered at the base of my throat. Christ. Why did she always look at me like she was deciding on the most efficient way to vivisect me?

I dropped my eyes to the book in her hands. "How's your next victim? Are you enjoying reading alone?"

"I'm not alone. You're here, unfortunately."

"God, you're so pedantic."

"Better than being inaccurate, especially when using accurate language is your job. Anyway . . ." Chan flipped over the advance readers' copy and considered its cover art: a bell jar with an albino weasel suspended inside, the title in elaborate capitals, DEUS EX ANIMALIS. It wasn't one of the buzz books with the twelve-foot posters, nothing by a marquee author. Glancing at the ARC's spine, I didn't even recognize the publisher. I felt a pang of sympathy for this Ariana Okoro person, wherever she was, oblivious to her fate.

Then Chan said, "Yes, I'm enjoying the book. She's funny, this author."

I'd been so busy devising righteously angry responses, I found myself with absolutely no reply to this simple statement of enjoyment.

"Oh," I said.

"She gets carried away with her dialogue," Chan went on, "but she has such an ear for it, I can't blame her." Her eyes were intent on the cover, both fixed and distant, as though she were sliding out through a fissure in reality and seeing the world of the book unfold in front of her. This wasn't the Selina Chan in the cartoon villain's mansion I'd pictured, holding every novel at arm's length with a premeditated expression of distaste, which any author had to clear some impossibly high bar to alter.

Chan seemed to remember that I existed. She glanced up at me. I realized with a sharp pang of discomfort how close we were, how I could see the dot of eyeliner caught in her lower lashes and the pink crease at the bow of her lip, the few light freckles laid on the tops of her cheeks.

I found myself saying, "That was weird. With Christian, on the panel."

"Very," she said.

A pause. Nearby, the bartender was firing soda water out of a small red gun into a tumbler. Why was I considering telling her that I'd never liked Christian's books, either?

Why was I still standing here, looking at the bright wet sheen on her mouth from her drink? I felt strangely aware of the taste of apple on my tongue, the lingering sweetness, as though in counterpoint to the gleam on her lips, that leftover gloss of gin.

"Well," she said, voice tart, sliding the advance copy into her tote bag, "I'm going back to Brooklyn. I assume I'll see you online, unfortunately."

I stepped back, my annoyance returning. "Yep. Bye."

She strode for the door. On the bottom step she paused, took her phone from her purse, and studied its screen, unreadable. I thought I saw her shoulders tighten. Then she vanished upstairs into the lowering blue evening.

Chapter Ten

Selina

Search results for: Selina Chan

10m ago **@richardpapensvape**: lol that panel video. i love how **selina chan** so completely does not care about these impotent men and their feelings. low-empathy icon. emotionless queen

14m ago **@infpcatlady**: I mean, people hated **Selina Chan** for years before this, though? Did we all forget that being an asshole doesn't make you smart or aspirational, even if that asshole is a woman??

27m ago **@LolaXu**: Ok everybody, if you want to sign my petition asking @TheParisReview to take down Parker Navarro's disgusting story about **Selina Chan**, HERE'S THE LINK!! Tysm to everybody who thought of more points to add about how this is borderline sexual harassment and maybe also a death threat???? **[LINK]**

41m ago **@ChristianGateheadAuthor**: On the heels of Saturday's panel, a new interview with @ElectricLit about the decline of our literary culture and, yes, **Selina Chan** and her ilk. **[LINK]**

51m ago **@2223333windo**: **@SelinaChan** bitch

The *City* office occupied the top floor of the Baumgartner, a historic nineteenth-century building a stone's throw from Union Square, whose austere limestone dripped with black rain marks. When you exited the elevator on our floor, you were greeted by a vast oaken wall, CITY MAGAZINE carved into its polished surface. Each letter was six inches deep and a foot high. Some mornings, I still stopped opposite the two enormous words and let their impact ring through me. I thought about the writers who had paused in that spot, taking in this monument to *City*'s work.

The Monday after the Wiseman Festival, I hesitated longer than usual. I told myself that this place had chosen me for a reason.

When I reached my office, I found the door open. Scott was standing at the window, gazing outside with his hands folded behind his back. This would have looked more impressive if my window hadn't been three feet from the adjacent building, with a view of a brick wall and a drainpipe oozing slime.

I knocked twice on the doorjamb. "Morning."

"Selina. Hi." Scott turned to me with a troubled air.

"How was your weekend?"

"Not especially noteworthy, but let's speak about yours. Hayden sent me the video of the festival program."

I tugged the door shut. "Was she not happy with it?"

"No, no, she was thrilled. She said something about a clip blowing up on TikTok."

"I thought I'd die before I ever heard you say the words 'blowing up on TikTok.'"

"And yet." Scott took the chair in the corner with a groan. "Did you see the morning's updates?"

"You mean Christian Gatehead's interview?" I tossed my purse onto my desk. "Or Lola Xu's petition making me out to be a tragic martyr?"

"Both. Look, Selina, I'm concerned that this feud is beginning to overstep some boundaries for you."

"I don't care what Christian Gatehead thinks about me."

He adjusted the knot of his tie, his silence oozing skepticism.

"Seriously," I said, "I've taken worse."

"You shouldn't have to 'take' anything. Something like Saturday is a world away from your job description."

"Right, but if it's benefiting *City*—"

"You're a critic. What benefits *City* is your criticism."

I angled myself away from Scott to unshoulder my backpack, not overfond of the way he was watching me, as though I needed a rescuer. Still, he made a fair point. As recently as two months ago, I'd spent my days reading new releases. Drafting reviews. Cooking dinner without opening social media and reading about every way in which I was insufferable or evil or pitiable or laughable.

I sank into my office chair, feeling exhausted. I'd slept terribly since Saturday, my parents' call circling my head like a buzzard. They'd emailed a follow-up as I'd left the bar. Xiao Yan—We are sorry to hear about the fight. We want to know how you are handling it. If you call we will talk again. From Dad and Mom. I hadn't replied and didn't know if I would.

"What about Hayden?" I said.

"I already spoke with her," Scott said. "She . . . well, her ideal scenario was that you sign this petition and sue *The Paris Review* for libel, but I told her you'd be more interested in being roasted alive over a slow flame."

"You know me so well."

"I try." Scott took a small mock bow. "Anyway, as an alternative, she agreed that it's not a bad idea for you to lie low. Right now, public sympathy for you and *City* is high. You were just doing your job, and here come these men making vindictive public attacks and writing . . .

unusually detailed short stories . . . you see the angle. And if you fire back, the goodwill could vanish. So, she thinks you could cool things off while she figures out next steps."

"What next steps?"

"Unclear. She did also suggest that, short of mentioning the petition, you post something on your social media reminding the world that you're a human being with feelings."

"So, she's saying play the victim."

Scott sighed. "She's saying let people be on your side, Selina. Is that so hard?"

I didn't answer.

He stood. "If Parker Navarro responds to the petition, or to the Gatehead piece, we'll cross that bridge when we come to it. For now, I want you doing coverage of the Booker and the Nobel. People think it's Murakami's year. Sound good?"

"Okay. Yes, understood."

Scott hesitated. I pulled my laptop from its protective sleeve, avoiding his eyes, though I could feel him watching me.

"Let me tell you something," he finally said. "I joined the staff of *City* in 1987. The first time I gave a book a really blistering review was eighty-eight, I think. The week after that review ran, the author mailed a four-page letter to the office saying he hoped I never wanted to work in fiction publishing, because his uncle was the publisher at Random House and he'd see to it that nobody in New York would so much as sniff a manuscript with my name on it."

My hands had stilled on my laptop. In the seven years I'd worked at *City*, I could count on one hand the number of times Scott had said anything this personal.

"What did you do?" I asked.

"I showed the letter to Sandy Reilly. She was the editor then. And Sandy said to me, 'Scott, are you planning on leaving *City* in the near future?' And I said, 'Well, no.' And she said, 'Then you just keep writing like you have nothing to worry about.'"

Scott opened the door. "It's a gift," he said, "to write like that. You'd better not lose it."

A week passed, but Navarro didn't respond to the Gatehead interview or Lola Xu's petition. He didn't mention me in any more articles or venomous short stories. On social media he devoted himself to more normal forms of self-promotion, like inflicting excerpts from *High and Dry* on the public. At meetings, Hayden kept dropping hints about "marketing cooking up exciting things behind the scenes" and, more cryptically, about "important takeaways," but in the meantime, my job returned to normal. I felt marginally more sane, as though some enormous hand were untwisting the clamp that had, for the past month, contained my head.

The Monday before Thanksgiving, the editorial staff arrived in the library to find Erica Robson, *City*'s head of marketing, tugging a projection screen over one of the bookshelves. Erica was tall and rangy and alert, eighteen-inch microbraids swaying down the back of her patterned pantsuits. She gave off the air of somebody who could face a tornado without so much as a raised eyebrow. Trying for fifteen years to make *City* profitable could do that to a person.

"Afternoon, everybody," Erica said.

"Is this the part where we find out what Hayden's been making y'all do downstairs for the last three weeks?" said Kellie.

"Yep. New site feature. It's really not the worst idea, though." With a click of Erica's remote, my review of *High and Dry* appeared onscreen. "The question was how to take advantage of articles that catch fire. The day after Selina's video, this review got two and a half million page views, but since we give people four free articles a month, most of them didn't have to engage with the paywall. So . . ."

She scrolled down to the bottom of my article. After the end mark, a graphic of a piggybank contained a box that read:

Tip this article: [$1].

[Add comment . . .]

"Wait," said Kellie, "do we actually make tips?"

Erica grimaced. "No. Sorry, that's just the language they wanted to use."

Kellie blew her bangs off her forehead like a horse dislodging a fly.

"Any other questions?" said Erica.

"Add comment," I said, eyeing the second box. *City* had never had a comments section, something that brought me more joy every time I browsed the comments of the *Times* and *The Washington Post*.

Erica met my eye. "Don't worry, they're not public comments. I had to fight for that one. They'll come through to email, like a thank-you note. I figured having a say might encourage people to pitch in, and if you're spending money on the site, you're pretty likely to be supportive and not . . . you know."

"Teeming with verbal abuse?" I said.

"That's the one. You don't have to read the messages, but there's a new tab in your emails if you want to check them."

A flurry of clicking and laptop-opening as we all navigated to our inboxes. "Oh, look," said Mike to Joyce. "This is very genteel, isn't it?"

I leaned over to read his screen.

Tip alert: $3

From: Robert (Chicago, IL)

Happy that City Magazine has introduced this "feature" to express appreciation for pieces of "especially fine journalism." I can only hope that "number of tips" will result in higher end-of-year bonuses! Keep up the good work, Mike!

"Quotation marks," said Joyce, with sympathy. "Always a killer."

Curious, I clicked on the Tip Jar tab at the top of my own inbox. A dozen emails appeared, and halfway down the list, a familiar name caught my eye.

Tip alert: $5

From: Parker (New York City, NY)

To tide you over when City folds.

I snapped my laptop shut and looked back up at Erica's presentation, trying to recapture the thread.

After the meeting, alone in my office, I reopened my laptop to study the message. What was Parker trying to accomplish, exactly? All those years of pirating my writing, and he'd caved just to make this petty jab?

I narrowed my eyes at the screen. Maybe he expected me to screenshot the comment, post it online with an insulting response, and generate more free publicity for his book. If I told Hayden, she'd probably encourage me to do exactly that. But unfortunately for both Hayden and Parker, I'd been enjoying the relative calm of the last week and a half.

Yes, I told myself, exiting my email. There was no need to respond at all.

No need, except that now I was imagining the self-satisfied expression he'd probably been wearing as he'd submitted the comment. I was remembering his belligerent look at our panel, when he'd recommended Aiden Linville's *Desperations* to that poor crowd of people. This was the person currently mocking me by email.

Lips pursed, I opened my phone, tapped into Venmo, and searched

Parker Navarro. Just like that, he appeared at the top of the list. That same brooding headshot.

I hit Pay, then entered $5. I drummed into the message field: Your next advance.

Are you sure you know this user? Venmo asked me.

I tapped Confirm and set my phone face down on the desk, hard. I needed to focus. Scott was expecting a review of that Ariana Okoro book. I needed a draft by the end of the day.

But as I opened my laptop, I found myself clicking back to Parker Navarro's social media. *This is unproductive,* I told myself, even as my fingers flicked to scroll, flicked to scroll, flicked to scroll.

> **@ParkerNavarroWrites**: Had a wonderful time at @WisemanFoundation @WFLF. Thanks to all who came!

> **@ParkerNavarroWrites**: Appreciated this review of High and Dry in the @AustinDispatch! Written by @CBHenderson, a generous reader and electrifying writer.

I switched to Replies.

> **@ParkerNavarroWrites**: @RobotCatsUnite Hahahaha yes! Made me laugh on the train!

> **@ParkerNavarroWrites**: @JennDiagram I've never read it, although clearly I should!

The page went on and on like that. Laughter, permissiveness, acceptance, absorption. Exhausting. And on his main feed: the voice of some wide-eyed ingenue, a person whose sole purpose in life was to react rather than to generate a thought of his own.

This annoyed me in a way I wasn't used to being annoyed. Parker Navarro was already an egotist and a bad writer. He didn't need to make himself seem *even worse* than he actually was. This version of him was nowhere near the real thing, the person who, at our panel, had at least displayed the ability to put an idea into words, the person who had approached me in the bar to confront me about *Asylum Piece.*

I was still wrestling with that overlap in our tastes. It shouldn't have meant anything that he'd read *Asylum Piece* half a dozen times, but somehow it did. Sometimes a book forms such a foundational part of you that to meet somebody else who loves it, who really cares about it, feels like stumbling into a stranger in another country who comes from your hometown. At some point in the past decade, Parker Navarro and I might have been rereading at the same time, tugging out our paperbacks and letting them accordion open, grateful that, though other books might let us down, this one never would.

It was strange to know that Parker had come to the book from Marcy D'Artagnan's *City* review, too. Unwillingly, I pictured him then, adolescent, a copy of *City* stuffed into an overfull backpack and *Asylum Piece* open before him on a high school desk. I'd been sixteen and desperately lonely the first time I'd read it. Like me, had he been blasted back in his seat by the sheer possibilities of language that slender book revealed, like a pilot experiencing the kickback of a jet engine?

I realized I'd been staring, unseeing, at an @ symbol on his profile for upward of a minute. Sixty seconds of my life I'd never get back, thinking about a teenage Parker Navarro.

I closed the tab and got back to work.

Chapter Eleven

Parker

My phone buzzed with an alert from Venmo:

Selina Chan paid you $5.00. "Your next advance."

I stopped in the middle of the subway platform. Someone knocked into my shoulder, and I hurried into the shadow of an I beam.

I knew I'd started this round, baiting her with the tip jar, but it still felt bizarre to see a private message from Selina Chan sitting in my palm. As I jogged up from the platform, filtering between a group of backpacked women speaking French, I pulled her up on social media.

@SelinaChan: You can now leave tips on your favorite articles at the @CityMagazine website. To clarify, these tips don't drop into the writers' pockets, but they'll contribute to the magazine's ongoing health.

@SelinaChan: @JohnDreyfus: Still developing my opinion.

@SelinaChan: A list with some interesting choices (#4, #27) and a number of glaring omissions (Bolaño, Ward, Cusk). **[LINK: The 50 Best Novels of the 2000s]**

I shook my head, hoisting my backpack up on one shoulder as I emerged in the Flatiron District. Had any non-robot in the history of social media ever sounded so aggressively unavailable? Her posts were so removed, so distant, as though even her own feelings were items that she had to reach into a glass case to access.

But I knew better. She might have liked to pretend she was above the rest of us mortals, but I'd caught her in the bar, staring into the book she was reading as though it exerted a gravitational pull on her. In that moment she'd been present, immediate, reachable.

An email had arrived while I'd been underground. I paused on Fifth Avenue to read, loitering by the window of a flagship clothing store, where dozens of spidery mannequins were drowning in their expensive coats.

To: parkernavarroauthor@gmail.com
From: brian.falwell.33@thebaynow.com
Subject: Blast from the past

Hi Parker,

How are you? I'm not sure if you remember me, but we went to Jefferson together. I was pretty good friends with Tyler Pressman, and if I'm remembering right, you and I bumped into each other a few times when he had those astronomy parties senior year, haha.

I'm emailing because I've joined the editorial team of The Bay Now, a newish arts and culture magazine based in South SF. Obviously, we've all been following your feud with Selina Chan, and I watched the livestream of that festival on Saturday. I could just see the story there! I'm champing at the bit here to do a profile.

I'm sure you have lots of demands on your time, but it'd be an honor to have you in our pages!

Take care, and say hey to Tyler for me,

Brian

I lowered my phone and watched a passing biker nearly mow down a couple of tourists, who leaped coltishly back onto the sidewalk while he yelled obscenities over his shoulder. None of this really registered with me. I did remember Brian, an easygoing eighteen-year-old with a holographic-stickered longboard and an infectious laugh. In the past couple of weeks, the feud's exposure had died down, but that petition about the short story was still doing the rounds among Selina Chan's fan club, and Bill was sending me a digest of media requests every few days. I couldn't answer everything that came in, but turning down someone I knew from high school seemed callous.

In any case, there was no time to respond now—I'd be late to meet my editor. I starred the email for later and turned from the sunlit avenue onto a narrow street, dim even though it was high noon, with blue shadows strafing down the buildings from the scaffolding. Halfway down the block I shouldered into a Greek restaurant decked with iron café tables, where live vines spiraled around rafters painted sunrise yellow. The stone ceiling was curved, cavelike, and mosaics underfoot surged into curling cobalt waves.

"Parker!"

I saw a hand waving from the window and hurried over, my mouth immediately dry. I hadn't seen Lauren since *These Extraordinary Times* had bombed. She gave the impression of a sculpture someone had built out of wire and silk thread: a delicate, almost fragile person whose fine silver hair formed a thin layer over her skull. She treated me to a brief, incongruously brutal handshake. "You're early."

"Yes, sorry, hope that's okay."

"Of course it is. Sit, sit . . . I'm happy to see you," she said to her menu, peering through her reading glasses at the appetizers. "Before we toast to your successes, I do have a question about current events. I assume you've been following the petition that's been circulating online?"

"Definitely, yeah. Bill and I are keeping an eye on it."

"And what do you think?"

Lauren's eyes were still roving over the soups. I realized what her studiously casual attitude meant: Coronation was afraid that I was about to get taken to court.

I laughed. "No. It's—nothing's going to happen. Selina Chan isn't going to sue me."

Lauren's eyes flicked up. "You don't think she has it in her, hmm?"

"That's not it. Just—" I struggled for words. "It's not her style. She already wrote that letter to the editor. She's not going to do anything else." I paused. I didn't know how to explain why, having had exactly two blistering conversations with Selina, I somehow knew that she was about as likely to sue me as she was to make a post saying, *Parker Navarro wounded my tender feelings!*

"Trust me," I said. "The petition's dead in the water. She's not interested."

Lauren seemed satisfied. "Well, the team will be happy to hear it." With a casual wave of her hand she summoned our waiter, who jotted down Lauren's lemonade, my coffee, and an olive tapenade. Then she set down her menu and regarded me directly. "Parker, I have to apologize again for what happened at the festival. What an unfortunate blip."

"Right. Um—yeah, it wasn't ideal."

"We were all relieved to hear that the panel went well, in any case."

Making my napkin into incoherent origami in my lap, I tried to think of a diplomatic answer. Kristen had called the change "last-minute," but how last-minute could it have been, with Selina's and Christian's names printed in the festival programs? Couldn't my team have sent an email that morning, giving me the opportunity to cancel before I was standing twenty feet from the one person on earth who most despised me?

Lauren went on. "I heard there was a line down the aisle for your signing. Isn't that right?"

"I . . . Yeah. That was great." I heard the gentle reminder in her words, that Saturday had been a positive for the book, but the idea only made me unhappier. Just for the purpose of racking up a few more preorders, Coronation had thrown me to the wolves with no preparation. I was lucky that the wolf in question hadn't made a point of ripping me to pieces.

It was deeply depressing, the idea that Selina Chan had acted more considerately on Saturday than the people who were supposed to be in my corner.

I was just mustering up the nerve to say something along these lines when Lauren said, "Parker, I know the past month and a half has been unusual, but your willingness not to back away from the spotlight really has changed the direction for *High and Dry*. I have some news to that end, actually."

"You do?" I hesitated. "What is it?"

"We heard yesterday that Anna Delaney wants *High and Dry* for her February book club. They'd like you to sign eleven thousand tip-ins for a special edition."

Shock whited out my conflicted feelings. "Oh my God. Eleven thousand—are you serious?"

"I am. I hope you don't mind that we accepted on your behalf. I'm sure your hand will recover."

I let out a stuttering laugh. "They can pulverize my hand with a hammer if they're selling eleven thousand copies of the book."

"That's the spirit. I think." The waitress returned with our drinks, and Lauren clinked her lemonade against my coffee. "Cheers, Parker. Well deserved."

"Cheers, yeah. I don't know what to say. This is . . . Wow."

"Wow is right. And while we're talking business—I wanted to discuss something else." Lauren slid a paperback across the table, an advance copy with cover art of a decaying cottage door. HOUSE HEARTH HOME, read the title, and at the bottom:

from the author of Our Gods Our Heavens
JULIETTE LIAO

I grabbed up the book. "Wait, thank you. I love Juliette Liao." She wasn't the most famous author in the world, but *Our Gods Our Heavens* had been the best book I'd read in its release year, and I'd eaten up the half dozen books on her backlist with increasing outrage. Why hadn't this woman been selling millions of copies since the 1990s? Why weren't prize committees bowing at her feet?

"You're a fan, then," said Lauren.

"Huge fan."

"I'm glad to hear that, because I wanted to ask a favor. Juliette was supposed to do a launch event with Christian Gatehead just before Christmas, but Christian's received bad news about his mother's health. He's leaving the city and doesn't expect to return until January." Lauren folded her arms on the table. "We'd love you to step in. I thought this might be a welcome change of pace from the publicity around the *City* feud."

"Oh, man," I muttered. If she was trying to bribe me into forgetting any hard feelings over the festival, she was doing a great job. "What date is the event?"

"Juliette is very particular about her publicity. The only date she gave us was December twenty-third."

The waitress returned at that moment, giving me time to mull. My siblings and I were supposed to spend Christmas in Daly City with our mother, then New Year's in Manila with our father and extended family.

No matter how much planning we poured into the holiday trips, they always wound up a mess. Christi's kids complicated every meal, and Kevin always brought along some terrible new girlfriend, and

Elena always brought along a more tolerable but weirdly codependent new girlfriend, and Justin and his wife inevitably fought on the first day, which irritated everyone else into a spiral.

This was always the time of year I felt happiest to be single. I'd spent two Christmases with my last serious girlfriend, and after the chaos of every event, I'd wanted nothing more than to crawl into bed together in gentle, mutual silence. But Kate—a resident in internal medicine, maybe overused to diagnosis and treatment—had wanted to pry out every discomfort of every day, as though reliving these things in minute detail would improve them.

"I understand if you have travel plans," said Lauren.

"I do. I'm supposed to fly to San Francisco on the twenty-first."

"Well, if you were to fly out on the twenty-fourth, Coronation would pick up the flight."

"Right, okay," I said, not thinking of the financials. I was envisioning the dining room in my mom's apartment on December 21, crammed with people, and the tempers that might spike without me there, because I had specific methods for defusing Justin's more tasteless jokes, and Elena opened up to me in ways she didn't with our siblings, and I was the only one who still listened to Mom's grievances about Dad without cutting her off midsentence.

It felt selfish how badly I wanted to do this event. I imagined sitting at the front of a silent bookstore across from one of my heroes, able to ask her every question I'd ever wanted to ask.

I thought, weirdly, of Selina Chan at the convention panel, straight-backed and unmoved.

"Yeah," I said before I could stop myself. "I'll do it."

That afternoon, energized, I began to write a new novel. With the book club news fizzing like champagne in the back of my mind, it was beginning to feel real: that *High and Dry* could become an honest-to-God bestseller, that Lauren might buy another book from me after all. I dropped into the seat by my living room window, opened a fresh journal, and began. This was an idea I'd been turning over for a while, but the specifics had finally snapped into focus.

A miniaturist, a woman in her sixties, lives in a remote Canadian village. A young man seeks her out, begging to learn her art. He comes from artistic fame in another country, but not the United States—an Indian actor, maybe? A Brazilian pop singer? But the miniaturist has no interest in his fame and assigns him a series of exasperating, apparently meaningless tasks as training in her art. This psychically disturbs something in him, and he begins to experience visions of his life as a baby while growing into a promising student. Late in the book he spends a full year perfecting a sculpture the size of his thumbnail. But the miniaturist's health begins to fail. The student takes care of her. In the end, though, he's the one to die, having tried to cross a forest in winter to get medical help for her. But he has made this one tiny immaculate work of art.

I surfaced from the outline and the six pages I'd written in a kind of delicious fever.

And? said a low, serious, familiar voice in my mind. *What's the purpose of all this?*

I shook the thought away, annoyed, and returned to the question of the student's origins. I liked the idea of the Brazilian pop star—but that meant this would be my third novel that didn't center on Asian characters. *These Extraordinary Times* had been about a white suburban family in the 1980s, though of course that hadn't saved the book from being declared "woke."

I assumed I would write a project starring Asian characters someday. But it did strike me as funny that, had I decided to write a novel set in the Philippines, I would be taken as some voice of authority on the subject, when I'd spent under three months there, cumulatively. As for writing something centered on a Filipino American, maybe I just didn't like the idea that anyone might read one of my characters and picture that person with my face.

I moved on to a less fraught subheading, jotting down ideas for the meaningless tasks the student could undertake. He'd sit in silence for days on end. He'd categorize pine needles. The miniaturist would have him assemble, then disassemble, an old wooden puzzle in her attic until he was teetering on the edge of sanity.

And the purpose? Selina Chan's voice insisted.

I snapped the notebook shut, feeling disoriented. I'd gone too deep with this fight, let her creep too far into me. I couldn't let her infect my work.

Anyway, the concept *did* have a purpose: to shred the idea that people should seek out lives of consequence and permanence; to show the seductive shape of idolatry, then whack it open like a piñata.

And has anything to that end happened in your first six pages? said the voice.

With something like dread I flipped open the notebook and reread what I'd written.

No, was the answer. In the first six pages, the celebrity had arrived at the miniaturist's house, and as he'd stood on her doorstep, I'd delved into recent time, and I'd shown his journey on a series of delayed trains. He'd made observations on those trains: about the scenery, about his fellow passengers, about the tan lines on his wrists.

Did I need the trains?

My pen hung suspended over the page as frustration built in me, water surging against a dam. Did this change even have anything to do with my own tastes? Was I seriously going to spend my one wild and precious life trying to satisfy an imaginary version of Selina Chan?

Did I want to get this right, or did I just want to escape criticism?

I threw down the pen and scrubbed my hands through my hair. I wished I could dismiss her reviews, the way Arthur and Bill and everybody else in my life had, but I couldn't. I couldn't dismiss *her*. She wasn't a crank with a cruel streak or a click-mining provocateur. She was something else, something that penetrated, something that saw too much.

She isn't changing me, I told myself. I could evolve artistically on my own. If I made this change, it would be because of something original to me, untouched by her.

I tried to believe this.

I marked black slashes across four straight pages and slammed the notebook shut.

Chapter Twelve

Selina

The holiday season dawned, luminescent. Gutters glazed over, white gold with the reflections of elaborate storefront displays, and my eyes passed neutrally over miles of brilliant glass. I'd bought gifts for Jacob, Cassie, and Lyra in August, so as usual, Christmas was largely irrelevant to me. While Kellie and Joyce chatted in the office kitchen about their flights westward and which books they'd ordered for their nieces and nephews, I stood at the window and watched marshmallows dissolve into cocoa.

"What about you, Selina?" said Joyce in her tremulous way. "Heading off anywhere exciting?"

"If she were," said Kellie, "we'd find out about it four years later through an encoded telegram."

I smiled and sipped my hot chocolate. Kellie was right: I wasn't overfond of the expectation of intimacy and disclosure that spread through the office during the holidays. Still, I had a soft spot for the atmosphere. In the *City* library, we garlanded the bookshelves and dotted the windows with white removable paint, the only trace of snow in a wet, windswept winter. Outside, the temperatures hovered stubbornly above freezing, rain and sleet spat onto the sidewalks, and the subways grew hazy with humidity.

As for the feud, I was still staying in my lane, Parker Navarro was staying in his, Lola Xu's petition had stopped circulating—and Hayden had vanished from *City* meetings. This seemed ominous.

"Scott," said Kellie one morning, jerking a thumb toward the corner of the library. "Am I allowed to ask where she went?"

"Her most recent email was fairly positive," said Scott. "Readers seem to like the tip jar. Between that, our . . . busy autumn"—his eyes flitted to me—"and the holiday subscription sales, we may have some breathing room."

"Does this mean they won't cancel the anniversary party?" asked Brandon, one of our junior book critics.

"Cancel it?" said Scott. "They love the anniversary party. They're doubling the ticket prices."

After that, the atmosphere around the office became downright festive. I'd been worried about the anniversary party, too, always a bright spot in the dark gray flatness that was January and an obvious candidate for the chopping block if we were cutting expenses. For Nextward to give us the go-ahead was more than a relief. It suggested that everything I'd done this fall might really have loosened the noose around our neck.

"Quit while you're ahead," Cassie said one afternoon. "Go on social media and tag Parker Navarro and say the feud's over."

"What?" I said. "Are you serious? And let him win?"

"Told you," Jacob said to Cassie over his shoulder, halfway through changing Lyra's diaper.

"Dude, come on," Cassie said to him. "We shouldn't be enabling this."

"It's her life," said Jacob.

Cassie looked back to me with a fond roll of her eyes. "Classic."

"Classic," I agreed. Jacob had always taken pride in having very little sense of judgment. You'd hear him saying sentences like "It's all the same to me" or "Oh, I don't know anything about that" with a broad, easy smile. Profoundly unrelatable, but in times like this, he did remind me that some people were blessed with the enviable ability to relax.

The nights grew longer, eating away at the back ends of afternoons, so that by the time the *City* staff left the Baumgartner, dusk was already nestling among the tops of buildings. Everyone seemed to agree that this was depressing, but I didn't mind. New York's winters had nothing on Minnesota's. Decembers here were many-colored and loud; they had the decency to fill the gaps. When I detoured to crowded bookshops and grocery stores, I heard people on the phone asking each other about seasonal recipes and how to surprise their friends. Then I'd return to my little apartment and put something quiet on the speakers. Apron up, crack open a grease-stained cookbook. I'd hand-cut ravioli square by carefully pressed square. I had lists of movies from the year I wanted to catch up on; there was always something to do. I climbed a ladder in my front room with my hand sander. I'd almost finished with the crown molding, which meant it would soon be time to paint.

And like I always did at this time of year, I texted Auntie Sylvia and my cousins, feeling the cautious limits of their messages. They never asked what sort of footing my parents and I were on, but when Auntie Sylvia said, What are your plans for Christmas this year, the larger question curled around the smaller.

Around Thanksgiving, I'd spent some time with my parents' email and drafted—then deleted—several responses. As Christmas crept nearer, the idea of replying returned, knocking against some edge in my mind like a piece of driftwood that had bobbed back to the docks.

A week before the *City* offices were due to close for the holidays, I cozied up in bed with a mug of spiced cider and reopened my father's message.

We are sorry to hear about the fight. We want to know how you are handling it. If you call we will talk again.

I turned the phone off and let it sit on my chest, warm and sleek and heavy, rising and falling with my breath.

I didn't think I blamed my parents anymore for the distance between us. At twenty, of course I'd blamed them. During winter break of my junior year, when I'd outlined my career intentions, I'd fantasized about enthusiasm or warmth or, God forbid, some level of belief in my abilities. Instead, my parents had stared at me from across the living room, appalled, as though my decision to major in English literature was equivalent to desecrating somebody's grave.

"You're going to leave Columbia," said my father, "with a degree that you could get from any old school?"

"No," I'd said, "I'm going to leave with a Columbia diploma."

"Selina," my mother said with a frantic edge to her voice. "What are you thinking? Where is this coming from? I can't watch you throw away such a bright future."

My father had looked to my mother, hollow-eyed. "We should have stopped this in high school."

"I'm sorry. Stopped me *reading*?"

"Stopped you from putting this hobby over everything else!" said my mother. "Make new friends? No, too busy with books. Going and having good experiences outside the house? Too busy alone with your books. What did we move to this country for?"

As if I hadn't tried to make friends. But I had no interest in defending myself to my parents, which would have required admitting what high school had been like for me socially. The small, boring humiliations of going to a football game, a party, a dance, only to stand several feet too far from any given group, holding my elbows in the palms of my hands, trying on jerky little smiles whenever somebody looked my way. The bigger humiliation of discovering that the people

I'd considered friends did not consider me a friend. Alternating between too-long silences and terrible honesty that I immediately regretted, between classes, in the gym changing room, with people I barely knew. My shameful arrogance at fifteen, because I could get a good grade; those poor people who had to put up with me, both students and teachers; the ways in which I had still, somehow, felt injured by other people's dislike, despite often agreeing with them about the faults in my character.

Against all this, books were a refuge. I could not interact wrongly with a book except by failing to give it my attention.

"So," I'd said to my parents, "the fact that studying literature is fulfilling to me means nothing to you? The fact that all my professors and teachers think this is the right decision—that means nothing?"

"We aren't paying two hundred thousand dollars for you to read books!" my father said.

I sat very still. I unfocused my vision and let some part of me retreat into a cage in the center of my body.

"Why not?" I asked.

"What?" said my father.

"Why won't you pay two hundred thousand dollars for an English degree, even though you're perfectly happy to pay the same amount for prelaw?"

"Selina, you can't be asking that seriously," said my mother. "Prelaw at Columbia gets you into a top law school, and then, there you are. That's a good job. A stable career."

"So the issue is that you don't think I can find a stable career in an English-related field."

"What stable career is there? What? Writing a book?" She laughed. "Writing advertisements or scripts for TV anchors? We don't want you to be scraping and struggling and unable to build a life when you're twice the age you are now!"

"But you're assuming that's what'll happen. Even though tens of thousands of people have jobs exactly like the ones you just wrote off, and have normal lives, even if they don't make two hundred thousand dollars a year. You're assuming it's not going to happen for me."

"Why are you assuming it *will* happen?" my father said. "There are fifty applicants for every one job in—what is it you want to do, publishing?"

"Journalism."

Both of my parents shut their eyes as though I'd said "terrorism."

"I'm not being arrogant for wanting to do this," I said. My voice was beginning to strain. "I'm not being presumptuous for—for having an interest, or for listening to my professors when they tell me I have a valuable perspective."

"'A valuable perspective!'" my mother burst out. "You know who has a valuable perspective? A lawyer with a good degree and the influence to make other people listen to their perspective!"

I sat, rigid, trying to tell myself that we had different cultural frames of reference. I tried to remind myself that they were pragmatic to a fault, and that when I'd received my Columbia acceptance, the expectation of a high-powered future had been bundled into their delight. I'd blindsided them. I knew that. But I knew, too, that if I never tried to follow this path, I'd regret it forever.

"I'm not changing my mind," I said.

"I mean it, Selina." My father's face looked as hard and brittle as fired clay. He looked like me. "We won't be part of this."

"Fine."

They watched me stalk toward the hall, fishing my car keys from my jacket pocket. I was at the door when my mother declared, "We'll be here when you're ready to admit you're wrong. Though, with you, God knows if that will ever happen."

I would remember those words for the rest of my life. The accusation was a perfect snare. Clawing my way through my early twenties, I would rather have died than crawl back to my parents and tell them that I'd made a terrible mistake. Yet I had to lie there at night, remembering my mother's words, and acknowledge that no matter what I did, she had still found a way to be right about me, about my stubbornness, my silence.

True to their word, from that moment on, they didn't pay another cent toward my tuition. Naively, I'd thought that after the cutoff, Columbia would consider me independent, and I could get help from the financial aid office. I was wrong. On paper, I was still assumed to have access to my parents' combined salary of $170,000. My application for a dependency override, which would have removed their income from the picture, was rejected, because I had no evidence of an abusive childhood.

And so I took on eighty-two thousand dollars of student debt to finish my last three semesters. They were a bloodshot blur of work-study hours, shifts at an off-campus job, and caffeinated all-nighters. I stayed in New York during breaks to work. My parents sent innumerable texts and novella-length emails begging me to reconsider, long after reconsidering was a feasible option—begging, as though they weren't still the ones with every ounce of power over my life. Even stranger to me was that their pain seemed real. They seemed to be undergoing a mourning process for a person I'd never planned to be.

They didn't attend my graduation, which came as no surprise. By graduation we were barely speaking.

Well into my late twenties, my relationship with my parents had been a source of deep angst and extensive therapy. These days, I could at least understand the knee-jerk worry they'd experienced about my future. Watching the brilliant writers around me lose their jobs, go back to school at thirty-five or forty, retrain in some other, more stable discipline, I understood.

Still, I felt that the connective tissue between my parents and me had atrophied fourteen years ago. Our periods of attempted closeness had resulted in endless friction. Their stilted responses to descriptions of my work. My short temper at their enthusiasm over my cousins' bright futures. But the periods of polite semi-distance—impersonal birthday greetings and holiday script recitation—had made me twice as miserable.

Even this attempt of theirs to reconnect made me feel heavy and empty, like a steel box. Cleaner to hold some things at arm's length.

I stood too quickly. Dizzy, I swept a book from my nightstand and went for the door, leaving my phone behind.

It was nine thirty on a Thursday night, and the Slippery Cork, my neighborhood dive, was half-empty. The bar had installed its usual wooden Santa by the door. This was an eight-foot-high statue with violently rosy cheeks, its blue eyes round and staring, its mouth open in what was probably meant to imply a "Ho ho ho!" But when taken all together, the expression suggested that Santa had seen some dread horror not meant for human eyes.

"Nadia," I said to the bartender as I took my usual stool beside the taps, "have you ever considered just putting up a tree? Some ornaments?"

"No," said Nadia, taking my favorite gin down from the back wall. She was in her fifties, red-haired, with a nose ring and a smoker's rasp. "People love Haunted Santa."

"You should put him up at Halloween and do something normal for Christmas."

"I should throw your ass out of here for being rude to him, is what I should do." Nadia upended a silver cone of lime juice into the shaker and began to pack it with ice. "Just reading tonight, sweetheart? Or are we meeting someone?"

"Reading." I took the advance copy from my purse and flashed her the cover: Juliette Liao's newest.

"Never heard of her."

"She's a genius."

"I'll take your word for it." Nadia knocked the steel cups together with the heel of her hand and began to shake. "It's been a while, huh? Since you had anyone in here."

For some reason, I didn't mind when Nadia asked me these kinds of questions. Something about the hard boundaries of our relationship relaxed me. We could clock in and out. She could walk away for hours to tend to other people. Everything was warm, and nothing had to be personal. "Maybe I'm taking my dates to another bar," I said.

"Yeah, right. You've got loyalty."

I smiled. Nadia didn't push the question, but she was right. It had been years since I'd made any attempt at a relationship, since I'd decided that my romantic life would be best left as an entertaining series of flings. And as the flings had become progressively less entertaining, those had petered out, too. I hadn't gone on a date in over a year.

I barely missed the experience, the revolving door of hope and discomfort. But sometimes I did feel sad about my own disinterest. Part of me had accepted that what I was looking for didn't exist: a man who was a reader, who wasn't put off by my career or my opinions, who read and loved women authors. A man who loved what he did, whether that was ornithology or programming or getting under the hood of beater cars. Someone who didn't mind disagreement, who actually seemed to have fun engaging with my thoughts. Someone who would ask questions about small things in my life as though they mattered. Someone who seemed to like me.

Nadia set my gimlet on a coaster. "Hey. You okay?"

"Fine. Yes."

She took my card. "Leave it open?"

"Thanks." I took a determined drink and settled in to read *House Hearth Home*. This was the main attraction for me this Christmas. A chance to see Juliette Liao, who hadn't done an appearance in eight years and who was coming to the city right before the holidays. I'd had the event in my calendar since September.

Granted, she'd be speaking with Christian Gatehead, which in my eyes was like van Gogh discussing art with a chimpanzee that's learned to paint with its own feces. But I'd put up with seeing Gatehead again if it meant I got to see her, too.

I cracked the book open, and she whisked me away, far from the clinks and chatter of the bar, through centuries, into a cabin in Missouri in the 1810s. I followed her into the switchgrass and up to the edge of the river. I became somebody else. Somebody better. The best books always convinced me of this: that I was in the presence not of greatness but of goodness, something so warm and expansive that it counterbalanced everything else that people were capable of. Nobody wrote that way like Juliette Liao. Nobody made me feel so close to other people, like I could understand everybody, like anyone could understand me.

I paused midpage at the thought. That had come from somewhere. An op-ed, maybe? Something in a journal?

I kept reading, though the thought persisted as I spooned down paragraph after beautiful, delicate paragraph.

A hundred pages in, I remembered.

To get that response . . . it feels like you're also separate from other people. Like other people can't understand you, or maybe you'll never understand them.

I stirred my gimlet with its straw, listening to the click of the ice, frowning into the glass.

Parker Navarro. What he'd said on that podcast had been percolating in me.

Weeks after the Wiseman Festival, I occasionally caught myself thinking about his comments during our panel, too. The way he'd spoken about fiction not as a calling, not as an art, but as a place that your body enters and exits, a fertile, private place.

Even a stuck clock is right twice a day, I told myself, but as I sipped my drink I thought of him leaning on the seat beside me at the bar that night. The way I could speak and watch the words ripple into him, his reactivity, his expressiveness. The way he'd looked at me not with the resentment I'd come to expect from authors I'd critically brutalized, but with a hard intensity, as though he were waiting for me to say something specific, as though, if we'd frozen time, he would have waited hours to hear the right words.

Chapter Thirteen

Parker

Elena

Parker no offense but why are you just now telling us you're not getting in until Christmas Eve?

Parker

I'm sorry, Lena. This event is important to me. I figured you could work around my new dates. We don't have reservations for anything those first few days, right?

Kevin

Ohhh Mom is going to be pissed

Kevin

Less time with the favorite

Parker

Our parents don't have favorites, Kevin.

Kevin

Easy for the favorite to say

Elena

Yeah it's just, you could have told us weeks ago lol. Katy and I wanted to cook a big dinner for everybody the night we all get in bc she needs to go up to Palo Alto the next morning. I guess that's not going to work?

Christi

Elena, we wouldn't have been able to meet up on Tuesday anyway. The kids are going to be out like a light after seven hours of travel. You should know this

Elena

Oh sorry, Katy and I neglected to plan our lives around Jenna and Manuel lol

Christi

I didn't say you should plan your lives around Jenna and Manuel. But if you're planning dinner for a group of people, you should consider all their schedules.

Christi

Also, if we're getting up for Simbang Gabi, I assume nobody wants to stay out late the night before.

Kevin

yeahhh babyyyy the only thing better than mass is mass at 5:30 am

Kevin

how many years do you think it'll be before Mom lets us do the evening services like normal poenple?

Kevin

*people

Justin

poenple

Justin

lol

Elena

Maybe we could convince Mom to do the evening mass just on Wednesday??? Then that'll free up Tuesday night more

Kevin

so, mass at 7pm on Wednesday AND 5:30am on Thursday? are you out of your mind

Justin

Will you guys calm down we'll figure shit out when we're there.

Christi

WE will not figure anything out, if you're included in that statement.

Elena

Lol yeah when have you literally ever contributed to planning, Justin?

Justin

jesus fine I'll just shut up I guess

Parker

Justin, you don't need to shut up. It's true that we'll be able to do some planning when we're on the ground. Elena, when does Katy get back from Palo Alto? I'm sure we can figure something out that works for all of us, plus the kids.

Elena

She comes back down Christmas Eve. Around the same time you land

Parker

Okay, awesome. Would you two want to do the big family feast as Noche Buena dinner instead? Though totally understand if you don't want to cook before mass.

Elena

Yeah that could maybe work except Mom will def still want to do gifts at hers. So it'd be a lot to have everyone over at our Airbnb, and then go to Mom's to present swap, then Misa de Gallo, then Katy and I go home to clean up after twelve people . . .

Parker

What if we cooked at Mom's that night? Then we could all pitch in to clean the next morning when we meet up.

Kevin

Wowwww am so excited to do ten million dishes on Christmas can't wait

Elena

Kevin you have no appreciation for anyone or anything. So typical. Here I am, trying to plan to cook for YOUR ungrateful ass, and you're complaining about POTENTIALLY having to wash like, MAYBE four dishes.

Christi liked Elena's message

Justin liked Elena's message

Kevin

Nobody asked you to make this dinner Elena, but I guegss now you get to play the martyr so thank god for that

Kevin

Also why are you liking that message Justin you've never touched a dirty dish in your fucking life

"Parker, you okay?"

"What?" I looked up from my phone at Arthur, who was lying on the sofa, reading something about the Etruscans. He'd swaddled himself in several blankets, making him look like a patchwork quilt come to life. New York had hit its first real cold snap of the season, the kind that clings to you hours after you've come in from the chill.

"Yeah," I said, "I'm fine. Why?"

"Because you look like you're passing a kidney stone."

"Have you seen a lot of people pass kidney stones?"

"Just you, right now."

I tried to smile. "Sibling group text about Christmas planning."

"What's happening, someone cancel Christmas?"

"You'd think. I'm getting in a few days late."

"Huh. And how is that a problem?"

I shrugged and glanced at my phone screen. The group chat was still lighting up with furious messages, and Elena and Kevin had each texted me separately to complain about the other.

"Maybe I should just turn down the event," I muttered. "It feels sort of selfish not to be there for the holidays."

"What? Come on," said Arthur. "It's not like you're missing Christmas. You're allowed to have a life. You need to let your siblings be adults for once and sort out their own shit."

I didn't answer. Arthur took this tone sometimes, a kind of urgent supportiveness, but rather than reassuring me, his suggestions invariably left me even more stressed out, as though I were not only failing at the problem at hand but also acting in a way that Arthur thought was childish or unreasonable. He was looking for his bookmark now, and then he'd mark his page in the Etruscans and make this into something it wasn't, the first step into an imagined downward spiral, like I was another cause he had to advocate for.

"No, you're right," I said, forcing a sigh. "Yeah. They'll figure it out."

Mollified, Arthur returned to his book, and I returned to playing referee, this time with my face purposefully blank.

As the twenty-third crept closer, the cold snap deepened, and I spent hours planning my questions for Juliette. I wanted to spark a real conversation, not just a courteously embellished yes or no. I wanted to show her the ways I'd loved her work. I wanted so badly for her to like me that it was pathetic.

The week of the event arrived, and my friends bled out of the city. By Tuesday, everyone from the Bay Area had flown back west, and on Wednesday, Arthur wheeled his suitcase to the door and pushed a wrapped rectangular prism into my hand.

"Book?" I said.

"Book," he said.

"Book." I handed over his gift, too, then slid a nail under Arthur's messily folded wrapping paper to cut through the tape. A hand-drawn cover came into view. He'd given me a copy of *ChiArts Young Voices: A Poetry Collection*. "Wait, incredible," I said, flipping to the title page, which wore the shaky, unpracticed signatures of all twelve contributors. "Oh, I can't wait to read this. Any recommendations?"

"I don't play favorites," he said, ripping through the wrapping of his own present to reveal a copy of Mark Bittman's *How to Cook Everything*.

"Bring it to L.A.," I said. "You can test the recipes out on your parents."

"Trying to escape being the guinea pig?"

"No," I lied.

Arthur laughed and obligingly stuffed the cookbook into his suitcase. "Thanks, man," he said as he cracked the door. "And good luck at the event tomorrow. I hope people show up. We're supposed to get flurries."

Thursday dawned gray and freezing. Still huddled bleary-eyed in my flannel sheets, I tugged my phone under the covers to check the weather. Arthur's flurries were nowhere in sight. Instead, a winter storm warning was splashed across my weather app.

I sat up in bed. "No," I said, throwing the covers off myself. Cool air cut through my T-shirt. I tapped into the forecast, groping my way through the apartment, muttering, "No, no, no, no."

The snow would start this afternoon and wasn't projected to end until tomorrow night. I was supposed to fly out of LaGuardia first thing in the morning. JetBlue hadn't emailed yet, but it was only a matter of time.

I tried to rope in the panic, opening the notebook on my kitchen table to review my questions for Juliette. I'd deal with the blizzard tomorrow. One storm at a time.

By the time I made my way to the Upper West Side that evening, buffeted by horizontal wind, three inches of snow had carpeted the sidewalks, and the air had taken on that muffled quality, like we'd all been transported to a New York City hidden beneath a thick comforter. I arrived with half an hour to spare at the store, a new indie called the Dog's Ear. Overlapping rugs and trailing plants gave the shop the air of a maximalist's living room, and a rheumy-eyed Labrador was melting off a chair in the nonfiction section.

The manager, Chester, an older man with orange-rimmed glasses, stood chatting near the shuttered café area with a woman whose back was turned. She was small and heavyset, wearing a collection of fraying, grayish clothes that made her look draped in centuries of dust. Her shoes were wildly impractical quilted slippers, and she held an enormous green woolen coat in the crook of her arm.

"Oh, you must be Parker," said Juliette Liao, turning to me. "How are you? It's so good of you to come all the way out here in this mess. I'm Juliette."

I was momentarily speechless. Juliette's eyes had delicate bags beneath them and six decades of smile lines fanning out from their corners, and as she regarded me, I imagined intricate processes of association and retrieval happening behind those deep brown irises, the type of connection I'd seen mapped out in all seven of her books.

"Hi," I blurted out. "It's no problem, really, the subway is running fine. I can't tell you how great it is to meet you."

"Likewise. I don't think we'll have an especially large crowd," she said, glancing to the snow-filled window. She didn't sound too bothered by this prospect.

Over the next half hour, six people trickled in from the silver-dashed darkness. They seemed scared of the front row. Clustered near the back of the seating area, they steadied stacks of Juliette's books in their laps, unwinding scarves, brushing snow from their shoulders.

I kept scanning the sheet-glass storefront. Eight million people lived in New York City. Surely a few more of them could handle a little snow? I wanted this shop to be full to bursting, to show New York's appreciation for Juliette's work.

She caught me looking. "Worried about the attendance?"

"I'm sure people are just running behind because of the weather."

Juliette chuckled. "Oh, you're sweet."

The door swung open again—I felt as much as heard it, the wind clawing away our precious heat—and I glanced over my shoulder, hoping for a dozen latecomers.

Instead I got one narrow figure in a black felt coat, red-cheeked from the cold, a crimson knit hat pulled low over her serious brows.

I recovered from Selina Chan's appearance more quickly than I had at the Wiseman Festival. Tight-jawed, I watched her take a seat in the back row and smooth the static out of her hair with two fingers. She unbuttoned her coat and shrugged her narrow shoulders out of it. Beneath, she wore an overlarge cable-knit sweater, dark red, like the gloss on her lips.

"Are you two ready?" asked Chester.

I tugged my eyes from Selina and nodded.

Chester took his time introducing us, the seven-person audience patiently absorbing Juliette's extensive list of fellowships, their eyes straying every so often to the gap between the bookshelves where we waited. Finally, they clapped us out into the shabby velvet armchairs at the front.

I could feel Selina's eyes on me, but I was surprised by how steady I felt. Maybe I'd worn out the worries this week with the rewriting of my questions, or maybe it was the small audience, but I didn't feel on edge. The feeling reminded me of a good day's writing, when you're so deep into your love for something that even the nerves can't reach you.

I gripped my advance copy of *House Hearth Home* and met Juliette's eyes. I felt, again, the immensity of the presence in front of me. She settled back into the embroidered cushions and looked at me with luminous serenity.

"First of all, Juliette," I said, "I want to thank you for writing this book. Whenever I come to your work, I know I'm going to a place where nothing else can reach me."

She inclined her soft, round chin. "That's kind of you, Parker."

"In case we have anybody here who doesn't know the gist of the book, would you describe it for us?"

"Of course." Juliette lifted a hardback into her hands. The jacket hushed against her dry skin. "*House Hearth Home* is a frontier novel set just after the War of 1812. It follows a woodcutter who's searching for a Duckbill Maple, a rare tree, to build a crib for his newborn daughter. This interweaves with the story of his wife, who will outlive him by twenty years, and their daughter, who will outlive him by sixty, and the species of tree, which outlives him by about a century, and the crib itself, which outlives them all by several centuries."

"Yes. Amazing." I opened my notebook. "I have some questions about that overlap of lives. There's only a brief window at the start of the book where all these—consciousnesses, I guess, exist at the same time. And these very Christian characters are obsessed with the idea of eternal life, but the book is more preoccupied with nostalgia for slender windows of time. Did you mean to set those two ideas in conflict?"

"Not conflict, but in contrast, of course." Juliette smiled. "The book and its characters do not worship at the same altars. If there is divinity on earth, I don't think it comes from the eternal; it comes from the ephemeral. We have only this brief moment together." She glanced toward the front window, where the wind was ripping at the awning. "I'm glad to spend this particular moment here, by the way," she added mildly. "I haven't done an event in years, but frankly I can't imagine better conditions."

The nine of us laughed, Juliette twinkled, and the snow clung to the corners of the window, smoothing the view of the street into a wide dark oval. We spoke for half an hour about the seven drafts she'd written longhand, about how the book honored her late husband, about the months she'd spent in Missouri for research, then turned to the audience for a surprisingly lively Q and A, considering our numbers. For a fleeting half hour I'd won back the feeling I used to have as a kid, hiding away in Poppy Street Books: that there was no world outside the bookstore, no world I'd rather inhabit than this one.

When the Q and A ended, the audience queued for the signing. Juliette carried on unhurried conversations with each person as she dedicated the copies. Selina stood at the end of the line, black coat on, and after reaching the front, she handed her copy of *House Hearth Home* to Juliette without acknowledging me.

I waited for Selina to say something about *City Magazine*, to tell Juliette who, exactly, she was.

She didn't. She said, "Could you sign this to Selina, please? S-e-l-i-n-a."

"Of course," said Juliette. "Thank you for being here, Selina."

"Thank *you*," Selina said too quickly. "The book was—I mean, it was—it really moved me. All your books do. Have. Since I was a teenager."

I stared at the point of her nose and the curve of her cheek, the only features I could see beyond the fall of her hair. I hadn't been aware that Selina Chan could engage in human behaviors like "stuttering" and "being uncool in front of a person you admire."

Trying to be surreptitious, I slipped my phone from my coat pocket, navigated to the *City* website, and searched Juliette Liao. Selina had published a review of *House Hearth Home* late last week. I'd missed it. She hadn't posted it to social media.

I began to read. Beside me, Selina worked her way effortfully through small talk, but in my hand was the articulate fullness of her appreciation. To read Juliette Liao is to be in the presence of such intelligence that you feel small, and then, often in the same paragraph, in the presence of such sensitivity that you feel yourself expanding.

I felt that satisfying feeling of juncture, the sensation you get when you've been trying to put your finger on the right word and it finally floats up to you out of the dark. This wasn't a personal essay. There was nothing about Selina's life in here, about what Juliette's books meant to her. But the devotion rang through every word, the care she'd taken in drawing lines from *House Hearth Home* to Willa Cather and the Zen sutras.

I glanced over at Selina, feeling a begrudging respect. Maybe, in the past few months, I'd begun to forget this: that criticism could be beautiful, not just a collection of reactions but a way to organize and illuminate the world.

I didn't have to like Chan to accept that she was a good critic. There was actually something sad about it, something stalwart and defiant about how fiercely she clung to this art form, which was, by all accounts, dying.

My phone buzzed in my hand. I glanced down.

1 New Message in Chan Pan Support Group

I felt a pulse of discomfort and returned my phone to my pocket.

The voices beside me had come to a coda. I glanced up to see Selina saying, "Well, it was wonderful to meet you." As her eyes fell on me, her face turned to cold glass. "Parker."

"Selina."

Juliette looked between us with surprise. "Oh, do you two know each other?"

"Yeah. We—yes," I said, trying to force civility into my tone. "Selina's a critic with *City Magazine*."

Juliette's papery eyelids fluttered rapidly. "Selina! You've been withholding!"

Selina let out a small laugh that sounded nothing like the derisive snap she'd aimed at me in the past. The sound was low, almost private. "Strangely enough, when you lead a conversation saying that you're a critic, it tends to set authors on the defensive."

"Can't imagine why," Juliette said.

Selina laughed again, and I managed to smile. Chester was at the register, closing up, and the other audience members were trickling toward the doors. Juliette stood from her armchair, slipping on her woolen coat. "Well, what are you two doing now? The snow delayed my flight, so I haven't eaten. I'd love to treat you both to something."

Selina and I stared at each other for a split instant, and I knew somehow that we were thinking the same thing: that however much we hated each other, we wanted to spend time with Juliette more.

We looked back to her as one. "No, please," I said, "I'll treat you."

"Yes," said Selina, "Parker will treat you."

I felt a bizarre desire to laugh.

Juliette waved her hand. "Coronation gave me a card, bless them. Come on—let's make a break for it, before the snow gets worse."

Chapter Fourteen

Selina

Outside the Dog's Ear, the snowfall had worked itself up into a blizzard. Juliette, Parker, and I made it a block and a half before caving to the wind.

"It's freezing," Parker called over the relentless blast of snowy air, like the steward of the obvious he was.

"There," I yelled back, pointing to a sliver of gold up the block, a window cut into the ground floor of a blurred brick apartment building. As we approached, the light shimmered into detail, revealing a decal curving over the window that read OLD JOHN's. On the other side: square-paneled ceiling, saddle leather booths.

I yanked the door wide, and Parker ushered Juliette inside. Bundled in her coat, she looked like she could have floated away with the wind, like a balloon spun out of wool.

The door snapped shut. Everything quieted. We glanced around, breathing hard, our faces chafed red.

We stood in an old-fashioned diner. Checkerboard tiles, a glowing drinks menu hovering like a cinema marquee over a small marble counter, menus clad in sweaty faux leather. The place was apocalyptically empty. One bundled-up man nursed a black coffee in a back corner. Christmas jazz whispered over fuzzy speakers, tripping from blue note to blue note.

"Three?" said the host, a woman in her early twenties.

"Three," I said.

She showed us to a booth, where we shed our layers onto the banquettes. Juliette and Parker took opposite sides of the table.

With the enormous coat piled on the seat beside her, Juliette already looked crowded, so I reluctantly slid in next to Parker. I caught that bittersweet scent. The dots of snow caught in his hair shrank, then melted to nothing.

We ordered drinks. Trumpet runs flurried from the speakers, and under the onslaught of wind, the sheet glass windows hummed.

"So," Juliette said, "Ms. Undercover *City* Critic, did you enjoy the event? Good questions, don't you think?"

"Oh. I mean . . ." The words caught on the back of my teeth.

"Yes?" said Parker. I felt the deep urge to shove him into a snowbank.

". . . Yes. They were good questions." I fashioned a bland smile. "Maybe you missed your true calling as an interviewer."

He exhaled through flared nostrils. Juliette, combing her dampened hair with her fingers, didn't notice. "Speaking of your calling, Parker, what have you been working on recently? You have a new book due out soon, don't you?"

"Yeah, in February! *High and Dry*."

"Have you read it, Selina?" Juliette turned her smiling eyes on me.

I wondered, yet again, how this had happened. Why had she assumed Parker and I were friends? I'd thought I had a talent for exuding the utter absence of friendship.

"Yes," I said, "I've read it."

"She didn't love it," said Parker, forcing a valiant laugh. "She, um—she thinks I have a tendency to overwrite."

"Ah," said Juliette. "Well, the best friends are the ones who will be honest with you. Honest and kind, of course."

I opened my mouth and closed it again.

"So true." Laughter edged Parker's voice. "Honest *and* kind. That's really the key, isn't it?"

"I think I'll have waffles," I said.

We happened to glance at each other at the same moment, and I fought the instinct to grimace. These booths were too small. Parker's eyes were full of amusement. I was close enough to see the freckle in his left iris.

At that moment, the waitress arrived with a decaf for me, a chocolate milkshake for Parker, and a glass of house white for Juliette. I ordered my waffles and gulped coffee, burning every square millimeter of my mouth.

My eyes watered as we looked back to Juliette.

"Tell me: What's *High and Dry* about?" she asked, and as Parker sketched the concept in a few sentences, she bobbed her head. "I see. I'll be interested to read it."

Parker's face went slack. He looked like he'd ascended into heaven. "Wow. Yes. Can I send you a copy?"

"Don't be silly. I'll preorder it. You can send me a postcard to tuck inside, though." Juliette spread her napkin in her lap. "Houston bus routes . . . where did that come from? Are you from Houston originally?"

Parker had just spooned about half a pint of milkshake into his mouth. He made a repulsive gurgling sound and held his hand over his lips.

I sighed. "No. He's from the Bay Area. Daly City."

A confused flicker of Parker's dark lashes. He looked my way, nodded.

"And Selina? Where are you from?"

I took another sip of coffee, feeling self-conscious. In my peripheral vision, Parker's face was still angled toward me. "A suburb of Minneapolis."

"Really? I don't catch a Midwest accent." Juliette tilted her head, her silver-threaded hair brushing her collarbone. "What was it like growing up there, I wonder?"

"It encouraged imagination."

Juliette smiled at Parker. "Cryptic, isn't she?"

"Tell me about it," he said.

"You value your privacy," Juliette said to me.

"Yes. Exactly."

"We have that in common. I've looked around online, of course . . . It's interesting, social media, but I think there's something religious about the urge to confess yourself online. Not for me, ultimately. And I'm very choosy with press, for which I'm sure Coronation despises me."

"What do you tell them?" Parker asked. "When they ask you to do interviews, I mean?"

She regarded him with curiosity. "Well, I tell them no."

Parker laughed. "Right. Yeah. I should try that."

I gave him a disbelieving look, but he seemed serious.

"You don't enjoy interviewing?" Juliette asked.

"No," he said. "I think I kind of hate it, actually."

"Do you?" I said before I could stop myself.

Parker's brows furrowed. "Yeah. Why?"

"Well," I said, trying to file the edge off my voice, "press seems to come so naturally to you."

His frown deepened. I knew what he was thinking: *Play nice, Selina, this is Juliette Liao.* But I hadn't even meant it as a veiled insult.

"I'm serious," I forced out. "You . . . you have a very relaxed manner with press. Like you get along with them."

"Oh." Parker's frown faded into confusion. "Well, sure, I like meeting people, but the point of press isn't to meet people, right? It's to add something to my books. And I've never come out of an interview feeling like I've deepened or enriched anything I write." He stirred his milkshake, the long spoon humming against the glass. "It's like I go into a fugue state, and then a week later I have to reread what I've supposedly said, and it reads like some alien consciousness studied my life and gave an interview in character."

Juliette chortled. I examined Parker's profile. Maybe he was just playing modest in front of his hero, but for some reason I didn't think so.

I remembered his jogging foot at our festival panel. The way he'd palmed the microphone from one hand to another. An excess of energy, I'd thought, of enthusiasm. Maybe not.

So? I thought, tearing open another sugar packet and snapping it into my coffee. Even if Parker Navarro wasn't a media vulture, he was still the entitled man who'd demanded I apologize for daring to dislike his books.

"Do you ever feel that way after interviews?" Parker asked Juliette.

"No, I think our reasoning is quite different. I have no problem with what I say, but I do think excessive exposure distracts from my work."

"Got it," said Parker. "So you're like Selina."

I paused with my mug held an inch from my lips. "What?"

"That's why you're so private, right? Didn't I read that somewhere?"

I hesitated. I didn't think I'd ever admitted on the record that I thought a highly visible persona distracted from criticism.

"Well, yes," I said eventually, lowering my mug. "With very rare exceptions, I think reviews are more meaningful when they're not cluttered up with the reviewer's biography. In an ideal world I'd be able to clear my background out of the room and focus on the book."

Juliette swirled her wine and sipped. "I don't envy critics. I would find it extraordinarily difficult to set aside my own taste."

I crossed my arms on the table. "You wouldn't have to, though. Your taste is still what makes your criticism."

"And what is your taste? What do you like?"

"Wow. Hard question. I suppose my favorites tend to be books about people who feel lost, or people undergoing ego death."

"Well, and comedies," Parker said, looking annoyed. "She likes farces and satires."

I blinked at him, lost for words.

"I've read a lot of Selina's reviews," Parker added to Juliette. "She wants to look so serious, but she writes about funny books like they reinvented the wheel."

Juliette laughed. "Selina, you've been rustled."

"Apparently," I said. He was right, of course. A book without humor was like a full day without a smile.

The night felt dreamlike all of a sudden, the fact that I was sitting here with these two people under a swing trombone cover of "A Holly Jolly Christmas."

"How about this one?" Juliette asked me, circling the point of her index finger in Parker's direction. "What's Parker's style?"

Parker's shoulders tensed.

"Well," I said slowly, "I found out that he likes Anna Kavan, which is a point in his favor."

"Oh, what a wonderful writer," said Juliette. "I know *Ice* has been gaining some readership recently."

"Finally," said Parker.

I glanced at him before I knew what I was doing. "There was a good article about Anna Kavan in *Harper's* on Monday."

He gave me a startled look. "Oh. Um, I didn't see it."

A beat of silence. Then the waitress appeared bearing enormous platters of steaming food. "All right! Waffles . . . steak frites . . . veggie burger."

As she set the burger in front of Parker, he leaned back to accommodate her. When she'd gone, we began to eat, fresh gusts of wind making the window wobble again. I glanced out at the nearly empty street. "Juliette, were you supposed to fly out tomorrow?"

"Luckily, no. I'm staying with my sister until the twenty-seventh, just around the corner. But were either of you traveling?"

In the corner of my eye, Parker was watching me again. Warmth tickled my collarbones. I wasn't ashamed of my life, but I remained acutely aware that it was not a normal life.

"No," I said. "I always stay in the city for the holidays."

I waited to see smugness on Parker's face. *Pathetic*, he'd think. Terminally alone, like the woman in his story.

Instead I caught fleeting curiosity in his expression.

Feeling abruptly uncomfortable, I worked open the silver dispenser and drowned my waffles in syrup.

Juliette said, "What about you, Parker? Traveling?"

"I'm not sure. I was supposed to fly to San Franscisco to meet up with my family tomorrow morning, but JetBlue canceled."

"Oh, I'm sorry." Juliette set down her fork and knife. "What a disappointment."

"It was worth it," Parker said quickly. "I mean, even if I'd known the storm was coming, I would have stayed for the event."

"Well, I'm glad you feel that way, but I wish it hadn't compromised your plans."

"Yeah." Parker picked up his burger, but he studied the grease-slick bun without biting into it.

"What is it?" Juliette asked gently.

"Oh, no, it's nothing. I mean—" Parker's eyes strayed to me. I sawed into my waffles and fixed my gaze downward, but it was impossible not to listen.

"I just have a big family," he told Juliette. "They, um—there are always a lot of moving parts."

"Ah," said Juliette, "that sounds familiar. Worried about the chaos?"

"A little." We ate without speaking for a moment, our cutlery chiming softly against the ceramic plates. Then he said, "But I guess it wouldn't be family without something being kind of broken. Like you wrote about the family in your book. The longest uncompleted project of their lives, right?"

Something warm darted down my back. I kept eating.

Juliette hadn't written that phrase in *House Hearth Home*. I had, in my review of it.

There was no reason to feel wrong-footed by this. Nothing was stopping Parker from continuing to read my criticism.

It was discomfiting, though, to hear him recite my words that way, quiet and pensive. Even more so for him to misattribute them to one of his favorite writers.

Juliette was chewing, clearly trying to remember when she'd written that particular line, but Parker, looking out the window, hadn't realized. "I wonder what they're doing now," he said, sounding far away.

I examined the compartments of my waffle, each glossy meniscus in each little cup of syrup. His strained words reached a remote, unfamiliar place in me. I wondered whether my parents had bought a Christmas tree this year, and whether they were planning to have Christmas dinner with the Zhous, an elderly couple who represented the other fifty percent of Chinese people in our neighborhood. I wondered if my parents had thought about me as often as I'd thought of them these past weeks. I wondered why I felt so afraid.

"Isn't it beautiful?" said Juliette, smiling out at the glittering snowfall, and for a while we sat there, unspeaking, watching the road turn cream under the streetlights, like an empty page.

* * *

Parker and I should have taken the same train toward Brooklyn—he was a few miles north of Bed-Stuy, in Greenpoint—but once we'd all said goodbye inside the restaurant door, he said, "I should deal with this," gesturing with his phone.

As I rode the subway home, I pulled up my father's email for the hundredth time.

Xiao Yan—We are sorry to hear about the fight . . .

Parker's discomfort in speaking about his family had been oddly reassuring. Of course my own family wasn't normal, the financial rupture, the years of resentment, but I didn't have many points of reference for "normal." Jacob and Cassie both hailed from perfect nuclear families who, every Christmas, pooled their resources to rent an enormous house in Vermont and spent a week in unrealistically photogenic happiness.

I pressed Reply.

Hi Dad,

I apologize for my late response. I've been collecting my thoughts, but I appreciate your reaching out again. I thought of you and Mom over Thanksgiving.

The ongoing argument with Parker Navarro has obviously represented a great deal of upheaval for my usual routine, but I've been handling the aftermath by working with City's editor and our representative at the parent company. I'm happy to say that this exposure has wound up being a positive for the magazine. My personal feelings, while complicated, don't matter in comparison. In any case, rest assured that I'm doing well.

Wishing you both a happy Christmas.

Selina

I hit Send. I returned my phone to my pocket. I blinked back the burn in my eyes and rested my head against the vibrating subway window. My feelings were agitated, but as I thought of a soft piano rendition of "Silver Bells" and being shielded from whipping wind by thick glass, the taste of syrup on my tongue, my heartbeat slowed. I saw the sway of Juliette's earrings, the way she smiled at me as though there were nothing wrong with me, though, of course, she didn't know me. And Parker, condensation trickling down his glass into his folded fingers, the instant of curiosity on his perpetually unguarded expression. This from someone who knew, at least a little, what I was.

I found myself holding to that. I held on for minutes. Then the conductor announced my station, and I went back home to my life.

Chapter Fifteen

Parker

I knew my siblings had begun to fight when they started texting me separately.

Kevin

Bro do you think you'll get here at all?

Mom says hi

Specifically its like "hi parker my favorite
and best son I love SO much"

"oh how I wish you were here"

"or that any of my other terrible children spoke
Tagalog with me"

Elena

RIP my Noche Buena dinner with the
whole fam :(

Not trying to put this on you park, just hoping you can still make it so you're not stuck out there alone!!!

Justin

lost in new york for christmas huh? say hi to joe pesci lol

btw listen. dad told me a pipe burst in his place right before he flew out. I went over and it's pretty bad. repairman says $700. no pressure if things are tight, I'll figure something out.

I knew Justin hated sending these texts. At thirty-six, he was still renting in L.A. with his wife. He'd moved there to make it as a cinematographer and instead wound up opening a small barbershop, which was always just on the right side of solvent.

Parker

No, no worries, I got it.

Parker Navarro sent $700 with Apple Pay

Justin

ty

I spent Christmas Eve pacing my apartment, refreshing Google Flights, watching cars brutalize the whiteness of the snow. My neighbors salted the sidewalks and transferred heap after heap of gray sludge into the gutters, only for fresh layers to fall within the hour. I exercised with the blinds drawn, hoping the workout would stop the churning of my stomach, but instead I pulled a muscle in my elbow and had to sink the joint in a bowl of ice for half an hour.

Hi, Mom, I texted one-handed. I'm so sorry. There aren't any flights NYC to SF tomorrow. I could probably fly out in two days, but everybody would be on their way to Manila.

And Manila was looking less likely by the hour. The tickets to the Philippines had cost $2,100, and changing the flight to a New York round trip would cost another thousand dollars. I still had no actual source of income. I needed *High and Dry* to sell copies; I needed to sell this next book to Lauren. I needed not to throw away that kind of money on airline fees.

My phone skittered across the table.

Mom

Miss you so much ☹

Christmas Eve isn't the same without you!

Parker

I miss you too, Mom. I'm so sorry about this. Can we all have a Christmas video chat tomorrow?

Mom

Yes if course we will video call

Of course

Going to see Kevy and Baby's godparents in the morning

But I'll ask your brothers and sisters
about video time!

Lunch maybe

I folded my arms on the table and nestled my face into my forearms. Chaos and all, I loved Christmas, its cut-paper lanterns and its extravagant, hours-long meals, the endless playing of "Christmas in Our Hearts" over my mom's speakers. The holiday had a way of showing me every side of my family at once, like cubism, Christi's rigidity cut neatly into her pragmatism and reliability, Kevin's immaturity unfolded alongside the games he'd conjure up to the kids' delight.

It was sinking in: I was going to miss Christmas with my family this year, for the third time in my life and the first that didn't involve a pandemic.

My phone buzzed again. I grabbed it up, but the notification wasn't a tracked Google Flight or a family argument. It was a Venmo alert.

Selina Chan paid you $5.00. "Eggnog for one."

For the first time since I'd woken up, my travel plans jarred from my mind. I reread the message several times.

Why was Selina Chan sending me a sarcastic Venmo, unprovoked, on Christmas Eve?

I wondered where she was right now. In her apartment? She'd mentioned living in Bed-Stuy. What did her apartment actually look like? Sometime between seeing her reading alone at a bar for two hours straight and watching her pluck at her sleeve as she'd met Juliette for the first time, the image of the supervillain in her mansion had dissolved, but I wasn't sure how to replace it.

I tapped through to her Venmo profile to find that here, in this remote backwater of her online presence, she'd foregone the intimidating headshot. The profile showed some sunny photo of Selina with her hair down, standing on a pier, wearing a T-shirt. She was smiling, with teeth. I felt like I was seeing a turtle without its shell.

I hit Pay and sent her back five dollars: "MTA fare to ice skate alone."

Five seconds passed. A notification dropped down from the top of my screen.

Selina Chan left a comment on your payment: "ha."

I lurked by the window, snow glaring brilliantly into the corner of my vision. What was she doing? Was that it?

Then another notification peeked down at me.

Site alert: New Message

I tapped it, and my email opened.

Your site, Parker Navarro: Author, has received one new message:
Contact: selinachanlikesbooks@gmail.com
Subject: That article I mentioned at the diner.

Message: **[LINK: Revisiting the Work of the Underread Master, Anna Kavan]**

I dropped onto the sofa and drank the piece in one long go. My thoughts felt clean and hard, like I was studying for an exam.

The instant I finished, I returned to my email, but I'd only typed a few words into my phone when I got frustrated—something about the smallness of the screen, the slowness of my thumbs—and grabbed my laptop from the coffee table.

To: selinachanlikesbooks@gmail.com
From: parkernavarroauthor@gmail.com
Sent: Dec 24, 3:01 pm
Subject: Kavan Retrospective

Good piece. Makes you wonder if most writers could reinvent themselves this completely.

Why are you messaging me, by the way?

To: parkernavarroauthor@gmail.com
From: selinachanlikesbooks@gmail.com
Sent: Dec 24, 3:02 PM
Re: Kavan Retrospective

Because nobody else I know has read Asylum Piece, and New York is covered in twenty inches of snow. Sometimes a person has to take drastic action to stay sane.

To: selinachanlikesbooks@gmail.com
From: parkernavarroauthor@gmail.com
Sent: Dec 24, 3:03 PM
Re: Kavan Retrospective

Great. Well, while I have your attention: Has anyone ever told you it's comical that your email address is "Selina Chan Likes Books"?

To: parkernavarroauthor@gmail.com
From: selinachanlikesbooks@gmail.com
Sent: Dec 24, 3:05 PM
Re: Kavan Retrospective

It's accurate. I do like books.

I've probably liked more books than you've read.

To: selinachanlikesbooks@gmail.com
From: parkernavarroauthor@gmail.com
Sent: Dec 24, 3:06 PM
Re: Kavan Retrospective

Unsurprising, since you spend your life doing antisocial things like reading in bars.

Let me guess: you're spending this terrible Christmas Eve reading.

To: parkernavarroauthor@gmail.com
From: selinachanlikesbooks@gmail.com
Sent: Dec 24, 3:08 PM
Re: Kavan Retrospective

I am. Jenny House has a new book out next May. I got an ARC at the Wiseman Festival. Her last book was an immense disappointment, but this one is exciting and kinetic.

And you?

I felt a pinch of discomfort. I hadn't told the Chan Pan Support Group that I'd seen Selina yesterday, although I wasn't sure why I'd kept quiet. They would have thought the dinner situation was hilarious.

Jenny would have been relieved to know that she didn't have to gear up for another pan. Still, I didn't pick up my phone.

To: selinachanlikesbooks@gmail.com
From: parkernavarroauthor@gmail.com
Sent: Dec 24, 3:11 PM
Re: Kavan Retrospective

I'm mostly reading articles about cancellation credit for Cathay Pacific. Great works of creative genius.

A few minutes passed, but Selina didn't reply.

I shut my laptop, realizing that, in the twenty minutes since she'd sent me that article, my systems had settled. The thoughts of my family still roiled, but less violently, and as I studied the miniature Christmas tree that Arthur and I had shoehorned into the corner beside the TV, I began to think of the week ahead with something other than misery.

I'd never actually been in New York at Christmas before.

The idea of a full Christmas Day unbound from my family's requirements was a little overwhelming. I could watch a Christmas movie without knowing Justin would mimic every schmaltzy line and Elena would talk through it with her girlfriend and Kevin would take every criticism personally. I could cook something without Christi adjusting my heat settings.

Another text came through, this time from Arthur: Bro. I just realized. Did you get stranded?

Yeah, haha, I said.

Oh shit.

No, it's okay!

His ellipsis blinked for a long time. Then he said, If you need company I can fly back early. There'll probably be flights in a day or two right? Just say the word

An embarrassed heat crept up my neck. It was true that I didn't, historically, do well with aloneness—the breaks I'd spent alone at Yale hadn't gone well for me—but I hated feeling like this, like something clinging to Arthur's ankle while he tried to live his life of cheerful independence, as though I were always one emotional trigger from dissolving into a puddle of need.

Hey, definitely don't change your vacation plans! I said. I'm actually looking forward to spending the holiday in New York this year. It'll be relaxing.

I felt a pang of guilt as I pressed Send. I stood, restless, needing to do something with my hands. I put on "Christmas in Our Hearts" over my speakers, unpacked my suitcase, and lined my family's presents on my dresser to ship after the New Year. Soon milk was simmering on the stove for cocoa and the Christmas tree lights were reflecting against the windowpane. I made myself sit down. I told myself, enjoy this.

* * *

I woke up early on Christmas morning, sunbeams trailing in through windowpanes swirled with frost.

There was nowhere to be. Nobody to handle.

Whole minutes elapsed. My pulse grew slow and even.

I turned over and went back to sleep.

Seven faces just about fit into the frame of the video call, although the camera was juddering in that characteristic way that meant somebody had put our mother in charge.

"Mom," said Christi's voice, sharp and high like the chime of a crystal bell, "if you turn it like that, it's going to—"

The camera switched to profile view.

"Oh no," said my mom. "Make it go back. Make it— Baby, can you fix—?"

"Yeah, here." Elena sighed. "Mom, let go. Just—"

"What if we use *my* iPad? It's newer," said Kevin.

"I'm Kevin, and I buy everything Apple shoves into my face," said Justin.

"Shut up, greentext," said Kevin.

Elena must have wrested the iPad out of our mother's grip and set it on a stable surface, because the nauseating blur resolved into a spread of familiar faces. Kevin and Justin were elbowing each other in one corner of the screen, Justin half a foot taller, his shaved head gleaming under the electric chandelier; Kevin was sporting a patchy mustache that looked like someone had pressed an inky thumbprint above each corner of his mouth. Elena, in a blue sequined dress, was whispering something to Christi, who had her kids grouped before her, arms linked protectively around their shoulders. "What do we say?" Christi said in that insinuating parental way.

"Merry Christmas, Tito," Jenna and Manuel chorused, with the flat affect of a five- and seven-year-old who had much better places to be.

And in the center of the image was my mother, silver currents running through her black hair, forehead sunspotted, her head lowered to look into the camera as though she were peering through a magnifying glass. "There you are! We miss you so much, Pijay."

I felt a rush of affection. "You too, Mom. How was mass last night? And gifts? Dinner?"

"Beautiful. Baby made enough food to feed the block." She pinched Elena's arm. "And Katy, and Katy," she added hastily when Elena opened her mouth. "Did your book thing go well, Pijay? Your reading?"

I considered telling her it wasn't a reading, but that seemed pedantic. "Yes, yeah, went really well."

"It wasn't a reading, Mom," said Christi, "it was a conversation with another author. One of Parker's favorites."

I grinned. "Thanks, C."

Christi gave a tight smile. "See, I listen."

"A favorite!" our mother said. "Very exciting."

"Anyone we've heard of?" Justin said.

"Stephen King," I said.

"Wait, really?"

"No."

Elena, Christi, and Kevin snorted. Justin made a dismissive gesture at the camera.

"Did you have fun last night, Manoy? Nene?" I asked the kids.

Their heads bobbed. Manuel's enormous brown eyes strayed shyly away, but Jenna burst out, "Tito Kevin got me a dinosaur."

"Oh, for real? What kind?"

"Stegosaurus," she said, mangled by her lisp.

"Awesome. Can I see it?"

Jenna ducked down beneath the table and emerged with a stuffed mint-green stegosaurus the size of her body. When she squeezed its head, it emitted an electronic groan.

"So cool. What's his name, Nene?"

"Roarasaurus."

I raised my eyebrows at Christi. "I guess he can wander around the cargo hold on the way back to South Carolina?"

"He'll have to. We don't have an extra checked bag." Christi glared murder at Kevin.

Kevin, texting, didn't hear her. When he realized we were all looking at him, he said, "What?"

"Anyway," said Mom, "when are you coming to visit, Pijay?"

"I don't know. Since the book comes out in February, the next couple of months are going to be pretty crazy. Maybe March?"

"We'll have to get it on the calendar!"

"Definitely."

A moment's silence.

"I wish I were there," I offered, beginning to feel the strain. Scanning my family's body language, I could see the discontentment running along the channels between them, like I was a plane flying above an oil spill in a delta. Kevin and Elena weren't speaking, that was obvious. And when they all got to Manila, Justin's wife, Courtney—whom Christi called Princess Courtney in private—would start making her little comments about the humidity and the traffic and the air conditioning in our Tita Eugenia's place, and the trouble would really start.

"Wish you were here too, Park," Elena said, picking at a scab on her elbow. She'd turned twenty-six last month, but something about the way she looked plaintively into the camera just then made her look years younger, like the fresh-faced girl who'd walked the stage at her graduation.

"I'll meet Katy soon," I said. "Promise. I can take the train up to Boston."

"Cool. That'd be fun." Elena made herself smile. She was miserable. I could feel her unhappiness rushing off the screen like wind.

"I see how it is," said Kevin, half joking. "*Some* girlfriends are more important than other girlfriends."

"Bro, you haven't even told me your new girlfriend's name."

"Oh. Huh." He scratched one half of his mustache. "Well, her name's Maria."

"And she is lovely!" Mom gushed, which I guessed meant she was Filipina.

"See?" said Kevin. "And she is lovely."

"Excited to meet her. Will you be around in March?"

"More like will she be around in March," muttered Elena.

Hurt flashed across Kevin's face. He opened his mouth.

"Lena, it's Christmas," I cut in.

Her purple-lipsticked mouth pursed. "Sorry," she mumbled.

Kevin grunted.

"Well," said Christi in that purposefully breezy way that broadcasted her irritation, "we should let you get going, Park. Love you so much! Kids, say bye."

"Bye, Tito Parker," Jenna and Manuel chorused.

"Merry Christmas, Merry Christmas," my mom said, her hands pressed to her heart. "Maligayang Pasko, Pijay, love you."

As everybody else joined in, the speakers blared indistinguishable noise. My eyes found the Christmas tree behind them, the geometric star at the top, and the parols hung around my mother's living room, glowing constellations of paper. "Love you guys," I said repeatedly, unsure they could hear me, until the call ended.

I closed my laptop. My apartment seemed to echo in the quiet. I pictured my family standing up from the sofa, breaking into twos and threes in the living room, chitchat and logistical conversations masking loaded silence.

I came back into my body, into my empty room, with a shameful sensation of relief.

The snow had stopped this morning. I wound a wool scarf around my neck and headed out into the clean cold air for my walk. Crossing the park, I passed a couple whose reddened hands were joined and swinging, and I remembered Christmases with Kate, the exhaustion I'd felt every night when I'd shut off the light, staring into the dark, waiting to sleep.

I'd spent so much time in that relationship telling myself I was happy. It had been the same with Cecilia, my girlfriend for half of undergrad, and Vivian, whom I'd dated for a year right after school, and whom I'd dutifully accompanied to raves every other week, despite being a person who, left to my own devices, would probably seek out a chemical waste treatment plant before a rave.

I hadn't dated anybody seriously since my breakup with Kate. We'd split up several months before the book deal for *These Extraordinary Times*, at which point my life had changed so dramatically that I'd had no room in my mind for relationships. In the past few years, I'd intermittently tried the apps, which had led to a couple of one-night stands and a dozen first and second dates that had felt pleasant and meaningless, like massages.

It was easy to look at these couples in the park and fantasize about dating again, but maybe I wasn't cut out for partnership. By the end of all my relationships, I'd felt unmoored from myself, as though the effort of forming myself into the right partner had made me forget what I was, if I was anything. At least, on my own, I knew that I was myself.

On the way home, I checked my phone. My Bay Area group chat—

which, for some reason I couldn't remember, we'd named "The Obviously Evil Bird Archive"—was an avalanche of Santa emojis and photos of enormous meals from Christmas Eve. I was typing replies, crunching past a stand of snowy evergreens, when an email alert popped up.

I paused at the open gate to the park.

To: parkernavarroauthor@gmail.com
From: selinachanlikesbooks@gmail.com
Sent: Dec 25, 2:10 PM
Re: Kavan Retrospective

I'm guessing you'll like this book. Its author also doesn't know how to streamline a paragraph. **[LINK: Heron at Night by Charles Roxbury]**

I sighed.

To: selinachanlikesbooks@gmail.com
From: parkernavarroauthor@gmail.com
Sent: Dec 25, 2:11 PM
Re: Kavan Retrospective

I've actually read that book already.

To: parkernavarroauthor@gmail.com
From: selinachanlikesbooks@gmail.com
Sent: Dec 25, 2:12 PM
Re: Kavan Retrospective

From your lack of a comeback, I'm assuming you did, in fact, like the book.

To: selinachanlikesbooks@gmail.com
From: parkernavarroauthor@gmail.com
Sent: Dec 25, 2:13 PM
Re: Kavan Retrospective

I did like the book. You're the worst.

To: parkernavarroauthor@gmail.com
From: selinachanlikesbooks@gmail.com
Sent: Dec 25, 2:14 PM
Re: Kavan Retrospective

Merry Christmas to me.

I shook my head and jogged across the snowy street, a reluctant smile tugging at my lips. As much as I hated to admit it, she could be kind of funny.

Inside, I kicked off my boots, but I didn't move to do anything, just stood beside the door and thought about my reply.

To: selinachanlikesbooks@gmail.com
From: parkernavarroauthor@gmail.com
Sent: Dec 25, 2:17 PM
Re: Kavan Retrospective

Does this mean you didn't like the book?

Do you usually send unsolicited recommendation emails to people you don't like, suggesting books you didn't enjoy?

To: parkernavarroauthor@gmail.com
From: selinachanlikesbooks@gmail.com
Sent: Dec 25, 2:18 PM
Re: Kavan Retrospective

No, I liked the book. Reading it was like watching a precocious child make a brightly colored presentation about his favorite bird.

And of course I don't usually do this.

I felt something compress in my chest. I took an aimless step forward. Some part of me recognized that I was hungry, and should eat. Instead I stared into my phone.

To: selinachanlikesbooks@gmail.com
From: parkernavarroauthor@gmail.com
Sent: Dec 25, 2:20 PM
Re: Kavan Retrospective

Good, because this is an exceptionally weird way to spend your Christmas. I'd hate to think you do it for just anybody.

To: parkernavarroauthor@gmail.com
From: selinachanlikesbooks@gmail.com
Sent: Dec 25, 2:21 PM
Re: Kavan Retrospective

Do you usually spend Christmas emailing your least favorite critics back within a thirty-second window?

To: selinachanlikesbooks@gmail.com
From: parkernavarroauthor@gmail.com
Sent: Dec 25, 2:22 PM
Re: Kavan Retrospective

I usually spend Christmas juggling four siblings, their partners, my niece and nephew, and either my mother or father, depending on who gets us for the day itself. I have a lot of time on my hands this year.

Clearly I'm not the only one.

To: parkernavarroauthor@gmail.com
From: selinachanlikesbooks@gmail.com
Sent: Dec 25, 2:24 PM
Re: Kavan Retrospective

No, you're not the only one.

By the way: Are you aware how different you sound over email?

To: selinachanlikesbooks@gmail.com
From: parkernavarroauthor@gmail.com
Sent: Dec 25, 2:24 PM
Re: Kavan Retrospective

In comparison to what?

To: parkernavarroauthor@gmail.com
From: selinachanlikesbooks@gmail.com
Sent: Dec 25, 2:25 PM
Re: Kavan Retrospective

In comparison to how you talk in real life, and how you post on social media, and how you write your novels.

To: selinachanlikesbooks@gmail.com
From: parkernavarroauthor@gmail.com
Sent: Dec 25, 2:27 PM
Re: Kavan Retrospective

Care to describe the differences?

To: parkernavarroauthor@gmail.com
From: selinachanlikesbooks@gmail.com
Sent: Dec 25, 2:28 PM
Re: Kavan Retrospective

It's this dramatic absence of laughter, filler language, and exclamation points.

To: selinachanlikesbooks@gmail.com
From: parkernavarroauthor@gmail.com
Sent: Dec 25, 2:29 PM
Re: Kavan Retrospective

I think that might just be how I email you, Selina.

To: parkernavarroauthor@gmail.com
From: selinachanlikesbooks@gmail.com
Sent: Dec 25, 2:29 PM
Re: Kavan Retrospective

I'm touched.

Lingering by the dining table, I considered putting down my phone. There was no need to respond to a two-word email. Yet I had the sense of wanting to get one over on her, to win this interaction, which was stupid, since in a private conversation there was no real metric by which I could gauge a win. But the instinct lingered.

Her attention intrigued me, too, maybe because it made so little sense. I imagined this was how it would feel to walk through a zoo, catch the eye of a panther, and find it padding over to the enclosure's glass to communicate with you by sign language.

To: selinachanlikesbooks@gmail.com
From: parkernavarroauthor@gmail.com
Sent: Dec 25, 2:30 PM
Re: Kavan Retrospective

You sound different in writing, too. For instance, in your review of House Hearth Home you talked about Juliette's new book in full sentences, something that didn't happen at any point the other night.

To: parkernavarroauthor@gmail.com
From: selinachanlikesbooks@gmail.com
Sent: Dec 25, 2:31 PM
Re: Kavan Retrospective

Haha. Parker, I know.

That's why I write. Because what I say in real life is a shadow of what I can articulate in writing. I hardly ever know what I think until I write it down.

To: selinachanlikesbooks@gmail.com
From: parkernavarroauthor@gmail.com
Sent: Dec 25, 2:32 PM
Re: Kavan Retrospective

If I say I agree, I assume you'll mock me for not seeming to know what I think even after the writing process?

To: parkernavarroauthor@gmail.com
From: selinachanlikesbooks@gmail.com
Sent: Dec 25, 2:34 PM
Re: Kavan Retrospective

No. It's Christmas.

If you want mockery, you'll have to email me on a different, less festive day.

My mouth was threatening a smile again. I drifted toward the kitchen and began to paw mindlessly through the cabinets, thumb still poised over the screen.

To: selinachanlikesbooks@gmail.com
From: parkernavarroauthor@gmail.com
Sent: Dec 25, 2:36 PM
Re: Kavan Retrospective

Are you suggesting that you, Selina Chan, have festive traditions? What, do you wear a Krampus costume? Climb down from the mountain to sabotage the Whos of Whoville? See the ghosts of Christmas Past, Present, and Future, who portend the dread life that's to come if you keep panning people's books?

No, wait, it's actually funnier if you do normal things like caroling. I would pay a lot of money to see you sing "We Wish You a Merry Christmas" in a stovepipe hat.

To: parkernavarroauthor@gmail.com
From: selinachanlikesbooks@gmail.com
Sent: Dec 25, 2:36 PM
Re: Kavan Retrospective

Name your price.

To: selinachanlikesbooks@gmail.com
From: parkernavarroauthor@gmail.com
Sent: Dec 25, 2:38 PM
Re: Kavan Retrospective

Stop, don't tempt me with the possibility, I'll get too attached.

To: parkernavarroauthor@gmail.com
From: selinachanlikesbooks@gmail.com
Sent: Dec 25, 2:40 PM
Re: Kavan Retrospective

Ha.

Yes, I do have Christmas traditions. I ice skate at Rockefeller Center in the morning. Then I go home, watch a Christmas movie, and spend the afternoon cooking something special.

To: selinachanlikesbooks@gmail.com
From: parkernavarroauthor@gmail.com
Sent: Dec 25, 2:41 PM
Re: Kavan Retrospective

What's today's menu? Child marrow, served rare?

To: parkernavarroauthor@gmail.com
From: selinachanlikesbooks@gmail.com
Sent: Dec 25, 2:42 PM
Re: Kavan Retrospective

I wish. Child marrow is so expensive these days.

This year: Duck confit over saffron risotto, roasted beets, Cabernet Sauvignon pairing. Crème brûlée with homemade blackberry ice cream.

To: selinachanlikesbooks@gmail.com
From: parkernavarroauthor@gmail.com
Sent: Dec 25, 2:43 PM
Re: Kavan Retrospective

My God. The degree to which you are a parody of yourself.

To: parkernavarroauthor@gmail.com
From: selinachanlikesbooks@gmail.com
Sent: Dec 25, 2:44 PM
Re: Kavan Retrospective

I only get one life. I want it to be full of what's good.

To: selinachanlikesbooks@gmail.com
From: parkernavarroauthor@gmail.com
Sent: Dec 25, 2:46 PM
Re: Kavan Retrospective

Oh, I know.

I didn't know why, when I pressed Send, the back of my neck felt momentarily hot. I didn't know why I stood aimlessly tapping through my phone, waiting, for five full minutes.

I didn't know why I looked up with the feeling of emerging from a different reality, but when I did, my apartment seemed fresher somehow than it had this morning; my bookshelves occurred to me, jumping out in my vision as though they'd just been installed, and the same happened with the cookbooks on the shelves, and the Blu-rays that Arthur had lined up under the TV. I thought of the jazz club a few blocks away I'd somehow never visited, of the hip-hop dance and leatherworking classes I'd pinned to the corkboard in my room and never attended.

At dinner, Selina had said she always stayed in the city for the holidays. Of course she had rigorously developed personal traditions. Of course she would take the train to Rockefeller Center for a skating session on her own, without a care in the world. I doubted she'd have been bothered to be snowed in for an entire month.

What was I going to do tonight?

I supposed I'd take a leaf out of her book and do whatever I wanted.

Chapter Sixteen

Selina

I received Parker's next email the day after Christmas, in the bath.

To: selinachanlikesbooks@gmail.com
From: parkernavarroauthor@gmail.com
Sent: Dec 26, 10:36 PM
Re: Kavan Retrospective

This condescending review made me think of you, for obvious reasons.

[LINK: The Fire Beneath Her Feet, Gabrielle Martin—Review by Xavier de la Cruz]

Generally I didn't take my phone into the bath, but I'd been reading a library book on Libby, and it had been building to its cheap and obvious climax. Now, naked, I felt oddly vulnerable as I read the email. I wondered what Parker was doing. 10:36 PM seemed late to be sending emails to people he hated.

I opened the linked review and read it.

To: parkernavarroauthor@gmail.com
From: selinachanlikesbooks@gmail.com
Sent: Dec 26, 10:49 PM
Re: Kavan Retrospective

I suppose I'm living down to your expectations when I say that the above review is well-written, and I appreciate both its clarity and its succinctness.

To: selinachanlikesbooks@gmail.com
From: parkernavarroauthor@gmail.com
Sent: Dec 26, 10:50 PM
Re: Kavan Retrospective

That email sounds like you wrote it using the predictive text feature.

I scoffed, put my phone on the sink, and hoisted myself out of the bath. As I dried myself off, the phone let out another chirp.

I picked it up quickly, grabbing my towel into place with my free hand.

To: selinachanlikesbooks@gmail.com
From: parkernavarroauthor@gmail.com
Sent: Dec 26, 10:52 PM
Re: Kavan Retrospective

but he was right, that book is pretty bad.

To: parkernavarroauthor@gmail.com
From: selinachanlikesbooks@gmail.com
Sent: Dec 26, 10:55 PM
Re: Kavan Retrospective

Surely not? Is Parker Navarro saying something negative about a book?

You're right, though. Terrible book. Meandering MFA project that should have been killed in its overpriced workshop. Sometimes I wonder what the National Book Award committee is thinking.

An instant after I pressed Send, I wondered if that had been wise to put in writing. Kellie had reviewed *The Fire Beneath Her Feet* for *City*, so my distaste for it wasn't public. I shifted my weight on the dampening bathmat and wondered if I could expect the next notification to be from social media. Something along the lines of *@ParkerNavarroWrites has tagged you in a post: If anyone thought Selina Chan was less awful in private, I've got news for you.*

My inbox refreshed, Parker's name in boldface again.

To: selinachanlikesbooks@gmail.com
From: parkernavarroauthor@gmail.com
Sent: Dec 26, 10:56 PM
Re: Kavan Retrospective

Oh, I would kill to know what happens in those committee rooms.

It's funny. With the glaring exception of my books, you actually seem to have good taste.

To: parkernavarroauthor@gmail.com
From: selinachanlikesbooks@gmail.com
Sent: Dec 26, 10:57 PM
Re: Kavan Retrospective

Thank you. Did you find that out when you read my entire review archive?

To: selinachanlikesbooks@gmail.com
From: parkernavarroauthor@gmail.com
Sent: Dec 26, 10:58 PM
Re: Kavan Retrospective

God. I don't know why I told you that.

I tied my robe and reclined on my bed in a pool of warm lamplight, my muscles relaxing.

To: parkernavarroauthor@gmail.com
From: selinachanlikesbooks@gmail.com
Sent: Dec 26, 11:00 PM
Re: Kavan Retrospective

No, please, tell me more about your disturbing internet habits. Did you Google "Selina Chan age" when you were writing your short story? "Selina Chan alma mater"? "Selina Chan height"?

To: selinachanlikesbooks@gmail.com
From: parkernavarroauthor@gmail.com
Sent: Dec 26, 11:00 PM
Re: Kavan Retrospective

34, Columbia, 5'9". Next.

To: parkernavarroauthor@gmail.com
From: selinachanlikesbooks@gmail.com
Sent: Dec 26, 11:01 PM
Re: Kavan Retrospective

I think I'm starting to understand. These late-night emails are a ploy to get more information out of me, which you'll use to write a sequel to your fanfiction.

To: selinachanlikesbooks@gmail.com
From: parkernavarroauthor@gmail.com
Sent: Dec 26, 11:02 PM
Re: Kavan Retrospective

Pretty sure I'd have an easier time heisting information out of a bank vault.

I put down my phone, fighting off a smile. There was nothing to smile about. We were two bored people snowed into a city at a standstill while our friends and family were off enjoying their vacations. That was the only reason I would ever spend time emailing Parker Navarro, and the only reason he would email me.

Still, he presented an unexpectedly entertaining distraction. With *City* closed until the New Year, my social life had made its usual December transition from "quiet" to "borderline nonexistent." Yesterday morning, I'd exchanged all of six texts with my cousins—Merry Christmas! Hope you're surviving the blizzard! et cetera—before Peter and Amanda had made a polite exit, and I'd gone back to scrolling through a list of 100 Christmas Movies to Watch Before You Die.

Later in the day, arriving home from Rockefeller Center with my ice skates knotted over my arm, I'd had a short video call from Cassie. She and Jacob were sweet to make time, considering the scope of their family retreat. During the FaceTime, I'd seen an entire platoon of seven-to-ten-year-old nieces and nephews tearing past the rental chalet's enormous stone fireplace, whooping, pursued by a pair of rippling basset hounds.

In that instant, as I'd watched the six-inch blur of color in the palm of my hand, a small part of me had wished I was in Vermont with them, although I'd never admit to the feeling. I already suspected my friendship with Jacob and Cassie could be described as codependent. Presumably they wouldn't have done things like call on Christmas if I weren't estranged from my parents.

Six texts, then, and a ten-minute video call. Besides these interactions, I'd had no human contact since Juliette's event. So maybe it was this social quiet that had me mulling email topics to Parker Navarro the next day, while I stood, motionless, in the hardware store, contemplating shades of ivory paint for my apartment's trim. I composed and rewrote sentences in my mind as I passed through the self-checkout and walked home. As I took the elevator up to my unit, a series of images came to me of Parker in some hypermodern apartment up in Greenpoint. Emailing me while he depressed the lever of his kettle. Reclining on some leather sofa. Sitting by the window, looking out, thinking about what to write.

To: parkernavarroauthor@gmail.com
From: selinachanlikesbooks@gmail.com
Sent: Dec 27, 12:38 PM
Re: Kavan Retrospective

So, here's something I wondered as I read *These Extraordinary Times*. Did the section about oyster-diving near the end originate as a short story?

To: selinachanlikesbooks@gmail.com
From: parkernavarroauthor@gmail.com
Sent: Dec 27, 12:40 PM
Re: Kavan Retrospective

No. What made you think it did?

To: parkernavarroauthor@gmail.com
From: selinachanlikesbooks@gmail.com
Sent: Dec 27, 12:44 PM
Re: Kavan Retrospective

To be honest, I thought the section would have made a good short story.

At the time, I thought, maybe that's the answer to the unsolvable mystery that is this book. I thought, maybe Navarro wrote a good short story and then decided he needed to wind up to it with seven hundred pages of unrelated family dramatics and bad sex.

That's another question. Were you trying to write the most unappealing descriptions of sex ever put to the page?

To: selinachanlikesbooks@gmail.com
From: parkernavarroauthor@gmail.com
Sent: Dec 27, 12:46 PM
Re: Kavan Retrospective

Absolutely. It's funny! Bad sex is galling and hilarious.

That's not my experience of sex, if that's what you're asking.

Leaning against the counter by my painting supplies, I felt a strange warmth run up my forearms, as though two hot palms had slid up toward my shoulders.

To: parkernavarroauthor@gmail.com
From: selinachanlikesbooks@gmail.com
Sent: Dec 27, 12:48 PM
Re: Kavan Retrospective

Delighted for you. At least I don't have to read your next book through the lens of neurotic sexual misery.

To: selinachanlikesbooks@gmail.com
From: parkernavarroauthor@gmail.com
Sent: Dec 27, 12:51 PM
Re: Kavan Retrospective

Very true. I'd argue that you don't have to read my next book at all. Think of how peaceful your life would be. You wouldn't need to spend weeks generating five hundred insults, then winnowing them down to the fifty that eventually make it into the storied pages of City Magazine.

To: parkernavarroauthor@gmail.com
From: selinachanlikesbooks@gmail.com
Sent: Dec 27, 12:52 PM
Re: Kavan Retrospective

It's adorable that you think I need weeks to generate five hundred insults.

To: selinachanlikesbooks@gmail.com
From: parkernavarroauthor@gmail.com
Sent: Dec 27, 12:54 PM
Re: Kavan Retrospective

Do the insults come to you while you read, or do you finish a book before unsheathing your claws?

To: parkernavarroauthor@gmail.com
From: selinachanlikesbooks@gmail.com
Sent: Dec 27, 12:55 PM
Re: Kavan Retrospective

While I read. They spring up from the rage and despair of the moment. It's more organic that way.

To: selinachanlikesbooks@gmail.com
From: parkernavarroauthor@gmail.com
Sent: Dec 27, 12:55 PM
Re: Kavan Retrospective

Rage! Rage?

To: parkernavarroauthor@gmail.com
From: selinachanlikesbooks@gmail.com
Sent: Dec 27, 12:57 PM
Re: Kavan Retrospective

Rage. As I said the other day, I have exactly one life. We should all feel outraged when the irreplaceable moments of our time on earth are misspent.

To: selinachanlikesbooks@gmail.com
From: parkernavarroauthor@gmail.com
Sent: Dec 27, 1:02 PM
Re: Kavan Retrospective

So, let me get this straight. You're on a quest to optimize every instant of your life? To live every moment in pursuit of maximizing your utils? You don't see the value in disappointment or partial success, even just as, like, threads in the fabric of the human experience?

I also have to say that you're a lot more morbid than I thought. I might have to revise my short story.

Have you considered converting to a religion that believes in reincarnation?

To: parkernavarroauthor@gmail.com
From: selinachanlikesbooks@gmail.com
Sent: Dec 27, 1:09 PM
Re: Kavan Retrospective

If the combined powers of Victor Hugo and Marilynne Robinson couldn't bring me to faith, Parker, I just don't think the concept of death is going to cut it.

I admit I have a morbid streak, but I also believe that morbidity is just another word for realism. We're all an inch from death at all times, and I don't think it diminishes us to recognize that. Actually there's something dignifying about the idea that, teetering on a precipice, we still reach for something sweet. Like the man in Tolstoy's fable, on the tree, tasting honey above the dragon.

As to your accusations of optimization. Yes, I see the value of disappointment and partial success. But while we're talking about the whole fabric of the human experience, I also see the value in anger and even some level of defensiveness, which remind you to value your own life and time and perspective, and not to prostrate yourself at other people's altars.

He didn't reply for a while. I prepared myself for a wall of text about my self-centeredness. Instead what arrived was this:

To: selinachanlikesbooks@gmail.com
From: parkernavarroauthor@gmail.com
Sent: Dec 27, 1:20 PM
Re: Kavan Retrospective

Printing this out and annotating it. The perfect basis for my next fanfiction.

I caught the laugh before it left my mouth. Paintbrush in hand, I settled to the floor and glossed long ivory strokes over the baseboards, but as the minutes passed, my eyes continually strayed to the phone balanced on the arm of the sofa.

The emails continued over the next few days. The strangeness of speaking with him didn't lessen. If anything, the conversation felt stranger and stranger, as I began to see snatches of Parker Navarro's private life, his daily self-imposed walks and his extended vegetarian grocery trips. The Nouveau Burger is worth the effort of checking four different stores, he insisted.

Some part of me began to imagine we were trapped in an elevator together, halfway up a skyscraper, and that everything we were saying was out of some kind of necessity, but at the same time I knew that wasn't true at all. We could have stopped. I didn't know why he wasn't stopping.

Surely you have friends, I said once, speculating on why he kept emailing me.

I do, he said. Dozens of friends. Possibly even hundreds, you don't know.

I'd expect nothing better of you.

Better? Selina, it's good to have friends. Take my word on this one, since I know it's way outside the scope of your interests.

I have friends.

Prove it, he said.

I sent him a photoshopped picture of myself in a stock photo of Friends Laughing Around a Boardroom Table.

Holy shit, he said. You make jokes?

Dozens, I said. Possibly even hundreds; you don't know.

Did you just fix my comma splice in your callback? You hopeless nerd?

I'm a journalist, Parker. We don't get to use comma splices and claim it's for "sound reasons."

On the thirtieth, Jacob and Cassie returned to the city, and I waited for myself to stop replying to Parker's emails. We went out for dinner that evening, Lyra in the high chair beside us, and when my phone buzzed at the table, my hand twitched toward it.

Frowning, I pushed the phone into my purse, but even as Jacob charted Lyra's rollercoaster of a nap schedule during their trip, part of me was wondering what Parker had written, then feeling irrationally exposed for thinking about our emails in front of Jacob and Cassie, as though they'd be able to read my thoughts from my expression.

"Overall, though," Jacob was saying, "we're feeling pretty used to what she's got to throw at us. So we're going to take a stab at a real trip in February."

"You are?" I said, coming back to myself. "Where? That's exciting."

"Thailand!" said Cassie. "Well, I'm thinking we start in Thailand. Then down the peninsula?" She glanced at Jacob, who smiled in his noncommittal way.

"Won't it be a nightmare during the New Year?" I said.

Cassie's shoulders bobbed. "I assume the intercity travel and stuff will be, yeah. But honestly, the crazier the better. We were just realizing it's been two years since we were farther out than Vermont."

We talked through a dozen bullet points on Cassie's itinerary. I had to be honest and suggest that hiking in Malaysia in the ninety-degree heat might not be received too well by a notoriously fussy twenty-month-old, to which Cassie scoffed and said, "I'm the one who had the C-section. She's got nothing to complain about." Then, in a sweet, gooey voice, plastering kisses onto Lyra's downy head—"You have nothing to complain about, do you? Do you? Despite your literally never-ending complaints?"

"Mama," said Lyra proudly.

"Exactly." Cassie gave Lyra a last kiss and turned back to me. "Anyway, what's going on with you, Lina?"

"Yeah," said Jacob, "what'd you get up to during the snowstorm?"

I lifted my shoulders. My pulse tapped gently in my wrist. "Nothing much. I finished repainting the molding in my front room."

"Oh, awesome!" said Cassie. "Do you have pictures?"

My phone buzzed in my purse again. "No," I said quickly. "Not yet. I can send some later."

"Or show us tomorrow night," Jacob said. "You're coming to the party, right?"

"Of course, yeah. Should I bring anything?"

"A drink, if you want," said Cassie. "But don't go crazy. No hundred-dollar bottle of Bordeaux, or whatever."

"Ninety-nine-dollar bottle of Bordeaux. Got it."

The next evening, I zipped myself into a white cocktail dress and curled my hair, listening to Vivaldi. Snow was falling again. I felt content and distant, like somebody at a museum looking into a favorite exhibit glowing in its glass box.

A chime behind me, and the glass seemed to fracture.

To: selinachanlikesbooks@gmail.com
From: parkernavarroauthor@gmail.com
Sent: Dec 31, 8:20 PM
Re: Kavan Retrospective

So, do you have an equally high-maintenance list of New Year's Eve traditions?

To: parkernavarroauthor@gmail.com
From: selinachanlikesbooks@gmail.com
Sent: Dec 31, 8:21 PM
Re: Kavan Retrospective

My Christmas tradition list is not high-maintenance. It consists of three things.

To: selinachanlikesbooks@gmail.com
From: parkernavarroauthor@gmail.com
Sent: Dec 31, 8:22 PM
Re: Kavan Retrospective

It consists of duck confit and a carefully paired Cabernet Sauvignon.

To: parkernavarroauthor@gmail.com
From: selinachanlikesbooks@gmail.com
Sent: Dec 31, 8:23 PM
Re: Kavan Retrospective

What am I going to do, pair it with white? I'm not a child, Parker.

Anyway, my only New Year's tradition is going to my friends' house party. They throw one every year.

To: selinachanlikesbooks@gmail.com
From: parkernavarroauthor@gmail.com
Sent: Dec 31, 8:25 PM
Re: Kavan Retrospective

The friends from the photo? Which ones? The bearded giant shocked by an empty spreadsheet? The woman laughing at a line graph with no Y-axis label?

To: parkernavarroauthor@gmail.com
From: selinachanlikesbooks@gmail.com
Sent: Dec 31, 8:26 PM
Re: Kavan Retrospective

Yes, those are the ones. Dear friends. Cherished friends.

I assume that you and your thousands, possibly even millions, of friends are drowning in plans?

To: selinachanlikesbooks@gmail.com
From: parkernavarroauthor@gmail.com
Sent: Dec 31, 8:27 PM
Re: Kavan Retrospective

You'd think. Those assholes are all still in California.

Enjoy the party.

Smiling, I pulled on my heels and headed for the train.

By the time I arrived, ankles straining, at Jacob and Cassie's place, two dozen well-dressed people had already dispersed throughout the loft. As I entered, Cassie exclaimed, "Selina! This dress. I love it!"

"Thank you. You look amazing." She was wearing a black canvas jumpsuit with a red silk scarf tucked into its neck, like a cravat. "You look like a hot mechanic. More than usual, I mean."

"You know just what to say to a girl. You want a beer? Or we've got gin in the freezer."

"I also brought this." I handed her a bottle of sake. "I've been chilling it."

She checked the label. "Sweet, I haven't had this kind before. Thanks, dude!" She hugged me. "Come on back, let's have some."

"Where's Lyra?" I asked as I followed to the kitchen island.

"Back there. Behind our best wall of soundproofing." Cassie cracked open the sake and poured off a couple of glasses. "We'll see if the sleep holds."

"Fingers crossed." I clinked my glass against hers.

"For real. Oh, Kieran! Do you remember Selina? I think y'all met last year."

"Yes," said the man who'd stopped at Cassie's shoulder. He was blond and clean-shaven, with a guileless smile and an unplaceable accent. A childhood of moving countries, I remembered. "You're the critic."

"I am."

"I saw you in the news a couple of months ago," he said as the door buzzed again, and Cassie hurried away. "You really eviscerated that man."

"Just doing my job."

"Lethal." He shook his head. "Goodness. I could never."

This was nothing new. Before I'd deleted my dating apps, I'd heard this wary tone every so often on first dates, as though the men had realized they were out to dinner with a serial killer. Still, I'd take the fearful ones over the men who suggested, with patronizing smiles, that it must be nice to get to read for a living.

"Have you ever read a book you hated?" I asked Kieran.

"Sure."

"So much so that you warned a friend about it?"

"Yeah." He was smiling now. "Okay, I see where you're going with this. But the scale is different. Aren't you scared that authors will—you know. Hate you?"

"Lots of them do." I took another sip of sake. "But that's the deal when you write anything, I think. People are going to hate your work. They're going to hate you. That goes for authors and critics."

"Fair," said Kieran, still smiling.

I'd heard this word a lot on dates, too. *Fair*, like I'd won a point in some tennis match I hadn't realized I was playing. I would think I was opening up a topic to discuss, and my dates would say, "Fair," apparently thinking it was the end of the line. The only option was then to pivot away from something I'd hoped would interest us both.

I was about to ask how the past year had gone for Kieran when my phone chimed.

"I'm sorry," I said, "I should . . ."

He seemed relieved to retreat. I dug in my purse for my phone and opened my email.

To: selinachanlikesbooks@gmail.com
From: parkernavarroauthor@gmail.com
Sent: Dec 31, 9:16 PM
Re: Kavan Retrospective

How's the party? Have the line graphs been decoded, boardroom table cleared, photos snapped, airbrush applied? All the usual New Year's activiitesd1?

I stared at this email for a minute. Then I began to laugh.

To: parkernavarroauthor@gmail.com
From: selinachanlikesbooks@gmail.com
Sent: Dec 31, 9:17 PM
Re: Kavan Retrospective

Parker, are you drunk?

To: selinachanlikesbooks@gmail.com
From: parkernavarroauthor@gmail.com
Sent: Dec 31, 9:18 PM
Re: Kavan Retrospective

It's New Year's Eve and I'm sending emails to the closest thing I have to a mortal enemy. Of course I'm drunk. (How did you know?)

To: parkernavarroauthor@gmail.com
From: selinachanlikesbooks@gmail.com
Sent: Dec 31, 9:20 PM
Re: Kavan Retrospective

I read closely. It's one of my favorite New Year's activiitesd1.

To: selinachanlikesbooks@gmail.com
From: parkernavarroauthor@gmail.com
Sent: Dec 31, 9:21 PM
Re: Kavan Retrospective

Oops.

Counterpoint: Who emails at a party? What are you doing?

To: parkernavarroauthor@gmail.com
From: selinachanlikesbooks@gmail.com
Sent: Dec 31, 9:22 PM
Re: Kavan Retrospective

I'm helping a poor, downtrodden man in his hour of need. Really, you should be praising my selflessness.

I paused in my typing. When I lifted my head, I surfaced into the laughter and the 00s Party playlist and the huge, snow-littered windows of Jacob and Cassie's loft. But for five minutes I'd been somewhere else, that dark, quiet place I tipped into during these conversations.

I pictured Parker sitting alone in a silent apartment and felt something brush the edge of my stomach.

My fingertips had warmed from the sake. Before I could overthink it, I wrote, The party is actually in Greenpoint. If your hour of need is really extreme, feel free to come. My friends' names are Jacob and Cassie. They invite around fifty people, so you wouldn't be imposing. Then I attached the party flyer Cassie had spent a not-insignificant amount of time making in Canva.

To: selinachanlikesbooks@gmail.com
From: parkernavarroauthor@gmail.com
Sent: Dec 31, 9:23 PM
Re: Kavan Retrospective

Really?

I'd come.

To: parkernavarroauthor@gmail.com
From: selinachanlikesbooks@gmail.com
Sent: Dec 31, 9:24 PM
Re: Kavan Retrospective

Text 612.555.8739 when you get here.

Either he left immediately or he was Jacob's next-door neighbor, because not even fifteen minutes had passed when I got a text from an unsaved number. Hey, it's Parker. I'm downstairs.

I reread the string of numbers a few times, disconcerted. Had this been a mistake? Parker Navarro was texting me. He had access to my life. Here he was, listed beside Jacob and Cassie and my cousins.

I didn't know why this felt so distinct from email.

I drained the last of my sake and buzzed him up. Standing by the door, I put my phone away, took the phone back out, began to save Parker's number, hit Cancel, and put the phone away again. Yes. This had been a mistake. What floor was he on? Maybe I could head him off.

The door swung open.

There he stood, two feet away. He'd clearly just pulled off a black beanie, which was snow-speckled in one hand, the other sunk in his dark hair. A triangle of wool scarf peeked out from the neck of his coat.

He looked at me for a startled moment. I didn't move, abruptly hyperaware of how much we'd been speaking this past week, how jarring it was to be opposite him, no longer imagining his facial expressions.

"Hey," he said.

"Hi. Come in." I stood back.

"This place is . . ."

"Yes. Jacob's parents are real estate moguls, so."

"Right, got it." Parker took off his coat. The man had an apparently endless supply of good sweaters. This one was goldenrod. His neck was faintly reddened where his scarf had rubbed the skin. "Where can I—"

"Here." I opened the closet. As he hung his coat, I asked, "Do you drink sake?"

"Not regularly." Parker shut the closet door. Faced me.

I realized I had no idea what to say. He felt different in person than over email, so much more obviously the man who'd looked me over with raw dislike at the bar, who'd snarled out his hatred for me at Cipriani. My body seemed to remember those encounters, my palms prickling, my pulse rushing, as though at any moment one of us would snap.

I knew he felt it, too. I could sense something wavering in him from the quick motions of his eyes. I'd seen him with other people. I knew how quick he was to fill space, to pour out meaningless niceties, to smile and agree and smile and agree. But that instinct was caught somewhere in his body.

His eyes traveled down to my dress, my heels. "You walk from the train in those?" he asked.

"Yes."

"How'd that work?"

"Are you familiar with how ice climbers use pickaxes?"

One corner of his mouth twitched. We both looked away. The confused heat in my body quivered, like the air above a bonfire disturbed by wind.

He held up a bottle of wine. "Where should I put this?"

"This way," I said, waving him toward the kitchen island. "How drunk are you, by the way?"

"Not very. Maybe four out of ten."

"Okay. So I don't need to warn Jacob and Cassie."

"I don't think so."

We wove between two strangers. I poured him a glass of sake and refilled my own and didn't suggest a toast.

As he took the glass, Parker's eyes strayed down to my dress again. Some band of muscles in my torso tightened.

"So," I said.

But his eyes had landed over my shoulder, and behind me, Jacob said, "Selina?"

I turned quickly. "Jacob. Cassie. I invited—I mean, Parker didn't have anywhere to go tonight."

"Thank you guys for having me," Parker said. His voice had changed, higher and clearer and flavored with a bright new smile. "Your apartment is gorgeous."

"Thanks!" said Cassie. Her facial expression could not more clearly have asked what the fuck was going on.

"I'll be honest," said Jacob to Parker, "I didn't realize you and Selina were on speaking terms."

"We're not," I said. "This was an act of extreme charity."

"This is actually just me trying to confirm that Selina has friends," Parker said.

"We're rare, but we exist," said Jacob. I could tell he was already warming to Parker, that fucker. "She has high standards."

"Oh, I'm aware," said Parker.

Cassie laughed, then broke off with a guilty clearing of her throat.

"It's fine," I said. "Parker can be funny, once in a blue moon, when he puts his entire soul into the effort."

"Exactly," said Parker. "It's the same way Selina scrapes up a single moment of kindness."

Jacob chuckled. "Selina's very kind. She gives us free books and babysits our kid and reads all the grant stuff I send her within the hour."

"Jacob," I said.

"What?"

"You don't need to"—I made an irritable gesture with my sake glass—"defend my honor."

"If you say so, killer." Jacob ruffled my hair. "We're going to go mingle, but don't murder each other, please. I hate it when the ball drops and I have to deal with a body."

"You got it," said Parker.

Jacob and Cassie filtered back into the crowd as I fixed my hair.

"How do you know those two?" Parker asked.

"Jacob and I went to undergrad together."

"Does he do that a lot? Mess up your hair?"

"Only when he wants to annoy me." I narrowed my eyes at Parker. "Don't get any ideas."

“I’m not. I like my hands attached to my wrists.”

I suppressed a smile. Synthesizers bounced between us; among the voices, the glassy taps of toasts.

Parker said, “So, you haven’t told anyone that we’ve been talking.”

“No.” I lowered my glass. “What, have you?”

“No.”

The sake was beginning to set in. As Parker glanced over his shoulder toward the windows, I watched the light shift on his forehead, across the curves of his cheekbones. His hair had begun to stray from where he’d pushed it back, a lock scattered over his forehead.

I thought about introducing him to some of Jacob and Cassie’s friends. I was acquainted enough with most of these people to approach them without feeling entirely stiff. They would like Parker, obviously. He would bend over backward to become likable to them. He would ask them questions, smile easily at them. They would think his job was romantic, because it *was* romantic, being an author. Authors were the people wandering down imaginary roads, and we were the ones watching, drawing attention to the artifice. Critics could be astute, respected, but almost never were we loved.

Yes. I should do it. I should introduce Parker to people whom he would like more than he liked me.

For some reason the idea annoyed me, and I said, “They have a good view from that window,” and moved toward the corner, glancing back occasionally at him following me.

The window was tucked behind a record player and partially hidden by an eight-foot-tall fiddle-leaf fig tree. I rested one shoulder against the glass and looked out at the shining stripe of Manhattan rising above the roofs of the opposite block. Parker did the same.

“So,” he said, “rate this past year on a four-star scale.”

I considered. “Two and a half. It was a good reading year, and I cooked a lot of new recipes, but the past few months have skyrocketed my blood pressure. Thank you for that."

"Thank *you* for more months of existential panic over my career."

"Please. You're an artist, Parker. If I weren't the source of existential panic, you'd find it somewhere else."

"Did you just call me an artist?"

"Yes. But in a pejorative way, not a validating way."

He'd begun to smile. "You can't do that in person. You can't, like, edit your tone after the fact. I heard you."

My lips were drawing outward, too, betraying me. "Fine. Yes. I don't think you're a complete hack." I sipped my sake. "What would you rate the year?"

"I wouldn't. Unlike some people, I'm not really into reductive judgments."

I caught my laugh in my throat.

"What was that?" He turned his ear toward me. "Did I just hear—"

"You didn't hear anything."

"Sure. Sure."

A weird silence elapsed. We both drank. I watched his left hand dip into the pocket of his jeans. He wore a silver ring on his fifth finger.

"So," I said. "Do you have New Year's resolutions?"

"Yeah. I do." His lips hovered over the rim of his glass. "I'm guessing you think New Year's resolutions are trite and meaningless?"

"Mostly. And I'm guessing you make little edits to your New Year's resolution based on who you're talking to?"

He shook his head, smiling. "Wow."

"Feel free to tell me I'm wrong."

"No, I . . . Yeah. I don't know what it is with you."

Our gazes brushed and I became aware of how close we were standing. My heels brought me onto his eye level. I could have been looking into a mirror. He had shadows under his eyes; a smile line was drawn down into his left cheek like a sculptor had taken the tip of a pencil and traced it gently onto clay.

At the same moment we looked back out at the city. Behind us, the party clinked and laughed, underscored by a looping orchestral sample and a deep bass thump. Across the river, the lights glimmered.

"I always wanted to live here," Parker said. "Like, so much that it almost feels childish to actually do it."

I looked over at his light-lined profile and for an instant saw through to someone younger. A confusing mishmash of images followed. The hillside he'd told me he walked in Daly City, south of San Francisco, where he'd grown up. The hammock he'd mentioned in his bedroom.

He gave me a guarded glance. "What?"

I shrugged and looked back at the skyline. "I came here when I was eighteen and assumed the city would fix all my problems. Childish, too."

Slowly, Parker's shoulders loosened. "Teenage Selina Chan's problems." He spoke quietly, but his voice pierced the noise of the party. "My imagination's failing me here."

I half smiled, my eyes still fixed across the river. "What's your New Year's resolution?"

"Write at least half of the next book."

"You're working on something new."

"Yeah." Parker leaned against the wall. "I actually—"

He cut himself off.

"What?" I asked.

He held my eyes for a split second, then looked down into his drink. "I'm going to get another. Do you want something?"

"Sure. I'll try the wine you brought."

"Okay, but you have to promise not to pan it."

"You know I can't make that kind of promise."

"Worth a shot."

But I did like it, the red he'd brought. It was tight and acidic and I could feel it staining my lips. Parker asked what I was reading lately and I told him I was catching up with Kazuo Ishiguro's *Klara and the Sun*, and he exclaimed in outrage when I called the book a second-tier version of *Never Let Me Go*, but then we got into *Never Let Me Go* itself, its frankness and tender naivete and endless gentle feeling of suffocation, and time began to whip by like whitewater. The conversation turned from clones to lab-grown meats to my least favorite college class—biology lab; I had a squeamish streak—to Parker's, a philosophy seminar whose professor, he said, would routinely spend fifteen minutes adding qualifiers to a single uncontroversial sentence. Then college. The ego games. The paralyzing freedom. As our glasses emptied, I felt as though entire universes of conversation were cracking open, colorful and enormous, as though we could chase any thread of any sentence and wind up in a place I'd never been. Then, suddenly, heads were turning toward the far wall at a surge of sound.

Parker and I glanced over, too. Cassie was turning up the volume on the TV so we could hear Times Square. I glanced at my phone, disoriented, and realized that it was 11:58. Somehow two and a half hours had evaporated. Onscreen, a red-cheeked man and a woman in a parka were swaying to an acoustic rendition of "What a Wonderful World," wearing bulbous blue New Year's–themed hats emblazoned with the Planet Fitness logo.

"Wow," said Parker. "The passage of time, sponsored by Planet Fitness."

"So beautiful," I said. "So poignant."

"So hard to cancel my membership."

I laughed. Parker looked at me strangely, an almost confused smile on his face.

"What a Wonderful World" ended, and the presentation cut between shots of the crowd. The glittering silver podium appeared with its glittering silver sphere, the mayor and several people in black coats gathered around. They pressed.

As the countdown began, Jacob and Cassie's apartment began to rev up like an engine. I scanned the groups rising from their seats, facing the screen, dashing to refill their glasses for a toast. Couples were gravitating together, beginning to melt into each other. I experienced a feeling of risk, as though I were holding my hand too close to an open flame.

When the countdown clock reached twenty, voices around us started to join in. Parker and I started chanting, too. I wasn't looking at him, but I could hear the smile in his voice, and the ring on his pinky glinted in my peripheral vision as he lifted his wineglass.

The ball dropped, glowing in the dark, fifty voices settling into a rhythm. I raised my voice too—"*Five . . . four . . . three . . . two . . . one!*"

The room exploded into a racket of celebratory yells. Everywhere around us, hands were joining, lips meeting.

I glanced over at Parker and found him looking at me. The noise of the room seemed dull somehow, clouding up in my ears.

He let his gaze slip to my mouth. Startled, before I could stop myself, I did the same, my eyes falling to the not-quite-smile still on his lips. Neither of us moved. Abruptly I felt hyperconscious of my motionless body, the angles of my shoulders and arms, the strange position of my wrist as my glass kissed my bicep. The itch of my dress near my shoulder, one slipped strap. The bluish shadow dipping over the corner of Parker's mouth, cast off by the party lights.

Then someone restarted the music. A dance beat cut through the air, and in a corner, someone threw open a window and whooped out onto the noisy street. Down the road, cheering burst, far-off and echoing, like a firework.

Parker lifted his glass. I clinked without thinking, drank down the last of my wine without thinking. I felt the urge to move, to say anything. I looked away and said, "I should get home."

"Yeah." Red was brushed on his cheeks. "Me too, don't want to impose on your friends. Um—let me walk you to the train."

"Right. Okay. I'm guessing you want to watch me slip on the ice?"

"Guilty."

We navigated through the crowd in uncertain silence. I hugged Jacob and Cassie goodbye, ignoring their inquiring looks, and then Parker and I were out in the cold darkness, heat sloughing off my body, breath curling from between his lips like smoke. We started southward down Newel Street. Sharp wind cut the space between us.

"You must live close," I said. "I'd barely hit Send on that email when you showed up."

"Very close. I'm ten minutes that way."

"By McGolrick Park?"

"Just across from it, yeah. I'm next door to that coffee shop, Little T."

I couldn't help a laugh. "Jacob and Cassie and I are there all the time."

"Cool. I've been warned."

"Very funny."

We passed an apartment whose drawn curtains showed the shifting silhouettes of a house party, then a garden unit whose cracked door emitted the *thump-thump-thump-thump* of house electronica. We checked down a one-way and crossed at the red light, and he said, "Second-tier *Never Let Me Go*, I can't get over that. You're unbelievable."

"Am I? Why?"

"Like, Kazuo Ishiguro hasn't won enough of your goodwill for you to like his other books out of hand? Genuinely, I don't understand that. Where's your loyalty!"

"Unquestioning loyalty makes you a bad critic, Parker." I steadied myself against a stop sign and adjusted one of my heels. "I can't just love something because it comes from someone I've loved before."

"You don't ever *want* to give somebody a pass?"

"I—maybe." I hesitated. "I mean, if Anna Kavan had ever published a bad book, I would have found that a little bit devastating to read."

"What if Jacob published a bad book?"

This drew me up short. I searched for words for a moment before saying, "Jacob doesn't write fiction."

"Play along with the thought experiment, Selina. What if he did? What would you do?"

"Well, I wouldn't write about it in *City Magazine*, first of all, because it would be a conflict of interest."

Parker looked up at the night sky and laughed. "You're terrible at this thought experiment. You know I meant—" As we were about to turn the corner onto Nassau, he broke off.

Just in front of us, a golden rhombus of light lay on the snow, cast out by an open door down a few steps to our left. I heard the chatter of muted voices, and I thought, a bar, but then my eyes found a small, dirty sign: THE BOOK BAR. Through the doorway I saw bookshelves.

"Wait," said Parker. "I didn't know this place existed."

"Neither did I."

We traded a look. The look was conspiratorial. I felt softly aware of my lightheadedness, the tipsy blur of my thoughts. Then we wordlessly stepped through the low iron gate and down the steps, each one a slick of ice pitted with green salt.

I stepped into the warmth, Parker close behind me. The place was low-ceilinged and rough, a labyrinth of unfinished wood and dim bare bulbs. As we moved down the main aisle, the voices grew louder, rounder, along with the chatter of a TV playing the New Year's celebration, until the book-lined pathway opened up into a half-full dive whose creaking stools and rickety tables were crowded against packed bookshelves. I loved the place immediately. The books' spines all faced out. White creases split their titles from years of reading.

I realized Parker was watching me. I unbuttoned my coat, my face prickling.

"Want a drink?" he asked.

"Just soda water. Thanks."

We exited the bar with glasses in hand and turned down the fiction aisle, which was so narrow that we had to move single file. Obscure paperbacks from the nineties faced out with book-talkers hanging beneath, while one reluctant copy of last year's biggest bestseller had been shoved anonymously into the G section.

"Fun selection," said Parker ahead of me. "I like this store."

"What makes a good bookstore for you?"

"The weirder the better, definitely." He glanced up at the higher shelves, his cheeks flushed. "I love when a place feels like a well-kept secret."

I smiled. When I didn't answer, he glanced back over his shoulder. Our eyes met. I inhaled, smelled his cologne, held my breath.

"This is kind of late for me," Parker said.

"Me too. I'm not usually up past midnight. Unless I'm being hectored with emails by some author with nothing better to do."

I caught one corner of his smile as he faced forward again. "Do you email anyone else? Or am I your only victim?"

"My parents."

The words had come out before I could think about them.

Parker kept moving toward the end of the aisle, where, at the corner, fiction turned into memoir. "Are they phone-shy?"

Even as I thought about lying or evading, I found myself remembering the way he'd looked out the diner window at the falling snow.

I remembered my words in his voice. *The longest uncompleted project of their lives.*

"No," I said. "We have a difficult relationship. They called me after the Wiseman Festival, and sent an email, but that was the first time we'd spoken in a couple of years."

Now his steps did slow. When we reached the corner, he stopped, silent. I busied myself with taking off my coat, grateful that he wasn't just saying the first bit of pablum that came to mind.

"Did you answer?" he asked eventually.

"After about six weeks." I didn't admit that our evening with Juliette had shifted some piece of machinery in me, that maybe, without the diner humming peacefully in the back of my mind, I would have left well enough alone.

I suddenly worried that he'd push, that he'd want to get to the bottom of me. I worried that even I didn't know what was at the bottom, that down there in the pit of me was something—not terrible, not monstrous or frightening, *that* I could have dealt with—something small and curled and sad, like a little girl in a corner. I didn't actually think I could stand to see that in myself, let alone for anybody else to see it.

But Parker didn't push. He pointed to something just out of sight, around the corner. "Look."

The aisle was narrow, but he didn't move. I took a step closer and found myself imagining a wobble of my heel. I could see myself tripping forward, landing against him. He'd catch himself against the shelf, another lock of hair tumbling out of place onto his furrowed brow. I imagined looking up into his intense, sensitive eyes.

I stayed even and upright. I tilted my head to peek around the corner.

Written across the raw wood endcaps were hundreds of authors' names. *Love you, Book Bar!* they'd written, or just their looped and well-practiced signatures. I thought I saw Juliette Liao's artful scribble on the next endcap down.

I opened my purse and handed Parker a pen. "Here."

As he took it, his fingers brushed mine. The moment of contact was long and slow, almost leisurely, his fingertip traveling up and over my knuckle. I couldn't tell whether the slowness was intentional or whether he was just like this, unhurried, so used to contact and closeness that he was oblivious to the things that in my insulated existence felt like a shattering.

I wondered for a single bizarre moment if Parker Navarro was flirting with me. If, when we'd left the party, he'd thought we were leaving together the way two normal people might leave a party together.

I thought about those hands keying into a laptop, *She inches her fingers down the yielding contours of her waist.*

He wrote on the wall in small, narrow letters,

well-kept secret

Then he signed, *P NAVARRO*, an almost unreadable knot.

He offered me the pen. I added *Selina Chan* in highly legible cursive underneath.

We studied our names on the wall. "That look like a truce to you?" Parker said.

"I think so."

His shoulder tipped against one shelf, and he said in a scratchy, uneven voice, "It's funny. I've never been in New York for the holidays before." He must have been properly drunk at this point, because his eyes didn't move from mine, as bright and focused as they had been in the Bar Car, when we'd been an inch from each other's throats.

"Because of your family?" I asked.

"Yeah. My mom and dad split up when I was twelve, so, twice the planning my whole life." He exhaled. "I miss them so much. I miss

Manila. You know how sometimes you like getting forced into doing things you'd normally never do? When my siblings and I, I mean, when we get up for the morning masses leading up to Christmas or stay out half the night, there's this sort of camaraderie to it. Like they all really like each other."

Parker hesitated. His brow furrowed, and he gave a sudden, self-effacing smile. "Sorry. I don't know why I—I mean, you don't want to hear . . . yeah."

As I watched him brush splinters from his coat, understanding hummed through me. He hadn't said anything objectionable, let alone something that needed an apology.

But, of course, this was how Parker acted with everybody whose opinion he cared about. He sanded off every edge to avoid remonstration. And with that truce written on the wall, he was beginning to do the same with me, too.

It made me unexpectedly sad. I looked at him and experienced that peeling back of time again. I saw a twelve-year-old kid with perceptive eyes, looking around at his family and seeing the universal absence of forgiveness.

"Parker," I said.

"Yeah?"

"You don't ever have to apologize to me for your opinion."

He studied me, a couple of millimeters left in his drink, the dark liquor thin enough to look blond. He was so still just then, photographic.

"Yeah," he said quietly. "I guess that's not what you want, is it?"

I gave my head the smallest shake and felt a slow, warm clench under my stomach, and on the heels of the feeling, something like alarm, something that made me tilt away from the bookshelf and take a step back.

"I should get home," I said.

He blinked, the stillness broken. "Right. I've got to close out."

He tossed back the last of his drink, and immediately, unwillingly, I looked at his throat, the way his Adam's apple bobbed, the shadow under the line of his jaw. My neck flushed hot. I took another step backward, turning away, as he said,

"Happy New Year, Selina."

Chapter Seventeen

Parker

I woke up on New Year's Day at an Arthur kind of time. My upstairs neighbor's elliptical was transmitting its heavy, rhythmic whir down through the ceiling, and I wasn't exactly hungover—I'd chugged two glasses of water when I'd arrived home—but I wasn't exactly normal, either. Something quivered in the center of my skull, and when I pulled myself upright it oscillated like a needle, and the instant I was on my feet, last night poured over me like a cool sea wind.

Selina Chan and me, framed in the window of her friends' apartment. Selina Chan a step behind me in the bookstore aisle, the metronome of those insane, brutal-looking heels, *click, click*, like the ticking alligator always just behind Captain Hook in Neverland. The ice white of her dress, high-necked and thin-strapped, clinging to her waist and hips, and the shine of her hair, loosely curled.

The moment she'd looked at me and said, *You don't ever have to apologize to me for your opinion*, and I'd realized—feeling like a house whose shutters had all slammed open at once in some gale-force wind, admitting some flood of illumination—that this was why I'd been unable to stop speaking to her this past week, why I'd felt so good the morning after our first confrontation, why I kept crawling back to her, again and again, for more. This was why our mutual anger, and more recently this sharp-edged, amorphous thing between us, had felt so freeing, even exhilarating: Selina Chan had never wanted me filtered. In fact, the whole basis of her criticism had always been that she wanted me less filtered.

And she'd seen me trying to prune back the truth last night, and she hadn't wanted it, because that was Selina Chan. Someone who wanted the real thing, even when it wasn't nice.

In that moment, I'd looked at her and tasted such a potent shot of understanding that the bourbon in my hand could have been water.

In the bathroom I washed my face and regarded myself in the mirror; I barely saw myself. I saw her on the threshold of the party, still-faced, her somber mouth.

Even more inexplicable: I'd had *fun* with her. I'd liked it, all of it—needling her, waiting for her to smack the tennis ball back, the energetic pleasure of the give-and-take; wandering the bookstore aisles together; saying anything I liked with her, feeling liberated, as though I were unbound from some constraints I unknowingly buckled on around other people. I'd liked the innate weirdness of seeing her at a party with her ordinary-seeming friends—I'd expected them to be tenured professors who thought Franzen was mainstream trash and spent all their time dissecting *Ulysses* over Armagnac.

I came back to myself, standing stock-still in front of my mirror. I gave my head a hard shake, slapped my cheeks with cold water, and went to the front room to visit my laptop.

The publication of *High and Dry* looked a lot closer from this side of New Year's, and I'd been neglecting my social media. As I wrapped up a breakfast burrito and opened my browser, I wondered—what was

I feeling about this book on the horizon? This book that felt utterly unknown to me now that I'd written it?

@ParkerNavarroWrites: High and Dry publishes in under two months, which means my next seven weeks will consist of trying to peer over the peak of the rollercoaster at rails that haven't been laid down yet. If you've read the book in advance form and left kind words, thank you. Your enthusiasm helps with the nerves!

Notifications began to accumulate, a dozen likes, then a hundred. I kept refreshing the page, unsure what I was waiting for until it appeared in front of me.

@SelinaChan: @ParkerNavarroWrites You're wringing your hands over this?

Beneath, she'd posted a screencap of an orange banner on *High and Dry*'s Amazon page. Number-one new bestseller in Literary Fiction, apparently.

The quivering thing in the center of my skull began to vibrate. I shifted forward in my seat, a strange satisfaction humming over the surface of my skin.

@ParkerNavarroWrites: @SelinaChan Yes, Selina. Sometimes we human beings experience emotions like "nervousness" when we have incomplete knowledge about something important. Let me know if you need more info!

@SelinaChan: @ParkerNavarroWrites Despite the book's many, many flaws, it appears that sales are the last thing you need to worry about.

@ParkerNavarroWrites: @SelinaChan And it's all thanks to you.

My phone buzzed. I felt a jolt in my fingertips and flipped it face up, already knowing what I was going to see.

1 New Message from ☠☠ Selina Chan ☠☠
I can't believe that my biggest material
contribution to this literary year will be ensuring
that High and Dry hits the NYT list.

Why was I feeling the urge to laugh at this?

A normal person, I said, would add "no offense" to that text message somewhere.

But it's an offensive text message, she said.

That's our entire thing, Parker. Offensive messages.

Maybe you drank enough last night to forget.

Something pulsated in the sensitive space between my heart and my stomach. I felt the cold glass sweating in my hand, the scrape of the bookstore's unfinished wood against my temple. My fingers remembered the softness of her hand as I'd brushed it. Of course she couldn't really feel like ice or marble or enamel, but that instant of contact had still somehow startled me, the warmth of her skin. Had I imagined the color rising in her cheeks?

I set down my phone. I couldn't actually be thinking about Selina Chan in this way.

I couldn't, at this moment, be imagining what might have happened if I'd pushed a little farther, traced my fingers over her knuckles, run my hand up her arm—if I'd stepped forward into that impenetrable layer that seemed to surround her.

My phone dinged again. I swept it up, wondering if I'd missed a chance, if I'd let this rhythm between us falter—but the message wasn't from Selina.

New Messages in Chan Pan Support Group

Carla Lew

Parker I just saw your posts. Wtf.

The demon can't even let you have

a nice New Year's Day??

Aiden Linville

pictures please, what did she do

Carla Lew

[image]

J.J. Purnell

Does this count as harassment?

Jenny House

Ugh, I'm so sorry, Parker. Let us know

if we can do anything

I felt a cold prickle over the back of my neck.

Parker Navarro

Thanks y'all but it's not a problem!

Those posts felt like more of a joke.

Parker Navarro

Hope everybody had a fun New

Year's

I thought of Selina looking out at the Manhattan skyline, her glass held to her collarbone, weary and half-ironic as she'd said, *I came here when I was eighteen and assumed the city would fix all my problems.*

My burrito had gone cold. I ate mechanically, telling myself the sour feeling in my gut was from last night's drinks—wondering, in reality, how Selina would have reacted if she'd seen the things this group chat had said about her.

I drained a glass of water and tried to shake the discomfort. Selina wouldn't have been surprised. She knew the impact her reviews had; she knew the anger wrapped up in that. As I set my glass on the counter, I tried to think of some witty, offhand answer to her texts, but even as I typed in a few aimless letters, another message arrived, this time from Arthur.

Bro I just saw Selina Chan being a dick to you online again. If you want to vent, feel free. I'm at my gate for the next 45 minutes so I've got time

I hesitated, then typed, Thanks

He replied seconds later: Seriously. For her to have the audacity to BE the reason you're nervous about the book coming out, and then to act like it's stupid for you to worry? Fuck that. Fuck her

I was rereading the text when he said, But also if you weren't thinking about it that hard, that's great!

Yeah, sorry, I said. I'm actually borderline hungover

Oh for real? What'd you do last night?

I thought for a moment, then wrote, My friend Julian had a house party. How about you?

Took it easy. I had to get up at 8:00 😩

Nobody's ever suffered like you've suffered, Arthur.

So true 😩 😩 😩

Fly safe, I said. Then I turned off my screen and hunched over the counter, feeling like the conversation had wiped some fogged-up window clean in my mind, so that I could see clearly again.

Everyone in my life was reading Selina's posts as mockery. Was I being overgenerous, reading them as something like banter?

I tugged my coat from the hook and laced up my boots. On our salted doorstep, I reread her texts, and this time they didn't have the laughing, secretive tone I'd lent them the first go around. They sounded arch and scathing.

It's an offensive text message.

That's our entire thing, Parker. Offensive messages.

Maybe you drank enough last night to forget.

The wind raked across my face. I parted my lips and drank in the cold. Was Selina right, as always? *Had* I forgotten what this was?

It was just that I was trying to remember the version of her I'd met in October, the one who'd induced white-hot loathing from tiny behaviors like the handling of her purse or the turning of her head. I was trying to figure out what it meant that she'd invited me to a New Year's party, and why I grabbed for my phone immediately whenever I thought she'd texted me. I was trying to figure out the difference between what I was doing now and what I'd been doing in November, when I'd woken up and checked her social media like it was the weather, obsessed by the thought of the next moment we'd interact.

My temples had begun to throb. I headed down the block, phone still in hand, and scrolled through the next few days of Google Flights. With New Year's in the rearview, the prices of a San Francisco round trip had cratered.

With two taps, I was booked. I needed to get out of New York. I needed no further evidence that I was going stir-crazy than this: Even as I looked around at my neighborhood billowing with motion, the weaving of cars, the swaying of stoplights smacked by wind, the steaming of the halal stand on the corner—even as I walked faster and faster into the city that had revved back into life around me—I felt as though some part of me remained absolutely still, frozen opposite her in the darkness of last night.

I pushed my phone deep into my pocket, her texts unanswered.

Chapter Eighteen

Selina

The *City* office reopened on January 3, for which I was grateful. In the past two days, I'd checked my phone so often for a reply from Parker that by the time I went to sleep on Sunday night, I was fighting off embarrassment. But the next morning, my routine came back to me like a faithful pet. The blare of my alarm, the whining of the subway as I read my way into Manhattan, the bleary welcomes of my *City* coworkers. I was happier than usual to see Kellie swinging around the doorframe of my office, and to engage in the usual polite script.

"Did you have a good break?" I asked.

"Spectacular. My partner and I went to Iceland and saw the Northern Lights. I bet it's the feeling astronauts get when they see Earth from orbit." She jerked back, eyes wide, as though she'd been caught in a searchlight. "Flattens you. How was break for you?"

"Uneventful."

"That's all I get? You should work for the CIA."

"Conflict of interest. I'm already working for MI6."

Kellie laughed. "That tracks. By the way, Mike told me the anniversary party is black-tie this year."

"What? Why?"

"To justify the hundred-and-twenty-dollar tickets, obviously. I'm trying to figure out how to tell Nextward Capital Associates that they don't pay us enough to expect floor-length gowns."

I smiled.

"What?" she said.

"Nothing." I turned back to my computer. "It's good to be back."

I made my now-routine morning pass through social media. Random House had won a bidding war for a novel imagining the life of Milly Bloom, the daughter of the main character of *Ulysses.* A blockbuster romantasy author had been given her own imprint at Bloomsbury.

I clicked over to my mentions.

@LolaXu: @SelinaChan Got my hands on this. It's everything you promised and worse, lol.

She'd attached a photo of an advance copy of *High and Dry.*

I winced and hit Reply, but after several minutes of halting beginnings, I still hadn't found what to write. This was my mistake. I'd stoked Lola's investment in the situation with Parker, and I'd never responded to that petition in November. I'd assumed my silence would make it clear what my thoughts were, but maybe I should have been explicit that I didn't consider it a prosecutable offense for a fiction writer to write a piece of fiction.

Before I could decide what to say, my phone chimed in my desk drawer. My personal email.

I pulled the drawer open and grabbed up my phone—but the email wasn't from Parker.

To: selinachanlikesbooks@gmail.com
From: Charles.Chan111@gmail.com
Sent: Jan 03, 9:18 AM
Subject: Re: Author fight

Happy New Year Xiao Yan. Yes we had a very nice Christmas. We used your mother's iPad to call your Yeh Yeh. Then Lao Lao and Lao Ye. All healthy. Auntie Sylvia is spending some time in Tianjin until end of CNY. then back to Seattle. All asked after you. We were happy to pass on how you are doing well. But, your mother has been reading the posts you make online recently. Is this really part of your job, to make people so angry? Is it not better to solve arguments in private? We were always afraid of this, in such a negative job. What will happen if you say something you cannot take back? From Dad and Mom.

I read the email twice, feeling as though I were shrinking. In that moment, I was standing on the porch steps of our house in Minnesota, duffel bag on my shoulder, gathering the courage to ring the doorbell. I was twenty-eight, visiting home for the first time in eight years. I would leave again two days later, promising myself never to return.

Yet here I was, somehow surprised.

I wondered why I still cared about my parents' opinion of my work. I felt as though I'd spent my entire adult life waiting for some scrap of validation from them, and that was childish, wasn't it? To continue to care?

Earlier on, their worries about my career had at least made sense. After Columbia, I'd strung my life together on freelance article writing and waiting tables at a French bistro, which combined had me earning $45,000 a year—just about enough to cover my debt payments and Brooklyn's cost of living. I was paying $750 in rent to live with three roommates in a semi-functional garden apartment in Crown Heights. Not that I ever admitted this to my parents, but my so-called career had felt aimless and frightening then, an ever-turning carousel of rejection—a threat that my mother had been right.

But small stepping stones led me through my twenties. At twenty-four, I landed a part-time assistantship at a now-defunct literary magazine called *The Long View*, and at twenty-five I had my first real break as a critic: I sold an essay to *Guernica* reviewing a small run of nonfiction books about gun violence. That day, I spent an extravagant twenty-one dollars on a bottle of wine and texted my parents in triumph. Their muted response maddened me.

But I could feel the momentum building that year. I found new rhythms in my writing. I finally felt that I'd read enough books to have a real intertextual well to draw from. Several months later I placed a review in *Ploughshares*, and the following year, when I was twenty-six, *City* accepted one of my freelance pitches for the first time. Soon they added me to their bank of contributors, and when I was twenty-seven, Joyce emailed to tell me that an assistant editor position had opened, and that, if I was interested, she would pass my resume to Scott.

My parents and I were in one of our periods of closer contact, then. When I got the job, I texted them with something between joy and spite. I used exclamation points. I had won.

I had won; so why, every time I spoke with them, did I still feel so defensive?

It was in this state that I'd planned the trip home. In my mind, working for *City* would fix everything. They'd wanted stability? Here was stability. They'd wanted an impressive career that they could mention to the extended family? Here I was, writing for one of the best magazines in the country.

But I arrived home in Minnesota to a barrage of doubts instead. Was I sure this magazine was a safe bet? Was I still living in that tiny, run-down place in Brooklyn? They kept reading about newspapers shutting down. What if I used these skills to transfer over to something more reliable?

It astonished me how they couldn't admit that they'd been wrong, that I'd done everything I'd meant to. And now, six years later, here was the same relentless quest to poke holes in my life. I read the email a third time. Of course they'd made no acknowledgment of the feud helping *City*—the main point I'd conveyed in my last email.

If I replied I would become bitterly angry, I could feel it already. We would fall into this again: that they still couldn't conceive of the person I'd become, as though they still saw some veil hanging in front of me and, projected onto that veil, a glowing vision of what they could have had.

I was a fool for failing to anticipate this. I never should have taken my father's call in that bar.

I dropped my phone back into the drawer and closed it.

Three days since New Year's, then four. I waited for the anticipation of Parker's next message to fade, but the feeling stuck in the back of my mind, an unreachable itch, and by the time the weekend arrived, I felt deeply irritated with myself. I'd known that my back-and-forth with Parker had an expiration date: the moment when the people whose company we enjoyed reentered our lives.

I hadn't expected this problem to arise: that I *did* enjoy Parker Navarro's company. That, in fact, I found him consistently funny and his opinions continually surprising. That the idea of never learning more about him frustrated me.

That Saturday, Jacob and Cassie invited me over for brunch. Usually I could count on these to be calming experiences. Cassie would sing along to Japanese pop music while cutting strawberries, and Jacob would thumb through their bottomless catalog of teas. We'd chat about some movie that Lyra had watched six times on repeat, or about the interpersonal politics of Cassie's lab, or about the megalomaniac director at Jacob's nonprofit, whom Jacob steadfastly described as "not that bad." This week, I knew the conversation would be different.

"So," said Jacob, the syllable loaded with suggestion, over the rim of his coffee mug.

"Jacob," I said, warning.

"No! Details!" Cassie demanded, brandishing a yogurt-covered spoon at me. "How did this happen? *What* happened?"

"Look. I ran into Parker at Juliette Liao's event right before Christmas. Juliette insisted on treating us to dinner afterward, which was extremely uncomfortable, but I mentioned an article to Parker about a book we both like, then followed up with a link afterward." I folded my arms. "We exchanged a couple of emails, and I realized he was alone on New Year's, which seemed sad. That's the entire story."

Cassie scoffed. "Well, you left the party together, so it's not the entire story."

"He walked me to the train, Cassie."

She and Jacob exchanged a skeptical glance.

"What's with the skeptical glance," I said.

"Oh, nothing," said Jacob, lifting Lyra onto his lap.

Cassie heaped raspberries into a bowl. "The skeptical glance, Selina, is because it was cool to see you talking with someone who could keep up with you. Like, he didn't do the rabbit-in-the-headlights face."

"No," I admitted.

"And I'm guessing he didn't do the thing you hate where people close off a topic by saying 'Fair.'"

"No. Sure. After drinking half our weight in alcohol we were able to carry a conversation. Amazing."

Jacob bounced Lyra gently on his knee. "So . . . how many emails is 'a couple of emails'?"

"Like—I don't know, maybe—"

Cassie laughed. "*Oh* my God. Dude. You are so full of shit. It wasn't a couple of emails."

"What?" I said, but now I could feel it: My face had flushed. "Fine! Okay. We sent *a number* of emails. Because he was stranded in the city, Cassie, and everybody besides me was with their families at Christmas."

"Right, so that's why he was emailing you, supposedly. Why were you emailing him?"

I made an irritated sound and looked out the window, but Cassie wasn't the one I was annoyed with.

"It doesn't matter," I said. "He thinks I'm a terrible person, remember?"

"Didn't seem like it. Seemed like he was hanging on to everything you said."

I flicked my hand. "He's an author. Authors do outrageous things in the name of having experiences to repurpose later. They're like magpies. Or weird neurotic squirrels. Anyway, since New Year's, we've stopped speaking, which is exactly what I expected."

Cassie sat beside Jacob and set the raspberries and yogurt in the center of the table, looking unconvinced. "What do you mean, 'stopped speaking'?"

"I mean we—" I cast a despairing look upward. This was going to sound so adolescent. "I mean, Cassie, that I texted him, and he didn't text me back."

"Oh, so you're *texting* now! Like normal people! Not just emailing!"

"I have literally just told you that we aren't texting."

She stuck out her hand. "Give me the phone."

Jacob finally broke. "Yeah, okay, I've got to see this."

My face burning, I opened our conversation and shoved my phone into Cassie's hand. "There. Enjoy."

Jacob, grinning, craned his neck to see the screen as Cassie muttered the messages aloud. "Offensive messages, our entire thing . . . Selina."

"What?"

"There's nothing here to reply to. It's not like you asked him a question. You just, like, made fun of him and didn't say anything else."

My cheeks warmed. "That's kind of the way we interact."

"Problematic," said Jacob.

I glowered at him. "You are extravagantly unhelpful."

Jacob chortled and tossed a few raspberries into his mouth.

"If you want to keep talking, just text him and ask him something," said Cassie, handing my phone back.

Coming out of her mouth, the suggestion sounded casual and ordinary, which disturbed me, because in my head, the idea of contacting Parker without any pretext felt distinctly uncasual and completely out of the ordinary. It made me feel panicky and defenseless, the way I felt in the doctor's office rolling up my shirt sleeve for a jab.

"Mm," I said, trying to maintain my composure. "What do you think, Lyra?"

Jacob bounced her on his knee again. Lyra looked up at me with solemn eyes and said, "Da."

"Means 'yes' in Russian," said Cassie.

"Traitor," I said to the one-year-old.

I arrived at our pitch meeting the following Monday to discover that Hayden had returned. She was sitting in her corner for the first time in a month, her laptop perched on a lapdesk, and when Scott strode into the library, he didn't address her reappearance.

Something about Scott's demeanor made me uneasy. He was cordial, asking us all how our weekends had been, but his effortful smiles shrank as soon as they'd formed, like elastic dough that couldn't hold shape. Eventually he lifted one palm toward Hayden and said, "We have some new plans from upstairs."

"*Hi*, everyone," said Hayden, still typing. "I hope you all had good holidays. Mine was great . . . I went to Italy. *Such* amazing food!" She finally lifted her eyes from her laptop. "So, exciting news. I'm here to unveil a new content strategy I designed over the New Year."

The library stilled, except for Joyce, picking at the fibers of her cardigan. Beside me, even Kellie had gone stiff, like a hunting dog on the scent.

"Everyone at Nextward agrees that we have some important lessons to learn from fall. Mainly that this magazine benefits from being more up to the moment." Hayden chopped the side of her hand into her opposite palm. "People want to see *City* as contemporary and accessible. No elitism, no navel-gazing. So, our new strategy is going to revolve around grabbing more headlines. Getting in on the ground level on anything buzzy or controversial in media. We want your hottest takes. Your edgiest ideas. I've already talked to Scott about opening up space in most of your schedules so we can get more coverage on this side of the culture beat." She turned her laptop outward to show us a spreadsheet.

I gazed into the scattering of multicolored cells, then lifted my eyes to Hayden's relentless smile, feeling farther and farther away from her, as though my chair were being tugged slowly backward through space. No, Hayden and I didn't like or respect each other, but I'd thought we'd at least understood each other. I'd thought we'd reached an accord: I would play by her rules, and she would not take *City Magazine* and saw open its surface and gouge out everything inside.

Why had I ever believed this? My sudden feeling of naivete startled me.

"Sandro"—Hayden turned to Sandro Nuñez, our film and television writer—"I've been thinking, like, why aren't we talking more about big moments in TV and movie news? In December, Marvel announced their first trans superhero. The engagement was out of this world. Huge opportunity to add our voice. Why didn't we?"

Sandro blinked rapidly, at an apparent loss for words. He spent most of his time editing Life Offscreen, our bimonthly interview series with everyone from Hollywood directors to camera crew, an industry mainstay that had been running since the sixties. We used to have more day-to-day film coverage, but Nextward had fired both of our junior film writers last August, leaving Sandro to manage a stable of freelancers who were paid $150 an article.

"And Kellie!" said Hayden. "I have a list of bestsellers on the doc for you to tackle. There's one called *Devil's Diary* that had the whole internet on fire last week. Something about incest? I don't know. Could be a really juicy article, anyway. The author was just blundering her way through responding to everything, which, I mean—that's exactly where we want to be."

"Hayden," I said.

"Yes, Selina?"

"I'm sorry. I don't understand how this . . . this content strategy squares with what I've been promising our readership for the past three months."

"What don't you understand?" she asked, still smiling.

"I've been telling people that *City* represents something that's disappearing." My eyes prickled. Alarmed, I straightened in my seat. "I've been saying that in a world inundated by articles that are superficial, or reactionary, or essentially regurgitated, we're different. This—"

"But *City* isn't different," said Hayden.

Silence rang throughout the library.

"What?" I said.

"*City* doesn't exist in a world of pure, untainted ideas." Her voice sharpened. "Like every other publication, it exists in the real world, which includes overhead costs and infinite online competition and a dozen other high-minded journals that are all eating into the same tiny demographic that'll pay for the kind of writing you're describing." Hayden closed her laptop and rose to her feet, her eyes never leaving mine, and I had the sense of our arrival at the center of something. "Look around, Selina. You're sitting in the most expensive city in the country, in a legacy office that's just dying to be rented out to a tech company with millions of dollars of seed funding pouring out its ears. Do you want *City* to stay in business? Then you need to evolve."

"But I thought that in December, everything was—"

"What you thought isn't my problem." Hayden shouldered her bag and went for the door. "Thanks for your input, but I wasn't asking for a debate. I was breaking the news. I'll send you the details by email."

Chapter Nineteen

Parker

Like every other house on our block, my mother's place was a small, neat cube. The Walker house to our left was robin's-egg blue, and the Vargas house to the right was the pale yellow of vanilla ice cream; ours was mint green. Side by side they looked like complementary paint chips. Duffel bag on my shoulder, I climbed our front steps from street level to the second floor, where our door was set back from the road, in the shadow of a terrace dripping with wisteria.

I hesitated on the square of concrete porch, looking at my phone. When I'd landed at SFO, my screen had lit up with delayed texts from the flight. A dozen had arrived from the Bay Area group chat, several from my siblings, forty from the Chan Pan Support Group, four from Arthur, and one—my eyes had fixed on it immediately, as though everything else were noise—from Selina.

Would it break our truce, said the message preview, if I came to your book launch?

What did this mean? We hadn't spoken in over a week. I'd spent the time trying to parse my feelings about New Year's, getting nowhere. Why was she asking about breaking the truce? Was this some threat for vicious articles to come? Did negative reviews of book launches exist?

Or was she—*ridiculous*, I thought, completely stupid—was she asking me to invite her?

I slipped my phone into my pocket and rang the bell. The sunset turned the roofs to black paper cutouts, and down the hall, the kitchen lights glowed. The faint strains of folk music probed through the door, joined by hurried footsteps, then the flip of the lock.

My mom threw open the door and exclaimed, "Pijay!" The rush of air, and her full-body tackle of an embrace, smelled so distinctly like my childhood—toasted bread, frying garlic, my mom's lavender lotion, the air freshener with the blue bottle—that suddenly I was remembering the rest, too. The scuffed Adidas I'd worn to pieces through high school, and the family desktop computer in our living room where I'd worked on my unreadable preteen writing projects, but secretly, in the middle of the night, because during the daytime Christi and Justin monopolized it to use MySpace. When I opened my eyes and drew back from my mother, looking down at the deep wrinkles in her beaming face, it was like being struck in the face with my adulthood.

"Come in, come in!" she said.

"Thanks." I toed off my shoes in the hall. "Wow, it's so clean."

"Had to get ready for your visit! How was the flight?"

"Pretty good. I wrote for a while." I followed my mother into the kitchen, set my duffel bag against the wall, and sat down at the narrow table across from the oven. "Feels sort of liberating to get out of New York."

"Is it the book release? Or what's been happening online?"

"Not the book. The book's okay." I watched her unload the last few wineglasses from the dishwasher. "Have you been following the stuff online?"

"Well, not all the time. Puts my blood pressure up. I just want to sit some of these people down and set them straight. And that woman, egging them all on." She kneed the dishwasher shut, looking much more like an MMA fighter finishing off an opponent than you'd really expect from a woman who was sixty-six years old and five foot zero. "I don't know how you stand it."

"Yeah, I—I don't know. I was in a weird spot over the holidays."

"Well, you're here, now. You don't have to think about any of that. Here, you must be hungry." My mom opened a cabinet, climbed onto her stepstool, and took down enough of my favorite snacks to last a year, Oreos and polvorón and dried mango strips and tortilla chips with a jar of green salsa.

I laughed. "Mom, I'm only here for three days."

"You can take it back with you!" She spread the bounty on the table. "Here, eat, eat."

"Thanks. You're the best. How's the hotel been?"

She sat opposite me. "Oh, you know the holidays. Booked solid. Third-party reservation problems, guests destroying the place . . ."

As she described a couple who'd wrecked their room and blamed it on the staff of the Harbor Inn, I watched her silver-lacquered nails drum against the plastic tablecloth and felt my contentment fade. Four years ago, I'd assumed that if I paid off this house, she'd retire early and never waste another second of her life worrying about hotel guests who vomited on their bathroom floors. But my mother sent part of every paycheck back to the Philippines for my grandfather, to the care facility where Lolo had lived since a pair of minor strokes, and as a fixture at the local Catholic church, she was generous to a fault, always contributing to funds for new immigrant families or buying baby clothes for single mothers.

Trying to find a more cheerful subject, I asked, "Have you seen Kevin since he got back?"

She sighed. "I haven't. Didn't he tell you? He lost his job."

"No. Seriously? Is he okay?"

"I don't think so. Hard to tell. You know Kevy. He mopes, he lashes out."

"That's awful," I muttered. "I really thought this one would work out." After San Francisco State, Kevin had spent most of his twenties in sales positions, getting bumped from company to company around the city. Two years ago, he'd sunk his meager savings into a data science boot camp, and a few months ago he'd finally gotten his first job as an analyst at a security firm.

"He'll find something else," my mom said. "Everyone wants a data person."

"Hope so."

I didn't realize I was massaging the spot between my eyebrows until my mom clasped my shoulder. "Pijay, you look tired. Go lie down, I'll call you when dinner's ready."

"Okay. Yeah. Thank you." I shouldered my bag, avoiding her eyes. I'd spent the past few days imagining the comfort of being back here, especially without the family to juggle. I didn't know what was wrong with me.

In my old bedroom, I set the duffel on the dresser and lay down, feeling claustrophobic. The double bed, pushed under the window, took up the room's entire width. The only other furnishings that fit were a bedside table and dresser, so my mother and I had installed shelves up to the ceiling, which still overflowed with the detritus of my teenage years, clear bins filled with socks and miscellaneous pens and scratched DVDs in busted cases, the skateboard I'd tried to adopt as my identity when I was fifteen, about two hundred books.

I'd moved into this room, originally a storage closet, at fourteen. That was the year Justin had moved to L.A. for college, igniting a debate over which of us would inherit his room—Christi and Elena had shared at the time, and so had Kevin and I. Christi, at fifteen, was the obvious choice, but Kevin had made some incoherent argument about girls not needing privacy. When the argument veered into the personal, I'd insisted on moving in here. Kevin could keep our old room, Christi could inherit Justin's, and Elena could spread out. Everyone else was happy, and I was happy enough.

I didn't know why I was imagining Selina propped in the doorway, studying me.

My phone found its way into my hand, and her message preview reappeared onscreen. *Would it break our truce . . .*

I let out a short sigh and switched to my thread with Kevin. I was supposed to be here to clear my head, not to circle the same questions that had made Brooklyn feel like it was folding in on me.

Hey, I texted Kevin, I heard about your job. I'm so sorry. I'm in town for a few days—we could get Chibog or something? Let me know if you want to talk.

A minute later, he replied. Yeah thanks it sucks. My ex boss was such an asshole. Happy new year youre fired

I'm sure you'll find something else soon. You're extremely employable.

Lol what? he said. You have no idea. Data sounds good but a lot of these jobs are getting automated and the market blows. Yeah probably if I went to Yale or Amherst I could just pick up the phone but some of us can't.

One scan of this text and a rapid, nervy pulse began to beat in my stomach. I reread it a few times. Why was he angry at me? What had I said wrong?

I get the sentiment, I said, but I never got a job through Yale, and as far as I know, Elena hasn't gotten one through Amherst.

Check again shes only working at her startup thing because she went to school with someone's rich ass cousin. And you probably could have done the same thing except you chose to be an English major lol

My grip was constricting on my phone. I typed a few letters, not knowing what to say. It seemed enormously selfish to get frustrated with Kevin when I'd texted with the express purpose of consoling him.

I was beginning to type Yeah when the ellipsis appeared on his end again. He typed for longer than Kevin was generally known to type. Down the hall my mother's knife beat a rhythm on one of her ancient cutting boards.

An enormous bubble appeared, kicking the rest of the conversation out of sight. The Elena thing is just insane bc she was a sociology major. Ik she got grants but she spent 60k of our parents money and took 80k of debt to get a soc degree which is FOR REAL a dead end degree unless youre doing academia. and now she has this great job and mom and dad are all "baby is such a grown up businesswoman, so driven and responsible" give me a fucking break. I actually WAS responsible and made sacrifices and didnt go to Northwestern because I KNEW we couldnt afford it and now im fucking unemployed and ofc thanks to you Elena doesnt even have to deal with the debt she signed up for. Shit is driving me crazy.

I could feel my pulse throughout my body now, in my palms, in my throat. The walls seemed closer, the room darker.

I pushed myself off the bed and strode back to the kitchen. My mother, aproned at the counter, was swaddling a glistening brick of tofu in paper towels with neat, practiced motions. "Mom," I said, "I—I'm going to take a walk. Stretch my legs from the flight."

"Okay, sure! Dinner at six or so." She let a series of heavy cookbooks thud down on the wrapped package, beginning to press out the moisture.

Outside the sky was black, although it was barely 5 PM. A single car a couple of blocks away drifted through an intersection, and I caught snatches of faraway ocean as I walked, faint as the sound of cloth rubbing against itself. It wasn't until I turned out of the residential side roads onto the wide, flat pathway of Mission Street that I realized where I was going.

I checked my watch. 5:18. Poppy Street Books was usually open until six. I'd wind between the shelves, the page-scented air stirring around me, until I reached the back corner by the biographies, where

I'd sink into that enormous leather armchair and feel the weight of reality slip from my back, the way it had hundreds of times before. I imagined that if I replaced myself in that spot, I could access some feeling of refuge that had tided me through eighteen years here.

I passed a gas station and a pond of white light, then crossed over a median whose runty, leafless trees shuddered in the evening wind. There, half a block ahead, the awning at the intersection of Mission and Poppy fluttered.

But as I approached, my steps slowed. The bookstore's front window was dark.

I stopped at the door. A sheet of paper taped inside the glass said, *We are closing our doors after forty-two amazing years!! Thank you Daly City!!*

Little by little, the fast shallow heartbeat in my ears faded to something slow and dull, like the tap of one knuckle against a slab of wood. I touched the ridged metal bar on the door and let my fingers rest there until they turned cold.

I made an aimless turn. The wind was sliding up the sleeves of my jacket. San Francisco wouldn't freeze you like New York, but January wasn't exactly balmy or forgiving. Ahead, light flowed down from the streetlamps like sheets hanging from clothespins.

In a daze I wandered back up Mission Street and into the Quick-Stop. More flickering fragments of memory here. Maricel and Tyler and I had roamed these gleaming aisles every other Friday evening at seventeen, pissing off the unlucky cashiers with hissed jokes and explosions of laughter. I passed shelves of chip bags, the same four logos in eight colors apiece, and came to a standstill in an aisle of gummy sour and caramel packages jam-packed on their white hooks.

Finally, with no other recourse, I took out my phone and reread the wall of text from Kevin.

How long had he been harboring this resentment? When had he even found out about the loan payment?

Had Elena told Christi, too? Justin? Our parents? Did anyone else in our family feel this way, and if they did, what was I supposed to say?

Heart pattering, I force-closed Kevin's thread and waded into the rest of the internet, looking for anything else to latch on to, cycling through tagged posts on social media, pressing likes and reactions, scanning my group chats but absorbing only the basic strokes. Three aisles over, some automatic scanner's voice was telling someone over and over to please remove the unrecognized item from the bagging area. The LEDs beat down on my hands, rendering them colorless. I realized that I wanted desperately to talk to someone, but every text entry field on my screen looked like the response line on some unending exam, a test to find the perfect thing to say about Aiden's health insurance or Xiangyu's job applications, chance after chance to fall short, to knock cracks into my friendships and relationships, to let someone down.

My heart had begun to sound in my ears again when I reached the last of my notifications, Selina's unread text, a small blue dot beside her name.

I wavered, then broke. I opened the message.

Would it break our truce if I came to your book launch?

The whole system of traffic that was my thoughts seemed to draw to a halt. Here, at least, I could write whatever I wanted. All the acrimonious things Selina and I had hurled at each other, and she was still sending me text messages, as though I could say anything and it wouldn't matter.

Why, I typed, are you planning some elaborate sabotage I should know about?

I hit Send.

Moments later, her ellipsis appeared.

She said, I'm sure I could come up with something, if that's what you really want.

I don't think it counts as sabotage if we plan it together, Selina.

A moment passed. Then:

Selina Chan laughed at your message

The muscles in my shoulders loosened. I settled back against the shelving as her next message arrived: That's a shame. I need help assembling this Trojan horse I bought from IKEA. They sent me two hundred pounds of raw pinewood and a hex wrench the size of a toothpick.

I began to smile. That's what you get for ordering the Ödeshög, instead of the famously more streamlined Grönsved model.

Ah, right, my mistake, she said.

I'd help you get through the 92-step assembly pamphlet, but I'm actually in California.

There was a pause, then, Visiting home?

Yeah. My dad's still in Manila, but I'm staying with my mom for a bit. Might see my brother.

How has it been? she asked.

It's been great! I typed, but as the words appeared, I remembered her eyes on New Year's, and that she didn't want my apologies, my elisions. I felt, somehow, that this was the one line I didn't want to cross with her. I didn't want to lie.

I deleted the text and started over.

I've only been here for a few hours, I wrote, over the course of several effortful minutes, but they haven't been ideal.

What made them less than ideal? she asked.

Some holiday horror stories from my mom's hotel job. She's not as close to retirement as I'd like. Also, my favorite bookstore here closed down, and my brother is apparently frustrated that I helped our sister with her student loans.

I stared at this draft text, feeling as though I'd slid sideways into a vivid dream. How had I arrived at these topics so quickly, topics I'd barely even broached with Arthur?

I hesitated, pressed Send—and then felt an immediate stab of disbelief. What had I just done? Of course she'd only asked to be polite.

Even as I batted around erratic thoughts about editing the message, her response appeared. I suppose with seven of you in that part of California, the financial pressure must have been pretty immense, especially around the time you went to college.

And I remembered who I was talking to. My thoughts slowed. Selina Chan wouldn't ask a question to be polite. She said what she meant, always.

I was able to type, Yeah. The money situation was worse after the divorce, worse during college. A little better after my book deal. I didn't know Kevin was bottling this up about Elena's loans, though. I'm still trying to figure out how to answer.

Are you and Kevin close?

I'd say so, I said. I've never had big fights with any of my family.

She typed for a while. So long that I imagined her standing in line at a coffee shop, frowning at her phone, wondering why exactly I was telling her my life story. I was taking up so much air in this conversation.

Before she could send her reply, I said, I'll figure out what to say to him. Anyway, how's New York? City must be getting ready for the anniversary party, right?

Her ellipsis disappeared, then reappeared. New York is cold, she said, and City has lots on its mind, yes. But I wanted to ask about the bookstore that closed.

I shifted my shoulder blades against the metal shelves. Yeah. Poppy Street Books, I said eventually. I went there a lot as a kid.

Did it shut recently?

I'm not sure. I just walked there from my house and the place is empty. They've taken out the shelves. It looks like a cavity.

She typed. I closed my eyes. She would say she was sorry, and I would have to either say the dignified lie, that I was fine, or debase myself by trying to articulate any of the immature ways in which I didn't feel fine.

My phone buzzed. I opened my eyes. She'd said, What are you doing now?

Puzzled, I blinked a few times as the dialogues I'd been imagining faded away. I'm standing in a gas station convenience store across from the sour gummies.

Do you think you'll buy any sour gummies?

Oddly, a smile pulled at my lips. I don't know, lol. Why?

It seems like you should do something nice for yourself.

I'm not a big sour gummy person, I said. But I appreciate the idea.

A notification dropped down from the top of the screen. Selina Chan paid you $5.00. "Sour gummy equivalent."

Excuse me, I texted her. Are you being thoughtful? What is this???

Elaborate act of sabotage, she said.

I hit the laugh react on her text, then said, I do want to know what the extremely euphemistic "City has lots on its mind" means.

She typed for a while. What arrived was, City is OK, really. Good luck with your brother.

My smile faded. The sign-off seemed so abrupt, even cold.

I said Thanks and tucked my phone away, feeling off-kilter. She didn't want to admit anything to me, which shouldn't have been a surprise, but still somehow felt like an unpleasant reminder.

Before I left, I did buy a box of M&M's, which I held on to in my jacket pocket as I walked home, feeling the contents shift and slide inside.

Over dinner, I said to my mom, "Poppy Street Books closed."

"Oh, that's right," she said, giving my forearm a little squeeze. "I'm so sorry, Pijay. I meant to text you. You loved that place."

"Yeah."

I kept my face serene. Why I'd brought it up, I didn't know. I'd come all this way to see her, and she'd taken all this cleaning and cooking upon herself to make my visit a happy one. She'd made tofu sisig for dinner, my lifelong favorite.

"I don't know what you do to this," I said, pointing my fork at my bowl. "I can never get it to taste this good."

After dinner, I took a long shower and slid into bed, staring up at the shelves, at my high school diploma, cobwebbed in the far corner.

I found myself thinking of the journalist from Daly City who'd emailed me. *I'm sure you have lots of demands on your time, but it'd be an honor to have you in our pages!*

I turned over in bed, the little guilts of the afternoon knitting into a hard lump in my stomach. It was hard not to see Poppy Street's closure as symbolic. During my longest stretch away from California, the period of my life that I'd been most self-obsessed, when I hadn't even joined my family for the holidays, Poppy Street had closed. Some ungrateful part of me was still trying to escape the place and the people that had raised me, treating them like a burden instead of trying to give back.

I fished out my phone and found the email.

Hey Brian, I wrote, so sorry for the late reply. I've been struggling to keep on top of my emails, but I'm actually in Daly City the next few days! If you still want to do an interview, I'd be happy to grab coffee? Thanks for reaching out.

Then I opened up my text with Kevin. I'm sorry, I wrote. I didn't know you felt that way about Elena's loans, but I get why it must have been frustrating. I wish you'd gone to Northwestern too. You know I would have done the same thing for you.

After about fifteen minutes, Kevin said, Yeah I know. I'm not mad at you, ik it was cool of you to do that for her. the whole thing just sucks. Lunch at Chibog tomorrow? You have to pay though lol

I got you, I said. I always did.

I walked the San Bruno Mountain trail the next day with nothing but my water bottle and a copy of Daisy Hildyard's *Emergency*. My lunch with Kevin had been mostly commiseration. I worried my way up the trail, but by the time I stood up from my reading spot an hour later, my thoughts had calmed. I spent the way home wondering if, when I got to my phone, I'd find that Selina had texted me again, reopening the door she'd shut yesterday.

She hadn't sent anything. What had arrived was an email from Brian Falwell: Hey, thank you so much for getting back to me! This is great timing. Your new book is out soon, right? I can time the profile to publish right around then!

I drove down 280 the next morning to meet Brian at 85C, an Asian bakery where I maxed out my daily sugar intake with a brilliantly marbled Thai tea. Brian drank drip coffee. He looked almost identical to the way I remembered him from high school, tanned and round-faced and dressed in casual wear: Stanford hoodie, joggers clinging to his knobby ankles, neon sneakers. He had not one but two bouncing knees and an eager, wide-eyed expression that made me feel like we were on the brink of some incredible discovery together. Off the record, we talked high school for a while, the reputations of clubs that would probably be unrecognizable to us now, friends and acquaintances.

"Wait, wait," he said, snapping his fingers, "you're not still dating Cecilia, are you? Cecilia—what was her name? Mc—something?"

"McCrory," I said with a laugh. "Yeah, no, we broke up in college. She went to Bryn Mawr, and—"

"Oh, long distance sucks."

"A lot, yeah. I spent half my sophomore year on trains to Philly."

Brian looked wistful. "Man, she was beautiful, though."

Cecilia *had* been beautiful, and flighty, and the first girl in my life to show interest in me. I'd spent my second year of college terrified of losing her, even as I grew more confused and upset that I was the only one traveling to maintain our relationship.

Another half hour passed before we arrived at the topic of writing. I'd scanned a couple of Brian's pieces, and he seemed like a good profiler, not too interested in poetic flourishes or creating grand narratives about his subjects' lives. As he asked me about Yale, a continuous stream of shorthand appeared on the notebook in front of him.

"Okay," he said, once I'd described the five years it had taken to get *These Extraordinary Times* down on paper. "I don't want to jump ahead, I mean, I want to get the context and everything, but . . ." He shook his head. "Hearing it took that long, and knowing what happened with Selina Chan? That's brutal."

I sipped five grams of sugar through my straw. I'd known we'd get to the feud eventually. Last night I'd found myself dismantling and reassembling sentences in my mind, ideas of how to describe the fight, now that Selina and I had a truce. But somehow I still didn't feel prepared to talk about her.

"Yeah," I said, setting down my drink. "Yeah, it definitely felt brutal."

"I've read a lot of your press to get a sense of the timeline, but that day the first *City* review came out . . . can you describe what went through your head?"

I hesitated. "So, um—I want to preface this by saying that I've actually been talking to Selina a little more in the past few weeks."

"Whoa. For real?" He jotted a note.

"Yeah. We have a truce going."

Brian laughed. "Wow, okay, I did not expect that." He set down his pen. "If you don't want me to mention a truce, I won't, but can I ask how it happened?"

"No, yeah, maybe better not to mention it—I don't know how she'd feel about it. But we were both stuck in the city over the holidays."

"Right. There was that storm."

"Exactly. And she . . . I don't know. She's a complicated person. Apparently she stays there every year, you know, on her own, and she doesn't seem to have any problems with that. I guess part of me is kind of impressed by her."

"Begrudgingly?" said Brian.

I laughed. "Yeah, less begrudgingly now. Anyway, that's the context. As for the review . . ." Brian picked his pen back up and waited. I winced, rubbing one hand through my hair. "I'm still of two minds about everything that's . . . I mean, I remember that day clearer than any single other day, I think, from my twenties. My college graduation, the day Bill flew out here, the actual book sale—I don't remember any of those as clearly as the day of the review. Maybe some of that is the drastic before and after, right? Like, when I woke up that morning, my whole future seemed rock-solid, guaranteed, written in permanent ink, and by the time I went to sleep that night, it was all gone.

"At the same time, I mean . . . it *is* Selina's job, and all she cares about is doing it with integrity. And obviously that has to mean being honest, even if . . ."

"If it feels like . . ." Brian said, nodding, jotting notes.

"Yeah, even if on my end, it feels like this is the worst possible thing that could happen to you as a writer. So, I had this knee-jerk response. Like, you just think, 'What are this person's qualifications,' 'What kind of a person does she have to be to . . . to do this to people.' But she's not trying to speak for everybody. She's just a person with an opinion. Which is something that I've told myself so many times in so many contexts now, and some days it makes everything feel more manageable, and other days it makes everything worse."

Brian's eyebrows had risen, but he kept writing. "Wow. Yeah. Okay."

"Sorry." I laughed. The back of my neck felt hot. "I guess I've been trying to process a lot of this."

"No, no worries, man." He set down his pen and took another sip of his coffee. "Are you trying to decide whether to let things go?"

"I don't know." I hesitated. "Maybe it's the opposite. Like I'm trying to figure out what to hold on to."

The rest of the day was a blur of fog. In late afternoon, my mother and I walked westward toward the sea, and she asked, unprompted, "Pijay, have you been seeing anyone?"

"Not really."

"Not really. What does that mean?"

I curled my hands in my jacket pockets, glancing up the street at the headlamps, diffuse ovals through the fog. "Nothing. Yeah. It means no."

"You know I liked Kate."

I laughed. "That was five years ago, Mom."

"Still! You took such good care of each other."

I didn't answer. My relationship with Kate had been defined by her life in residency, urgent, rigid, and scheduled. I'd dropped everything to see her when she was available. I'd molded my life around the shape of hers like wet clay pushed against a hard object. It bothered me, sometimes, that nobody in my family had seemed to recognize this, the way I'd started to slip-slide so completely into her life.

"What about you?" I asked. "Are you dating?"

"Me?" My mom laughed. "Of course not."

"Wait, why of course not? I thought you met someone at that book club."

"Oh, *Alan*. Pff. Wrong for both of us." The wind lifted my mother's hair, blowing a few strands across her face. She caught it back and bundled it up at the crown of her head with one of her plastic clasps. "To tell you the truth, I find it a lot easier, being alone. There's no trouble, no dramatics. After your father, everything was such a relief . . . the relaxation of it, you know. My systems had been in overdrive for so long."

I'd heard some variation of this from my mother since I was twelve years old. I didn't know why, now, the words disturbed me.

"Um, that overdrive feeling," I said. "How do you know whether that's a positive or a negative?" I paused. "Because it's not like being interested in somebody is a quiet feeling, either, right? So, I mean, how do you know if you're feeling agitation or excitation or whatever it is for the right or wrong reasons?"

My mom looked up at me, a sad tilt to the creases around her eyes. "Well, I don't know, Pijay. I never knew." She laughed. "That's why everything happened this way, isn't it?" And she slipped her arm through mine and walked me to the sea, where we watched the waves turn over and over.

I flew back to New York the next day. I'd imagined California would open my head up and scrub my skull cavity clean somehow, but as the plane hit the tarmac at JFK, I felt no measurable difference in my thoughts, in my level of contentment, clarity, anything. I opened my phone. The notifications began to roll in. Chan Pan Support Group, Sibling Megatext, The Obviously Evil Bird Archive, Arthur, Bill, Dad, some unsaved number that was probably spam, nothing from Selina.

She wasn't obliged to text me, of course. She'd started our previous conversation, so maybe the onus was on me to reach out, if I wanted to speak with her again.

And I did. I could admit that much to myself: I wanted to speak with her, the way I'd want to scratch an itch, the way I'd want to satisfy hunger, but I didn't know where that instinct came from, or whether it was the type of instinct that led anywhere good.

Unthinking, I opened the spam text, only to realize that it wasn't spam.

> Hi Parker! Sorry this text is so late. Bookstores get crazy around the holidays. But it's Emily from Word 😌 I wondered would you want to have dinner sometime? Again, no pressure if you think it'll make anything weird for the launch! We can also keep it totally professional!

I was still deciding how to respond when I unlocked our apartment door an hour later. "Hey, he's back," said Arthur as I unlaced my sneakers. He lay on the sofa in a half-open bathrobe, his work laptop balanced on his stomach.

"I'm back," I said. "Listen—are you busy?"

"Nah. Why?"

"This woman who works at the bookstore asked me out."

"Oh, for real?" Arthur levered himself up on the sofa. "The one with the curly hair, or the one who's like fifty years old?"

"Arthur. What do you think?"

"Right. The fifty-year-old."

"I hate you."

"Same. So, what'd you say?"

"Nothing yet." I dropped my duffel and settled into a chair. "I don't know. I'm . . . she's running my book launch, for one thing."

"Good point. Don't shit where you eat."

"Bro. Could you not describe my love life as taking a shit?"

"Do mine ears deceive me? Does the renowned author not know what a metaphor is?"

I rolled my eyes, smiling. "Anyway, even without the launch, I'm . . . I don't know."

"Why don't you know? She's hot and likes books. Isn't that, like, all two of your boxes checked?"

For the first time, I considered trying to explain to Arthur what had happened with Selina over the holidays, but I could predict his reaction down to the beat. He'd howl me out of the room, urge me to say yes to Emily purely because she wasn't Selina Chan.

"I guess I've been thinking I . . . I might be interested in something else," I said, looking down at Emily's text.

"But you don't even know this woman. How do you know you want something different?"

"Yeah. That's true, you're right." I hesitated, then stood. "I'm going to unpack."

As I headed down the hall, Arthur called, "You should do it, Park. You're the one who's always talking about how apps are a textureless way to meet somebody."

"And they are," I called back before shutting myself away in my sanctuary.

Having settled into my hammock, I reread Monday's conversation with Selina, trying to decipher her intentions, which seemed slippery and changeable. It felt like trying to interpret the shift in a summer wind. I watched the ceiling sway with the movement of my hammock. That night, discovering the empty space where something I'd loved had been, I hadn't turned to my family or friends but, inexplicably, to her. Stranger was the fact that she'd made me feel better, her small, calm texts puncturing my feelings of distance and self-pity.

Yet I couldn't even admit to Arthur or my mother that I was talking with her. The agitation I felt whenever she spoke to me—was that the overdrive my mom had described? My body seeking out a high-conflict situation because it couldn't distinguish between an adrenaline rush and desire?

I felt suddenly desperate for clarity, any hard answer, any obvious truth. I found myself closing our texts and navigating to the *City* website and, out of four years' habit, reopening her review of *These Extraordinary Times.*

As I reread, the hum in me quieted, then died out.

At three hundred pages, the book might have been a disappointment. At nine hundred, it feels like a cruelty.

The words hurt as much now as they had four years ago. In fact, they found new places to hurt, because now I imagined her looking me in the eye and speaking them.

Selina had once told me she didn't do retractions. I knew she chose every word with care. She could easily have written a pan without punchlines, without a drop of ridicule, but this was what she'd always maintained: That I was an insult to literary culture, not just talentless but beneath contempt. That I'd failed at the one thing I'd ever loved.

I stood up so quickly that my vision swam. No, a few polite questions on Monday didn't make Selina Chan a kind person, no matter what her friends said. Had I brainwashed myself into thinking she was anything other than disdainful and unsympathetic, just because—why? Because she was beautiful? Because she could be funny? Because she had a bad relationship with her parents? A truce was one thing, but was my self-worth really so low that I'd feel *interested* in somebody who'd written about me like this?

That seemed like the mindset of a desperate person, but I didn't have to be desperate. I had a career that impressed ninety-nine percent of people. I'd had enough girlfriends and second dates to know that, despite the way I'd felt growing up, I actually wasn't bad-looking, and since signing up for my overpriced gym, I knew I was in the best shape of my life.

Didn't I think I was good enough for somebody like—like Emily, somebody who smiled when she saw me?

I reopened Emily's text. Hey, Happy New Year! I wrote. It's great to hear from you. Dinner sounds fun.

Oh I'm so glad! she said. What's your schedule like?

We set a date for the following weekend, and I set my phone face down on my bedside table and began to unpack my bag. I felt clear-headed, unconfused, undisturbed. I felt ready for the steps ahead, and I could anticipate how it would feel to take them. This was how it was all supposed to be.

Chapter Twenty

Selina

The articles had begun to appear late last week, mixed in at the bottom of our front page, like arsenic in the sugar bowl. A scan over our titles went like this:

"Borges Spoke to Me in Winter—Essay"
"The Plow and the Mountain: Jennifer Croft on Translating Nobel Winner Olga Tokarczuk"
"Ranking Kendall Jenner's Beach Reads"
"Scenes from 1810s Munich in Newly Unearthed Lithographs"

In the days since, Hayden's requested articles had crept higher and multiplied. By January 21—the day of *City*'s anniversary party—the piece just below the masthead was "10 Bookish Gadgets Under $15 on Amazon That You Have to Try!"

I found myself wondering what Parker might think. I had to wonder. Since last Monday, we hadn't spoken.

That night, I'd considered telling him about Hayden's new directive, but he'd been shouldering so much in California. I hadn't wanted to pile my own issues onto him, too.

I couldn't understand what had happened. He'd seemed strangely intent on turning the conversation to me, as though his problems and feelings were barely worth the few sentences that he'd taken to describe them. I'd thought he might text me the next day to restart the conversation. Instead, silence.

"Why didn't you invite him to this?" Jacob asked while he, Cassie, and I walked toward the *City* anniversary venue. The magazine had booked our usual event space in Greenpoint, a five-hundred-person hall not far from Jacob and Cassie's apartment.

"Because," I said, "I only get two comp tickets, and I invited you."

"One of us could have stayed home," Cassie said. "Could've saved on the babysitter."

"I don't even know if Parker's back from California."

"You could have—"

"Jacob, I wasn't going to uninvite one of you just for an excuse to text a man who doesn't want to talk to me."

Cassie straightened her sequined suit jacket with a convulsive shiver. Jacob settled his arm over her shoulder. "Well," said Cassie, "his loss."

I laughed.

"What?" said Cassie.

"Nothing," I said, but I was thinking about all the people Parker had described to me over the last few weeks, the dozen childhood friends who now lived in the city, his siblings and parents and roommate, the authors he'd befriended recently, a constellation of people loved by him. The idea that I could somehow represent a loss in his life was laughable.

"Is everything booked for February?" I asked. "Did you decide where to stop in Thailand?"

"We are booked and ready," said Jacob. "The hotels are so cheap it feels criminal."

They outlined their plans as we walked through a melting world.

The past few days had seen temperatures in the forties, and the last of the Christmas snowstorm was finally trickling from roofs, dripping down stairways, sliding off banisters, rolling down the gutters in long glittering snakes. We passed by the glowing window of a laundromat, its white-blue interior deserted except for one woman hauling armloads of linens out of a dryer.

The venue stood on the next block, an artful spike of gray stone with a line of rideshares standing out front. A measly little red carpet spanned the six feet of sidewalk between the road and the heavy driftwood door.

Just inside, a table was laden with extravagant party favors. *City*-branded tote bags had been stuffed with signed copies of *Pathogenius*—Joyce had pulled a few strings—as well as *City*-branded pens, notepads, and postcard books featuring vintage *City* covers.

"Are we allowed to take these?" said Cassie. "Or are they for the people who paid for tickets?"

"Don't be so loud about it," said Jacob, helping himself to a bag. "People will hate us."

As we moved into the venue, past flower beds that had been raised out of the concrete floor, into a sea of bare twinkling bulbs, I spotted Scott in a tuxedo, Kellie in a cream linen dress, Hayden wearing crimson.

"Selina Chan," said a low, cordial voice. A slender, deeply tanned man in a canary-yellow suit had sidled up to us.

"Anthony, hi," I said, shaking his hand. "Jacob, Cassie, this is Anthony Villano. He writes for *The New York Times Book Review*."

"And I've been trying to poach Selina for years," he said confidentially to Jacob and Cassie. "What do we think? Is this the year?" He leaned closer, his smile turning to a sympathetic grimace. "It can't be long now for *City*, right?"

"What do you mean?"

"Oh." Anthony thumbed his glasses up the bridge of his nose. "Well, I know *you're* not responsible for the, ah . . . change in direction of the coverage." He let out an apologetic laugh.

My face warmed. *The New York Times Book Review* had presumably never posted anything as degrading as "10 Bookish Gadgets Under $15 on Amazon That You Have to Try!"

"Yes, we've had less creative control recently. But *City* is perfectly healthy." I waved to the elaborately decorated railings on the mezzanine. "I'd think that was clear."

"Really?" said Anthony. "I thought this was compensating for something. I mean, that ticket price . . ." His eyes strayed to the opposite side of the room. "Oh—I'm sorry, I have to catch Simon. *Simon!*"

As he hurried off, my cheeks continued to prickle. I scanned and spotted Scott again, near the musicians. "If it's okay with you two," I said to Jacob and Cassie, "I'm going to have a word with Scott."

"Sure thing," said Cassie. "We'll see who we can offend the most by not knowing who they are."

By the time I reached Scott, the warmth in my face had spread down to my neck. I unwound my scarf. "Selina," said Scott. "Love the dress."

"Thanks. Listen, Scott, I just talked with Anthony Villano, and he was acting like it's obvious that *City* is about to—to—I don't know." I dropped my voice, looking around at the glimmering formalwear. "Go bankrupt."

Scott buffed out a smudge on his wineglass instead of replying.

"Scott." My voice rose. "That's not happening, is it? Please tell me it's not happening."

"No, no." He raised his hands. "Well, not imminently."

"What do you mean, *not imminently*?"

Scott set his wineglass on a high-top. "Hayden got word over Christmas that the rent on our office is hiking in March. Something to the tune of eight percent."

I couldn't speak. I didn't know the exact rent on our office, but I knew eight percent represented tens of thousands of dollars a month.

"So . . . yes. The ticket prices, the new 'content strategy' . . . these are Hayden's last-ditch efforts to keep us solvent. In her way, I think she's trying to help."

Around us, the string quartet's melody floated up to the high stone reaches of the room. The *City Magazine* banner on the wall rippled as a small group of people passed beneath it, laughing and sipping tomato-red cocktails. Pretty sounds circulating through this hollow structure. I watched with disbelief.

"Maybe this strategy of hers will work," said Scott.

"Maybe. Yeah." I tried to collect myself. I knew that whatever I was feeling, Scott must be feeling it tenfold. "I guess, let's not assume anything catastrophic will happen."

"Exactly."

I excused myself and moved through clouds of perfume and cologne, holding up the navy silk of my dress. But the more I looked for Jacob and Cassie, the less I wanted to find them. They'd spent so much of the past four months worrying about me, my reputation, my position. I missed the days when I was nothing to worry about, for anybody.

I was attracting a number of nods and polite hellos, which I returned. Then a hand brushed my shoulder. A red-haired woman in a group of five. I recognized the long narrow slope of her nose, her downturned eyes.

"Selina, hi! Mary Clark."

"Right. *The Guardian*," I said. "It's good to see you."

She waltzed through a few niceties about the party, the drinks, the lights. Then, with relish, she said, "And it's been so fun to follow along with this feud between you and Parker Navarro."

"Oh . . . Thank you," I said, thinking of Parker standing alone in a convenience store. His family. His inexplicable silence.

"I kept wondering, you know—what on earth is she going to say tomorrow?" Mary laughed. "What part of this man's career is she going to end next?"

"I'm a photographer," added a man beside her, rocking backward and forward on his heels as though preparing to take a leap. "And I've got to say, it's fascinating to get a peek behind the veil. These author-critic relationships, obviously I know they're not friendly, but . . ."

". . . but you really think he's the scum of the earth," said a woman across the circle. They all began laughing again.

The smile was frozen on my face. I remembered Hayden saying, *It's a feud, Selina. It's all about you.*

She'd been right. Even among other journalists, nobody had cared about my high-minded ideas of proving the value of our work, defending our history. That was never going to save us. People had followed what I'd said because they were finally getting access to the things I'd tried to keep hidden my whole career. My personal frameworks of opinion. My private biases. My petty cruelty and—in this moment, it seemed perfectly obvious—my profound shortsightedness.

"Selina?" said a voice at my shoulder. Jacob and Cassie had found me, Cassie finishing the dregs of a cocktail.

She took one look at my face and said, "Maybe we should think about heading out."

"No," I said immediately, "we can stay."

"We were actually getting texts from the babysitter. Sorry to steal her," she added to Mary's group. Then she casually took the coat from my arm, draped it over my shoulders, and steered me toward the door.

"We can have a nightcap at ours or something," said Jacob, flowing along at Cassie's side. "Thanks for the invite, by the way. Great wine."

I nodded, mute.

When we were out in the night, returning down the sidewalk into the relative quiet, Cassie said, "What were they talking about?"

"Nothing. The feud. Parker."

"Must be weird, now that you don't hate him anymore." She paused. "You don't, do you?"

"No," I said quietly. "No, I think I seriously misjudged him."

"You sure?" said Jacob. "I saw the video. He wasn't exactly Prince Charming, with the yelling, and the calling you a monster, and everything."

"Well, no, he shouldn't have confronted me. But it *was* questionable of Scott to assign me his second book, considering what happened with the first one." I buttoned my coat and folded my hands beneath my elbows. "The thing is—I thought Parker hunted me down because he was this shallow egomaniac. You know, some of these writers, they love writing so much less than they love their own image. Their end goal is to charge seventy-five-thousand-dollar speaking fees and never talk to somebody outside publishing again. And some of them *do* come from these backgrounds where they're just drowning in money and entitlement, and I thought that was Parker, but—"

I glanced into the laundromat again, now completely empty, an oasis of light glancing off steel.

"Turns out it's not?" said Jacob.

"No. It's not." I looked down at my shoes. Embroidered flats. The heels had really taken it out of me on New Year's Eve.

The thought of New Year's made me slow, then stop.

"Hey." Cassie gave me a bracing squeeze on the bicep. As a rock climber she was probably unaware that her bracing squeeze felt like a normal person's death threat. "This is a good thing, Selina. It's a positive development to realize somebody's not as bad as you thought they were."

"Right. Yes. But I'm still the person who's been going after him and his book, repeatedly, for—I mean, for what, then? To try to turn things around for *City*, like that was a realistic goal?" My parents' email floated across my mind. "To get the last word?"

Jacob and Cassie exchanged another look. A weight was accumulating in the pit of my stomach. I'd been called a bitch since I was fifteen years old, and twice as often since I'd entered the disproportionately male sphere of criticism. Parker had even said it himself, though not in so many words, called me arrogant and cold.

Maybe his story in *The Paris Review* had shown me as I really was. Whereas maybe he had always just been a kind, intelligent person who deserved an apology.

"Hey," said Jacob. "You didn't do anything wrong. Criticism is your job, Selina."

"I know that. But taking on his second book . . . it felt like punching down. Part of me even knew that. I tried to tell Scott and Hayden, but they overrode me."

Cassie raked her fingers through her ponytail. Where Jacob had softened under my distress, she'd firmed up. "Well, if you feel bad about it, you can always apologize now. Right? Hey." She waited for me to glance over at her. "Right?"

"Yes. That's true."

"There we go. Let's get home, I'm freezing my ass off." She moved into the crook of Jacob's arm again.

I watched them arranged like subjects in a painting, Cassie's black hair spilling messily past her neck, Jacob's eyes pushing up into crescents as he smiled, his hand dappling Cassie's cheek with shadow as he brushed back her bangs. They glanced over to make sure I'd fall into step with them.

I wanted to say, *I love you two, do you know that? And do you know how much?* But I'd have needed a lifetime to articulate it.

An hour and a hot cider later, I left their apartment into the cold, dripping night. Wet gusts traced my forehead, my cheeks.

Halfway to the train, my steps slowed. I came to a halt beside a halal cart and looked up the street toward McGolrick Park.

After a week of silence, texting Parker an apology felt faintly desperate, as though my only reason for apologizing was that he wasn't speaking to me. But he'd said his apartment was beside the coffee shop opposite the park. He was virtually on my way home, and while 9 PM was late, it wasn't inappropriately late for a five-minute talk.

Before I could think about it too hard, I was heading up the street toward the shouts and laughs emanating from the bar on the corner, toward the whisper of naked tree branches rubbing against each other in the wind. I turned up my coat collar and wiped a trickle of snowmelt from my brow.

Two identical brick apartments flanked the coffee shop. The second, beside its column of buzzers, listed NAVARRO / LEUNG on the ground floor, 1E. The lights were on. His roommate? Or was Parker home from California?

I didn't buzz. I turned back toward the park, flexing my fingers inside my leather gloves. I didn't have to do this; our truce could be enough. I didn't technically owe Parker this conversation.

But I remembered the way he'd looked at me in that subterranean maze of shelves on New Year's Eve, the heat that had stirred in me when he'd said, *That's not what you want, is it?*

Did he talk like that to other people?

Why did I want him to keep talking like that to me? To keep messaging me late into the nights?

Why did I want to tell him what had been happening with *City* since the New Year? Why did I feel that he would immediately understand the gut-deep, almost irrational fear that the idea of the magazine's bankruptcy induced in me?

I stood on the steps for minutes, silent, trying to decide whether to retreat or move forward. Then the door of the building swung open and a man in his sixties held it open for me, and I said automatically, "Thank you," and walked inside, feeling as though the choice had been made for me.

I passed the dented mailboxes set into the foyer wall and entered an antechamber out of which led an old wooden staircase with a carved banister. I faced the door marked 1E and tugged off my gloves and, wishing I weren't wearing a floor-length silk gown, worked a few tangles out of my hair, trying to feel more prepared.

Go, I thought, and rapped three times on the door.

The muffled sound of a male voice. Then footsteps, growing closer. I swallowed and found my mouth dry.

The rattle of a lock, and the door swung open, and Parker was there in front of me, dressed in dark jeans and a LONDON REVIEW OF BOOKS T-shirt, his hair messy.

He froze. For a moment we just stared at each other. It occurred to me how beautiful he looked, this rumpled, private version of him.

"Selina," he said.

"Parker. Hi."

"Hey." His eyes strayed toward his apartment. So did mine. In the visible wedge of the place I caught the corner of a ceiling-high bookcase, a rug with blocks of geometric color, a modestly sized television paused on the acting credits of a movie. Two art prints in thin black frames above a saddle leather sofa.

"Um," he said. "Why are you—sorry, I—"

I'd never seen him so flustered. I searched for some on-ramp into the conversation, something that wouldn't just fling me headfirst into the apology on his doorstep. I wanted to go in, for us to find that compulsive New Year's rhythm. Jacob would have called me predictable, but yes, I wanted to do this right, or not at all.

But before I could speak, a high, sweet voice came from behind the door. "Parker? Who is it?"

Parker glanced back and eased the door wider. A dining table came into view.

Standing at its far corner was Emily from the festival. Easy-laughing, kind-faced Emily. She held two stacked plates in one hand and a pizza box in the other, clearing the remains of dinner.

When she saw me, her brows flew high. "Oh my gosh! Selina Chan, right?"

"Yes," I managed to say.

"I'm Emily Shapiro. I saw your panel with Parker at the Wiseman Festival. It was so interesting!"

Parker looked back to me, unreadable.

The heat had leached from my face. I felt strangely distant. Two empty beer bottles stood on the table, and Emily's coat dangled half-off one of the chairs, as if it had been flung there.

"Thank you," I said. "You're a bookseller, right?"

"Yeah, I work at Word. It's about twenty minutes that way." She pointed through the wall behind her.

"Right."

"Sorry, I interrupted," Emily said, making to retreat with the dirty plates. "I can—"

"No, please, you didn't." My own voice sounded smooth and blank. "I was just leaving *City*'s anniversary event around the corner, and I remembered. Parker mentioned a while back that he had a copy of Clarice Lispector's first book, and the library hold list is seven weeks long, so"—I made myself look back to him—"I thought I'd ask to borrow it."

"Right. Of course," said Parker. "Let me . . . yeah."

He left the door hanging open and jogged deeper into the apartment, down a hallway I couldn't see. Emily set their dinnerware on the counter. "Do you want a cup of tea or anything? I mean, it's Parker's tea, but I'm sure he—"

"No, thank you. I appreciate it, but I'm on the way to the train."

Parker's footfalls again, still quick. He wanted this over with.

He reappeared holding *Near to the Wild Heart* and held it out.

"Thank you," I said, taking the book.

"Sure. Of course." His eyes fell to the cover. "I, um, I hope you like it."

"Yes. I hope so too. It was nice to meet you, Emily." I lifted a hand. "Have a good weekend."

"You too!" Emily said with real enthusiasm.

Parker nodded, but I couldn't look at him. I didn't wait for him to shut the door. I turned and headed out of the darkened foyer and into the eye-watering winter cold and it was only halfway down the block that I began to feel my hands again, and to realize that I was blinking unusually fast, and that my breaths were uneven.

I walked more quickly toward the train, yanking my gloves on, the world a blur around me. I could only see Parker's shock, his disturbance to find me on the threshold of his life. Mortification and realization were moving through me in slow, sickly, alternating waves.

Somehow, despite his text silences and our whole acrimonious history, I really had fooled myself into thinking he could be interested in me, purely because he'd been drunk and lonely on New Year's Eve. And maybe that night, if I'd tried to touch him, he would have reached toward me out of morbid curiosity, in the way that men used to, before I grew tired of feeling like a foreign land that people were always trying to document and interpret. But of course in his right mind he would search for someone sweet and kind and open, because everybody wanted to be liked in uncomplicated ways, and I'd never loved anything without twisting it into knots.

Chapter Twenty-One

Parker

"I'm so glad you two are on better terms now," said Emily.

I smiled across the table. "Yeah."

"I did tell you at the lit fest she probably wasn't that bad."

"Yeah, you did, yeah."

"That must mean no more feuding, right? What a relief with the book launch coming up, huh?"

A small, artificial laugh escaped me. "My publisher will probably ask me to start a second round for sales. But yeah. You're right."

Emily touched my shoulder as she headed to the bathroom. She shut herself in and the silence enclosed me. I sat motionless at the table.

Had Selina Chan really just knocked on my apartment door at 9 PM, out of nowhere? Had that actually happened?

I gripped my mug and stared forward, not seeing the beer bottles on their coasters. I saw Selina's face. Her instant of surprise when she'd heard Emily's voice.

Why had I felt so embarrassed, so exposed, like I needed to explain myself?

Emily jogged back down the hall and put on her coat. "I've got to get back for my roommate's birthday thing, but I had a lot of fun. Do you want to hang out again next week?"

I collected myself and rose from my chair. "Yeah, um, I'm free," I said, walking her to the door.

"Wednesday?" she said. "I get off at eight thirty—we could do a late dinner?"

"That sounds great."

On the doormat she rose up on her toes and kissed me, her lips cool and soft, and I felt that pleasant buzz in my fingertips, the same thing I'd felt an hour ago, when, lying on the sofa, she'd turned to me halfway through *Roman Holiday*, and I'd dipped my face to hers and kissed her with a kind of determination.

Once she'd gone, I washed out the beer bottles, wiped down the table, and opened my laptop. After one look at my draft I shut my computer and pushed it away, disgusted, for some reason, by the sight.

Arthur slouched out of his room at eleven and crossed into the bathroom. "What's up," he said, emerging with his toothbrush sticking out of his mouth. "You have a good night with bookstore girl?"

"Yeah. She's nice, it went well."

"Thought so. Heard the movie going." He wiggled his eyebrows. "What's her thing?"

"Um, she's from Michigan and studied English in college, and she has two sisters. She's into the indie rock scene. She plays guitar, which is cool."

"Cool, yeah." Arthur went into the bathroom and spat.

Lying in bed an hour later, inhaling the floral hint that Emily had left on my T-shirt, I tried to think of her. But it was Selina's instant of surprise that kept intruding into my mind.

I'd never so much as taken Selina's hand. For God's sake, she'd never so much as given me an indication that she liked my company.

Didn't she? said some idiotic part of me. We'd sent 128 emails over a week. Then New Year's, and our conversation while I was in California. Did all this sum to anything besides Selina being pleasantly surprised that she didn't hate me?

I passed a restless weekend on my laptop, trying and failing to write. In cafés and libraries, I tried to write. Deleted. I wondered if, rather than self-identifying as a writer, I should tell people I was a deleter. *Wednesday night*, I told myself. A second date. This was going to be fun. Why couldn't I have fun? Maybe *High and Dry*'s upcoming release was making me incapable of recognizing and appreciating fun. Selina didn't message me about the Lispector.

On Monday night, I began to wonder if that book had been the real reason she'd come.

I knew the question was trouble as soon as it occurred to me, but I couldn't put it back in the box. Doubt began to eat up minutes. Swaths of minutes. Why else would she have visited my apartment?

I ruminated on her cryptic expression in the Book Bar. *You don't ever have to apologize to me for your opinion.* How long had I looked at her after that, feeling as though she'd reached forward and taken some vulnerable part of me in her hand?

Wednesday came as a relief. That afternoon, Bill called to tell me that I'd been invited to be the keynote speaker at a book festival in Seattle, whose chair had, apparently, adored *High and Dry*. I felt steadier than I had in days as Emily and I walked from Word to a vegetarian restaurant a block away, then settled into a corner where we could look through a glass window and see a brick oven in the kitchen.

"So, besides the good news, how was your day?" Emily asked.

"Not that productive. I mean, I spent about seven hours trying to write a paragraph, then got rid of the paragraph."

"Ah, I'm so sorry!" she said. "Are you okay?"

"Oh, yeah, of course. I bet most people would be horrified at the amount of time authors spend failing to write."

"It must feel so cool, though. I mean, doing the thing you love."

"It does, yeah. I'm beyond lucky." The words came easily. I'd said them before. I poured her some water and asked, "How was the store?"

"Pretty good, pretty good. Had a lady doing that thing where she asks for a book she saw four months ago, but she doesn't remember the title, author, or genre."

I laughed. "Did you figure it out?"

"I don't know!" She laughed too. "Like, we tried. She bought this book, and she was like, I'm pretty sure this is the one. So, I hope it was the right one."

"Yeah, hope so."

"Right?"

"Yeah." I took a quick drink of my wine. She was watching me, smiling, in a way that reminded me of Kate, this pause a gentle prompt that she was ready for a segue. "You, um—are you ready for your sister to visit?"

"So ready. We're looking at doing Ellis Island. She's never done the tourist stuff before. I mean, neither have I."

"Oh, yeah, it's a cool museum," I said.

"You've been there? How was it?"

"Um, thought-provoking." I hesitated. "It felt sort of ghostly to me. Not in the sense of anything paranormal. But there's something about the architecture, or maybe, like, the pilgrimage aspect of taking the ferry out there, that put me in this mindset of . . . I don't know. Being more aware of the people who passed through a hundred and fifty years ago than any of the people who were physically there with me. Maybe that's just the sign of a good museum? I don't know. I'm not sure if that makes sense."

"No, for sure!" Emily took a drink of wine. "That sounds so interesting. I'm excited to check it out!"

I asked about her parents, who were vacationing in Florida. She asked about my siblings, and I described their jobs. I kept waiting for some engine to start, something that would propel us into some different territory, but I couldn't describe that other place. If someone had asked me what I wanted from her, from this, I wouldn't have been able to answer, and so I sat there feeling as though my restlessness and dissatisfaction were completely unfair to her.

After we'd finished eating, she reached out and took my hand. I smiled instinctively.

"I listened to that band you mentioned," I said. "Hannah and the Peach Trees. I liked their first album."

"No way!" she said. "What'd you think?"

"Cool sound. I liked how that distorted guitar keeps punching into the first half of the album, and then the second half has that rougher edge."

"Oh! Yeah. What'd you think of the lyrics?"

I hesitated. "I'd have to listen again. With the filter on the vocals, I didn't hear a lot of them. Are they—do you listen to them for the lyrics, mostly?"

"Yeah, their lyrics are so good."

Oh, God, I thought, *why am I having such a bad time?*

I looked at her hand in mine and tried to focus on it. The little tattoos on her knuckles. I'd asked her about those last Friday.

I squeezed her hand and let go. "Hey, I'm sorry, I should be getting home."

"No, totally fine! Me too. Um—"

We sidled around the table and bundled up in silence before moving toward the door together. "Listen," I said once we'd exited onto the sidewalk, "I . . . I don't think we should see each other again."

"Oh." Her lashes fluttered in surprise.

"Sorry, I just—"

"Did I do something? Or, like, say something, or—?"

"No, not at all. I think you're really cool. And beautiful. It's just . . ." I balked. She was going to get upset, or angry. What was I doing, ending things with somebody so completely my type, because of—what? Some inarticulable feeling of discontentment? I could have gone on another date like this, a dozen more, and told Arthur they'd gone well, and I wouldn't even have felt like I was lying.

What did I want, if it wasn't this?

"Hey. Parker." Emily raised her hands. "It's okay. I know this is sort of a weird time, with the book coming out so soon."

"Right, yeah. I really am sorry. I probably shouldn't have said yes, with everything that's been happening."

"No worries." She opened her arms. "Hug it out?"

I hugged her, then watched her go with an immense, miserable feeling of relief.

By the time I arrived home, Arthur had shut himself in his room, and I could hear the guttural exclamations of a video game bleeding beneath his door. I stripped off my drizzle-dampened outerwear, took a long, hot shower, and slid between my bedsheets, and as though I'd always known I was going to get home and do exactly this, I navigated to my text messages and opened my conversation with Selina.

January 10. Her curt, inexplicable signoff. *City is OK, really. Good luck with your brother.*

I began to type.

What do you think of the Lispector?

Before I could think myself out of it, I hit Send.

My pulse began to sound in my ears. My gaze flicked from the phone screen to my darkened bedroom window, which looked out the back of the building, past the fire escape. Telephone wires laced the stars. It was almost eleven o'clock, and I hadn't texted her for more than two weeks. She would probably reply in the morning, if at all.

The phone buzzed in my hand. I felt a hit of energy like a pistol had just popped at a starting line.

Hard to process the imaginative power of a 21-year-old writer who somehow seems to know everything about being alive.

I know, right? I wrote. I'm so glad I didn't read this when I was 21. I would have broken in half.

Agreed. Thanks for the loan.

The ellipsis appeared as she kept typing. Then it vanished.

I waited. Nothing.

I said, No problem.

I paused, then typed, But you didn't come over on Friday to borrow that book, did you?

My neck was prickling. I shifted between my sheets, overwarm. I hit Send.

No, she said.

Then why?

Her ellipsis appeared. My eyes started to burn; I didn't blink for twenty seconds, thirty. She was going to say something mundane, I told myself, something impersonal. Don't anticipate. There was nothing to anticipate.

A wall of text appeared, and adrenaline shot from my chest to my extremities.

I came by to apologize for not pushing back more forcefully against City assigning me High and Dry to review. To tell you the truth, when my editor assigned me the book, I expressed my doubts multiple times because of the way my previous review had been received, but he overruled me. That said, I suspect I could have argued with more conviction and passed the review on to one of my colleagues. I'm sorry I didn't take that step. It would have been more ethical, more professional, and a kinder thing to do.

The adrenaline faded. I felt as though I were sinking into my mattress, the comforter weighing me down, the darkness of my bedroom pressing in on me and my phone.

I was filled to my farthest reaches with absurd disappointment.

I closed my eyes and turned off the phone screen and rested its warm edge against my forehead. How could I be unhappy with an apology, the thing I'd craved since the first time we'd met?

The disappointment curdled into shame. I knew why. I'd wanted her to have come over for another reason: just to see me.

Like a masochist, somewhere between the hundredth email and the walk home on New Year's, I'd begun to want this from her. To want her.

But why would she want me? Some writer whose work she didn't even respect? Of course she'd been focused on the things she'd always cared about so passionately: critical professionalism, moral correctness. Meanwhile, some self-important part of me had wondered if she'd seemed off-balance because she'd seen Emily and me together.

Obviously Selina Chan didn't care who I was involved with. On New Year's, the instant I'd said something borderline suggestive—about what she might want—she'd left. She'd probably been embarrassed that I'd been drunk enough to say something like that.

I turned onto my back and stared up into the dark. I saw Selina, hovering ghostly against my vision, the shine of navy blue silk against her thighs, the set of her chin and the wine-reddened creases in her mouth. I closed my eyes and the vision clarified, and then, in my mind, I was sliding my hand over the side of her neck and leaning forward and tasting her lower lip. Drawing her through the door.

I rocked onto my side again. I turned on my phone and tried to focus. Selina had obviously put a lot into this message, this message that represented such an astonishing disappointment.

Thanks, Selina, I typed. An apology is a valuable thing, coming from you. I should also say I'm sorry for cornering you at the Maynard-Roth party to yell at you.

Oh, it's nothing that every author hasn't fantasized about.

Fantasized about. And now I was seeing her in the glimmering green dress she'd worn that night. I was feeling her fingertip impact my chest, remembering how, even then, I'd wanted to run my hand through the dark silk of her hair.

I'm a lucky man, I said, hating myself.

You are. I saw your post with the Anna's Book Club special editions yesterday. Has your hand recovered from signing all those tip-ins?

Absolutely not. Five sprained knuckles and a broken wrist.

Wow. How do you sign your books? With a solid punch?

I began to smile, even as the embarrassment and disappointment compacted into a painful little stone in my chest.

Uppercut-right hook combination, I said. It's good luck.

I don't think you need luck, Parker. You have something much better: months of rage-fueled publicity.

How does our truce factor into the rage-fueled publicity?

I was wondering the same thing. If you'd like to write another insulting short story, I can edit it for you this time.

Very sneaky, I said. You know, a couple of my friends asked if our initial fight was staged.

Ha. Why?

They thought I was too mild-mannered for it to be real.

It's like they don't even know you, she said, and for some reason I imagined her low, amused voice saying the words directly into my ear, and I turned over in bed with an aggravated noise.

This was seriously bad. It was obvious to anybody with eyes that Selina was beautiful, but until now, she'd seemed so distant, so untouchable—too far away to envision any of this.

But now some floodgate had broken, and some part of my mind had realized that the idea of touching Selina Chan was thrilling and transgressive, the hottest and most confusing thing I could possibly imagine. As we texted, I battled image after image. Selina pressing me hard against her friends' plate-glass window, her lips ghosting over mine. The idea of gripping her waist, lifting her onto my kitchen counter, sliding my hands up under her dress. Selina touching my chin to keep my eyes on hers, wearing her heels. Nothing but her heels.

It was long past midnight by the time I managed to get my imagination under control. As exhaustion dimmed the fire of my thoughts, I thought back to the bookstore, to what Selina had told me about her parents.

Did your parents ever email you back? I asked.

I wondered if she'd dodge the question, but she said, Yes.

Then: They were upset by my posts online and asked, for roughly the millionth time, whether I regretted picking the wrong career path yet.

You didn't pick the wrong career, I said.

She didn't say anything. I added, Selina, I might never have met another person who's more obviously in the right career.

Thank you. That means a lot.

After a moment she went on, I try to imagine doing anything else and it's like trying to imagine living in somebody else's body.

When did you start writing? I asked.

In high school. You won't be shocked to know that I was a weird kid. We joke about my not having friends, but that was pretty much true back then.

I hesitated. When I'd probed in California, she'd pulled away, but this seemed even more like an opening than her reference to *City* had been then.

When you say 'back then,' I said, you don't mean your entire childhood, do you?

For a moment, no response, and I thought I'd struck the wall again, some barrier of privacy that she'd never allow me through.

Finally, an ellipsis appeared, and a minute later, the message:

Well, the experience wasn't as dramatic as that sounds. I was a borderline silent kid with weak social connections that didn't transfer over between schools. In high school, I was on the periphery of a group for a while, but I discovered after a couple of years that they'd spent a lot of time privately making fun of me. Which at the time was upsetting, but pretty soon felt unsurprising more than anything else. It wasn't as though I ever felt in step with any of them.

I sat with this message for a minute, trying to pick apart the swirl of scenes it conjured. Then anger rose in me. Jesus, I said. Selina, you don't have to describe that like it's acceptable. They sound terrible.

They weren't, though. They were just normal high schoolers pointing at the nearest abnormal thing. Tale as old as time.

I can't believe you feel rage about reading a bad book, but not about this.

She laugh-reacted to this. Well, the experience led me deeper into reading and writing, so, it was worth it. My journal entries back then were more like lists of observations than essays or reviews, though. I think they gave me a sense of control, like the world wasn't just something happening to me but something I could catch on to, or observe deeply enough to understand it.

Participating without participation, I said.

Yes, exactly, she said. What about you?

I started writing in high school, too, I wrote. For fun. To explore. To hear how the words crashed into each other. To open up space.

Space for yourself?

Yeah.

She asked me how my family was, which was how I knew she understood what I'd meant, and one in the morning passed, and she told me how nighttime sounded in Minnesota, and it was with her crickets in my ears that I fell toward sleep, miserable and buzzing, imagining her somewhere across the city, pillow against her cheek, curve of cell phone light upon her dark eyes.

I woke up to learn that Selina had panned the book of the season.

The book—*Next Time Lucky*, by some Booker-shortlisted Brit named Martin MacEnroe—was a multigenerational family epic, which Selina described as "Tolstoyesque, if Tolstoy had assumed a readership with the attention span of fruit flies." I read the review with an escalating sense of guilty amusement. This woman.

My social media had grown correspondingly loud.

3m ago **@ParkerNavarroWrites** I thought you'd be interested to see Chan yet again showing off how bad of a critic and person she is

4m ago **@ParkerNavarroWrites** @MartinMacEnroeBooks you two should be friends lol

6m ago **@ParkerNavarroWrites** Must be a day that ends in 'y'. . . . Selina Chan is being an intolerable literary hipster again. . . . . . .

I watched the posts unroll, realizing that I disagreed with every single one.

I hit Reply on the post calling her an intolerable literary hipster, but I remembered this user. She'd tagged me in the days after the video with her sympathy. I'm so sorry this is happening to you Parker! I preordered your book and I'm really really excited to read it!! It seemed so hypocritical to turn on this person now, to chastise a stranger, when not even a month ago, I'd thought the same things about Selina.

Even as I exited the app, my phone buzzed.

New Messages in Chan Pan Support Group

Aiden Linville

should we add Martin MacEnroe to this chat?? poor guy

Jenny House

I met Martin at a launch last year. He was lovely! Of course, that doesn't mean anything to Selina Chan.

Carla Lew

I am FUMING

Carla Lew

Just picturing her stupid smug face in front of her laptop as she thinks 'oh I'm REALLY going to torture somebody today, ha ha ha'

J.J. Purnell

It would be one thing if she were supposedly a nice person, but by all accounts, she's even worse in real life. I heard from a couple of friends of mine that she iced them out at an event. Superiority complex.

Aiden Linville

in the immortal words of Maya Angelou, when someone shows you they're a soulless bitch, believe them the first time

Aiden's text drew me up short. Messages continued to materialize, rapid-fire, my throat tightening with every bubble, every swooshing alert. Maybe we'd grown too loyal to each other in this group, defensive to a fault. I couldn't imagine Aiden calling Selina a bitch when we'd first started chatting. I should have said something weeks ago.

I began to type.

Parker Navarro

Okay, wait, confession. I did this event at the Dog's Ear right before Christmas and Selina Chan showed up. We talked afterward, and she isn't that bad.

Carla Lew

WHAT???? parker . . . . you're not serious right . . . .

J.J. Purnell

Isn't that bad in what way?

Aiden Linville

if selina chan is holding you at gunpoint, try to secretly share your address. we'll save you

Parker Navarro

She just takes her job very seriously.

Parker Navarro

She actually apologized to me. She said City shouldn't have assigned her my second book and she shouldn't have taken it on to review.

Jenny House

Well, that's the least she could do.

Aiden Linville

i'm glad she wasn't terrible to you for the millionth time, parker, but that's not really a consolation, lol. an apology to one person doesn't magically undo years of being publishing's resident harpy.

Carla Lew

I'm with Aiden on this. Yeah, she SHOULD have left your second book alone! What is she going to DO to make up for what she did? Like, I'm noticing she hasn't admitted fault publicly (because it would make her look bad) or backtracked in any way (because I DO think she's a narcissist who's incapable of exhibiting humility)

J.J. Purnell

You're a sweet guy, Parker. Just make sure you're not being played, okay?

Jenny House

But we support you even if you've been brainwashed by the Chan cult!

Aiden Linville liked Jenny House's message

Carla Lew liked Jenny House's message

J.J. Purnell liked Jenny House's message

After typing and deleting a few beginnings, I hit Like on Jenny's message, too. I was never going to convince these four to feel anything positive about Selina. This would have to be good enough.

My heart rate settling, I switched over to my conversation with her. We'd talked so late last night that I'd woken up past 10 AM again, which meant she was in Manhattan now, in the *City* offices.

When I was a kid, I'd envisioned the world within every book so vividly. Any old story could paint a full-color picture with a few vague words. Now, it was a rare book that excited my imagination that way.

But I typed, I saw the review. Have you been hunted down with pitchforks yet? People love that book.

And she said, almost immediately, Sorry, can't talk. Being burned at the stake.

And I saw her there, at a desk that I imagined was spotless smoked glass, and I pictured her hair bound in a knot at the base of her skull, and I saw her in that silken navy dress she'd worn when she'd come to my apartment last weekend, and its neck was open, and there was a seed pearl necklace sinking into the dip between her collarbones, and she had that secretive half smile on her lips as she looked down at her phone. My imagination was so full of her it felt halfway to inspiration.

Chapter Twenty-Two

Selina

I shouldn't have been responding to Parker this way.

I was a curiosity on the edge of his life. Any given evening we didn't text, he might be curling up around Emily Shapiro, on his sofa, in her bed. When I was in line at the grocery store or descending the subway steps, I'd imagine them like that. His hair messy from the way she'd run her fingers through it. Her fingers spread against his naked chest, his hand gripping her waist or thigh. They were going on sweet, wholesome dates for nice people. She was kissing confectioner's sugar off his mouth. His mouth—he'd tilt it easily against hers.

This was humiliating.

I had never felt so humiliated in my life as I did by this: spending hours texting a man who was in the act of falling for somebody else, because whatever he gave me still felt better than nothing.

Since my apology, we'd been texting every day, and I'd begun to accept, torturously, that he wanted to be friends. Why had I done this to myself? I didn't want to be his friend, although, yes, of course I did, because nobody had ever managed to make me laugh so often, alone in my apartment, pausing at the cutting board, wiping slivers of carrot from the tips of my thumbs over and over again so I could answer him, rendering my life slower and more inconvenient and, undeniably, happier.

Apparently I didn't just enjoy his company. Apparently I wanted the version of my life that had him woven into it.

I told myself it was better this way. Even if he had been single, and miraculously interested in me despite everything we'd said to each other, the optics around getting involved with a writer I'd reviewed seemed less than favorable.

Yes: much cleaner to be friends, and stamp out these feelings in my own time. I just had to hope they faded before I made myself sick with sleep loss. I was spending a few nights a week at the Slippery Cork now, soothed by the rhythms of my fellow regulars. "What's with you?" Nadia asked one night, replacing the dartboard where Haunted Santa had been.

"Why?"

"You're here all the time."

"No reason," I said.

"Okay," she said, and when she didn't push, I felt embarrassed by my disappointment.

January was coming to a cold, dry conclusion, and the *City* office was somber. So far, I'd been spared getting assigned to the listicles and what Kellie referred to as "the drama beat," but I knew my days were numbered. Hayden now sat beside Scott at the round table during our meetings, vetoing idea after idea. Her vetoes were met with a dull, resigned silence. We all knew about the rent hike, now.

In the first week of February, Hayden turned to me at a pitch meeting, and I knew that my time had run out.

"Selina, I have a proposition for you. Hear me out."

"Promising way to start a proposition."

She held up a hand. "I've been mulling this over, and I think you should request an interview with Parker Navarro, with his new book coming out."

The sound of his name surprised me into silence.

"Okay, no immediate objection! That's a good sign."

I sighed. "I'm listening."

To my left, Kellie cocked an eyebrow. Her wry looks always had this grim edge to them, these days. "Could be interesting," she said. "You two could talk about what last fall was like."

"As long as you can both keep it civil for an hour or so," said Scott.

"Okay, but is *civil* interesting?" said Hayden. She tapped her pen on the round table, a rhythmic *tick, tick*. "I mean, he spent a lot of time bad-mouthing you in fall. You kept it pretty clean, pretty focused on his book. But this guy is just like all mediocre men who think they deserve to fail up, right? If we can show how entitled—"

"No," I said.

She broke off. The rest of the staff glanced my way.

I avoided their eyes. "A . . . mutual acquaintance gave me a better sense of his background. I'd given him flak for his advance, but he used a lot of it to help his family."

Hayden set her pen down. "Well, fine. But we want to give people something to click and share."

"Mm," I said. It occurred to me that I could admit that Parker and I were on friendly terms now. But maybe, in this small, inadequate way, I wanted to keep him to myself.

"We do want it to be printable, Hayden," said Scott. "Selina, maybe I could sit in with you, or—"

A little laugh came out of me. "No, we don't need a mediator . . . I'll—it'll be fine."

"Do you want me to email his agent?"

"No, that won't be necessary. I'll reach out and let you know the details on timing."

After the meeting, I shut myself into my office and texted Parker.

How would you feel about doing an interview with City Magazine to celebrate the upcoming release of High and Dry? More specifically an interview with me?

A minute passed. Then he said, Celebrate? I think you misspelled litigate. Or denigrate?

Ha, I said. I'm serious, though.

You? Serious? I need to sit down.

Parker.

He laugh-reacted to my message. Then:

Yeah, I'll do an interview with you, Selina. Apparently my masochism knows no bounds.

"*Your* masochism?" I muttered. He had no idea. I was the one who was going to have to speak with him for an hour, trying to ignore my own inevitable reactions to the sound of his voice.

When are you free? I asked. The earlier the better, so that I can have the interview finalized before your release date.

You say that like this interview will help me sell copies of the book.

All publicity is good publicity, I said.

I'm beginning to think that phrase was invented by bad publicists.

I turned my chair away from the door as though, through solid wood, somebody might see me smiling at my phone screen.

I'm free tomorrow, he said.

Great. Would you prefer a video call or a phone call? I asked, but even as I hit Send, he asked,

Want to just do the interview over dinner?

I went still in my chair.

Sorry, he said almost immediately. We can do a call.

No, I said. Dinner is good.

An awkward pause.

I continued, Dinner is better for me, actually. I have two pieces to finish tomorrow.

Great, he said.

Another pause. I stood up abruptly, my palms tingling. Why had this become uncomfortable? It was a business dinner that happened to fall on a Friday. So what?

But then I imagined going to a restaurant and realizing that one of Parker's friends, or some author, or any person peripherally involved in publishing, was seated next to us.

On second thought, I said, it might not be the most prudent thing for us to have dinner in public.

Yeah, maybe not, he said.

Thirty seconds passed. The ellipsis appeared as he typed. I typed, too, then deleted, then retyped. I was pacing more quickly now, my mouth bone-dry.

I wrote, You're welcome to come over to my apartment for dinner.

My finger paused over the Send button. This was inappropriate. This no longer sat within the bounds of a business dinner that happened to fall on a Friday. It was just that I'd agreed to dinner, and the prospect of trying to hold eye contact with Parker in a crowded room felt agonizing.

I pressed Send just as a message arrived from Parker:

It's okay. We can do a call instead.

"Fuck," I said, and began to type: Yes. A call would probably be easiest. If evening is best for you, then

A message appeared from him. Oh—sure, I could come over.

I deleted what I'd written. I could feel my pulse near the top of my stomach, shallow and quick. He sounded taken aback. Or was that a tone of casual dismissal? Veiled reluctance?

If a call is easiest for you, then we can do a call, I said.

And I thought, *I don't want to settle for a call.*

And I thought, *Please just ask me to call you, how am I going to stand you walking into my apartment.*

And I thought, *Please come inside, please stay for hours, please find something in the corners of my life that makes you want me.*

He typed for a while. I wondered if he was writing a joke or a gentle letdown. Then he said:

Just tell me what time to be there.

After a lot of careful deliberation, I left work an hour early the next day.

"Leave work early?" Scott asked, startled. "Why?"

"If it's not all right, I can—"

"No, please, by all means. I'm just wondering if, somewhere, pigs are beginning to fly."

I smiled. "No, I just need to—I'm doing the Navarro interview tonight and I need to prepare some, some notes."

Scott's pantomimed shock faded, and to my surprise, he patted me on the shoulder. "Thank you for doing this, Selina. I know the last month has been . . . but I'm sure you'll make something wonderful out of it."

"You're not expecting me to play some trick on him for the clicks?"

"No."

"Good. I'm glad." I hesitated. Scott's weariness shadowed his face, deepening the pouches beneath his eyes, the sag of his cheeks.

I forced myself not to turn tail. I swallowed the cordial exit line that was always, in situations like these, on the tip of my tongue.

"Scott," I said.

"Yes?"

"Do you remember Marcy D'Artagnan's review of *Asylum Piece*?"

Scott settled back into his office chair, frowning. "*Asylum Piece* . . .

the Anna Kavan? Marcy would have reviewed that . . . fifteen years ago?"

"Eighteen. I—I just wanted to tell you how much that piece meant to me. And that"—I cleared my throat—"that it still means everything to me to be here every day. No matter how different things look."

Scott looked at me in astonishment. I ducked out before he could find his voice.

The difference in my departure time gave me enough leeway to beat the rush hour and nip into the Chinese grocery store a subway stop away for ground bean sauce. It would also give me enough time to steam the buns.

I found cooking meditative; it had never made me nervous before. Of course, I'd never cooked for someone who'd occupied my thoughts like this.

For that matter, I couldn't remember even knowing anyone who'd occupied my thoughts like this. In the couple of faltering six-month relationships I'd had in my twenties and the endless stream of first and second dates in between, my interest in men had always been something slow and measured, something I could, to a degree, evaluate and control. This was different, this spiky, erratic feeling that had me distracted at work, that had me losing track of paragraphs halfway through a book, that had me staring into the darkness beyond the subway windows and thinking about the sight of him, messy-haired, in his apartment doorway.

I stirred the onions in the skillet, trying to steel myself. Parker was used to being liked; he was probably used to being wanted, too. The important thing tonight was to stay steady and professional. Not to show myself.

He buzzed two minutes before seven. My heart in my throat, I pressed the button with the open-door icon and flipped the dead bolt.

I stood by the mat, thinking about Parker in the elevator, his hands in his pockets.

Two knocks on my door.

I tugged my hair down from its ponytail, then tucked it behind my ears. I forced myself to think of Emily, told myself that it didn't matter how I looked, but I still glanced back at my dark reflection in the oven.

I pulled the door open. Parker had a bottle of wine in one hand and a finished hardcover of *High and Dry* in the other. His shoulders lowered slowly, as though he'd just drawn a deep breath, and it occurred to me that he might be nervous about what I intended to ask him. I wanted to reassure him. I wanted to look at him for a long time, the lapels of his wool coat, the corner of his jaw.

"Parker," I said.

"Selina."

When had it started feeling like this to hear him say my name, like a shot of adrenaline? Had that been true since October?

"Come in."

"Thanks." He slipped his shoes off inside, surveying the kitchen, the living area. I wondered how my home looked through his eyes.

"Anything surprising?" I asked.

"Yeah. Where's the rack? And the iron maiden?"

I tried to suppress a smile. "They're collapsible. They fold up into the wall like a Murphy bed."

"Right, those classic Brooklyn space savers." He was smiling, too.

I looked away. "You can hang your coat in the hallway. There's a hook by the clock."

As Parker took off his coat, I turned back to the steamer on the counter. I didn't want to watch him, but when he emerged from the hall, I couldn't help it. He wore a black knit shirt that clung to his shoulders, his hair falling over one side of his forehead.

"It smells delicious," he said, scanning the table, the centered carafe, the reed placemats topped with symmetrically placed wineglasses, cups for water, and folded napkins. "This is way more than you needed to do. Not that I'm surprised."

"I'll take that as a compliment," I said, handing him a corkscrew.

"What's in there?" he asked, nodding to the bamboo steamer.

"Goubuli buns. My family's from Tianjin, so—street food. If you've ever had pork buns from a dim sum place, those are similar."

"Tianjin." He twisted the screw into the cork. "That's in the north?"

"Yes, a couple of hours from Beijing. Though my dad's side is from Hong Kong, originally."

"Do you go over there often?"

"No, I haven't been in, I think, fifteen years." I hesitated. Some part of me wanted to admit that without my parents by my side, I worried that I'd feel like a tourist in China, foreign to my own heritage, my own extended family, my own body. I considered admitting that these recipes, and Chinese books in translation, and even the language dying on my palate, sometimes made me feel like a tourist, too, as though these efforts to come closer only made me more aware of an unbridgeable distance. But to say any of this to him would have felt the same way: a painful try at closeness.

Instead I lifted the top of the steamer, and the white flower unfurled from inside, hot and moist. The buns hadn't collapsed.

"Are you hungry?" I asked.

"Ravenous." He popped the cork, and we sat.

As I looked across the table at him, everything that had happened since Juliette's event seemed to hang between us like a blue haze, but I wondered if Parker was thinking twice about any of it. In all likelihood he was thinking about the interview, maybe even about the ways I'd insulted *High and Dry*.

"How long did this take you?" Parker said as he picked up one of the buns.

"A lady never reveals her secrets."

"I thought that was magicians."

"Yeah, it's a close Venn diagram."

He bit into the bun and made an indecent sound. Warmth twined between my ribs. "Good?" I asked.

He swallowed. "Okay. Wow. Remind me not to make fun of your menus ever again."

I smiled. "You're allowed."

"Really? Why?"

"It feels like an intrinsic part of the dynamic now."

"You could just call it an inside joke."

"Right," I said slowly. "*In-side joke.* Is that something that people with 'friends' do?"

"It is. Don't worry, you'll learn."

He poured me a glass of wine. I watched his hand, his knuckles, the tendons drawing lines down to his wrist. The way a muscle in his forearm flexed when he set down the bottle.

"Thank you." I tasted. "It's good."

"Thank God. I didn't want you to have to break out the rack this early in the evening."

"No, you've bought yourself some time."

Our eyes met, and, smiling, I felt young and obvious, and I busied myself with spooning peanut sauce onto my plate. It occurred to me to say something about the book, or about Emily, to reestablish boundaries for my own sake.

"In regard to the interview," I said.

"Right."

"I have eight questions for you. You can look over them before we start, if you'd like."

"You mean, if I'm scared."

"If you were scared," I said, "you wouldn't be here."

"I think you're giving me too much credit."

I gave him an amused look. "Yes, Parker. That's what I'm known for: giving people too much credit."

Parker smiled, but he didn't answer.

I felt an unhappy tug. *Was* he scared of me? About a decade ago, I'd accepted that my baseline for interacting with other people was that they'd feel some level of intimidation or discomfort, but Parker? I didn't want that with him. I wanted the endless giddy serve and hard-hit return of our messages. I wanted the way he'd looked at me in Jacob and Cassie's apartment, or even in the bar after the convention, as though he saw me as an equal.

"Brought you a present," he said, pushing the hardback of *High and Dry* across the table.

"I do already have an advance copy."

"What, you're not overjoyed to get a finished version of your favorite book of the year?"

I flipped the book open to the title page. "You didn't sign it to me."

"Yeah, I thought maybe you'd want to give it to someone as a gift. Or as punishment."

I knew he was joking, but the words saddened me for some reason. "There are people who will love this book," I said. "Lots of people."

Puzzlement flickered in his eyes.

"I just want to be clear that I don't think my opinion is the only one that matters."

"I know you don't," he said.

My pulse quickened. I closed the book and slid it to my right.

"And I don't need to see the questions," he added. "I trust you."

My gaze strayed up onto his. His eyelids contracted slightly, as though I'd shone a penlight into his face. The moonlike lamp hanging above my table made him glow, like his skin was burnished, and his hair shadowed his left eye, and I didn't know when it had become this bad, I didn't know when I'd started wanting him so much.

But he had somebody, a nice girl, a good person, and I reminded myself that I was lucky even to have him in this limited way, to have reached a point where we could eat dinner and trust each other.

After dinner, we moved to the window. I'd positioned a two-seat table there beneath the cool, leaky glass. When we sat, he angled his legs outward so they wouldn't touch mine. I set my phone on the table between us. "Ready?" I asked.

"Ready."

"The written introduction will have a description of *High and Dry*, so we can go right into discussion."

"Great."

"Before we start . . ." I looked out the window, down at the street, where the grocery store awning was retracting. "When we were at dinner with Juliette, you said you never expressed what you'd like to in interviews. So, I wanted to say, there's no rush to answer these questions. You can take your time. I'm not"—I tugged at the sleeve of my dress—"I'm not going anywhere."

Parker was quiet for a while. Then he said, "Thank you, Selina," his voice a little rough, and I felt the words like the brush of his fingers against mine on New Year's Eve, slow and deliberate, and I hoped the tension in my body wasn't visible on my face.

I collected myself and pressed Record. "Thanks for agreeing to this interview, Parker."

"Thank you for having me."

"It's always a pleasure to talk about a book I loved, but when a book and I disagree, I usually find myself with a longer list of questions."

"Right," he said. "And what are the chances that I give such insightful answers to your questions that your entire outlook on the book transforms?"

"Low."

"So, you're saying there's a chance."

I couldn't help smiling. "Nothing's impossible. My first question is this: What transformations did *High and Dry* undergo during your editing process? I think it's easy for a reader to look at a novel and say that it needed editing, because the reader can imagine the book transforming in whatever way is convenient for them. So, I'm curious what did change here, from first draft to final manuscript."

"Well," Parker began. Then he stopped. Swallowed. He took a sip of water and gave me a look that was half question, half apology.

"It's fine," I said quietly. "Take your time."

He nodded, and his sight line moved up over my head, fixing to a spot on the ceiling as he thought.

"So, the project expanded by seventy, eighty pages," he said eventually. "My first iteration of the book had a more grounded approach to the passengers on the bus. The riders were trying to find lost family members, or they were flood victims with all their worldly possessions on their backs, that sort of thing. Some of that is still in the book, but as I worked through my early draft, I realized I wanted to go weirder and wilder. The more absurd the passengers become, the more absurd it is that Dave continues to drive as if nothing's changed, as if he's not changing through exposure to his warping reality."

"Thus the mutant alligator."

"Yeah, thus the alligator."

"This idea is important to you. The way people are bent on continuing down a predetermined road."

"Absolutely."

"Can you expand on that?"

His leg began to jog, his fingers tracing patterns on the table. I saw him sorting through his thoughts.

I felt a sudden, painful surge of contentment. This would have been a perfect night, I thought, if I could have stopped recording.

"I think resisting inertia is the predominating challenge of being alive right now," he said. "Obviously the book is preoccupied with how this presents in the context of labor, billions of people clocking into and out of their lives, signing over the majority of their waking hours. But you see it everywhere. It's easier to keep believing what you already believe than to absorb new information and react to it, and it's easier to keep scrolling than to put down your phone, and it's easier to keep gliding along any frictionless surface because that's a comforting state. People have such a strong aversion to disruption, even when what they're going through is actually so much worse than change."

I looked down into my water glass, thinking of myself even a single month ago, warring against what I was beginning to see in the man opposite me. The slowness of my reactions to my parents. My father's unanswered email.

"And for people who like what they have?" I asked.

"I'm sure they exist. I'm not sure they make for extremely compelling books."

Parker seemed to have relaxed. I asked him what he thought made a compelling book, and I asked why on earth he'd chosen not to bring back any of his side characters, and in the face of my bewilderment he laughed. "Why? Did you get attached?"

"I didn't have the chance to get attached, Parker. You wrote them on and off in a few pages apiece."

He shrugged. "Maybe the gamble of the book is that you'll like Dave."

"I didn't like Dave, that's true."

"Maybe this is the critical problem. I assume that if somebody hates Dave, they'll stop reading. They won't willingly spend six hundred pages in his company. But you're held hostage by your job."

"Am I held hostage by my job," I said, "or by you, who wrote a six-hundred-page book?"

"Why don't you like Dave, anyway?" Parker said. "What did Dave ever do to you?"

"He keeps driving. He doesn't react. Nothing he thinks or feels is ever externalized. I appreciate that you had thematic reasons for him to act like this, but it's extremely annoying, especially for six hundred pages."

"Careful, Selina. You're almost making it sound like I wrote exactly the book I wanted to write."

We kept talking. He began to smile after my questions, which I didn't understand. At points we wandered away from the topic to joke around, to laugh. This interview was going to be a nightmare to condense. Outside, people clustered around the nearby bars, and their exclamations echoed up toward us, sounding thin and far away. Eventually we reached the last of my questions.

"I'll cut this question if not, but would you like to tell the readers of *City Magazine* anything else about *High and Dry*?"

"Just that I'm having a launch event at Word in Brooklyn on February fifteenth."

I looked down at my phone, and the giddy feeling in my chest punctured. Emily sat at his table in my mind's eye, the bright spot in his life.

"Events aren't usually the sort of thing we print."

"Right. In that case . . ." Parker reached out and hit Stop.

I watched his hand withdraw. "How are the numbers looking for the launch?"

"Not bad. We're almost at capacity. I'm sure that's because we got Tessa Hargreaves to be my conversation partner. It should be fun."

"Oh, that's exciting." I steeled myself. I had to do this, had to say it. "It was nice seeing Emily the other day. Is she working the event?"

He paused. "I'm not sure. I haven't checked in with her in a week or so."

The silence in my apartment grew louder, then differentiated. I could hear the distant tick of my bedroom radiator, the gentle hum of the kitchen light. The faintest strain of a violin was seeping up from a different floor.

"You—you two don't talk much about work, then," I said.

"No, I meant we haven't spoken. We went on a couple of dates, but it didn't work out."

The words reverberated through my body. I didn't lift my gaze. I entered Navarro interview as the title of the voice memo and pressed Save. "Oh," I said, trying to sound like myself, but something seemed to be accelerating in me, vibrating, as though I were pressed back against a seat on a high-speed train.

I looked up and found Parker watching me. My breath lodged in my throat.

Don't, I thought. Nothing had changed. Yet everything felt different.

With a titanic effort I stood and took a few steps away from him, vaguely in the direction of the dining table. I said, "I suppose you've had a lot of time to write, then."

I heard the sound of his chair as he stood, too. "Yeah, enough to scratch the itch."

"This new project." I picked up my near-empty wineglass from the table. "Is it another story about a critic who gets what she deserves?"

Parker stopped at the opposite corner of the table, one hand curved gently over its edge. "It's not." He paused. "Why? Is that what I should be writing?"

I could only think, *He isn't leaving.*

We'd finished the interview, and he wasn't going to see anybody else, and he wasn't saying it was late and he should get home. Instead, he was continuing to watch me, very still.

I began to feel as though a hand had closed around my heart, squeezing every time it beat.

"I don't know," I said. "The descriptions were interesting, last time."

"Which ones?" he said quietly.

I held my glass to my lips but didn't drink. "You tell me." My throat was so tight, I didn't know how I was still speaking.

Parker took a step toward me and my heart began to speed.

It doesn't mean anything, I told myself, clinging to anything that would guard me. He would take the glass from my hands and pass into the kitchen. That was what was happening, not what I wanted.

"I did my best," he said. "But I had to imagine a lot of the details."

With another step he closed the distance between us.

"Like what," I said.

He took the wineglass from my hand, set it on the table beside me, and didn't step back.

I finally let my gaze rise then, from the neck of his shirt to his eyes, fixed intently on mine.

"This place," he said softly. He paused, his eyes straying down to my mouth, his head dipping by a fraction of an inch. "Your perfume."

If I had ever felt this way in my life, I couldn't remember it, like my torso had filled with surging waves, like every sensation was a static shock.

I let my head tilt back until it gently met the wall. I turned my chin half an inch to one side.

I watched something change in Parker's eyes, a dark glaze that made heat sear across my abdomen. He lifted his hand and slowly, deliberately brushed back my hair, his fingertips skimming my neck. Then he leaned down and set his mouth to the corner of my jaw and drew a quiet, shaky inhalation.

Tingling spiraled down across my collarbones. I imagined how his lips would feel, the graze of his touch. "Selina," he said, just beneath my ear, and then his other hand found my waist, and I turned my face toward him, and his mouth pressed deeply to mine.

My eyes fell shut. My mind hummed.

Parker moved closer, his hand tightening in my hair.

A mess of impulses fired in me. To wrap my arms around him, to fist a hand in the back of his shirt, to press myself up against his body so he'd know what I wanted.

But instead my hands rose and gently cupped his face, holding him, just feeling him here. He made a small, low sound. I felt like something had broken open in my chest, and what it spilled was molten, searing through me vessel by vessel.

Kissing was not supposed to feel this way, I wasn't seventeen, but when I breathed in, his scent seemed to fill me, that rich, sweet smell, almond and amber, intensifying this sensation like hunger. I slipped one of my hands around to the back of his neck, feeling the rigid muscles there against my palm, and tugged him down into me.

He responded. Pressed me up against the wall, slow and hard, one hand tightening on my hip. His tongue drew a line over my bottom lip with an unhurried confidence that made my face burn. I curled a hand around his bicep, scraping him with my nails, and he made another low sound into my mouth that made me push away from the wall, toward him, toward his palm, which was slipping down my thigh.

Parker let go my hair and wrapped his arm around me, his forearm locking into the small of my back. He pulled me backward toward the love seat, our steps clumsy. His hand pushed under the hem of my dress as we went, mine under his shirt and tracing the flex of muscle in his side and back, the curve of his shoulder blade. He pulled away to yank his shirt over his head.

I reached up, closed my hand over the place his neck met his shoulder, and he sank onto the love seat, looking up at me flushed. The sight of him here, in my apartment, shirtless and hair rumpled, sent a warm shock down through me.

I stepped between his legs, then settled my knees on either side of his hips.

Parker's hands found my thighs and squeezed. He pushed up my dress as I settled onto his lap, cupped his face in my hands, and lowered my mouth to his again. His teeth closed on my lip, gently first, then harder. One of his thumbs slid under the elastic of my underwear at the hip, the other up my abdomen, and when his palm brushed over the thin lace of my bra I whispered, "Take it off."

"Impatient," Parker said, and when he kissed me again I could feel him smiling, and all I could do was melt deeper into him, pushing him against the back of the sofa. He moved his hips. I could feel how hard he was. One hand sprang the clasp of my bra, and he broke the kiss to lick the pad of his thumb before reaching under my dress again, under the loosely hanging fabric of my bra, circling my nipple with his thumb tip.

I leaned back, my eyes easing open, and watched him watch me. His other hand moved, still stretching the band of my underwear, to the front of my body. His fingers slipped down, slid wet against me, and the touch felt so good, I sank down against his hand, my breaths growing ragged. A small, controlled sound came from his throat. I saw him swallow, and his fingertips ran back and forth until I felt drunk on the pleasure of it, until finally he pushed his hand forward and sank his finger deep into me.

I groaned. Closed my eyes and moved on his hand. He wrapped one arm around me again, then tilted me until my back was flat on the sofa seat, one of my feet hooked over his hip. His finger stayed deep inside me, moving slowly, curling, touching a place that made me see white.

"I was imagining this," he murmured in my ear, "all night."

With his other hand he pushed up my dress. I pulled it over my head, flung it away. He leaned back to look down at me, then slid a second finger inside, moving faster.

"Parker," I said unsteadily. I reached up and touched his jaw, and like I'd tugged some invisible cord in him, he bent down and kissed me hard, his lips warm and wet now. I traced his lip with my tongue and reached down, searching for the button of his jeans. His hand brushed mine. I heard the buzz of his zipper, the rustle of cloth.

I cast a look at the hook on the wall, his winter jacket. "Did you bring a condom?"

"Fuck." His hand stilled between my legs. "No. I had no idea there was any chance of this happening."

"We can still . . . I have the implant. I'm up to date, if you—"

"Me too."

"Good." I trailed my hand over his hip, the skin at the top of his thigh, his hardness. He stilled, then pressed his hips forward, putting himself in my hand. I gripped tighter. He groaned into my mouth, bit at me gently, his fingers withdrawing from me, slipping against my thighs.

"You're so wet," he said onto me, sounding hoarse. "It's driving me crazy."

"I want you," I whispered.

"Say it again."

"I want you. Now—please."

He pulled my underwear down and lowered his hips between my thighs. I felt him brush my entrance. I was so sensitive, the air cold, his skin so warm. But with my last shred of clarity I touched the back of his head, and he looked up at me, his eyes full of desire, and held my gaze as he slid into me, inch by slow, full inch, pressure building inside me.

"Please," I said, opening my legs wider. He moved faster, deeper. I took his hand from my hair and moved it down toward my center. His thumb settled there and brushed, teasing, dipping, as I lifted myself up into him, the heat seeming to echo and multiply. Our noses brushed, his breaths rough against my cheek, and I said his name, and his mouth pressed hard to mine, and I held tight to his shoulder as his thumb hit that perfect spot again, and as he thrust into me I came undone under him, insensible, unable even to kiss him, so that his mouth moved over my chin and into the crook of my neck, his teeth teasing the skin there.

I cried out, gasped. Satisfaction jerked through me, tight and fast, then loosening out into steady, rhythmic waves. He kept pushing into me, riding me out, and I rolled my hips and felt his body go rigid, his mouth slackening against my neck. I lifted my legs around him, holding him deep in me.

The breath rushed out of him, and he crumpled, catching himself just above my body, on his forearms.

My heart pounded. Every inch of my body felt alive with minuscule bursting sensations, as though my blood were carbonated.

He pulled out slowly, gently, one hand still tracing my hip. "Selina?" he murmured onto my earlobe.

My eyes had fixed on one corner of my ceiling, a weathered spot of molding. I tried to steady myself, to understand why, suddenly, I wanted to pull a blanket over my body, to curl up in darkness.

"One second," I whispered. I hurried to the bathroom and cleaned myself up, not looking in the mirror. I looked down at my hands on the edge of the sink, at my thighs. I redid the clasp of my bra. The apartment was so quiet.

He'd felt so good. The warmth and certainty of his hands. I wanted to walk back into them. I wanted to shy away.

I brushed my hair over my shoulder, then returned to the sofa, where Parker levered himself upright, watching me. I perched on the seat beside him, my thighs pressed together.

"Hey. Was it all right?" Parker said.

The question felt so ridiculous that I looked up, startled. "All *right*?" I repeated. "Parker."

I saw tension ease in his face, and there was something amused in his voice when he said, "Well?"

"Well, what?"

He leaned closer and stroked a lock of hair back from my face. "Maybe I want to hear you say it."

I couldn't help a laugh. "That you're good in bed?"

"Yeah. I don't know, maybe that does something for me."

I licked my lips, which still tingled, swollen. I looked at his disheveled hair and the lean slopes of his body and his talented fingers. *Obviously*, I thought. Obviously.

His hand found my thigh, and it was downright unreasonable the way my breath caught all over again. "You are," I said unevenly.

He met my gaze, and I breathed through the intense feeling of exposure, finding that freckle in his iris, examining the fine lines at the corners of his eyes. "Really?" he said.

"The best I've ever had." I leaned toward him and brushed a kiss just on the edge of his mouth. "Honest."

He cupped my face in his hand. Kissed me gently. His hand splayed over my thigh and squeezed. "Can I take you to bed?"

"Please," I said.

Deep into that night, when we were both exhausted, lying in bed, I killed the light. I didn't know the time. We might have moved outside time completely. He faced me in the dark and stroked my hair behind my ear, away from the sticky nape of my neck.

"I haven't slept with anyone in a while," I told him.

"How long?"

"A little over two years."

"Want to make up for lost time?"

I felt momentarily wordless with relief. It was the first indication he'd made that he wouldn't leave in the morning, say he'd had a good night, and move on with his life.

"Sorry," he said, "did saying 'lost time' activate your death thing?"

I half smiled. "Oh, I was already thinking about that. Sex and death go together."

Parker sighed. "Is this where the rack comes out?"

"Yeah. Hands up. Stretch out for me."

He draped his arm over my waist. My bedroom was always cold. I pulled the blanket higher and moved toward his warmth, shifting one of my legs between his. I watched the curves of his neck and shoulders move as he breathed.

"Do you have any idea where that comes from?" he said in a sleepy murmur. "The death thing, I mean."

I considered a while. "I guess sometimes I have these disconnected feelings. Like other people have some innate tie to the world that I don't. And that's a morbid feeling, I think." I hesitated. "But when I read something really beautiful, that does make me feel connected. I read *Asylum Piece* and think, you know, somebody felt this, or . . . somebody knew me, even though she died sixty years ago, and feeling that way just suffuses everything with meaning. I don't think my parents ever understood that reading is one of the only things that makes me feel that way."

"How long has this been going on with them?"

I told him how they'd cut me off in college, about our fits and starts in the intervening decade. Somewhere in the retelling, I hit the limit of my ability to speak. "Sorry," I said quietly, "this is strange for me. I hardly ever talk about it."

"Don't apologize." Parker kissed my forehead. "I can't imagine. Just the total opposite of my parents."

I laid my head on the pillow beside him and let myself look at his sympathetic expression. My feelings for him just then, the intensity of them, terrified me.

"To be honest," I said, "part of the reason I don't like to talk about it is that I feel like the average person will assign it this dominating importance, and then that's all I'll be for the rest of my life. Someone with a dysfunctional family." I hesitated. "The way most people see me, even if that's a tyrant or an aesthetic snob or whatever, I think that's closer to what I am."

A small smile made the shadowed contours of his face curve.

"What?" I asked.

"I said that to Emily at the bar after the festival. I said, people know Selina how she wants them to know her."

I found myself smiling too. "What about you?" I brushed his cheek, and he moved infinitesimally toward the touch. "Do people know you the right way?"

"What do you think?" he said.

"I'm not sure." I hesitated. "The way people spoke about you online, and wrote about your work. It made me so frustrated. I felt like . . . but it's ridiculous."

"Tell me."

"I thought, they're not listening to what he's saying. They're not seeing everything I'm seeing. Or not understanding it like I do." I moved a strand of hair from his forehead, my fingertips lingering at his temple. "But maybe I was just imagining that."

He took my hand in his, kissed my palm, and whispered, "You weren't."

Chapter Twenty-Three

Parker

I stayed at Selina's right through the weekend, unable to make myself leave. Every time I considered going back to my apartment, this urgent, irrational feeling stopped me, as if the instant I walked out the door, what was happening between us would collapse, and she would snap out of some hypnotic trance and remember that she didn't need me, maybe didn't even want me the way she seemed to want me.

But she did seem to want me. On her bathroom sink, and against the wall, and tangled in the bedsheets that smelled like her grapefruit body wash, she seemed to want me.

"I can go, if you need," I said, Saturday night, lying strewn across the bed. She'd reappeared in the illuminated doorway wearing a nightrobe of emerald satin, her hair tousled.

"Do you want to go?" she asked, pausing in the doorframe.

"No."

I felt so free, saying even something as simple as yes or no to her, undefended, unjustified.

She came to the bedside, knelt down, and kissed me. "Then stay," she said.

Part of me still couldn't believe any of this. The idea that Selina

Chan looked at me like I fascinated her. The sheer fact of waking up to her head upon my shoulder, and the way I'd started to see her laugh, always turning away to do it, her eyes sometimes straying back to me.

The days felt bizarre and giddy, cut with too-bright sun. She took me to her favorite dive bar, where a steel-eyed Russian bartender scanned me in obvious judgment, and to her local bookstore, owned by a graying, motionless man who looked as though he hadn't left the desk in fifty years, and who, when Selina asked if he had a copy of Can Xue's *Frontier*, grunted, "Shelf 113," immediately, without checking. We bought coffee from a hole-in-the-wall whose brick interior hung dozens of portraits of Victorian women, painted over to imagine them holding steaming mugs. Selina and I cooked in between, simple, hearty meals with whatever she had in her pantry, one of us sitting on the counter while the other stirred at the burner. We walked fifty minutes to the riverfront on Sunday, a bitterly cold afternoon we spent shouldering between the intermittent slaps of wind off the water. When we got back to her place, we stripped off our freezing coats and flung them in no direction and burrowed back into her bed, making each other laugh and jerk with our icy fingers against each other's backs and stomachs.

"Parker, stop," she gasped, her eyes tearing, as I touched the back of her neck. "That's awful." She tried to retaliate, but her hand was growing warm against my chest, and I pushed closer to her, gliding my other hand up the smooth curve of her back, hoping her thoughts were steadily turning the way mine had been, nonstop, for two days. And soon enough her laugh faded, her eyes dipped to my mouth, and she pushed me onto my back and I grappled her on top of me, hungry for the sweet slip of her lip balm, and time slid out from under me again.

Ok where are you, Arthur texted me several hours later.

Sorry, I said, I met someone.

Bro who?? A bank robber in charge of a hostage situation??

Lol, I said, I'll explain later.

That night, Selina warned me her alarm would go off at seven on the dot, but at two in the morning we were still whispering. I couldn't help it. I wanted another day of this, and another after that. As the night deepened, I began to think exactly how much more I wanted; how, if Selina had touched me in that unexpectedly gentle way and said, *Let's go somewhere*, I would have canceled my launch event, ignored everything Coronation sent my way, and walked onto a plane with her. But I didn't want to crowd her. I had this feeling as though I'd held out my hand and a bird had landed there in my palm, and if I tried to bring it too close to myself, it would realize what I was and startle, flying off for good.

I woke up to her appalling radar alarm at seven the next morning. It was so awful, I started laughing, bleary-eyed, into the pillow. "Jesus Christ," I said, "is there not, like, a birdsong or string instruments option?"

Selina, already brushing her hair at the side of the bed, gave me an amused look over her shoulder. "I assume you live a life completely without alarms?"

"Yep." I stretched out in her bed and folded my hands behind my head. I liked the way her eyes played over my arms when I did that. "I wake up with the sunrise, most of the time."

"Of course you do. Parker Navarro, at one with nature." Selina moved to her dresser and snapped on one of her lace bras. "And today?"

"I should probably go home. Maybe go to the gym."

She zipped up a crisp sheath dress. "What are you going to tell Arthur?"

I stood, stretching. "What makes you think I won't tell him the truth?"

"A hunch." She approached and gave me a lingering kiss. "I know you like a well-kept secret."

I caught her before she could step away, held her beautiful face in my hands, lowered my mouth to hers again. "Are you going to tell Jacob and Cassie?"

"We'll see. They're traveling to Thailand in a couple of weeks, so maybe I shouldn't distract them . . . Also, they'll be insufferable about it."

"Did they give you a hard time about New Year's?"

"Of course. I kept telling Cassie how much you hated me and that she was making something out of nothing."

I ran my hands down over her waist and felt an unwelcome quiver in my chest. I had hated her. The pain and anger I'd felt as recently as a few weeks ago, rereading her reviews, had been real.

Some unsteady part of me wanted to ask if she still felt that about me or my writing—if some part of her still thought I was contemptible.

"What?" she said, her fingers stepping up the back of my neck and tangling in my hair. She'd pressed her hips forward into mine at my touch, and a hit of arousal confused my thoughts.

"I don't think you have time for what I'm thinking," I said, squaring my hips against hers, pressing her gently against the wall.

"I could be late for work for once in my life."

"What? Who *are* you?" I said, but instead of answering, she took my earlobe between her teeth, and I melted down toward her, drawing her into me, the cotton of her dress whispering over my chest.

When she left for work, I rode the subway back home. My apartment felt different somehow when I stepped inside, its colors dim, its air quiet. But my mind felt clear. I settled down to work on the sofa and wrote carefully for unbroken hours, feeling lucid and exacting, uncompromising.

When Arthur came back from work that evening, he threw his hat at my face.

"Finally," he said. "I was this close to calling the cops. Who's this girl?"

"You'll meet her soon," I said, spitting out wool.

He flung his scarf at me too. "Bro, come on. Do I know her? Is it bookstore girl? One of your San Francisco friends?"

"You don't know her."

Arthur rolled his eyes and grabbed his hat and scarf out of the air when I threw them back. "Fine. I hope she's better than Kate."

"Your faith in me is overwhelming. What'd you do this weekend?"

"Threw a massive rager. Reduced this place to dust and rebuilt it with these hands." He shucked off his gloves and waved his hands at me.

"So . . . you phone banked, went on a bad Tinder date, and binged another season of *Severance*?"

"Fuck off," he said. Then, grudgingly: "Two out of three."

I grinned and keyed in a shortcut on my laptop. Arthur nodded to the computer as he picked through our snack cabinet. "How's the writing?"

"Good," I said. "I'm going slow. It feels better."

"New book? Short story?"

"New book."

He bobbed his head.

"I was surprised you liked that short so much," I said. "The one about Selina Chan."

Arthur's eyes strayed back to me, and I wondered if something in my voice had given me away, if I couldn't even say her name anymore without revealing myself.

"It was good," he said. "Like, I don't know enough to say what the difference was, but it did feel different from your books."

"Better than my books, you mean."

"I liked your books. But—yeah. Maybe your books feel like they're trying to prove something, and that story felt like it was just saying something."

I began to smile.

"What?" he said.

"Nothing." I shook my head, looked back at my laptop. "I guess that's writing for you. Spending your whole life learning how to say something."

My phone buzzed, and I grabbed for it, knocking it off the table.

"Wow," said Arthur. "Whoever this woman is, she really did a number on you."

I laughed. "You have no idea."

I held out two more days before going back to her apartment. I barely made it through the door before needing to kiss her, needing to feel her hands on me again. Another week and a half lurched by like this, days of self-imposed deprivation broken up by nights together. We went out dancing that Saturday night, somewhere so loud and full and young that we felt invisible. We read a new book from a writer we both liked and texted each other highlighted quotes, commentary attached.

I've been going back to this sentence all day.

The way this rhymes with the sound of the creek in chapter four? Unreal?

And then, somehow, it was the week before the *High and Dry* launch. My *City* interview with Selina went live on Thursday morning, and after she got off work that afternoon, we holed up in her bedroom and looked at the reactions online together. I sat at her desk, socked feet up on the radiator, while she lounged on her bed.

According to the internet, I was a sellout and Selina was a bitch. I was such a good sport, and Selina was so funny. I was insufferably pretentious, and Selina was also insufferably pretentious. It was strange to watch them at it, painting new details onto caricatures that neither of us believed in anymore.

"Oh, look," said Selina, angling her laptop toward me. "This person accused you of sleeping with the enemy."

"For real?"

"I think they were being figurative."

"If only they knew."

A beat of charged silence. People would, of course, know at some point. Wouldn't they?

"Okay," said Selina, closing her social media tabs. "I think that's enough for me."

Still looking at her screen, I caught sight of a half-drafted email. "Sorry," I said, glancing back to my own computer on the desk. "Not spying."

"Aren't you? Isn't that the point of sleeping with the enemy?"

"Good point. I think my mission got sidetracked somewhere."

"It's to my parents," she said, lifting the laptop closer to me.

My smile fading, I hunched down toward the bed to read.

Hi Dad,

I

"Not my best work," she said.

"Hey. It'll come." I hesitated. "Are you still trying to defend your career to them?"

"Apparently, which is ridiculous after this long. I can't think of a defense that could change anything." Selina snapped the laptop shut. "For years I've felt like they're just waiting for my career to collapse, so that when it all disappears on me, everything they said will be vindicated." Frown lines curved down the middle of her forehead. "I hate being locked in this open-ended question of who's going to wind up right or wrong. This is my life."

"What career did they want you to have?"

"I was prelaw before I switched to an English major. They loved that idea." She gave me a furtive glance from under her eyelashes. "You're always solving things. For your family. What would you do?"

"I don't know if I solve things. Smooth them over, maybe." I paused. "What are your parents like? Their personalities, I mean?"

She drew a pillow into her lap. "They're very risk-averse people. They're always thinking about the future. My dad's a nephrologist, so they're pretty well-off, but when I was a kid, we lived in a little rowhouse and didn't go out to eat and only bought new clothes once in a blue moon. I know that mindset is where they're coming from. And obviously I would also love a financial cushion and a safety net. But—" She smoothed a ripple in her silk robe against her thighs. "This is probably ungenerous, but sometimes it seems to me like their entire life is a contingency plan."

"I don't know," I said quietly. "Considering what they put you through in school, I think it's more than generous that you're still trying to see this from their perspective. I wish they'd try to see more of yours."

Selina's brow relaxed. She rose and, standing behind the desk chair, tucked her chin into the crook of my neck. "Thank you," she murmured.

"You'll figure out what to say."

"Hope so." She kissed the side of my neck, then looked unabashedly at my laptop. "The new book?"

I fought the instinct to turn off my screen. Between what I'd transcribed from my journal and what I'd drafted into the Word doc, I had about twenty pages, which felt very vulnerable just then. "Yeah."

"May I read it?"

I scrolled back up to the top of the document, considering. "I think so. It's readable through page ten or so." I stood, kissed her. "I'm going to make some tea. I'll bring you some."

"Thank you," she said, but she was already reading, already somewhere else.

I watched the kettle come to a boil, part of me still in the bedroom with her. Mugs in hand, I returned to the bedroom doorway and watched her, seated at the desk with her head bowed over my laptop, meeting my miniaturist and my celebrity, focus making her face taut. The image I'd failed for four years to imagine.

Eventually she looked up at me.

"What do you think?" I asked, and the feeling of vulnerability intensified, as though I were standing naked in front of someone in plate armor. What if Selina hated this, too? What if she hated everything I ever wrote? She wouldn't lie to me. How could I live with that?

I sipped from my mug and burned my mouth and said, trying to sound casual, "At this point I don't know why I care."

"Of course you know why. You're a brilliant person. You want to make brilliant work that touches people." She arched one brow. "And for some reason, you seem to care about my opinion, specifically."

"Guilty." The words gave me enough strength to approach her, to set the mugs on her desk. "So?"

A smile touched her lips. "I like these pages, Parker."

"You do?"

"Yes. I think it's a really deft, restrained opening." She rested her fingertips on my wrist. "It seems like you know what you want to say."

"Yeah," I said, touching her cheek. "Yeah, I do."

I went out with my friends from San Francisco on Friday night, and Selina told me she'd be asleep by the time we finished—*Your youthful thirty-two-year-old energy, it's too much for an ancient hag like me*—and so I crawled into my own bed at the end of the night, missing her.

I woke up on Saturday to my door swinging gently open, the morning light dimmed by my shades, and Arthur's silhouette crossing from the threshold to the end of my bed.

"Hey," I said sleepily. "What's going on? You all right?"

"Hey."

I sat up and put on my glasses, and Arthur's features clarified. He looked serious. "Look, Parker, something's happening online. I want you to . . . to kind of brace yourself. All right?"

The overfamiliar feeling began in my stomach, the spiraling churn, the throb of my pulse. Arthur typed something into his phone. "There's this article. The guy says he interviewed you?"

"Wait, the—the guy from Daly City? The *Bay Now* profile?"

"Yeah."

"But I never heard from him. I just figured they killed the piece." I reached for the phone. "He seemed nice. What, did he make me seem terrible?"

"What?" Arthur frowned. "Parker, the profile's not about you."

He set the phone into my palm. A high-contrast photo of Selina looked over her shoulder at me, icy and unreadable.

THE DRAGON LADY OF PUBLISHING

by Brian Falwell

She's influential, revered, and—for someone of her stature—young and beautiful. With an hour's writing, she can torpedo the creative work of years. Selina Chan is, in the words of some readers, the only honest person left in publishing,

> but the publishing world itself tells a different story: of an overpowered, unqualified writer who, through a confluence of lucky circumstances, has come to enjoy a position of outsized control in a troubled industry. When I spoke off the record to a legendary editor who works with—in several insiders' words—"every writer worth reading," she told me she wasn't surprised I'd reached out to get a fuller picture of the woman with the iron pen. "How could I be shocked?" she said. "The only question is why, in an industry that's been quietly seething about this woman for years, nobody did this sooner."

"Oh, my God," I said hoarsely. My hands had begun to shake.

> Selina Chan was born in Minneapolis, the daughter of Jianguo "Charles" Chan, a nephrologist, and Xiuying "Michelle" Chan. The relationship between parents and daughter is a strained one; according to one source, Chan hasn't left her perch in New York City to spend holiday seasons with her family for years. Her high school teachers describe her as withdrawn, brilliant, and socially troubled, a description that would follow Chan into her years at Columbia University.

My disbelief started to turn to panic. I was the source. I'd asked Brian not to mention my truce with Selina, but the details I'd let slip about her life—the way she spent her holidays—I'd left that on the record. How could I have been so spectacularly naive?

The next nine paragraphs were filled with anonymous quotes from other writers Selina had panned, from editors airing grievances about how she'd treated their authors, even from Selina's former Columbia classmates. Brian spent a healthy paragraph examining "the Chan phenomenon" with Christian Gatehead, who tiptoed right up to the edge of calling Selina a diversity hire.

And there, at the end of the article, was my name.

> Chan's highest-profile conflict has, of course, been the ongoing clash with Parker Navarro, who met with me to discuss their feud. A young, articulate writer with an evident nervous hangover, Navarro has an easy manner that turns to hair-pulling distress as he describes Chan's first pan of his work. "I remember that day clearer than any single other day from my twenties," says Navarro. "My college graduation, the day Bill flew out here, the actual book sale—I don't remember any of those as clearly as the day of the review. This is the worst possible thing that could happen to you as a writer."
>
> Navarro, whose second novel has since enjoyed strong reviews from the *Los Angeles Times* and *The New York Review of Books*, voices the frustration that unified every writer I spoke to: "What are this person's qualifications? What kind of a person does she have to be to do this to people?" Eventually he concludes, "She's just a person with an opinion." The so-called Chan phenomenon is as simple—and, for the career artists devastated by her words, as brutal—as that.

I looked up at Arthur, my breaths shallow. "Right, so we knew all that already," he said, as though the article I'd just read was something normal, and not something that would have catastrophic repercussions for Selina. "But there's this thread responding to it." He tapped to a different tab and returned the phone to my nerveless hands.

I stared down at the posts, each of which had thousands upon thousands of likes. The view metrics were in the hundreds of thousands.

@LolaXu: THE DRAGON LADY OF PUBLISHING? Are you fucking SERIOUS? You people are literally sharing an article with an Orientalist title that would have been offensive last century and acting like it's some kind of gotcha??

@LolaXu: This no-name outlet just allowed this man to write that Selina Chan got hired by City through "luck" and "circumstance" with ZERO evidence? If she doesn't sue this guy into oblivion for libel I stfg I'm going to do it for her.

@LolaXu: I was just going to let this go, bc Selina has been quiet on socials lately and it seems like she's been trying to move on. And y'all know I am all about lifting fellow BIPOC voices, but I can't watch Parker Navarro keep playing the victim and destroying the reputation of one of the only prominent Asian-American women in media. I got an ARC of his new book and honestly? Selina was being generous. Just look at the way he writes about mental illness and race. THREAD. (1/7)

"Oh, God," I said.

Arthur settled slowly onto the end of my bed.

@LolaXu: Yeah, things are hard out there for Asian writers! And no wonder, when this is what Asian authors keep putting on the page just to get a deal from a major publisher!

"Floating among the back rails of the bus, now, a little Chinese woman, or maybe she was Korean, Dave could never tell, but he spent a lot of time looking at their eyes, wondering if they knew anybody in manufacturing out there, if they had some personal relationship to the preshrunk cotton T-shirts in his top drawer at home, fellow transpacific imports." (2/7)

@LolaXu: Did you feel good writing that, Parker Navarro? Did you feel like you were helping your community, reusing stereotypes that Asian-Americans have to deal with every day of our lives? And don't you love that he put this racist ramble in the mouth of a working-class, Latinx narrator, basically undoing decades of race and class solidarity? (3/7)

@LolaXu: Latinx-Americans aren't closed-minded racists. They understand racism, even if Parker Navarro doesn't. (4/7)

@LolaXu: But wait, there's more! Here's what Navarro has to say on the topic of depression and being suicidal:

"Sometimes he toyed with potential suicides, painted and hung them like baubles upon the unlit Christmas tree in his mind, amused himself by breaking them open, pop, pop, as he turned the corner from Pine to Seventh, electrocution with household appliance, neighbor's gun, paint his face like a clown's before he pulled the trigger, so whoever found him would know at least he wasn't a dour fuck about the whole thing, not like those people who splatter-painted their misery on the internet, he'd seen them, creating anthemic slogans from their animal ability to keep inhaling and exhaling, as though the audience should be impressed." (5/7)

@LolaXu: And this asshole has the nerve to paint Selina Chan as hostile and unsympathetic? When HE has no sympathy for people struggling with these REAL PROBLEMS? Honestly even Dave, worst character ever, deserves so much better. Where's the compassion for his suffering? Also where's the impact on the character's relationships? But Parker Navarro didn't give him any close friends or family, of course, because people dealing with mental illness are just here to feel like a burden and push everyone away!! (6/7)

@LolaXu: I'm so tired. There are so many amazing books out there that show healthy and supportive angles on mental illness and this is the one Asian writer publishing decides to anoint and pay millions to, when there are so many worthy BIPOC writers who will never have a fraction of the opportunity he's gotten? A man who thinks suicide is a joke, depressed people who have the audacity to talk about our experience are cringe, racism is okay, and then steps on other Asian writers in the name of his own ambition? We ALL deserve better. (7/7)

@hardertimes: @LolaXu Wow, thank you for the heads-up. If I wanted to read a book that sympathizes with racists, there are piles of fascists to choose from.

@RightyLoosey: @LolaXu Canceling my preorder, fuck this man, thank you for this

@chanelfour: @LolaXu Omg I sent him a nice message after the video and he seemed so friendly. Writers like this are so fake. Profit-driven pigs. My skin is crawling

@333marcar333: @LolaXu Guillotine

I set down Arthur's phone, feeling sick. My skin was clammy. The air felt thick, obstructive, in the back of my throat.

I looked up at Arthur.

"I know," he said.

He did. Arthur knew better than anyone the tunnels in my mind that I'd been dragging myself out of for fifteen years. Arthur, who'd returned from break in the spring of our senior year to find our apartment a labyrinth of filthy dishes and unwashed clothes. Arthur, who'd tried to fix things by cleaning my room, because I was in bed fifteen hours a day, and who had found the note I'd drafted sticking halfway out of a drawer. Arthur, who must have recognized one of those lines from Lola Xu's chosen excerpt. *I don't want you to act like I was a dour fuck about this whole thing. Do me a favor and sprinkle some humor over it if you can.*

And now, a decade later, part of me thought, *Why didn't I just do it then?*

And another part of me thought, *Has she seen this yet?*

And I picked up my own phone and typed her name into the app, and then I saw what was, somehow, the worst of it.

Chapter Twenty-Four

Selina

I sat at the window with my head in my hands, staring down at my phone.

When had Parker said this about me?

This magazine was based in San Francisco. Had he talked to the writer when he'd been home last month—after all our emails, after New Year's?

I stood up abruptly. No. The interview could have happened after our panel in November, which would explain Christian Gatehead's prominent placement.

Why does it matter? I thought, rereading the paragraphs describing him. *Navarro has an easy manner that turns to hair-pulling distress as he describes Selina Chan's first pan of his work. "I remember that day clearer than any single other day from my twenties . . ."*

Who could say I hadn't deserved this?

I tipped headfirst back into social media. Every moment, Lola's thread was picking up new traction.

@Chinchillaaaa: @LolaXu I already knew he was trash after that shit he wrote in his first book, he literally has a guy thinking about women like they're animals. Disgusting, evil person

@Sapiosapien: @LolaXu Not to be like "I knew Selina Chan was right the whole time" but I knew Selina Chan was right the whole time

Guilt rammed through the floodgates. Lola hadn't cared about Parker until my review of *High and Dry*. I'd laughed with her, emboldened her. I hadn't even tried to curtail her disdain when she'd tagged me in that post with his advance copy.

I pressed the heels of my palms against my closed eyelids, my head throbbing. I understood Lola, angry and disillusioned. I'd been each of these readers, exhausted by the exotic language that doused Asian characters, by Hollywood's clouds of blue-tinted smoke diffusing over women in historically inaccurate hanfu, by the sensation that I had been born into a narrow and doorless room. But I didn't see how this was reparative.

I hit Quote Reply on the post with the "little Chinese woman" excerpt, my heart in my throat.

@SelinaChan: @LolaXu Lola, respectfully, I think context matters here. Yes, this thought is racist, but the book's primary interest is in how people fail to confront the worst patterns of their lives. Two of the most sympathetic side characters are a Chinese teenager and her elderly father, each looking for the other. Later on, Dave experiences a moment of identification with them, which complicates what you've quoted here. You know that I think the novel is unsuccessful, but I don't think Asian readers have any need to take issue with it.

I hit Post, and the replies began to arrive, in a trickle at first, then a deluge.

@lemon_cello: @SelinaChan Are you brainwashed?? Did you buy everything this man said about you? You're going to defend the "Asian people's eyes are shaped the same" quote???

@65tunes: @SelinaChan After that article, I was so prepared to take your side, but wow, everybody here sucks. Yet another milquetoast liberal who thinks their respectable intellectual bona fides matter more than AAPI readers getting to read one book in their lives that isn't teeming with dehumanization. Fuck you.

@bunnbunn: @SelinaChan newsflash: racists aren't going to love you no matter how much you hate yourself

@JennyHouseBooks: @SelinaChan Selina, I've had my gripes with your criticism in the past, but that article went way over the line. Trust me when I say that you, of all people, shouldn't be defending this man.

I looked at the last message for a little while. Jenny House.

@SelinaChan: @JennyHouseBooks Hi Jenny, why do you say that?

Five seconds passed, and then two screenshots of a group chat appeared. The title of the chat was Chan Pan Support Group. I read the two messages in gray once. Then twice. Trying to understand.

Parker Navarro
I don't know why I let Selina Chan, of all people, get in my head

Parker Navarro
I guess I've just got to remind myself: I might have bad reviews, but at least I don't have to wake up

in the morning knowing my broken personality will alienate everyone in my life

And the second:

Jenny House
Parker, you just got back from California, right? How was that?

Parker Navarro
Good! I did an interview with a writer back home. I think it's probably my last word on this feud. Feel like there's not much more to say.

I felt a slow, gentle pain, as though someone were taking my heart in their hands and pushing it apart, the way you'd break bread. The week that I'd been thinking day and night about New Year's Eve, imagining inviting Parker to *City*'s anniversary, checking my phone compulsively in hopes that he'd text me—this was what he'd felt, even then.

None of it was real. I had invented the person I'd been falling for.

And everything we'd been doing the past few weeks—what was that, for him? A joke? Some kind of sick physical gratification?

My eyes began to burn. I breathed fast, looking upward, trying to compose myself. The text he'd sent to his friends was true, anyway. I had alienated everybody but Jacob and Cassie, and someday they would be gone, too, when they were tired of putting up with me. And I would be here. The only person in the room.

For a while I could do nothing but sit there and reread Falwell's article, and as I did, my attention zeroed in on a line I'd skimmed over on that first read. *According to one source, Chan hasn't left her perch in New York City to spend holiday seasons with her family for years.*

Who else but Parker could have given Falwell that information? Who else was now equipped with the tools to humiliate me so completely?

My phone buzzed. Parker was calling me.

I hit Decline.

He texted me. I watched the message previews show up on screen and didn't touch my phone.

Selina, please pick up.

I have to talk to you. Please let me expla . . .

He called again. I let the phone ring, feeling as though I were being tugged backward by a rope down a long tunnel, watching his silhouette shrink in front of me, encircled by a mouth of light.

Twenty minutes later, my buzzer sounded. I didn't buzz him up, just looked over at the speaker from my seat at the window, but he must have rung the rest of the building, and someone must have taken pity on him, because two minutes later an urgent knock was sounding on my door. "Selina? Are you there, are you home?"

I rose slowly from my chair. The burn in my eyes faded, and as I moved toward the closed door, my anger unfurled, cold and enormous.

I pulled the door open. Parker stood in the hall, panting, looking like he'd run through hell to get here. "Can I come in?" he said.

"No."

"Selina—"

"I said no, Parker. You can't come in."

"That article," he burst out. "The interviewer took me completely out of context. I swear to God, Selina. I knew him a bit in high school, and he let me think he was writing a profile of me. I had no idea I needed to have my guard up."

"You *know* this guy?"

"Only a little! I told him I didn't feel that way about your reviews anymore. I *don't* feel that way."

"You don't? Even though you've been texting your publishing friends, saying—"

"No, listen. Those texts were from November. We were still saying things like that about each other in public at that point. You were still calling me juvenile and hopeless in print."

"I said those things about your *story*, Parker. Your fictional story. I've never written anything about how your family or friends feel about—"

Down the hall, my neighbor stuck her head into the hallway.

My hand strangling the doorknob, I stepped back. Once Parker had strode inside, I shut the door and faced him. "Let me get this straight. You came here to say this isn't that bad? And here I thought maybe you came to say you were sorry for airing my family's dirty laundry."

"But I didn't mean to—all I said was that—that you spent holidays here on your own, and—"

"I don't want anyone to *know* that about me!" I hated how thin my voice sounded, how abruptly vulnerable. "I don't tell people that! You know that! Why did you talk about it at all? Let alone to a media contact you haven't spoken to in fifteen years?"

His fingers flew to his forehead, his face crumpling. "I don't know, I—"

"And what about these past few weeks? Acting like—like you really—" I felt his hands on my body, his mouth on my neck. Humiliation bloomed inside me. I was losing it. Losing my composure, my articulation, everything. "When this whole time, you've had this—this group chat with my name on it? Did you like checking in on how much your friends hate me? Secretly having the upper hand while we were—"

"Selina, no." He reached for me. I smacked his hand away, stepped back. "It wasn't like that at all. The last thing I said to these people was that they had the wrong idea about you. Do you want to see the texts? I'll show them to you."

I let out a miserable laugh. "Sure. Show me, if you want to. But I don't know if you do."

As he looked down at his phone screen, thumbing his way up through the conversation, he swallowed, and his brows drew together. I tried to imagine Parker drawing a hard line in the sand. I tried to picture him arguing with a group of people on my behalf, risking offense or unpleasantness to stand up for me.

"No," he said, his eyes closing. He looked sick. "No, okay, I don't."

I wanted to stifle the hurt somehow. I wanted to stop the question spilling out, but I couldn't. "What have they been saying about me?"

"Don't," he said hoarsely.

Pain and anger twined into a hard knot in the center of my chest. "What have you been watching them say?"

"Selina, it wouldn't have mattered if I—"

"It would have mattered to me."

"But they have these deep-seated—even compared to what we were saying last year, these people are way beyond—"

"I don't *care* about them, Parker!" I said, halfway to a shout. "Do you think their opinions ever mattered to me? *You're* the one I cared about! God knows why!"

He flinched. It felt good. My mind was a blank roar, and I smelled weakness, pain, pressed my advantage. "I should have known the whole time," I said through my teeth, "that there would be some two-faced, cowardly shit like this with you."

Something ignited in his hollow expression. Hurt sparking against anger.

"Are those texts," he said, his voice low and restrained, "really so much worse than what you wrote about me? For years, people have been taking what you wrote about my books and turning it into an attack on who I am. And I know you think it's different, because you didn't talk about me directly, but Selina, *it's all the same*. Nobody fucking *cares* that it's fiction. They don't care. If you say the book is idiotic, then I'm an idiot. If you say the book is a failure, I'm a failure."

"It's not my fault that people will take criticism and expand it past its actual boundaries."

"That's the world we live in! You *knew* that when you wrote what you wrote about my books!"

"And I already said I was sorry for that!"

"No, you didn't." His voice rose. "You apologized for taking an assignment. You didn't apologize for writing that I was *painful to read*, or what was it the first go-around? That the book I put my whole heart into was *a cruelty*? Maybe if you hadn't written something so self-satisfied, Lola Xu wouldn't even know my name, and people wouldn't be sending me messages saying if I think suicide is so funny, maybe I should fucking try it! This is all happening because of *you*!"

My breathing sped. My eyes burned.

In that moment of ringing silence, I knew we'd both said too much, too many things that couldn't be unsaid.

"Thank you," I said, quiet, my voice shaking, "for your honesty, Parker."

I opened the door. He stared at me, blinking hard, as though he'd just awoken from a nightmare.

Then he looked through into the hallway. He drifted out like he didn't know which way he was going. Glanced back at me.

"I did come here," he said hoarsely, "to say I was sorry."

He waited for me to take the last word. I didn't want it.

I stood there in the open door and watched Parker step into the elevator and out of my life, and then the mirrored doors closed, showing me myself, and I couldn't stand the sight. I had to turn away.

Chapter Twenty-Five

Parker

I told myself I was so lucky that this was the worst day of my life.

I reminded myself that other people had real problems. I told myself stories about those problems, about death, loss, and physical pain, as I sat there in my apartment with food in the fridge and money in my bank account and my family and friends in good health.

I hope this piece of shit never writes another word in his life

One-starred before reading because I don't support people poisoning other people with their internalized racism

Arthur made me lunch, which we ate in silence.

Bill called me and said, "This is what I meant, before, when I said it could be worse."

Unbelievable that Anna Delaney is platforming this guy

No it's okay I just heard she dropped the book

OK good, at least she isn't a hypocrite

Tessa Hargreaves sent word through her agent that she was withdrawing as the conversation partner for my launch. Not even an hour later, Bill received an email from the book festival in Seattle, rescinding my keynote invitation for September. Nobody from Coronation had been in touch with either guidance or reassurance. I felt as though I were hurtling down a long, straight road and watching the asphalt shatter ahead of me, cracking all the way down to the horizon line.

I called my parents, who didn't seem to understand what was going on, but when my mom said, "I love you, Pijay," I had to choke out "Love you, too" and hang up before she could hear anything else.

hey parker navarro how does it feel knowing you've set your community back fifty years?

It would be one thing if he was even a good writer lol

As somebody suicidal trying to get some shred of reassurance from talking about it online FUCK YOU, FUCK YOU SO HARD

This last person. I wanted to message them. I wanted to tell them about myself, about how I'd felt in college, so full of private envy for the people who could talk about their depression that I'd sublimated the envy into scorn, and I knew it was an imperfect reaction, but it was true. I wanted to tell them it was going to be okay. I wanted to crawl into a hole and die.

Maybe they were right, these people. I'd had my share of self-loathing thoughts. Maybe they'd leaked onto the page, and what I'd enshrined in this book was not anything artistic or beautiful but instead a catalog of every one of my worst instincts, and when I was dead, that would be all that was left behind. I *could* have written something more positive. I could have written a novel about being Filipino, with a heroic, complicated, vibrant Filipino main character. Maybe this instinct I had to pitch my imagination far into some other space ultimately came down to the idea of wanting to see myself dead. Maybe it came from the knowledge that, at the end of the day, I was a C-tier writer, a bottomless well of unfulfilled potential, an uninteresting person, and apparently also a bad person.

I should have realized this before now. I'd never written anything that had been widely loved. The only way in which I was loved was that, in a group of people, I could obligingly make myself absent.

Except with Selina.

And Selina. I'd gone to her apartment to apologize, desperate to know she still cared about me, and then, somehow, I'd yelled at her in my self-pity.

It wasn't Selina's fault that people hated me. It was my own. It was my writing they loathed, my choice to participate in that group chat and then, like a coward, to watch silently as they'd called Selina a harpy and a narcissist. Whereas Selina had immediately leaped to my defense online, knowing that Lola Xu's 120,000 followers would go for her throat. The contrast sickened me.

At the end of that unending day, Arthur came into my room and found me scrolling through my phone.

"Hey," he said.

"Hey."

"Maybe you shouldn't be online so much right now."

"You're probably right," I said, not looking away from my screen.

Arthur walked up with his hand outstretched.

"What?" I said.

"I think you should give that to me. And your laptop."

"It's three days before my book launch. I need to be in touch with people."

"I'll handle it. If they have questions, I can ask you. If your family or friends text, I'll let you know, and we can figure something out."

"Arthur"—I hunched lower in bed—"can you not do this?"

"Not do what? Look out for you?"

"You know what I mean."

"No." He reached his hand farther toward me. "I'm serious, Parker. You don't need to be seeing this shit."

"It's still happening, even if I'm not reading it."

"And, what, that makes it your responsibility?"

I wavered.

My phone dipped in my hand. Arthur swept it from my grasp. I watched him unplug my laptop and take it from my desk, and a feeling of powerlessness overwhelmed me. So much for the progress I thought I'd made.

"Arthur?" I said hoarsely.

"Yeah?"

"If I get any texts from . . . I mean, if . . ."

"I'll tell you who tries to get in touch, all right? Get some rest."

As he walked away, everything grew quiet and slow. I looked at my bookshelves, my favorite authors looking back at me, and the hammock in the fall of evening light.

I drew the bedcovers up over myself and thought of the hurt in Selina's face, and the way that, for the first time since we'd met, her words to me had fragmented. I'd done that. I'd shoved away the only person to look at me and see every part of me, because, as it turned out, I couldn't stand to be seen.

The strange quietness lasted right through Sunday. It hadn't been this difficult in ten years to get out of bed, get dressed, and walk out the door, but when I did, I found I didn't want to go home. I sat in the park chewing falafel, tasting nothing, watching dogs skitter by in their harnesses and small boots. The day was near freezing, but I'd layered up and didn't mind the feeling of my face growing icy. I walked three miles around Brooklyn, four, five, then sat on a bench at a bus stop and watched the J train hurtle along the elevated tracks, then went in to thaw at a little ice cream shop, where the woman behind the counter smiled at me like I looked normal, called me sweetheart.

As I walked back to my apartment in the evening I saw silhouettes in our front window. My steps caught. I didn't want to bump into Arthur's friends. I barely wanted to see Arthur, as unfair as that was, considering everything he was doing for me.

Maybe I could sidle through with a quick nod, shut myself in my room. Steeling myself, I unlocked our door and slipped inside, only to find that it wasn't Arthur's friends who'd come to our apartment.

It was my family.

Kevin and Elena flanked my dad on the sofa, showing him something on the TV remote. Christi and Justin stood in the kitchen, heads bowed together in a serious way that I hadn't seen since they were teenagers sneaking away to talk about our parents splitting up. And my mom was there, too, standing at the stove, cooking something that filled the air with the rich tang of soya.

Nothing about the sight felt real. I hadn't seen my parents in the same room since I was twelve years old.

"Hey, there he is," said Justin. His brash, hard voice felt bracing.

"Pijay," my mom cried, dropping her ladle into the simmering pot on the stove and rushing to enfold me in her arms. I stood motionless, shaken, letting my head drop over her shoulder, as the others approached.

"You okay?" Christi said in that brisk older-sister way as she clamped me in a brief hug.

"Of course he's not," said Kevin. "Parker's got a lot of feelings."

"Can we not, with the dismissive attitude toward feelings?" said Elena.

"Elena," said Justin, rolling his eyes, "nobody's dismi—"

"Stop," I said sharply. "Please, stop it."

My whole family looked toward me, wide-eyed.

It took everything in me not to apologize immediately.

I drew a slow breath. "Thank you for coming," I said quietly. "I love you guys. I also need you to . . . not to start anything. Please. Okay?"

Elena's eyelids flickered quickly over her large, brightening eyes. Kevin's feet performed a guilty little shuffle.

"Of course," said my dad.

I looked his way. Guillermo Navarro was a tall, square-shouldered man with deep purple circles under his eyes, the ones I was slowly inheriting. "Your mother," he said, "is making Pancit Canton. Should be done soon."

"Yes." Mom didn't look at him, her voice as careful as his. "It'll be ready in fifteen minutes or so."

"Thanks, Mom." I set a hand on her shoulder. "Need any help?"

"No! No, of course not. Sit, relax. Talk."

And we did. My parents sat diagonally from each other at the dinner table and didn't carry any conversation, but Arthur helped them loosen up, and eventually they passed dishes to each other without visible signs of dislike. I wouldn't have wanted this to happen at any other time, but when, near the end of dinner, Christi finally said, "Can you explain, like, what this whole blowup means for the book? And for you?" I couldn't have described how much it meant to see everybody's faces turn toward me with concern and affection.

I thought of Selina. *Do people know you the right way?* And in that moment, it didn't seem to matter if my family and I understood each other perfectly, because they were here, trying.

I explained what it meant that the book club selection had been canceled—the eleven thousand special-edition copies that would be destroyed—and what it might mean if my reputation tanked so hard that Bill couldn't sell anything else I'd written. I told them that I might never publish another word, that I might have to sell my apartment and move out of the city, depending on where I could find work. I began to picture it as I spoke, quiet and monotone, a teaching post in a small town, and maybe that would be okay, to have an unobjectionable life in calm obscurity, writing for nobody but myself again.

But as I described these possibilities, I still thought of Selina's eyes in the dark. And I wished she were here, looking at me the way she had just three days ago, with that unlikely tenderness, that fathomless understanding, as though when I spoke, she could identify every layer of meaning beneath my words, like a geologist tracing the strata of some compressed stone, all the way down to the core. She, more than anyone, would know what it meant for me to lose the life I'd built here.

I thought if I'd had her back, if I'd only had her here, I could have withstood all the rest.

That night I lay in bed, staring at my bedside table, at the limp end of my phone charger, and I wished I could have that horrible thing back in my hand, full of the world's hatred for me, full of every reminder of every way I'd fallen short, because at least I could have visited the *City* website and read something in her voice. I could have looked her up on Venmo and seen that picture of her smiling on the pier. I could have looked back through the messages we'd sent, brushed hands with the ghost of what she'd felt for me.

When I arrived at Word that Tuesday night for my launch, Emily said, "Hey," with visible strain. I couldn't interpret the strain as sympathy or dislike, so decided to assume dislike until she gave me another indicator.

"Hi," I said. "Thank you so much for still doing this, even without Tessa. I'm sorry, the past few days must have had some blowback on you guys."

"It's fine. I'm sure it's been harder for you."

This gave me nothing. I wondered what Emily wanted to hear. An admission of guilt? Was she being intentionally vague because she worried that I'd stake out some aggressive position on mental illness right in front of her? If I said something wrong, would she post it online and set off another wave of disgust?

"It was a weird weekend, yeah," I said eventually. "My roommate took away my phone and laptop on Saturday, so I haven't known what's been going on the past couple of days."

"It's been okay today." She offered a sympathetic smile and added, "I think it's starting to die down." And the fact that she didn't hate me filled me with embarrassing relief.

As 7 PM drew nearer, my family and friends started to arrive. Tyler and Maricel had bought a cake, and everybody else greeted me with cheery exclamations and said nothing about the internet. Two people trickled in whom I didn't know: a bearded man in a cardigan and a shy-looking teenage girl, who would never know how much their presence meant to me.

I kept watching the door, the busy street outside, as the minutes ticked down. Some tiny part of me was clutching to the sliver of a possibility. Every bobbing shape in the night was her dark head bowed against the wind. Every glint of light across the street, her phone screen.

At 7:03, Emily said, "Are you ready?"

"Could we wait a couple of minutes?" I said. "Just—just in case."

It didn't matter. She never showed.

Chapter Twenty-Six

Selina

For half an hour, I stood in the shadow of a USPS mailbox, shivering, looking through the window of Word. The image was a perfect, glowing diorama, the bookstore lights shining on Parker's messy hair, his smile. The audience was around two-thirds full. For that much, at least, I was grateful. I'd worried nobody would come.

Of course, if nobody had come, maybe I would have been able to make myself go inside. Maybe I could have convinced myself that he would rather have seen me than no one at all.

But I should have known that Parker would have a crowd of friends to support him. Friends who embraced him, friends who insisted on photographing him with his stack of books, even as he protested. His family even seemed to have flown in, his four siblings bookended by his parents, in whom I could see Parker's features.

He looked exhausted but happy. After Emily's introduction, he did a short reading, then closed the book and started to speak.

I wanted so badly to know what he was saying. But I heard, for the thousandth time in the past three days, *This is all happening because of you*, and I wasn't selfish enough to ruin a celebration with his friends and family simply because I wanted to hear his voice again.

I made myself turn away from the window and walk down the

block, my breath clouding in front of me. The train was southward, but I turned west, toward Jacob and Cassie's place. On Saturday, Jacob had texted our group chat, saying, Are you okay? We saw the profile. And you going to bat for Parker.

I'd said, Yes, it's fine, I shouldn't have gotten involved.

The idea of telling them what Parker had been to me, even for just a few weeks, had felt excruciating. But at this moment, the idea of returning to my apartment, filled with memories of him, felt worse.

A minute later I was buzzing and saying, "Hi, it's Selina, can I come up?"

I hurried up the steps. When Cassie opened the door, the sight of her worried face made something in me wobble.

"What's wrong?" she said.

My hand flew to the bridge of my nose. My eyes burned.

I let out a sob.

"Selina?" Her voice was sharp with alarm. As I stepped over the threshold and she wrapped me in a bear hug, she called back into the apartment, "Jacob!"

I held my eyes shut, enveloped in the scent of Cassie's coconut conditioner. I heard quick footsteps and the door closing, and Jacob saying, "Oh, man. What happened?"

"I don't know."

"Selina? Hey." His hand touched my back. I looked up, crying, my hand still over my nose and mouth. "Hey, did something happen to you?"

"No. It's—" I tried to breathe. "Just . . . Parker."

Cassie and Jacob exchanged a look. Then Jacob guided me toward the sofa, and Cassie hurried to the kitchen island to run me a glass of water, and soon she'd pushed it into my hand and was crouching by my side. "Wh-where's Lyra?" I said, glancing around.

"Asleep," said Jacob. "She's a little sick."

"Oh, no. When did—"

He shook his head, settling beside me. "Don't worry about it. She's okay."

"Hey," said Cassie, rubbing my thigh. "Hey. Tell us what happened."

And I did, although I had to stop intermittently to cry. I didn't know how to do this. I had never done this before. I told them everything, described every lovely facet of the fragile thing I'd broken. I couldn't believe how little I cared, anymore, about what Parker had said to some two-bit reporter or what insults toward me he'd let go unchallenged. He'd been willing to look past what I'd done to his career. How ludicrous, how prideful, that I'd thrown that grace away.

"His book launch is happening right now," I cried. "I went by. Past the window. I saw him."

"Selina," Cassie said quietly.

I put my face in my hands. I couldn't say it, it was too humiliating, but I couldn't believe that I'd ever had someone like Parker, that a person so kind and good had ever wanted me. It hurt so badly to have had him for that short moment. Now the moment had become a snapshot in time, like Juliette had described in her book, an illuminated window that I would look back on for the rest of my life, as it grew smaller and smaller behind me.

Two sobering days passed. While commuting I kept my face angled toward the windows in the train's sliding doors, trying to look out at the blurry details of the subway tunnels and not at the harshly lit reflection of my own wan face. After work, to the gym. After dinner, to the Slippery Cork. On Thursday, Nadia asked me, "How are you, sweetheart?"

"I'm okay."

She glanced down the length of the empty bar, then tossed her rag down. "I'm sure you don't need me to tell you, but people online don't know how to act."

I glanced up quickly from my drink. "You . . ."

"I saw that video that went around in October. I gave you a follow."

For a long moment I sat there, jarred. Of course, Nadia had read my name off my credit card biweekly for the last five years and could, at any time, have Googled the antisocial creature who crawled into her bar to read. There had been no reason to assume distance between us.

In the face of her reassurance, I wanted to feel closer to her. Instead I experienced a feeling of suffocation, that even here, in this place I'd come to feel like a safe, anonymous, perfectly scripted version of myself, I couldn't escape the mess of who I actually was. But I said, "Thank you, Nadia," and she gave me a pat on the wrist and comped my drink.

When that unending week finally drew to its close, the discourse online had mostly burned out. I'd been wondering if Nextward would fire me on the basis of the hit piece. Hayden had reassured me by email that they didn't mind the controversy, but that Friday, the *City* staff came in to find her at our morning meeting, looking grave.

"So, not *great* news," said Hayden. "We got word from the Densmore Foundation that they're considering pulling support for the upcoming year."

"*What?*" said half the table.

Hayden's eyes strayed to me.

"Because of the profile," I said.

"You'd think," said Hayden. "No, it's because the head of their board didn't love how you dealt with the Parker Navarro controversy this week."

"They're pulling support because I wasn't angry *enough* about *High and Dry*?"

"Selina, you're a public figure. You have forty thousand followers and *City Magazine* on your profile. You can't just say whatever you want."

"What's the point of having a social media account if I don't say what I want to say?"

"I don't know. Let's think. You support Parker Navarro when he has the popularity of Joseph Stalin, partially thanks to *your own* review, and you're shocked there's a ripple effect?" Hayden turned to Scott, her lips pressed together. "I'm trying to keep the conversation open with them, but between this and the rent situation, we need to start thinking about the office."

Silence spread from bookshelf to bookshelf. We were reaping what we'd sown. That felt patently obvious now: I should never have stoked the fires of the feud, never caved to my base instincts, no matter how good it had felt at the time.

"Why *did* you stick up for him, anyway?" Kellie said. For once there was no bounce in her inflection. I let out a leaden-sounding laugh, but I couldn't make myself answer. At least, now, I would never have to explain anything to Kellie or anyone else on staff. The people online who had already been circling the idea of Parker "sleeping with the enemy" would never be vindicated. My credibility, I reminded myself, was the cornerstone on which my life was built. Maybe I had nothing else, but I still had that. The shreds of my privacy. The idea of myself. A door I could keep locked forever.

I stopped by Jacob and Cassie's apartment that afternoon with a gift, wanting to thank them for dealing with my outburst. They were scheduled to fly out tomorrow afternoon, so I expected to find a half-disassembled apartment. When Jacob opened the door to the loft, though, I found no sign of disorder.

"Hey," he said. "What's up? You okay?"

"Yeah. Just wanted to drop this off to thank you both for Tuesday." I handed him the small gift bag.

"You didn't have to do that."

"Yes, well, it was an embarrassing night, so." I frowned up at his disheveled hair, his red-rimmed eyes. "You're sick."

"We all are." Jacob's laugh sounded hoarse. "Lyra's thing turned into a fever, and Cassie caught it, too. She had to call out sick today."

"Wait. Your trip . . ."

"Yeah. We canceled everything."

"Oh, Jacob." I felt a pang of sympathy. I couldn't imagine Cassie's disappointment. Even Jacob would have a hard time bouncing back from the prospect of Lunar New Year in a tropical paradise. "I'm so sorry."

"Yeah, thanks. It sucks."

"It really does feel like forever since you two got to live your actual life."

Jacob's gentle smile made him look even more tired. "This is our actual life, Selina. Neither of us would trade it." He fished around in the gift bag and drew out a Fresh Linens–scented candle in a frosted glass cylinder. His eyes brightened. "You know what, this is perfect. We can just light this tonight and lie in bed and watch a movie."

"None of you can smell anything," I pointed out.

"Don't use logic on me when I have the plague. Rude." He lifted the candle to me like a pint in a toast. "But thanks, seriously. We'll see you when no one's contagious."

"Perfect. Let me know if you need anything."

When he'd shut the door, I heard Cassie, muffled, calling to ask who'd buzzed. Jacob's congested voice trailed back to her, into the quiet reaches of their home, and a moment later I heard them laughing. Of course they wouldn't trade this, even for freedom.

That night, with a tight, repetitive ache in my chest like a muscular cramp, I spent two hours rereading my emails with Parker, and then our texts, all the way down to the end.

Selina, please pick up.

I have to talk to you. Please let me explain.

I pushed my phone under my pillow and lay in bed, watching the radiator. My eyes leaked, my nose burning. He had come over to fix things, and I hadn't let him. No wonder that, by the end of the fight, he'd realized the truth.

I didn't want to look at his social media. It didn't sound or feel like him. Instead I rose unsteadily from my bed and knelt by the radiator. On the second shelf from the bottom were the *N* authors. Parker's books sat wedged between Katie Navan and Curtis Nelson.

I tugged them out and let the new hardcover of *High and Dry* fall open in my lap.

My throat constricted when I saw the title page.

In his slapdash hand was written,

to my well-kept secret.
yours,
Parker

I touched the bleed of the ink and felt that pressurized pain in my chest again. When I opened *These Extraordinary Times*, I found the same inscription.

I hugged the books into my bed and turned on the reading lamp at the corner of my headboard. Shut off all other lights, so I was enclosed by a sleepy amber cone. Then I opened *These Extraordinary Times* and began to read.

I read fifty pages, then seventy-five, with increasing disorientation.

I could see the book I'd read four years ago. They were of course the same words in the same order, and I could identify the same lack of focus, the same jarring and evasive turns, that I'd criticized before.

But I could no longer tell what I thought.

It was as though I were standing six inches from an impressionist painting, gazing into the fine textures of the brushstrokes, too close to contextualize shapes or colors. In every sentence I could feel Parker's care or his joy. During a scene I'd insulted in my review, where the grandmother loses her makeup case in a bucket of fish at a sea lion performance, I heard Parker's voice reading to me, his low and smiling voice, like we were sharing a joke, and I imagined him awake in Daly City in his terrible studio apartment at six in the morning, squeezing in these words before his shift at the H Mart, cheap kettle gurgling in the background. I imagined the way his lower lip folded between his teeth when he worked. The makeup case toppled in among the fish, rouging their scales, and he overdescribed it, because he wanted to make sure I was right there with him. He was playing around, dreaming, toiling, feeling free. I couldn't separate any of it from him.

I loved it, I realized.

I loved these pages just because they had him in them.

I closed the book and stared down at the messy scrawl of its cover art, feeling adrift, disturbed. What was I without my ability to see clearly, think clearly, judge clearly? How could I fix this? How to get my perspective back?

I let the book open to the inscription again.

yours, Parker

My disturbance stilled like the surface of a lake after rain.

This was how it felt, then, to love someone: To sacrifice clarity. To let go the illusion of objectivity. To give every word the benefit of the doubt.

And with Parker, if I had to choose between a clean and confident judgment and this—this mess of contradictory feeling, this stew of complication; if I had to choose between the neat and comprehensible outside and the inexplicable inside, then, for the first time in my life, I chose the inside. I would love him right into my own uncertainty.

And even though he didn't want me back anymore, he'd given me this much. This understanding. It was something I'd never lose.

To: Charles.Chan111@gmail.com
From: selinachanlikesbooks@gmail.com
Sent: Feb 19, 10:23 PM
Subject: Re: Author fight

Hi Mom and Dad,

I'm not sure if you've seen the article about me in a magazine called the Bay Now, but unfortunately it mentions your names. I can't say how sorry I am.

Over the past month, I've thought a lot about your last message. I'm not sure I've told you this, but I've understood your worries about my career for years now. Criticism can be a volatile and thankless job, and you're right: Sometimes you say things you can't take back.

But whenever we've spoken about my work, you've always brought up my future. You worry about stability. Longevity. I don't know if you'll understand, but even if my career ends tomorrow, I'll still be proud to have spent my life building it. Something doesn't have to last forever to matter.

You asked in November if I'd call you back. Maybe we could find a time for that soon.

Selina

Chapter Twenty-Seven

Parker

My life had changed. I was no longer Parker Navarro, the author of the most hated book of the decade. Now I was Parker Navarro, the *New York Times*–bestselling author of the most hated book of the decade.

It was with this news, eight days after *High and Dry* published, that Arthur returned my phone and laptop to me. "I'm so proud of you, bro," he said.

"You mean for lasting more than a week without a phone?"

"Yeah. *New York Times* who?"

I sat at our dining room table, the devices stacked before me. "Thank you," I said. "Seriously. I'm sorry you had to—"

"I didn't have to do anything."

"Yeah, no, I just"—I let out a breath, angry with myself—"you take on so much already, and I told myself after college and the first book that I'd stop letting things get bad, and you're still here, like, having to look after me, or whatever."

Arthur shrugged on his coat. "You planned stuff for me when I got dumped. You cooked for us that whole month."

"Well, yeah, but that was a normal—"

"This is normal. That's what I'm saying. Not everything is a brain chemistry problem. Sometimes it's a 'life kicks people in the teeth and then they have to wait for their teeth to stop bleeding' problem."

I watched Arthur do up the buttons of his coat and tried to come up with some counterargument, but nothing came to mind.

"If you *want* to square things off," he said, "you can buy me one of those stupid twelve-dollar Japanese ice creams."

"That seems like a false equivalence."

"You're right. Three fancy ice creams. That's my price." He shoved his wallet in his pocket, clapped me on the shoulder, and left me to reenter the internet for the first time in a week.

I left my laptop shut and handled the phone gingerly, allowing myself only cursory glances at my email. But reading through my sibling and San Francisco group texts, settling back into the collage of text styles and voices, felt like a kind of homecoming, and soon enough Lauren and Bill called to congratulate me. I deleted the Chan Pan Support Group thread, then blocked all four numbers individually, feeling a deep satisfaction each time, as though I were turning the world's heaviest dead bolts with each tap of the thumb.

I wondered how Selina felt about the news. I tried to imagine what she would have said if we were speaking, but my imagination was an unacceptably poor substitute.

I'd dreamed of hitting the *New York Times* bestseller list since I was a teenager. I would have traded it for a lifetime of anonymity if, somehow, it meant I had her back.

Hunched over the dining table, I opened social media, steeling myself for the coolly unaffected, consummately professional posts that she would have made in the ten days since I'd seen her. But there was nothing. The last thing she'd said was, Hi Jenny, what do you mean?

Below, her defense of me remained undeleted on her profile, although hundreds of replies had accumulated beneath it, lambasting her. Of course, no matter how we'd fought, she wouldn't go back on what she'd said. She'd stood between the world's anger and me, trying—in a way no one ever had—to protect me.

A wave of feeling rolled through my body. It seemed impossible that I'd ever had her, this woman whose brilliance was matched only by her strength of character, and even more unbelievable that I'd allowed myself to lose her.

I knew now that I'd never get her back, but maybe I could move the needle the tiniest bit on how people saw her.

I opened up a new post. As I did, I felt a clear, cool anger, the kind of anger Selina had once described, the kind that demonstrates that you know you're worth something. I didn't want to talk about any of it, but for her, I would.

@ParkerNavarroWrites: I know I'm courting disaster by writing this—a response to the criticisms of High and Dry that have been discussed on this platform for the past week and a half—but if these admissions mean any less judgment aimed in the direction of Selina Chan, our generation's most clear-minded, thoughtful, and devoted critic, about whom I was completely wrong in October and for months afterward, then the disaster will have been worth it.

When I was 22 years old, I planned my suicide. I was devoutly preoccupied with how the suicide would look. I didn't want it to be one of those self-indulgent suicides. I doubt I need to say anything further about how this informs my character, Dave, and his attitude toward his mental health.

The passage about the elderly Chinese woman is cobbled together from experiences I've had with non-Asians. I find value in repurposing and exploring experiences I don't understand, and I find hope in imagining that the people who said these things to me might someday experience a shift in worldview, the way that, as Selina said, Dave eventually does, later in the book.

I hit Post, then dropped my phone on my bed, put on my coat, and walked out into the neighborhood. Already clouds of potential responses were forming in my mind, the ways in which my post would be seen as inadequate or disingenuous. The responses wouldn't come only from strangers. My siblings would text me soon, asking why I'd never told them. I'd made allusive comments to Elena in reassurance before, when she'd hit her own low points, but even she had never known how far things had gone when I was at school. I imagined she would call with no warning, multiple times; Christi would text hyper-articulate paragraphs; Justin would get angry and defensive in a way that revealed his worry. I pictured Kevin at a loss for words completely. I wondered if any of them would tell our parents, and what my friends from home would say, what they would think of me—but—enough. The truth was out.

As I skirted the park, the leafless maples, I turned my thoughts to Selina instead, and the world fell quiet. I wondered if she would even see what I'd written, if the post would mean anything to her. It couldn't undo what I'd said when we'd fought. The wind through the bare branches seemed to murmur her name. The sun had begun to set, and I wandered westward, down Nassau, to a familiar intersection.

I thought of Selina on New Year's Eve and drew a shaky breath, imagining I caught her perfume on the cold wind. Then I turned onto the quiet residential block and descended the narrow steps to the Book Bar.

The store was dim and near-empty, even shabbier by daylight. The bar at the back apparently made gestures at repurposing itself as a cafe during daytime. I ordered a decaf and used it to warm my hands, and I tried not to think of Selina's smile when she'd seen this place, like she'd fallen in love.

I moved down the deserted fiction aisle, but as I approached the corner, my steps slowed. Maybe I didn't want to see it, *well-kept secret,* that mark of the first time I'd looked at her and understood what she might mean to me.

I reached the corner, turned, and froze in place.

Selina was sitting a few paces away, curled in an antique armchair in the corner, reading by the light of a stained glass lamp.

She looked up and became perfectly still.

This corner of the store was warm. Her coat hung over the back of the chair, and she wore a soft gray T-shirt and jeans, and her hair fell over her shoulder. I could have stood there, transfixed by the sight of her, for hours.

"Parker," she said quietly.

I opened my mouth and found I couldn't speak.

"I'll leave," she said, closing her book.

My voice flooded back to me. "No. Please—it's okay, stay."

Selina rose to her feet anyway and gathered her coat over her arms, lifted her purse onto her shoulder. But she didn't walk away.

"I saw your post," she said.

"You did?"

She smoothed her hair back from her forehead and looked away. "It was kind."

"It was the truth."

Her fingers shifted on the strap of her purse, and it seemed like a preparatory motion, like she would disappear down the aisle, having, in one minute, wrecked my night, my week, my entire uncertain future.

"Wait," I said, unable to stop myself.

She grew still as I reached out and touched our names on the wall. Our truce.

I lowered my hand to move toward her, then stopped midstep, remembering how she'd slapped my hand away that morning in her apartment. Those minutes of rage and hurt seemed to roll in on us like a stinging fog, Selina snarling out that she should have expected nothing better, my accusation that she'd made this happen.

But she was here.

After that Saturday, I'd been sure that if we ever saw each other again, she would look at me with all the scorn and disgust she'd shown in the Cipriani library in October. Instead, she was regarding me with something bizarrely close to doubt, her lips pulling first to one side and then the other.

Hope laid a fingertip on my heart.

"Parker, what I wrote . . ." she began, and from the softness of her tone I realized that she intended to apologize, and disbelief reared up in me. *No,* I thought. That was the last thing I wanted from her.

"I read what you wrote," I broke in. "Over Christmas. Last month . . . What you wrote to me."

I saw her breath catch. She swallowed hard.

"Those messages," she said, "meant more to me than anything I've written in my life."

A gust of impossible hope swept through me, and suddenly my heart was beating hard, insistent, like an urgent knock at a door. I stepped closer. "Me too," I said hoarsely, barely able to work the words free. "If I've ever said anything that mattered, I said it to you."

I saw her sway by an inch, steady herself. The silence rang around us, and I couldn't have looked away from her for anything.

"I waited for you," I said. "The launch. I thought maybe you'd come."

"I did."

I looked at her, uncomprehending.

A blush faded in on the curves of her cheeks. "I couldn't make myself go inside. I thought, I couldn't ruin your night."

"But that was all I wanted. For you to be there." I finally closed the distance between us, close enough to take a shaky breath and smell the cream of her lotion and the sultry hint of her perfume, the sweetness of her shampoo. She lifted her chin, searching my expression with a kind of open need that I'd never seen her show.

"Did you mean it?" she asked. "What you wrote in my copies of your books."

Haltingly, I lifted my hand to her reddened cheek. "Of course I meant it." She closed her eyes and moved into my touch. I said, quietly, "I love you."

She said, "I love you, too," and my other hand found her waist, the softness of her T-shirt, and I just held on to her, unable to believe the feeling in my chest, like my heart was straining against its confines.

She leaned up toward me, and I tilted my head and kissed her, and my thoughts lit up like an electric grid, revolved brilliantly like a time lapse of the night sky. The truth swept around us like a cold, clean wind. When I looked back to autumn, all I saw was performance, but in winter, what we'd said in secret, that was the real thing.

This was the real thing.

Chapter Twenty-Eight

Selina

"Toni Morrison?" called Joyce, waving a small stack of Morrison novels around the library.

"Got them," said about half the staff, rising above the mumbled assent of the other half.

"More for me, then!" Joyce placed them in her box as I did the same with a copy of *Our Gods Our Heavens.*

On my knees, I looked up at the *City* library, at the steadily emptying shelves. Scott stood near the door. He appeared to be studying a copy of Min Jin Lee's *Pachinko*, but he'd been standing there long minutes, the crags and valleys of his face immobile.

"Think he's doing okay?" Kellie said.

I looked over at her. She was sitting with her back against an emptied shelf, her elbow resting on a closed box of books.

"No," I said, "I think he's devastated."

"Yep. He takes things hard." She toyed with the zipper on her leather jacket. "How about you?"

I watched Joyce and Mike haggle over a first edition of *Kindred.* The light through the mullioned windows tumbled off the dust in the air, disturbed by fourteen pairs of hands. The room had grown darker and darker as the colorful spines disappeared into boxes.

I wanted to say something intelligent and restrained. Instead, when I opened my mouth, a dejected sound slid out.

"There we go. I know." Kellie gave me a bracing pat on the knee. "But all is not lost, right?"

"Yeah." I turned over a translation of *Beowulf* in my hands. "How are you always so unfazed?"

"Unfazed? I'm plenty fazed." Kellie took the *Beowulf* from my hands and tossed it into her own box. "Ask me how fazed I am. Do it. I dare you."

I managed to give her a sidelong smile, and I asked her.

At the end of the day, Scott gathered us at the round table. "Now, on Monday, we'll probably hit some bumps in the road, but we'll figure it out. Just think of the time and money you'll save commuting."

Some appreciative murmurs, a couple of chuckles. I didn't join in. Of course I recognized the convenience of remote work. It wasn't even that I believed the magazine's operations would necessarily suffer, conducted over text and video. Having lost the Densmore Foundation grant, we were probably lucky that Nextward had decided to try this instead of bumping us into a coworking space and putting us through another round of layoffs. Still, it seemed to me that in losing this place, we'd lost a part of what we were, failing the decades of writers who'd come before us.

I lingered so long in my office that by the time I emerged into the hall, the whole floor seemed to echo with quiet. I was the last one here.

When I got out to the fourteenth-floor landing, my steps slowed. Parker was waiting across from the elevator, one hand in his coat pocket, his head bowed over an open paperback.

"Parker," I said, hurrying up to him.

He looked up, smiling. "Hey." He bookmarked his page and kissed me. "Surprise."

I kissed him again, my hands loosely encircling his wrists. "Thank you for coming."

"Of course. How was it?"

"Terrible. In all the ways I imagined and some others I didn't prepare for."

He looked toward the sheer face of the oak wall, CITY MAGAZINE carved in deep. "I'm so sorry," he said. "I know you loved this place."

I reached out to touch the edge of the *C*. "I remember my first day here. I got out of the elevator and saw this, and I felt like it had been here forever." My hand lowered. "Like it was going to be here forever."

Parker trailed his hand over the wall, too. I wondered what he was thinking, if, someday, I would see this moment crystallized in something he wrote.

He approached the glass door. I followed, and we stood looking through at the bare walls. The tessellated carpeting.

"The framed covers used to hang down this side." I pointed. "And that's the library at the end."

"Any chance of a goodbye tour?" Parker said.

"I think I can arrange that." I opened the door, and we stepped through. "Why? Do you want to see the office where I spent hours seething over your press clippings?"

He tucked my hair behind my ear. "Maybe I just like getting to see your sentimental side."

"Don't tell anybody I have one."

"Your secret's safe with me."

That night, we took the train to South Slope, where Scott lived, and where he'd decided to host what we'd called the Out-of-Office Party.

Parker and I walked up a long line of row houses in the cool March dusk, the air laced with a drizzle so fine that I could barely feel it on my skin. We pushed through a waist-high iron gate and rang the old, glowing bell at Scott's home, a brownstone that had been in his family for a century.

"I wonder if Jacob and Cassie are here yet," I said, listening to the chatter seeping through the door.

"Arthur's coming too. He'll probably be an hour late, though."

The door swung open, and noise, light, and music enfolded us. "Selina!" said Kellie. "And Parker Navarro. *Hello*. Hi."

"Kellie, right?" said Parker, shaking her hand as we stepped in.

"That's me. It's extremely fun to meet you." Kellie's laughing eyes strayed to me. "Selina's been so secretive."

We hung up our coats in the small tiled mudroom. "Really?" said Parker, his hand brushing the small of my back. "What did she tell you?"

"Your book came up at a staff meeting. You know, a month on the list . . . I thought it would be fun to poke Selina about it." Kellie led us through an oak door that looked like it could have withstood a battering ram, into a long, narrow, crowded living room, whose mantelpiece boasted an enormous abstract painting and twin vases of lilies. "So I said, your favorite book's been on the list for a month, what do you think. And Selina was like—what did she say?" Kellie stood up ramrod straight, wiping the impish smile off her face. "I'm very happy for Parker."

Kellie gesticulated with her empty champagne flute and made an incredulous face at Parker. "And we were all, like—*what?* Since when did Parker Navarro become *first-name-only* Parker? What are you hiding from us? And she goes, like, solemn face, witness stand, 'I haven't been completely forthcoming.'"

Parker laughed, and looking at him, I broke into a smile, too. I had never considered myself a jealous or possessive person, but there was something satisfying about having him here beside me, about everyone in this room knowing that, somehow, I was the one he wanted.

I thought I heard my name, and I turned, looking for Jacob or Cassie, but my eyes moved toward the front of the room, onto what I'd thought at first glance was Scott's dining table. But from this angle, I could see it was none other than the enormous claw-foot table from the *City* library. I moved slowly toward it. The pitted surface held a sea of champagne glasses.

"It's our round table," I told Parker.

"Well," said Scott's voice behind me, "we need somewhere to conduct those Friday eleven o'clocks."

I turned to Scott, my hand passing over the hard, ridged wood glossed with age. The pang I'd felt looking around our barren office seemed to fade. "I'm glad you took it with you," I said.

"The magazine is changing shape," Scott said. "Just a little metamorphosis, Selina. Nothing we can't handle. Now, this must be Parker."

"Yes, sir." Parker shook Scott's hand. "I love your magazine. I've been reading *City* since I was thirteen."

"That's what I like to hear. Not planning to write revenge fantasies about any of our other staffers, are you?"

An embarrassed smile spread over Parker's face. "Not unless I get requests."

"There you are," said a flushed-looking Cassie, darting around one of the data guys and tugging Jacob after her. Following them was a tall, shaggy-haired Chinese man, whom I recognized from Parker's photos as his roommate, Arthur.

I felt abruptly stiff, sipping my champagne.

At first, in the days after Parker and I had reconciled, I hadn't thought much of the fact that he would come over, night after night, to my apartment. He had a roommate; I didn't.

But at the beginning of March, we'd had dinner in Greenpoint, and I'd suggested that we go home to his place afterward. He'd set down his fork and knife, deliberating, and said, "Look, Selina. Arthur is . . . He's having a tough time getting past everything that happened."

I hadn't known what to say. I'd been coming to terms with the strange fact that many thousands of people, for the rest of my life, would react to my name with hatred or disgust, but for Parker's best friend to feel that way was different.

"He's been trying to talk you out of seeing me," I said.

"Yeah."

I'd never lost my appetite so quickly. *What if it works*, I thought. What if Arthur made such a compelling argument that Parker slowly came back to his senses and left me, this time forever.

"Hey." Under the table, Parker's fingertips grazed my knee. "It's not happening, Selina, obviously. He's going to love you, eventually. Just, right now, he thinks I'm . . ." He grimaced, running his hand through his hair. "You know. Caught up in the physical stuff, not thinking clearly."

"Are you?"

He lowered his voice. "You didn't seem to be thinking that clearly this morning, either."

I touched his hand under the table. His fingers twined with mine, and, drawing circles on my palm, he'd said quietly, "A little more time, and he'll see how clear I am on you. I promise."

Now, as Arthur came into the circle, I tried to loosen my shoulders. I told myself, *Be likable.*

"Arthur," Parker said, "this is Selina. Selina, my roommate Arthur."

"Hello." I moved my hand in an awkward wave. "It's nice to meet you."

"Yep. Hi." Arthur was looking over my shoulder with a determined expression, as though he were about to take bitter medicine.

I thought about small talk. Asking him about Macmillan or how he liked the wine. But his hands had hooked into his pockets, and Jacob and Cassie were giving him curious looks, and I did not have time in my one life to talk around clear discomforts.

"Arthur," I said, "could I borrow you in the hall?"

"I—what?" He glanced at Parker, who shrugged. "Um. Okay."

Leaving Parker chatting with Jacob and Cassie, I led Arthur into the small, deserted hallway that looped back toward the kitchen. When we were far enough from the door, I stopped and said, "Look, Arthur. I'm sure you still have some misgivings about me, considering what I wrote about Parker."

"Yeah. I do."

"Right." I set my champagne flute on an end table. "And maybe you think I'm responsible for what happened before his launch. I still feel responsible. So I understand."

Surprise showed on Arthur's face, his thin mouth loosening.

"Believe me," I said quietly, "you and I are on the same page, if you think I don't deserve him."

Arthur shifted. He shook his shaggy hair back and looked at the ceiling. "He did say you'd be intense," he said eventually.

"Yes," I said with a small smile. "I've been told that."

Arthur took a swig of his beer and sighed. "Okay, fine. Let's do this. It's nice to meet you, too." He stuck out his hand. "But also, if you hurt him again, I'll—"

"I know." I took his hand and shook.

"What's this shady backdoor deal that's happening?" said Parker's voice down the hall.

"She bought my affection," Arthur said as we made our way back toward the party. "She bribed me with a lifetime subscription to *City Magazine*."

"Completely untrue," I said, reaching Parker's side. "Good idea, though."

"Everything okay?" he murmured in my ear as Arthur moved ahead.

"It's good." I kissed him, then looked out into the glowing room ahead of us, at the circles and arcs and pairs of people, at Jacob and Cassie, laughing at some comment of Arthur's. I looked at this sliver of my life, and then back to Parker, to the warmth and care in his face, and I said, "It's all good."

The party slowly filled wall to wall. Authors and publishing professionals leaked in, some of whom performed double takes when they saw Parker's hand on my waist. It was easy not to pay them much mind. Cassie mentioned something about climate change, and Arthur eagerly leaped in with six different options to volunteer for climate policy, while Jacob, Parker, and I talked about how baffling it was that an experimental book from last year called *Alaya's Elephants* was getting a film adaptation with major studio backing and Saoirse Ronan set to star. Our corner of the room felt so comfortable that I finally understood why people felt compelled to stay at parties until two in the morning.

Around eleven, though, Jacob and Cassie headed home to relieve the babysitter, and Arthur spotted a friend in the crowd and disappeared. Parker and I stepped backward into the empty hall, just beyond the door, in the wavering light of Scott's vintage chandelier. Parker looked so handsome then, his hair rumpled, his tie loosened under his jacket, his gaze skating over my shoulders.

I glanced toward the door down the hall and traced my fingers over the knot of his tie, across his chest. He leaned in toward me. "What are you thinking?" he murmured in my ear.

"That I want you," I said, but I was thinking, *That I love you so much I could never find the words.*

Parker moved closer and slid his hand down my back, lighting fire where he touched me. "Now what are you thinking?"

"Take me home," I said, but I was thinking, *I'm already there.*

Chapter Twenty-Nine

Parker

Selina in the morning. As usual, she was right. I could have written a twelve-hundred-page book with no drive at all, and this would have been the subject: her body in the sheets, the slope of her waist into her hip, her dark hair loose across my pillowcase, the way she propped her elbow up on the pillow, half smiling, to look at me.

"Good morning," I said, my voice scratchy. "How'd you like the place?"

"I don't think you have enough books," she said, nodding to the floor-to-ceiling shelves.

"I can think of a way to fix that. Don't you have a few books?"

Selina reached out and toyed with my hair, cool-eyed. "I do. I'm open to joining forces."

It occurred to me what, exactly, we were saying, that I'd just joked about moving in together not even two months into an actual relationship. This should have felt like an absurd thing to do, but instead it felt like an obvious answer to an unspoken question, because I knew, I just knew, that this was it for me: Either I would have her for the rest of my life, or I would think about her for the rest of my life.

I breathed, feeling laid bare, as we looked at each other. Then my hand strayed for my phone, and I opened it to find a mess of notifications.

"Fuck," I muttered. "What now?"

"What?" Selina said as I opened social media.

Wordless, I showed her the picture I'd been tagged in. Somehow I wasn't even surprised. It was Selina and me at Scott's party last night, laughing with Arthur and Jacob and Cassie, my arm around her waist.

@SasuNaru113: I'M SORRY. WHAT? SO ALL THE DRAMA WITH THESE TWO WAS A PR CONSPIRACY?

@mentoscokegoboom: I knew it I knew it I absolutely fucking knew it

@swift_ly_falling: So do we think she got paid off to do the second negative review by his publisher? Like was the fight even real?

@Doubleganger: Of course the fight wasn't real, dumbass. The whole thing is a lie

@LolaXu: Interesting developments.

Lola Xu's post had six thousand likes and a slew of sly replies. Most of them were questioning Selina's credentials. Some were calling her an embarrassment to the critical profession.

I glanced over, considering how to defend her, how to respond, how to win. "Should we—"

Selina plucked the phone from my hand. For a moment I wondered what blistering response she was going to type.

Then she exited the page. I watched her delete the app, and the next, and the next. She tossed my phone into the hammock, where it swayed, an invisible weight.

She turned back to me and said, "What were you saying?"

I pulled her in, smiling, and as she kissed me, I felt something untie in me and slip away. Let the ocean of judgment keep recoiling and resurging outside these walls. Later, Selina and I would roll out of bed, and we'd get coffee next door. We'd drink it over one of the cramped tables in the humid back corner and I'd steal bites of her croissant while she made charmingly specific threats. We'd go to an art gallery in the afternoon and explore some exhibition that made me feel far away from myself. We'd swing through every bookstore we saw, and I wouldn't check whether my books were stocked in any of them. We'd return home and Selina would absentmindedly wander onto my bed to read an article or make notes for her next review, and I'd call my mother or father while sitting in the front window and watching spring slip one green finger through the white veil of winter. I was done scoring points in public, with a life like this in private.

By late April, *High and Dry* had dropped off the bestseller charts, but ten weeks on the list was a strong enough showing to ensure my future in publishing, at least for another several years.

First of all, the book had immediately earned out its fifteen-thousand-dollar advance. So, come this fall, and every six months thereafter, I'd get a royalty check—somewhere in the six-figure range this year.

Second of all, with these new and improved sales figures, Lauren convinced Coronation to buy my next two books on proposal, this time for fifty thousand dollars apiece. Bill tried to negotiate higher. Lauren told him not to push his luck.

In mid-May, Selina and I celebrated the new deal by taking the train up to Boston, where we overnighted in a tiny hotel and visited Elena and her girlfriend, Katy. As it turned out, Katy was a fan: not of me, but of Selina.

"I read all your reviews," she stammered, tugging at her hair.

"Thank you," Selina said, unsmiling.

Katy laughed nervously and went off to use the bathroom.

"How have you been, Park?" asked Elena, picking at the end of one of her braids. "With, you know . . ." She gestured vaguely at her head.

"Not bad. Seriously. I haven't had a really bad day since"—I glanced over at Selina with a small smile—"since February."

"You sure?"

"Yeah, I'm sure." In the days after my last post about *High and Dry*, my siblings had reacted in ways I hadn't expected. Christi and Kevin had sent shocked, sympathetic texts that had surprised me with their candor and sensitivity. Justin, normally allergic to phone calls, had rung me on a Sunday afternoon, and we'd spoken for an hour about my downward spiral in college. At one point his voice had grown narrow and buzzy, and he'd coughed a few times, muttering, "Sorry, I'm sorry." The last time I'd seen Justin cry, I'd been six years old and he'd been ten, his knee gashed open on a concrete driveway.

As for Elena, she'd told me she'd already suspected the truth.

"Well, thank God," she said, pouring me more wine, then Selina. "It's about time you both got a break."

We returned to Brooklyn to an apartment full of boxes. Over the course of April, Selina and I had talked about moving in together in language that included fewer and fewer jokes, and finally, at the start of May, I'd asked Arthur if he'd be okay with moving out.

"I knew this was coming," he said with a sigh.

"If it softens the blow," I said, "I just heard about a lease takeover for this convenient rent-stabilized one-bedroom in Bed-Stuy."

"Oh, really?"

"Yeah, the last tenant spent eight years upgrading the place."

He cracked a grin. "Sounds like her."

A few days later, Selina came over to give him the keys. "Please, be nice to the apartment."

"I'm very nice," Arthur said indignantly. "*You* be nice to my roommate."

She just laughed. By then, he knew her. By then, he loved her, too.

June spread over Brooklyn like butter, gold and balmy, and the last of Arthur's boxes disappeared, and Selina finished setting up the home office in his old room. She called her parents in there once every few weeks, and I heard her padding slowly back and forth, her voice even and restrained, and sometimes when she came outside afterward, she moved directly into my arms and leaned her face against my neck as I kissed her hair.

By summer, *City* had settled fully into the new rhythms of remote work. Once a week, Selina took the subway down to Scott's brownstone for the Friday staff meeting. "But otherwise," she admitted, "it's a lot less of getting breathed on during rush hour." Even better: With the tens of thousands of dollars the magazine was saving every month on Manhattan office space, they were no longer hemorrhaging money, and Scott had clawed editorial oversight back from Nextward Capital Associates. The day that *City*'s front page finally cleared of articles like "What Was with That Crazy Cameo in the New Batman Trailer?" Selina and I spent the afternoon on a picnic blanket in the park to celebrate.

I loved our life together. We read side by side on the couch with quiet music over the speakers, occasionally reading a striking line out loud to each other. We laughed over dinner tables with people we loved. Every day I felt like myself; every night, before I slept, I felt close to her. I annotated pass pages in the hammock while she made margin notes in bed. I watched her grapple with new favorites and disappointments. I learned exactly what went into her pieces.

And still, every time I read her work, I was struck anew by her clarity and precision, as though to read her was to walk down an endless path inside her. Some mornings, after reading her latest, I would come into her office and kiss her and say, "It's perfect." And every so often, reading my pages, she would text me, You're brilliant.

Maybe nobody else in the world agreed. Maybe we were unreliable sources now; maybe that was what it meant to be in love.

All I knew was that I'd finally found the right words.

I wanted to spend the rest of my life saying them.

Acknowledgments

I am profoundly grateful for the publishing teams who have toiled to bring *Bad Words* to shelves, and for my friends and family, who every day give me the gift of an emotionally rich and creatively inspiring life.

Thank you to Clare Mao, my champion agent, for your editorial insight and your belief in this book. I also owe my heartfelt thanks to Dorothy Vincent and Bailey Tamayo at Sanford J. Greenburger, and to Imogen Bovill and our other coagents abroad.

To my editors, Vicki Lame and Olivia Robertshaw: I am forever lucky that this book found you. Thank you so much for your vision, guidance, and enthusiasm. Huge thanks as well to the extraordinary teams at St. Martin's and HarperFiction. At St. Martin's Press, my thanks go out to Sarah Pazen, Cassie Gutman, Janine Barlow, and Lauren Riebs on the production editorial side; to Amelia Beckerman, Brant Janeway, Tracey Guest, Katie Bassel, Kiara Ronaghan, and Lexi Neuville on the marketing and publicity side; to Melissa Campion and Dominique Jenkins in Events; and to SMP's fearless leaders, Jennifer Enderlin and Anne Marie Tallberg. On the audio team, thank you so much to Katy Robitzski, Maria Snelling, and Drew Kilman, and for making the book beautiful inside and out, my thanks go to cover designer Olga Grlic and interior designer Devan Norman. At Harper, I am so grateful to Libby Haddock, Tink Blauth-Muszkowski, and Bec Gillies for helping to champion this title.

For the earliest reads and invaluable support, thank you to Caryn

Wiseman, Laura Schreiber, Phoebe Woods, Caitlin Murphy, Hunter Lehr, Andrew Milne, and Mandy Albert.

For writing excellent novels, excellent text messages, and/or excellent novels in text message form, thank you to Mackenzi, Bri, Emily, Justin, Traci, Miranda, Jeff, and Janet.

For chatting with me at crucial junctures about critics, criticism, art, or story, thank you to Amy, Aaron, Phoebe, Jeremiah, Jamie, Ashlan, Terry, Elliot, and the AE family.

For dinners and coffees and calls and walks, for making me laugh, thank you to Avi, Piper, Foss, Nate, Emma, Eamon, Rekha, Liam, Michael, Derek, Emily, Peter, Ben Jacoby, and Ben Locke.

For making Chicago home for eight years, thank you to Dyer, Sarah, Nina, Chelsea, Scott, Lauren, David, Rachel, and Rupa. I miss you!

For inexplicably not bullying me in childhood—I've reread the cursed GChats and know it would have been justified—thank you to my lifelong ride-or-dies, Anne, Rose, Noelle, Li An, Kshipra, and Lilith. Love also to Fran, Mary Claire, and Sheryl.

For everything else, my thanks and love to my mom and dad and Siofra and Sam, as well as to my extended family, especially Briony and Tamsin.

A final thank-you to Tim Brayton, chief film critic at Alternate Ending, whose criticism I've read since I was a teenager and whose work taught me why criticism matters. Selina could only hope to emulate your thrilling, devastating pans.